Lisa stumbled, losing a shoe. Her captors dragged her to her feet. A man came running after them, and when he passed under a lantern, its light flashed on a drawn sword.

Lisa's kidnappers dragged blades out of scabbards. Her arms were released as the newcomer jumped into the fray. One against five.

A terrible scream. Four.

"Kill him!" shouted a kidnapper. Metal rang and clashed in the night. The newcomer whirled like smoke between the swords, dancing with death. Another scream—another captor down.

Then . . . it wasn't possible! The newcomer lit up with a glow of his own, brighter than any lantern, illuminating the shuttered windows and narrow streets. He blazed like a golden sun and the kidnappers wailed as they realized they were fighting *gramarye*.

Books by Ken Hood

Demon Sword
Demon Rider
Demon Knight

Published by HarperPrism

THE YEARS OF LONGDIRK

DEMON KNIGHT

KEN HOOD

HarperPrism
A Division of HarperCollins*Publishers*

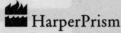 HarperPrism

A Division of HarperCollins*Publishers*
10 East 53rd Street, New York, NY 10022-5299

This is a work of fiction. The characters, incidents, and
dialogues are products of the author's imagination and are not to
be construed as real. Any resemblance to actual events or
persons, living or dead, is entirely coincidental.

ISBN 0-06-105759-2

HarperCollins®, 🔥®, and HarperPrism®
are trademarks of HarperCollins Publishers, Inc.

Cover illustration © 1998 by Donato Giancola

First printing: June 1998

Printed in the United States of America

Visit HarperPrism on the World Wide Web at
http://www.harperprism.com

❖ 10 9 8 7 6 5 4 3 2 1

CONTENTS

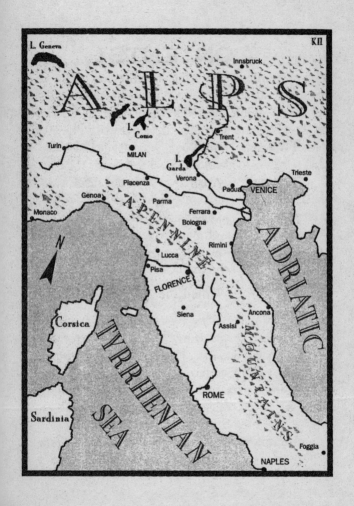

By the fall of 1524, Nevil had conquered all of Europe north of the Alps, but thirteen years of unbroken success had made him grievously over-confident. While he indulged himself in putting down rebellions with the extreme cruelty that had earned his name of the Fiend, he delegated the conquest of Italy to Varnius Schweitzer.

Schweitzer was a competent general and foresaw no difficulty in overcoming the Italian city-states, which had been fighting one another for centuries and seemed incapable of uniting for any reason. He crossed the Alps with about fifty thousand men and was opposed near the city of Trent by a hastily gathered coalition of Italians, Swiss, and Tyroleans. Facing a force less than half the size of his, led by a mercenary soldier he had never heard of, Schweitzer willingly accepted battle and thereupon suffered one of the bloodiest and most lopsided defeats in history. Within days all Europe rang with the name of the young man who had celebrated his own twenty-third birthday by overcoming seemingly impossible odds . . .

—Emil Marrat, *Longdirk: The Fighting Years*
(Edinburgh University Press, 1967)

DEMON
KNIGHT

ONE

JOURNEY'S END

1

Hamish Campbell was not looking for trouble that fine spring evening and did not expect any. Toby Longdirk attracted trouble like stables drew flies, but Toby had stayed behind in Florence to organize this year's fighting season. Hamish had come to Siena on a quiet little spying mission. If he were caught, he would be tortured and possibly hanged, so he was certainly not looking for trouble.

Lady Lisa, on the other hand . . . *Trouble* was not what she had in mind. *Adventure* would be a better term. But trouble was what she got.

Extraordinary consequences were to result from their meeting. Although it appeared to be due to the merest chance, it was not fortuitous at all. There were demons involved.

◻   ◻   ◻

Lisa had opened hostilities before noon. "Mother! It is Carnival! How can you possibly resist the opportunity for a little innocent merrymaking?"

Looking up from her embroidery, the Countess of Ely uttered one of her longer-suffering groans. "Very easily. We have not spent two nights under the same roof in the last month. We have just crossed the ocean in the dead of winter, and the last thing I want to do is go out and participate in a public riot. Have you practiced the virginals today?" Maud seemed tired, but then she always seemed tired now. However skilled, her maids could no longer disguise the grooves in her face, and her once-golden hair was quite obviously dyed, not merely touched-up as it had been until last summer. That was no excuse, because people wore masks at Carnival, and the handsome young men would be looking at Lisa, not her mother.

"It was *not* the ocean, we were never out of sight of land, we were three nights in a row in the horrible inn in Pisa, and before that we were shut up in that awful Savoyard villa leagues from anywhere for months and months, we have been in Italy almost a week, and I have yet to . . . um, experience any of the culture."

"Then I suggest you try a few madrigals. I saw some sheets beside the virginals."

"Just to look, I mean. Surely a sedate stroll—"

"No, Lisa! This is a very dangerous place for us, as I have repeatedly warned you, and we must remain indoors until safer arrangements—"

"Danger? Mother, you imagine things. You

behave as if the Fiend himself were personally hunting you, and that is crazy! Other people do not—"

"Lisa! You are a foolish, ignorant child! And a very ill-mannered one, to yell at your mother so. I have told you a thousand times . . ." She was still in full bleat when her daughter slammed the door on her.

The countess was haunted by imaginary terrors. For as long as Lisa could remember, the two of them had never remained more than a few months in any one place. Fleeing by night, as often as not. Traipsing from castle to château to hunting lodge to obscure city house, she had spent her entire life being dragged around the free nations of Europe. Burgundy, Swabia, Bavaria, Switzerland, Savoy . . . on and on. How could she ever make friends? Now Italy! Lush, beautiful, romantic Italy, the wellspring of culture. A land renowned for its art and music and sultry-eyed, handsome young men.

What she needed was a selection of sultry-eyed, handsome young men serenading her with lutes under her balcony, and how were they ever to find her if they did not even know she was here?

Not that the cramped, musty-smelling house possessed a balcony, or a garden full of gardenias either. Whoever their current landlord might be—Lisa had not even heard his name, let alone met him—he had very warped notions of the style in which a countess and her daughter ought to be quartered. The only local servant he had provided was a surly, spotty boy who spoke nothing but Italian. Frieda was doing the cooking, so Bavarian sausage, morning, noon, and night.

Ugh! Old Jacques, the coachman, had stayed behind in Savoy, worn out by all the years of traipsing. The countess's household was down to four stupid girls and one spotty boy.

Lisa tried again in the afternoon. And again after dark, when the sounds of music and revelry were heart-achingly plain in the streets—not the street outside, which was a smelly dead-end alley, but streets just maddeningly out of sight and reach. She made no progress, except that Mother began complaining of a headache. Halfway through dinner, she threw down her napkin, lurched to her feet, and in martyred tones bade Lisa be certain the house was secure before she went to bed. Then she vanished upstairs to lie down.

Lisa gobbled the rest of her meal, inspected both doors and the downstairs windows, and graciously informed Gina that she and the other servants could go off duty as soon as they had cleared the table. She retired to her room. She had already established that the bars were loose on the upstairs corridor window that looked out on the stable roof. All by herself, without any help at all, she donned her best apricot silk gown, the one with the epaulettes, slashed sleeves, and V-necked décolletage. Fortunately her hair was already pinned up, and she had a fetching satin *balzo* hat that left a little of it exposed in the front—hair as blonde as hers must be extremely rare in Italy. Adding her light blue cloak and a mask fashioned by cutting two eye-holes in a kerchief, she set off to investigate Carnival.

She had her ring. No harm could come to her while she wore that.

The stable roof part was a little trickier than expected. It ripped the hem of her gown, but May could stitch that up so Mother would not notice. The descent into the alley splattered a lot of disgusting mud on the cloak, but once around the corner, she was into Carnival—torches and music and dancing! Before she knew it, a group of laughing youngsters swallowed her up and swept her away. They pressed wine bottles upon her and whirled her around in dances. They laughed at her protests, jabbering cheerfully in Italian. They took her to a huge semicircular piazza full of crowds larger and louder and more riotous than any she had ever known. She was surrounded by people of her own age, being totally ignored by the older folk present. It was more fun than she had dreamed possible.

Suddenly it was terror, heart-stopping, choking terror. She was lost. She felt ill, but that was partly from too much wine. She had never intended to go farther than the corner. The men who had plucked her from there had vanished into the crowd. She had no idea where she was or where she should be and couldn't even ask anyone for directions. She had never been truly alone in her life before. When Mother discovered her absence, she would have no one to send out as a search party.

Calm! Stay calm! There must be a way out of this situation. All it needed was a little thought. (So why were her teeth rattling?) She still had her ring. No harm could come to her while she wore her ring, but it could not help her find her way home. Even if she knew no Italian, there must be someone around who understood one of the languages she could speak. But she did not know the name of the street she wanted, nor what the house looked like from the front. Fool, fool, fool! Shivering in the cool air, she left the piazza and plunged into the ants' nest of alleys—smelly, deserted, and pitch-black. She had come downhill, so she went uphill, half-running, half-staggering, heart thumping in her throat. Every road looked like every other. Here and there, a public-spirited householder maintained a lantern beside his door, but the gaps between were long and dark.

Hearing a movement behind her, she glanced back, saw nothing, and began to run anyway. There was a lantern ahead, but before she reached it three men emerged out of the shadows, obviously menacing. She turned on the spot, saw three more coming behind her. She screamed. Rough hands grabbed her. She scratched, kicked, and bit down on a set of foul-tasting fingers. Their owner said, "Bitch!" and back-handed her across the mouth. Very hard. Her head shot back as if it had been knocked right off, and she sagged and fell limply into thick, powerful arms. She tasted blood. She was giddy. She was about to vomit from terror. The ring? What had gone wrong with her ring?

Feet flailing on the greasy cobbles, she was dragged along to the light. Nails clawed away her mask.

"That's her!"

"Sure?"

"Yes! Bring her."

She opened her mouth to scream again, and the cloth of her mask was thrust into it. Two of her captors began running her along the road, back the way she had come, each pulling an arm. She stumbled, lost a shoe, and they held her up, still running. Six men, all masked for Carnival, but not true merrymakers, not drunk. There had to be some mistake! How could it possibly be she they wanted? But they had spoken in English.

A voice shouted: "Stop!"

Another man came running after them, and when he passed under the lantern, its light flashed on a drawn sword. The kidnappers dragged blades out of scabbards. Her left wrist was released as that man jumped into the fray. One against five.

A terrible scream. Four.

"Kill him!" shouted the man holding her, his fingers digging into her arm.

She kicked, squirmed, and beat at him with her free hand. He shook her until she fell to her knees, expecting her shoulder to break. Metal rang and clashed in the night. The newcomer whirled like smoke between the swords, living a charmed life, dancing with death. A howl of pain meant another one down—three left! But the odds were too great. He was retreating before the assault.

Then . . . it wasn't possible! The stranger lit up with a golden glow of his own, brighter than the

lantern, illuminating the shuttered windows and door-
ways, the staircases and balconies. He blazed like a
golden sun, and the kidnappers wailed as they realized
that they were fighting gramarye. The one holding her
threw her to the ground and began waving his arms
and shouting. His companions fled from the man of
fire with the molten blade. Was her ring working at
last? It hadn't saved her from the punch that still
throbbed through her head, puffing out her lip like a
melon. She pulled the rag from her mouth and began
to rise, hoping she could make a run for it, even with
only one shoe . . .

More gramarye, more conjuration! A thing like an
ape or a bear—something huge and pale-furred—
loomed up at the rescuer's back, twice his height. His
own light reflected in its eyes, on great fangs, on claws
like daggers. Sensing it, he glanced back and ducked
just in time as it swung a taloned paw at his head. Then
he sprinted toward Lisa, sweeping the last two
assailants aside with his sword. Roaring, the demon
lumbered after him.

Her rescuer jabbered some Italian and grabbed
her wrist with a hand that should have been fiery hot
but instead felt cool and dry. He turned to face the
monster, raising his sword in hopeless defiance.

Flick!

The street, the demon, the attackers, the dark . . .
all gone.

She was standing on a thick rug in a room lit by
three or four candles. Her savior was still holding her
arm and extending his blood-streaked sword to meet a

danger that had now vanished. He no longer glowed. He said, "Ha!" in a satisfied tone and turned to her, lowering his sword. Only a very potent hexer could burn in the dark with cold fire and evade demons and conjure her here to this palatial chamber of gilt furniture, frescoes on the walls, crystal and fine porcelain, thick rugs underfoot, and an enormous *bed* with its curtains open—and now his dark eyes glittered through the holes in his mask as he inspected his catch.

Lisa fainted into his arms.

2

Back in Florence, Toby Longdirk was attending the Marradi Carnival Ball, although he would rather have fought a squadron of *landsknechte* single-handed. A man who had been reared in a one-room hovel did not belong amid such grandeur. Standing beside Don Ramon in a reception line that wound among statues of bronze and marble across the grand courtyard, a hundred guests, with more still arriving, lined up to meet their host and hostess, he fidgeted and squirmed and kept wondering if he had forgotten to lace up his hose.

Yet his gilt-edged invitation would have fetched a hundred florins at public auction, because Pietro Marradi's hospitality was legendary, and this was the first grand function he had sponsored since the death of his wife. The Magnificent was the richest man in

Italy—probably in all Europe since Nevil had devastated most of it—a celebrated patron of the arts and a major poet in his own right. His palace was a treasure chest.

More than the grandeur was bothering Toby. Florence was a very beautiful city, but all cities were dangerous for him. In some dark corner of his mind he was conscious of the tutelary in its great sanctuary, only two streets away, and also of many lesser spirits in lesser sanctuaries. They were watching him, ready to strike if the hob escaped from his control for an instant.

The line shuffled forward, ever closer to the Magnificent.

"A moneylender!" the don sneered, not quite quietly enough. "A common draper! One inflicts irreparable injury upon one's honor by gracing his board." Don Ramon de Nuñez y Pardo could trace his excruciatingly elongated pedigree from the Emperor Romulus Augustulus. Toby Longdirk had been fathered by a committee of English fusiliers.

"Lunch is lunch," he said philosophically.

"It will be a miracle if we complete the evening without anyone being hexed, poisoned, or stilettoed."

True enough. And although Don Ramon thoroughly despised the likes of the Magnificent, he was quite willing to enjoy his party. Toby would endure it only because he knew something important was going to happen during the course of the night.

He shivered, for the air was cool, and he felt naked without cloak or jerkin. His multicolored hose clung tight as paint, but his waist-length doublet hung open at the neck to display the embroidery on his shirt. His face was razored smooth as porcelain, his hair hung to his shoulders under a hat like a mixing bowl with a brim. This was fashion. His tastes in clothes—now that he could afford to have taste—was naturally conservative, for no one his size needed to draw attention to himself, and yet this outrageous outfit had cost more money than an honest man earned in a year. Over the tailor's tears, Toby had insisted on subdued greens and grays instead of reds and mauves, but he had lost the rest of the arguments. Hip-length tunics were for the middle-aged and cloaks for the elderly, the tailor had maintained, and messer must not conceal such magnificent thighs, for which most young gallants would cheerfully execute their grandmothers with blunt spades. He had gone on to enthuse about Toby's calves and shoulders until Toby threatened to ram a bolt of Genoese silk down his throat.

Untroubled by any qualms of modesty, Don Ramon was never reluctant to make himself conspicuous, and admittedly his lithe form suited these revealing styles. His coppery hair and thin-horned mustache were set off by brilliant blues and greens, his pearl buttons inset with rubies. The golden plume in his hat was as long as his arm, his exposure of shirt close to indecent. Even so, his garb was not as extreme as that of some of the young men there, whose use of padding was unseemly or even ludicrous.

And the women! Every one of them was loaded with enough silk, satin, velvet, brocade, and damask to build a tent. How could they walk, carrying the weight of those skirts and sleeves? Their necklines were cut so wide and low that it seemed the slightest unwary movement would cause the entire ensemble to collapse around their wearers' ankles. It was a marvel.

"Magnificent!" murmured the don, indulging in some gawking of his own. "That one in mulberry?"

"What I don't understand," Toby whispered, "is how the gowns stay on them at all!"

"Ask not how they stay on, my boy, but how easily they come off!"

Much too easily in many cases, from what Toby had heard, but he did not have to worry about that.

The line shuffled forward. Peering over heads, he studied the Magnificent. For a despot, he was astonishingly unassuming. It was said that Pietro Marradi could wander unnoticed along any street in Florence—he was never fool enough to try it without his bodyguard—and that evening, in the somber tones of half mourning, he was a crow among kingfishers. He had no outstanding physical characteristics at all, except that he wore his forty years well. Officially he was merely a private citizen; in practice he was the government, ruling Florence without office or title, as his father and grandfather had done before him.

How did he do it? Toby watched in bafflement. The manners were flawless—the smile and bow were the same for ambassadors as they were for business friends or political foes—yet Marradi was too aloof to be charismatically charming. He was a celebrated patron of the arts, but no one could control a great city through its poets, painters, and sculptors. Money helped, but there were other rich men in Florence who seemed to have no political power at all. "I am not a duke or a prince," he had told Toby during their secret meeting that morning. "I am not the doge of Venice. I admit I have some influence, but my only tool is rational persuasion." He could have mentioned bribery, rigged elections, nepotism, favoritism, blackmail, coercion, and—once in a while—riot, gramarye, and assassination, but persuasion certainly seemed to be at the heart of it. Tonight he welcomed the Scottish peasant to his Carnival Ball with the same cool courtesy he had just shown to the exiled King of Austria.

"Sir Tobias! Our house is honored by the presence of Scipio reborn." His eyes were russet-brown like his hair and glittered bright as daggers.

Toby's knowledge of the classics was precisely zero, but fortunately he had asked Brother Bartolo to coin some suitable phrases for him to memorize. "It is for the feasting in Valhalla that the warrior fights, Your Magnificence."

Marradi acknowledged the mot with a graceful nod. "But what he wins is glory and the gratitude of the people."

Toby hastily reached into Bartolo's collection again. "I was but the sword that the hand of Liberty wielded."

"May Liberty ever be so well armed, Sir Tobias."

Having won the match two falls out of three, Marradi gracefully passed Toby to the care of his sister, tonight's hostess. Next . . .

Toby bowed to her, Lucrezia, Duchess of Ferrara. She was resplendent in cloth of gold, although her husband's death was more recent than madonna Marradi's. The gossipmongers declared that mourning would be hypocritical for her, and the only known sin that her critics never attributed to Lucrezia Marradi was hypocrisy. She was tiny, able to walk under Toby's arm in a plumed hat. With a small nose and a slightly receding chin, she had the face of a child, and those same gossips insisted that only gramarye could explain how she retained her youthful complexion and the fiery red-gold hair. She might have been a doll standing there in her superbly crafted gown and enough jewels to gravel a stable yard, honoring the giant with a disarming, coquettish smile. She could see how out of place he felt.

"Tobiaso, you are the handsomest man in the city."

"And you, *duchessa,* are the biggest liar." Feeling as clumsy as a drunken ox, he bent to kiss the childish fingers. Not all of her was childish. She held her hand where he would have a good view down her cleavage. He could almost see her toes.

"I was hoping you would appear in a lion skin."

Another classical allusion? "I washed it, and it didn't dry in time."

Lucrezia tinkled a laugh that sounded utterly genuine and might be as deadly as her most recent husband's last sip of wine. "I expect to dance with you tonight, *comandante!*"

"I am yours to command, madonna."

"Of course," said the rosebud lips.

Toby followed the don indoors, fervently wishing he were somewhere else, anywhere else. So many incredibly ravishing women, and he could not even dream . . .

3

The hexer had removed his mask. He was very tall and lithe, with waves of black hair and features just on the bony side of classical. He had placed Lisa carefully on the bed without ripping her clothes off or performing any demonic conjurations. He was doing something at the far side of the room, now coming over to the bed . . .

When he laid a wet towel on her bruised mouth, her eyes jerked open in surprise. His smile displayed one of the very few perfect sets of teeth she had ever seen.

"Do you really look like that?" she mumbled. How could a nightmare turn into a dream so quickly?

Surprise faded to a worried frown, as if he thought she might be raving. "Do I look like what?" He removed the towel.

"Aren't all hexers old and ugly and—"

He laughed. "I'm not a hexer! Just a soldier."

"A condottiere?"

"A humble man-at-arms. My name's Giacomo, and we . . ." He paused, surprised. "We're talking English? So call me James. Hamish if you want to be accurate."

First name only? But perhaps he was being tactful, hinting that it was better not to reveal too much. Her heart was pounding strangely.

"Er, I'm Lisa. Hamish? Is that Welsh?"

"Scots!"

"I beg your pardon. I thought all Scotsmen were seven feet tall and had red hair."

"Only the wild ones. I'm the domesticated variety."

His solemn manner bewildered her for a moment, then she laughed. "I am extremely grateful for your assistance, sir! You don't look like a soldier." Any she had seen had been scruffy scoundrels. His clothes were stylish but not showy, like his manners.

He shrugged. "I don't do much fighting. I'm mostly in administration."

She had wanted sultry eyes, she remembered, never guessing that eyes could be as sultry as these. Was he possibly one of the fabled condottiere princes? "You fought like a legend tonight. Against six!" A rapier was a nobleman's weapon. No mere man-at-arms could have wielded one as he had.

He shook his head almost bashfully. "I was in no danger at all. I have a guarddemon, see?" He raised a hand to show a ring with a yellow jewel. "My only worry was that my ring would zap me out of there before I could do anything to help you."

But the fact that it had not implied that he had been holding his own until the monster came. How could a mere man-at-arms explain these sumptuous quarters? He was at least wealthy, if not a noble, and he had behaved with perfect chivalry so far. Except that he had not summoned a chaperone. Would it be proper to ask for one, or rude? If he began making advances . . . how far did a lady's obligations go in these circumstances?

Probably a long way, she decided nervously. She fingered her swollen lip.

"Are you well enough to walk yet?" he asked. "We ought to leave here before someone comes. I expect they're all out at Carnival, but—"

Oh! "Where are we?"

Again that appealing smile. "I haven't the faintest idea. It must have been safe at the time, or my demon wouldn't have brought us here, but we should leave as soon as possible. It won't defend us against social embarrassment."

"Mine didn't defend me against anything at all!" She scowled at her ring. The stone was only garnet, but Mother had always said the gold setting would be very valuable even without the demon immured in the jewel. It had been less than useless tonight.

Hamish frowned, took her hand, and peered at it closely. "It's very old, isn't it?" He did not release her hand.

"It belonged to my grandmother. Mother gave it to me on my—" what would he believe? "—eighteenth birthday."

"Older than that. The setting looks Carolingian."

"How do you know that if you're not a hexer?"

"Mm? Oh, I read a lot." He grinned briefly, then turned serious again, frighteningly serious. "Are you royal, my lady? Ordinary people don't need guard-demons and certainly can't afford them." His eyes were no longer sultry; they were rapiers.

She had no choice but to trust him. If he meant to take advantage of her, he would have done so before now. "My mother is the Countess of Ely, and no, we're not royal, or rich. Not poor, of course. My father died many years ago. Mother has strange fears. She travels a lot, and never stays in one place more than a few months. She imagines a lot of enemies, that's all. That's why I have the ring. I was always told it would protect me. It must be a fake!"

He lit up the room with his smile again. "Not necessarily. My guarddemon is conjured to move me out of danger, but perhaps yours works by bringing help."

Did he realize what a wonderfully romantic notion that was? "You were the answer to a maiden's prayer tonight, sir."

"Ah, maidens are always telling me that. Come along." He pulled on her hand to help her sit up. She smoothed her gown, which was utterly ruined. Oh, she must look a sight! But he smiled, and she smiled back. She wasn't just dreaming this.

"Madonna, I will escort you safely to your residence. I will also steal some shoes out of that closet for you, if there are any there to fit you—you may have heard how skilled we mercenaries are at looting and pillaging. Otherwise, I am afraid you will have to hop." He headed for the closet. "In which *contrada* do you live?"

"I don't know."

He stopped and looked around. "You cannot even venture a wild guess?"

She shook her head and felt a huge lump rise in her throat, as if she were about to burst into tears. "We just arrived in Siena last night. I don't know the name of the street, or even what the house looks like. I came out the back. Over a roof."

"That makes things a little difficult!"

He did not believe her, naturally. She herself could not believe that she had been so stupid. She did not approve of people being stupid, especially herself, because she normally wasn't, but tonight she seemed to be blundering into every pothole in sight. "I wanted to take a look at Carnival. I had my ring. I was only going to the corner, wanting to watch the revelers going by. But some young men pulled me into a dance. I can't speak Italian. By the time I escaped from them, I was in the square, and I didn't know which way I'd come."

He did not laugh at her tale of folly. "But, Lisa, the attack on you wasn't just a random assault. Those ruffians knew who you were—I heard them. One of them said something like, 'That's her!' In English."

She nodded. "Yes."

"So it must have been gramarye of some sort, either a summoning or an ambush. The one holding you was a hexer. He invoked that demon. And he had it on a very loose rein—just a couple of words and gestures. That is extremely dangerous! I think you should take your mother's fears more seriously."

"You're saying I've been a terrible fool."

"I'd say your mother was the fool, for not confiding in you. She probably thinks of you as still being a child."

She looked up quickly, then turned away, afraid she was blushing. He was not making that mistake.

"I am very grateful for your help. You'll take me somewhere safe until we can find Mother?"

"Of course. Go and see if there are any shoes you can wear."

If he believed her story, would he be giving her orders like that? Or were the orders a sign that he did believe her story and thought she was stupid? "Very well, my lord. I'll give you some lessons in looting and pillaging."

He grinned hugely, and that made her feel better.

The closet was almost as large as the bedchamber, and its racks and rods and shelves held an impressive collection of gowns and cloaks and accessories, clearly belonging to a large woman. Anyone so rich would not grudge help to a lady in distress. Lisa found a pair of stylish buskins that she could walk in and not walk out of, and added a warm, dark-colored cloak of soft wool that fitted very well and would be much more suitable than her own for the sort of midnight adventuring that must lie in store. She discarded the *balzo* and exchanged it for a dark floppy hat that concealed her hair. After what must have been the fastest lady's dressing in history, she returned to the bedchamber.

"How do I look?"

Hamish stared at her for a moment in wonder. Then he sighed. "Lovelier than Venus. Beauty like yours drives men out of their wits."

"Thank you, Sir Hamish!" She *knew* she was blushing. "Brave knight deserves fair lady."

"Demons! I shouldn't have said . . . Lisa, I am not a knight! I'm not even an honest soldier—I'm a spy."

Her smile died, cold on her lips. "A spy for whom?"

"Not Nevil, I swear. Florence. But the Sienese might even prefer the Fiend to a Florentine. I'm not a nobleman in disguise, if that's what's in your mind. I'm a spy, and if the Sienese catch me, they'll rack me on principle."

The ruffians had spoken English, and so did he, but she had no one else to trust. She held out a hand so he could tuck an arm under it.

"Then I won't let them catch you. You're quite tall enough already."

"I'd like to stay the way I am, I admit. Now, the first problem is to get safely out of here. We'll just walk downstairs as if we owned the place. If a servant sees us, I'll do the talking. If I speak to you, smile as if I'm discussing Carnival."

The candle she was holding trembled and wavered. "And if we meet the owners?"

He shrugged. "I'll think of something." He opened the door with a cheerful grin. "Hold on tight in case I disappear."

4

Toby was out of his depth in recitals of music and poetry, but the jugglers and buffoons made him laugh. He saw many parts of the palace he had not visited before, gazing in wonder at great salons so decorated with frescoes that gods and heroes lurked on the edges of the crowd and cherubim flitted overhead. The air was heady with the scents of perfumed bodies, beeswax, and intrigue.

He knew many of the men already and was introduced to a hundred more, but the problem was never remembering a man's name, it was judging his importance, because the standard term of office in Florence was a mere two months, and titles tended to be meaningless anyway. Undoubtedly at least a quarter of the persons present were in the pay of other states and would be filing reports the following day, so he was much in demand as a potential source of interesting material.

The Veronese ambassador inquired smoothly why the noble condottiere spurned his old friends who had so well rewarded his magnificent services in their righteous struggle against the Venetian dogs.

"Florence pays better," Toby replied, just to watch the man wince. It paid in prestige, not money, but it was prestige he needed now if he were to influence events.

Within the hour, representatives of Ravenna and Naples, both former employers, made similar inquiries and received similar answers. They met frankness so seldom they had trouble dealing with it.

Frankness was barely enough when he was trapped in a shadowy corner by Lucas Abonio, who was a cousin of the Duke of Milan and brother of its *collaterale,* Ercole Abonio. The brothers could hardly have been more dissimilar, for Ercole was completely admirable, a shrewd and competent old campaigner, respected equally by his own men and his enemies. He had taught the young foreigner many things the previous summer while the Don Ramon Company fought for the duke against Florence—a trivial squabble that had been solved with a few thousand ducats and a few score dead mercenaries. Ercole was a true knight, Lucas a lurker in dark corners, a scavenger of scandal, a sniffer-out of secrets. He oozed along on a trail of intrigue like a slug on slime.

"Have you reconsidered our offer, *comandante?*"

Toby backed away a pace and collided with a wall. "You honor me beyond words, Your Magnificence. Alas, Don Ramon has already committed to the Florentines."

The spy bared a few yellow teeth. "Not according to my sources. The don's appointment was a temporary replacement for the late and unlamented Captain-General Vespucci. I have it on excellent authority that Florence has not yet met your terms for a new *condotta.*"

"Well, there is never any fighting in the winter."

"Exactly." Abonio lowered his voice and wafted closer on wings of garlic. "We are not interested in that mad don of yours, boy. Let Florence have him. It's you His Grace wants. Forty thousand florins if you bring the Company, twenty thousand if you come alone. For you personally. In addition to whatever we announce in public."

Toby began to shake. This was wealth beyond all the dreams of his boyhood. It was utterly crazy. He knew Milan did not want his abilities, although he was now willing to admit that he had abilities. His name alone had become a trophy, a token of prestige in the unending rivalry between the Italian states.

"Excellency, what good will money do any of us if Nevil triumphs? Pray inform His Grace that I am more deeply honored than I can say. I have given my word to Florence."

That was a point of ethics, irrelevant in a discussion of money, and it made Abonio smile with all the cuddlesome appeal of a rat.

"The duke is a man of his word, messer Longdirk. Only a fool would trust these republicans. They choose their officials by drawing names out of a bag!"

"But *Il Volpe*'s hand puts the names into the bag."

"When they do hold an election, his goons prevent his opponents from voting."

Toby chuckled unsteadily. "Exactly." What was the point of this discussion? No one could possibly run a city the way the laws said Florence was to be run. "What matter whose banners we hold, Excellency? I hope and trust that Florence and Milan will fight shoulder to shoulder against the same foe." He bowed, muttered more regrets, and prepared to leave.

"Lecco Castle?" Abonio growled. "A fiefdom of your own, for after the war, whether you bring your Company or not. The duke's daughter to wife, the fair madonna Isabetta. My brother wishes to retire from fighting soon, and His Grace will appoint you *collaterale* in his place. I have all these trifles to give you, in writing, with his seal on them."

Demons! Sweat! This was more serious. The *collaterale* was minister for war, probably the most senior state employee after the duke himself, and that was a huge step up for a mercenary. A castle had no appeal for Toby—what on earth would he do with a castle?—but if the Milanese started waving castles in front of the don, he would accept at once, and that would scramble Toby's plans completely. It was one more reason why the *condotta* must be agreed tonight.

"Excellency, my only ambition is to try and stop the Fiend from doing to Italy what he has done to the rest of Europe. I am convinced that Florence needs me far more than Milan does, for His Grace is a superb warrior in his own right and has your noble brother to serve him. Wealth and honors do not interest me." Stunning Abonio with that heretical haymaker, Toby hurried away from the torment of temptation.

At the banquet, every course was paraded in on golden trenchers by liveried flunkies—capon, veal, thrushes, pheasant, trout. Toby was seated well below the salt, down among minor merchants and their wives, but that bothered him not at all, for two years ago he would have been lucky to be allowed to beg for scraps at the kitchen door. His companions were thrilled to learn who he was, demanding to hear all about the Battle of Trent. He insisted that it was not a topic to be discussed in the presence of ladies. He was not at all sure that they were true ladies, though—hands caressed him under the table and toes nudged.

"Will the Fiend's armies return?"

"Certainly, and this time he will come in person."

Some of the women prepared to swoon. "Can you save us, *comandante?*"

"Italy can save itself, if it will just unite and support its fighting men."

Then it was the men who turned pale, because he was talking about taxes.

The dancing began around midnight. He enjoyed dancing. For his size he was agile and could twirl and pirouette and gavotte with the best of them. It was the proposals for encores that upset him. One or two of his partners straight-out suggested they run upstairs together and find a bed as soon as the music stopped, but most just dropped hints like millstones. He lost count at eight, and the three he wasn't sure of were probably being too subtle for him. Were there no faithful wives in Florence? Worse, his abstinence was soon noted, and beautiful young men began being charming to him. His glares made them melt back into the crowd very hurriedly.

Eventually, at long last, something meaningful did happen. He was accosted at the buffet table by a soft hand on his arm and an oily voice in his ear.

"My dear condottiere! Why on earth are you languishing out here among the riffraff? An honored guest like yourself should be with the real people."

Toby turned to look down at the greasy smile of roly-poly Antonio Origo and was very tempted to ask him who had let him in, because he had understood that Origo was *non grata* in Florentine society. He was the third or fourth richest man in the city and in theory also the chief magistrate, the *podestà,* but the wildly independent Florentines shunned him to show how they despised the Khan's nominee. His wife was reputed to have gone mad from grief, and he wielded no power whatsoever. That he had been included among the guests tonight was obviously a very significant development. It tended to confirm the rumors being whispered around of a special emissary from the Khan having landed at Naples.

"You honor me, *sovrano.* I just came to loot the tableware."

The *podestà* guffawed at this brilliant humor, little knowing how close to the truth it was. The hob loved pretty things, and in the days before Toby learned to control it, it would have been running amok in such surroundings, filling his pockets with gold and jewels.

Origo eased him away from the table. "Follow me," he whispered, and waddled off into the mob.

Wondering whether he was going to be hexed, poisoned, or stilettoed, Toby duly followed. The elegantly shaped tresses dangling below his guide's biretta included more than the usual number of nits. That must be symbolic of something.

5

They had left the house safely and unseen, Lisa shuffling awkwardly over the cobbles in her stolen buskins, with her hand resting on Hamish's arm, he strolling blithely, as if he had not a care in the world.

"Nice neighborhood," he remarked. He cocked an ear to the distant sounds of Carnival. "Let's go this way until I recognize somewhere."

Every one of the narrow, winding canyons looked the same to her, but she was not going to let him see how terrified she was. She forced her voice to be brave and steady. "Describe, sir, your normal procedure for rescuing damsels in distress—those who don't know where they live, I mean."

He flashed her a grin—undeceived but approving her effort.

"Normally I escort them to the Palazzo Publico and deliver them to the signory, but there are good reasons not to do so in your case."

"Because they don't know where I live either?"

"There's that. And whoever is after you may be watching there or may be in league with the signory. Also—there's the rack. After all these years of looking up to Toby, I don't want to start looking down on him. Selfish of me, I admit, but there it is."

"I don't want to put you in danger!"

"I put myself in. My decision. Don't feel guilty about it." He paused at the first corner to listen to the distant sounds of Carnival. "We go this way, I think. Instruct me, my lady. I am at your disposal, but I regret that I must leave Siena before dawn."

"Have you friends here who might assist me?"

He sighed. "Agents, not friends. It's my gold they love, not me, and none of them could be trusted with anyone as beautiful as you. I can have them try to locate your mother, but that will take a day or two."

"I understand." But Mother spent her life being not-found. Must not think about that!

"I think it would be better if you held this." He pulled a cloth from his pouch and offered it to her.

"But that's . . . why?" It was the kerchief she had used as a mask.

He shrugged self-consciously. "It might be useful. Something I read in a book once." Puzzled, she accepted it, but before she could query him further, he said, "Ah! Now I know where we are. That's the Galluza Palace. They're very respected citizens. The dowager's a woman of considerable influence in Siena. I'm sure she will not spurn a maiden in distress."

"You know her?"

They were passing under a lantern; he gave her a puzzled frown. "Lisa, I've told you. I'm only a man-at-arms."

"So you expect me to sit on the steps until morning and then get past servants who speak only Italian and drag a bad-tempered old harridan out of bed to hear a mad tale of gramarye and spies? And if the authorities may be in league with whoever's after me, then that may be the worst possible thing to do."

He sighed. "You synopsize the situation succinctly."

They walked on. Sounds of Carnival became clearer. Drunks were heading home, staggering all over the road, some still singing raucously. No one troubled the efficient-looking swordsman at her side.

"Take me to the sanctuary, then. I shall appeal to the tutelary."

"A very good idea. It's that way, on the hill west of the Piazza del Campo."

"You won't escort me?"

"I loosed a demon tonight, monna. I am in the service of Florence. The spirit will not be friends with me at all. At the very least it will confiscate my ring. It may help you, though."

But not necessarily. Many tutelaries refused to aid strangers. He was warning her politely that her plan was all fish feathers.

"If you're only a man-at-arms," she said angrily, "how can you possibly afford a guarddemon? And don't tell me you looted or pillaged it, because it wouldn't be worth having if you did."

He laughed and took her hand in his to squeeze. "I confess! I lied. It isn't mine. Our company hexer loaned it to me for this escapade, and when I return to Florence I must give it back. Truly, I am nothing more than a soldier."

She had never let a man hold her hand before, but these were exceptional circumstances. It was a strangely comforting sensation. "Then I offer you employment. Mother will certainly reward you handsomely for the help you have given me. We need some male retainers. Whatever you're being paid, I'll double it. I promise you a reward of . . ." She was not familiar with Italian money. Nor any money, really. "Enough to buy a first-class horse."

Hamish coughed harshly, as if he had swallowed

a fly. "Excuse me. A *really* first-class horse? One of the two-hundred-ducat chargers the don buys? That is a very generous offer. However . . . you must have heard of Longdirk?"

"The great general who defeated the Fiend's army last year?"

"He'd laugh if he heard you call him that. He is a great man, though. I work for Longdirk. I'm his chancellor."

Well, he had to work for someone. Condottieri could be anything from princes to brigands, and Sir Tobias Longdirk was at least famous. Or he was now, for no one had heard of him before the Battle of Trent. There was a gruesome story about a burning forest.

"What does a chancellor do?"

"Spies, among other things."

"Spies for whom? Who does Longdirk work for?"

"Whoever will help him fight the Fiend, but Florence needs him more than the others do. You see," Hamish said earnestly, "there's five big states in Italy— Milan, Venice, Rome, and Naples. And Florence. None of the rest count for much. Florence is the smallest of the five, and militarily it's far weaker than the others. It distrusts soldiers. It has never, ever, appointed a native-born captain-general, so hiring a non-Italian like Toby fits their tradition."

"Florence is planning to make war on Siena?"

"Oh, no. The cities must combine again. When Nevil sent Schweitzer last year, some of them cobbled together an alliance—which was largely Longdirk's doing, incidentally. They all knew him and trusted him, so they voted him in as *comandante*. He talked the Swiss into joining. Then he walloped Schweitzer, but this year Nevil's certain to come himself. Time is running . . . Sorry. I'm lecturing."

"Go on, please," she said automatically. "It's very interesting."

"No it isn't. I have this bad habit. Don't encourage me, or I'll harangue you all night on everything from acarology to zymurgy. Let's solve your problem first."

"I definitely want to hear about zymurgy later. How much does this Longdirk man pay you?"

"Four ducats a month when he has it. We're a few months in arrears at the moment."

"Oh. Well, my offer of the horse still stands. Two hundred ducats. And eight ducats a month. And I'll make up your arrears, too."

"Including my board and arms and horses? No!" he said before she could answer. "I'm joking." Now he seemed to know exactly where he was going, heading uphill, moving along the smelly alleys as fast as she could keep up. "I'm more than just one of Longdirk's men. He has an incredible knack of inspiring loyalty, but I can honestly claim to be his best friend. We were boys together. He was my hero, and he took me with him when he left Scotland. Nevil's been hunting us ever since, although it's Toby he wants. You can't buy me."

She knew what he wanted her to say. He was not going to suggest it himself, but he had left her no option.

"How far is it to Florence?"

"About fourteen English leagues. Say two days with the roads the way they are just now. We won't push the horses unless we have to."

"I'm a very good . . . 'We'?"

"Me and Carlo and Rinaldo. They're waiting at an inn outside the walls. There's no curfew tonight. We'll have no trouble at the gates."

We again! But he knew that she knew that she had no choice. Her heart was pounding as if she had a tertian fever.

"Master Campbell, I am very grateful for what you have done for me already, but I do wish you would make up your mind. If you are only a soldier of fortune, then name your price, and I will meet it. If you are a gentleman, then I must appeal to your chivalry. Which is it to be?"

He winced. "My lady, you don't want either. Most mercenaries would take your money and betray you. Most gentlemen would . . . be even worse. Don Ramon, for example—never mind. Please just accept me as a friend. I will gladly set my men to work on locating your mother, and I will be honored to escort you to Florence and give you shelter there until they do. I will accept no payment or reward except a few of those wonderful smiles of yours, because they are beyond price."

The rush of relief made her knees weak, but it also told her that she had made the right decision. Poor Mother would be frantic. And when she did find out what had happened to her wayward daughter—if she ever did—she would be utterly appalled. Riding off with a common *mercenary* to another city, another country? But what else was she to do?

"By all means let us be friends! You must call me Mistress Lisa, and I will call you Sir Hamish, for I think you really are a gentleman, a true gentleman. I have always found a man's manners to be a more reliable guide to his true quality than his lands or the number of portraits above his banquet table." She had also learned, over the years of a very lonely childhood, that solid men of humble status—grooms and servants— were often much more pleasant company and much more respectful to a young lady than certain gentlemen. Mother would regard that belief as rankest heresy, but Mother had never been backed into a corner by a snotty many-handed adolescent who thought he had the hereditary right to do anything to anyone. "I am very grateful and will smile like a stuffed cockatrice all the way to Florence if it pleases you."

"Oh, Lisa, I'm sorry, really sorry. I shouldn't have mocked you. You know the danger you're in, and you're behaving very bravely. Pay me if you want. I am in need of money. I shouldn't put on airs and pretend I'm not. I have a hole in my boot and can't afford to get it mended."

"I insulted you."

"No, no. I was presumptuous. But whether I'm your paid bodyguard or just a friend in need, I give you my word that no harm will befall you. I promise Longdirk won't use you."

"*Use* me?"

"Politically, I mean."

"I don't understand. How could he use me politically?"

"Oh, nothing," Hamish muttered. "Forget I said that. I read too many books, that's all."

6

Toby followed pudgy *podestà* Origo past unobtrusive guards to an unassuming door and into a warren of dimly lit smaller rooms where another sort of party was under way. In spite of his ability to look over heads, he had trouble making out who was present in the gloom, but they were all men, all standing, all discoursing in whispers.

"You know the noble Guilo, of course?" Origo vanished into the crowd with the air of someone who has just scraped something unpleasant off his boot.

Toby did know Guilo, a weedy, slightly pop-eyed young man, a very minor member of the clan. They bowed, flattering each other as *"comandante"* and *"magnifico,"* respectively. "Your Magnificence" was a servile way of addressing a man who lacked any official title, but it was understood in Florence that the Magnificent was one man in particular. He would be around here somewhere. And Toby had long since given up trying to convince the Florentines that his title of *comandante in capo* had been a field appointment, good only for the day of battle.

Obviously Cousin Guilo had been designated

sheepdog, to make sure the mercenary spoke with all
the right people and none of the wrong. When they
arrived at a group, the whispers would stop abruptly.
Fulsome greetings would lead into the standard
questions: Would the Fiend invade Italy? How soon?
Could he be stopped? How much was it going to cost?
Toby gave standard answers: yes, this spring, yes,
plenty. Then he would be led away, and the muttering
would start up again at his back.

They came at last to a brighter room, where a
single glance identified enough of the top politicos
of the city to show that this was the center of the
web. A massive, florid-faced burgher in the center
was pontificating in a wine-slurred roar. He was the
current chairman of the *dieci della guerra,* the council for war, messer Jacopo Benozzo, and the kindest
word the don ever used about him was "buffoon."
According to the unsupported word of Master
Hamish Campbell, his nose was much in demand in
winter for roasting chestnuts. Marradi himself stood
at the edge of the group—silent, unobtrusive, ob-
serving.

The moment of truth was approaching.

Until that day, Toby had left the negotiating to the
don, who was much better at it. Unlike Toby, he could
tell lies with a straight face, because he believed whatever he wanted to believe. Truth was anything he
needed it to be. He despised money in any form, considered fighting for money shameful, and thus genuinely
hated to agree to anything, especially with merchants
like Benozzo or even Marradi, who were lower than

the dirt under his horse. He drove them crazy. Why not?—he was crazy himself, oblivious to reality. Yet he was creepily perceptive at divining what Toby wanted to do and ordering him to do it. When they had first met, he had been leading an army that existed only in his muddled mind—noble knights, infantry, bands, guns, everything. Toby had made his dream come true, putting him at the head of the finest mercenary company in all Italy.

But that morning Pietro Marradi had summoned messer Longdirk to Florence, taken him into a very small private office, and shut the door. Alone, the two of them had negotiated the *condotta* that had been under discussion for months. Now all that remained was to ram it through the proper channels.

Introductions, bows, the usual stately minuet of banalities . . . War slid gently into the discussion. So did Antonio Origo. In fourteen years the Khanate had done nothing to oppose Nevil's rebellion, but the presence of the *podestà* in the inner circle suggested that this might be about to change.

"Yes, the Fiend can be beaten," Toby said for the hundredth time that night. "But only if Italy will unite. The cities must agree upon a *comandante* and give him the forces he will need. Time is running out. If Florence does not soon replace the late and sadly missed Captain-General Vespucci and start building a sizable army of its own, then it will not only be pitifully vulnerable, it will have no seat at the allies' table."

There! How did that feel? Marradi had told him to

.pull no punches, and punching was one thing Toby Longdirk did very well indeed.

"Indeed?" Pietro murmured. The listeners shuffled themselves quickly to include him in the group. "This news disturbs me." It could hardly surprise him, for nothing in Florence was concluded until he had approved every detail. "What is delaying the negotiations, messer Benozzo?"

The fat man wrinkled his grotesque nose in disgust. "The Spaniard. The man is a maniac!"

"He has very high ideals," Toby murmured sadly.

"And very few wits. However, we have made some progress."

Marradi waited for more. The buffoon began to bluster.

"We are making progress! We have agreed on the limits of the captain-general's authority over our *provisionati,* the proportion of his men's wages to be withheld as tax, the amounts of those wages to be issued in cloth and in grain, the form of muster rolls that will be presented and the frequency of our inspections, regulation of prices for victuals and the markets . . ." And so on, all meaningless details that were more or less standard in any *condotta.* He subsided like a punctured wineskin and at last fell silent.

"So much?" marveled the Magnificent. "Then there can be little left to decide. Cannot the rest be cleared up tomorrow so that we may seal the *condotta* and swear in our new captain-general? Say by noon?"

Toby watched in admiring silence. As he had risen in the world, he had come to appreciate power, and no one wielded it with greater skill than *Il Volpe*. There was power and power, of course. Toby knew *push* power, because he had had some of that all his life. The ability to force men when you had an army at your back was much like forcing with two large fists and a lot of muscle. But to make the army follow you, you need *pull* power, and that was quite different. He had learned in Spain that he possessed it, but he still did not quite understand how it worked. He had grown into it, he thought, and it seemed to feed on its own success. The Magnificent had it in bushels. His *pull* power was invisible, yet every man in the room could see it. Like a willow, it seemed frail and harmless, but it suffered nothing to grow too close to it. It worked inside men's minds to put chains on their limbs.

Power was the opportunity to make mistakes.

Benozzo squirmed. "If the Spaniard will see reason."

"I shall do my best to persuade him," Toby promised solemnly.

Marradi allowed himself a smile, which quickly spread to most of the onlookers. "Then I see no problem. Are there still knots in the wool, messer?"

"Cost, Your Magnificence. The size of the forces to be raised."

"Mm? And what does Sir Tobias think?" Marradi looked to Toby with no hint that the two of them had spent the entire morning haggling over this.

"Everything you can possibly afford, Your Magnificence! At least twenty thousand men." He felt a swell of protest rising around him. "With any less,

Florence will have no hope and certainly no voice at the table—not when Venice is raising forty and Milan at least seventy. Only a supreme effort by all the states combined can stop the Fiend. We'll need a miracle to hold him at the Alps as we did last year."

"You expect us to let you march off and leave the city undefended?" bleated one of the younger men.

Toby looked down on him in exasperation, remembering days when Don Ramon had returned from the negotiations in near-homicidal frenzy. "If every city thinks like that, then the Fiend will swallow you one at a time! If Florence will not send its army north, why should Naples?" He wanted to add, "You idiot!" but managed not to.

Benozzo was looking pleased. "The don was talking of five thousand lances."

"I doubt that we can find that many now. They are all sworn elsewhere."

"A moment, signori," Pietro murmured. "Pardon the ignorance of a civilian. How many men in a lance, *comandante?*"

Now what game was he playing? That morning he had displayed an iron-fisted grasp of military matters down to the finest details.

"Usually six, Your Magnificence. Originally, of course, it was three—the knight himself, his sergeant to hold his spare horse, and a page. The coming of firearms has brought heavier armor and a far greater toll of horses, so now the knight requires more spare mounts, and hence more attendants to care for them."

"I see. But only one man in six is actually a fighter?"

"That is correct, although nowadays they may dismount, and then two men handle the lance."

"How about infantry?"

"Very much the same, about one in five or one in six."

"How many men in the Longdirk Company itself?" Either Marradi was using Toby as a ventriloquist's dummy to educate the men who would have to approve the *condotta* and vote the taxes to pay for it, or else he wanted Toby to demonstrate that he was more than an oversize thug capable of swinging a battle-ax. Either way, it was lecture time.

"Three thousand, but the most we can put in the field is about five hundred—five hundred helmets, we say. This seems a shameful limitation, but any condottiere will confirm it. Of the five hundred, about half are cavalry and half foot. Our infantry companies include pikemen, crossbowmen, and arquebusiers. The don leads our heavy cavalry in person, and we also have four squadrons of light cavalry armed with crossbows. Either may dismount and fight on foot when conditions require."

Marradi nodded solemnly, as if all this were new and wonderful. "I can understand a mounted knight requiring five attendants, but surely a common man-at-arms can sharpen his own pike?"

"He will be in considerable trouble with Marshal Diaz if he does not, Your Magnificence! But he requires the support of shield men, ammunition carriers, munitioners, fletchers, carters, pioneers, buglers, cooks, pay clerks, barber-surgeons, gunners, stonemasons, provisioners, and armorers. He travels to battle on horseback, so he needs farriers, saddlers—"

"Stonemasons?" one of the younger men demanded.

"To cut the cannonballs. We have six light cannons. In good weather on flat terrain they require only ten carts and twenty pairs of oxen apiece, but to take them across the Apennines, say, would require far more. To move the entire Company . . ."

Toby could go on indefinitely. He had just begun describing the *casa*, with the paymaster, quartermaster, hexer, chancellors, and other essential staff when an almost imperceptible nod from Marradi told him he had made his point. If any man present had thought that Florence was hiring a disorganized rabble of hoodlums, he should know better now.

"And how many men will Nevil bring?"

"At least a hundred thousand." A more realistic estimate would just frighten them out of their wits. "Schweitzer had about forty at Trent."

"Not fighting strength?"

"No, total. About seven thousand helmets. I expect Nevil to bring three times that many." At least.

"And how many can Italy raise?" asked a fat-faced man.

"Enough to defeat him," Toby said patiently, "if it can bring them all to bear at the right place and the right time. If not, he will pluck the goose one feather at a time."

"But Florence can only bear so much of the burden," Benozzo protested. "Naples and Venice are much richer and—"

Toby's scowl stopped him. "Will you risk letting the Fiend's horde loose in your streets for the sake of a year's higher taxes? Nevil's men are mindless puppets, suicidal, driven by demons. You cannot match them one for one. The Fiend himself is an incarnate demon and rejoices in causing destruction and suffering."

"What is the least amount you will accept?" Pietro asked quietly. The maneuvering was over; the battle was about to commence.

"Sixty thousand florins a month. Gold florins."

They did not gasp. They had known the news was going to be bad. They were not smiling.

"For twenty thousand men," Toby said. "If I can find them. The best companies are already signing with other states—Alfredo's with Venice, the Black Lances with Milan, and today word of Jules Desjardins with Naples. These are bands I hoped to enlist. Soon there will be nothing but dregs left."

Il Volpe studied him carefully, seemingly ignoring the audience. "At three gold florins a man? Eighteen florins a month for every helmet?" That was many times the pay of a skilled artisan. The brilliant red-brown eyes challenged Toby to back down, as they had that morning.

As he had that morning, he stood his ground. "For a six-month contract with a six-month option. That does not include the upkeep of your own *provisionati*, but I require that they be under my command. I cannot undertake the defense of Florence on any lesser terms."

Less than three years ago he had been a penniless outlaw. Now he was bullying the richest city in the world.

Benozzo's snort would have roused a herd of mares. "Captain-General Vespucci, may his spirit find—"

"Was not hired to fight this war. Costs of arms and supplies, of fodder and armor, have risen enormously. Warhorses are trading for three hundred ducats."

Mention of prices caused the company to explode:

"The wool trade has collapsed!"

"The price of silk . . ."

"Taxes are already higher than . . ."

One large man managed to shout down the others. "A three-month *condotta?* The crisis will surely be over by then!"

Absurd! Toby folded his arms. "The men have to arm themselves, mount themselves, travel here from winter quarters. On a shorter contract the price goes up. No. Those terms, or I offer my sword elsewhere." Pull no punches!

Marradi spoke into the deadly silence. "This is your last word, *comandante?*"

"It is, Your Magnificence." The night had become even more unreal.

The despot looked thoughtfully around the group, one man at a time, and did not seem pleased. He pursed his lips.

"How much is Milan offering you now, messer Longdirk?"

The onlookers bristled in alarm. Toby should have known that no one kept secrets from Marradi in his own palace. A truthful answer would not be believed.

"Enough to buy the don if he hears of it, Your Magnificence."

"You would go with him?"

"Undoubtedly."

"I see. You leave us little choice. Paolo? Giovanni?" One by one, Marradi queried the onlookers. One by one they pouted, squirmed, then nodded. "So we are agreed?" He turned to Toby and offered a hand. "You have your *condotta,* messer."

Toby released a long breath and bent to kiss those delicate fingers. As he straightened, Benozzo made his snorting noise again.

"But you will not allow us to hail you as captain-general?"

"That title must go to the don, Your Magnificence."

"He is a raving madman!"

"And he would chop me in cutlets if I dared belittle his status in the Company. He is your condottiere, Your Honors. I am his high constable, no more. We share the duties—he takes the glory, and I do all the work."

One advantage of a total inability to lie was that one was believed when telling the truth. The audience looked puzzled, but not disbelieving. If anyone could understand how a man might wield power in the background while using another for a figurehead, it ought to be these Florentines.

"You were elected capo at Trent," Benozzo complained.

"The don graciously allowed me to accept the title. He prefers to fight as close to the enemy as possible, and he knew so large an army could not be led from the front line." That was true. It was also true that the other commanders would sooner have blown themselves out of cannons than ever elect Don Ramon to anything.

"We all realize," *podestà* Origo said with a smile that would have left an oily shimmer on the Mediterranean, "that you needed the Spaniard's name and reputation when you founded the Company. But why do you bother to hide behind him now?"

Toby needed a moment to work out the logic again and make sure he had not misunderstood the first time. Then he needed more time to calm himself lest an explosion of anger waken the hob. Finally he said, "It is true that I have refused offers of continued employment from Verona and Naples and others. When they paid me, I served them as well as I knew how, giving them full value. That was business. But I do not throw *friends* away when my need for them is past, Your Excellency!" He had not totally masked his disgust, for Origo flinched.

Il Volpe contrived a thin smile without showing his teeth. "Yet the citizens would be happier if the famous Longdirk were their official protector."

"My regrets, Your Magnificence." Toby set his jaw to indicate extreme stubbornness. That was something else he was very good at. It required no deception at all.

Pietro sighed tolerantly. "The baton to the don, then. We shall issue two silver helmets, though."

"You do me great honor, but again I respectfully decline. I am an easy enough target without that." Now the onlookers' bewilderment was becoming affront and suspicion. These men spent their lives chasing trappings of grandeur, and most of them would sell their own mothers for much less than what he was refusing. He was insulting them and their values. "Signori, in my native land we believe it is unlucky to count chickens still in the shell. Offer me prizes after the victory, not before the enemy is even in sight." Besides, he was a foreign-born stripling—how would seasoned Italian troops feel if they saw him in a silver helmet? He was also a lowborn bastard, although the bastardy part did not seem to matter in Italy.

"You will swear the oath?" Benozzo demanded truculently.

"I will gladly swear allegiance to the noble republic of Florence." He wondered if the oath-taking ceremony would be held in the sanctuary. His participation there would only be possible if the tutelary agreed that the hob was not a demon. If it decided otherwise, it might blast him to ashes. Worse, it might try to exorcise the hob and destroy his mind in the attempt.

7

The congratulations Guilo babbled as he herded the *comandante* to the door went unheard. Toby's mind was soaring far beyond the seventh sphere of heaven. In reality, if not in name, he was now Captain-General of Florence and held the fate of the city in his hands but no one could save Florence if Italy fell so he was in effect undertaking to save the whole peninsula but Nevil would never rest until he controlled all Europe so Toby was really undertaking—

Whoa! One lifetime at a time!

He would have to repeat the miracle of Trent. It was fortunate that Benozzo and his fellow commissioners did not realize how much of an incredible fluke Trent had been. The assembled captains-general and *collaterali* had elected the big foreigner *comandante* that day only because they thought the cause was hopeless, and he would be an ideal scapegoat. The cause had been hopeless until he had tricked Schweitzer into drawing up his forces on the downwind side of a pine forest and then been ruthless enough to exploit that mistake. Nevil would never fall into such a trap. Guilo closed the door with himself on one side of it and Toby on the other. The lock clicked. Nevil would—

The lock had clicked!

Surprise snatched Toby back from dreams and sent his hand groping for a nonexistent sword. He was alone in a long gallery, its heavy darkness salted with a very few candle flames gleaming like stars. One wall bore a parade of gilt-framed portraits, but the bronze and marble statues set between them provided a dozen shadowy hiding places. Heavy velvet drapes opposite meant bright windows by day but might conceal regiments of killers at night. He reached behind him to test whether the door had been locked and then decided not to—he could do nothing about it if it was, and it didn't matter if it wasn't. Certainly Guilo would be standing guard outside, whether the purpose was assassination or merely assignation.

Toby strode over to the nearest candelabra, a head-high tangle of bronze sea serpents, and lifted it as if to inspect the portraits. It weighed quite enough to smash skulls with if need be. There he waited, thinking back to what Guilo had said—something about another meeting, someone wanting to meet with him? And a smile. Not a murderer's leer, more of a silly smirk. No matter, the kid might not be in on the real plot.

Silence, except for faint sounds of an orchestra beyond the far door. The longer he was kept waiting, the less likely that there was an innocent explanation. How many would there be, what weapons would they use? Against bow or gun his size was more handicap than help; against blades, up to two or even three, he would have a reasonable chance with the sea serpents. Poisoned blades would be another matter. Then a flash of movement, a flicker of golden cloth just beyond a great hunk of contorted marble . . .

"You are keeping me waiting."

Lucrezia!

"I'm admiring your ancestors, *duchessa*. Which one was this? Why did he look like that? Did he have gout, or was he a lawyer?" The Marradi family could afford to marry well now—it was amazing how the highborn would swallow their pride and disgorge a daughter in return for a few sacks of gold—but it had sprung from humble roots. The don would dismiss this entire collection with a sneering remark about pedlars and fish merchants.

"Don't be tiresome, Tobiaso. You had just as many ancestors as we did, and you have just as little idea of what they really looked like. Now come here." She was artfully posed on a padded silk couch between two towering marble giants.

He strolled toward her, keeping the corners of his eyes peeled but fairly confident now that he faced nothing worse than grievous social embarrassment. "I do know what mine looked like. They looked like English soldiers. They were probably in uniform at the time."

"You expect to shock me, Tobiaso? When a man catches my eye I inquire into his history."

Shock her? Shock Lucrezia Marradi? According to Hamish, who was never wrong when he was being serious, she had two daughters older than Toby, had several times escaped conviction for hexing only because witnesses or magistrates had conveniently died, and had come home to Florence because her sixteen-year-old son had banished her from Ferrara for poisoning his father. She was a beautiful and fascinating woman. The gleam in her eyes could flatter a man to madness.

He set down the candelabra and grinned vacuously. "Wonderful party, madonna!"

"You are not drunk!"

She was, though. He was sorry to see that. It would make matters more difficult.

"Just intoxicated by your beauty."

She jumped up, a child doll staring imperiously at him. "Sit!"

He perched his bulk on the edge of the couch. She remained standing, and their eyes were level. Why did she have to hurt herself like this? He was twice her size and half her age.

Any man who felt sorry for Lucrezia Marradi was out of his mind.

Smiling coyly, she patted his cheek. "You never get drunk, you never sleep with women, and tonight you refused two of the most beautiful boys in Florence."

"You forgot the sheep."

"I'll send for one if you ask nicely. Why don't you want a silver helmet?"

Gramarye? Possibly. More likely she had eavesdropped on his rehearsal with her brother that morning. Didn't matter. "It would annoy the don. I have enough troubles without that."

"And the Milanese earldom?"

"Promises are cheap."

She moved forward to stand between his knees. Her perfume closed around him like velvet. "You are a strange and fascinating man, Tobiaso. You hide your success. Usually when peasants rise to higher station they scream their glory from the roof-tops."

"Or their wives do. I was outlawed at eighteen, monna. I learned not to draw attention to myself." He was sweating. There were enough jewels in her hair alone to finance a summer's campaigning, and the promises in her eyes were brighter yet. This was dangerous, deadly. Briefly he thought of being like other men, and his head swam with longing. Yes, he had the hob under control now, most of the time, but certain things he must avoid: demons, terror, rage—and passion. Already he could feel it stirring as his heart began to beat faster. Only once had he ever tried to make love to a woman, and the hob had gone berserk. Jeanne had died; half the hamlet had perished in fire and chaos. Never again would he dare succumb to desire.

"If my abstinence were from choice, *duchessa,* you would have melted it a long time ago."

Her pretty lip curled in mockery. "Are you admitting to a tragic battle wound, Tobiaso?"

Why must she pick on him? Although the life expectancy of her lovers was scandalously low, there were scores of men in the Marradi Palace tonight who would fight duels for a chance to bed Lucrezia. She was pathetic as well as deadly.

"Only a broken heart. Let us part as friends, madonna."

"Look!"

She gestured at the nearest statue, an oversize, overmuscled male brandishing a club and wearing only a lion skin that concealed nothing of importance. Doubtless this was a very clever use of a hunk of marble, but to an uncultured backwoods yokel it was obscene. He scowled at it.

"I could not locate a lion skin, Tobias," Lucrezia said throatily. "But I have a leopard skin waiting upstairs. You will pose for me."

"I am honored, but I don't want to spoil your fantasies."

"You will surpass them. You will be a superb Hercules."

"Is that his name? He's a bit paunchy, isn't he?" Toby flowed to his feet, clasping her shoulders and lifting her aside so he would not bowl her over. That was a mistake. She weighed nothing. His fingers registered the warmth of her skin, and he saw his strength excited her. Her eyes were bright, her lips moist and expectant. There was gramarye in her allure, making the hob stir under his calm like a shark in a still pool.

"Most beautiful madonna, Florence paid me an infinite compliment tonight by making me her defender, but what you suggest is more flattering still. Were it possible, I should never hesitate. There is no one else, believe me, nor could any woman come before you. Yet it cannot be. My heart breaks. I thank you, but I must bid you good night." He bowed and walked quickly toward the far end of the gallery and the sounds of the orchestra, hoping she had left the key in the lock.

"Stop!" More than the command itself, her tone made him turn. She was holding one hand close to her mouth, and spears of light flashed off the jewels of her rings. If she had a demon immured in one of those, then a few words would serve to unleash it. "You think you can spurn me like that, boy? You great barbarian lout! You are about to suffer. You will grovel naked at my feet, howling for release, for pain, for anything I choose to—"

"No!" Toby shouted. "You must not use gramarye on me, *duchessa!*" His fragile control over the hob would shatter if it sensed the presence of demons. Any gramarye would provoke it. "No, no, I beg you! You endanger the whole palace!"

Unconvinced, Lucrezia began whispering an incantation.

Anything might have happened then, had not Hercules hurled himself to the floor beside her with an earsplitting crash that jarred the whole building. Fragments of marble and mosaic tiles flew like hail; gravel rattled and boulders rolled. Lucrezia recoiled with a startled yell. The orchestra outside wailed into silence. For a frozen instant duchess and mercenary stared at each other in mutual dismay. A hundred people would come flooding into the gallery to investigate.

Lucrezia rapped out a command and vanished faster than a soap bubble.

So she was a hexer! That did not mean she had deliberately pulled over the statue, though. In among those rings she was wearing, she must have at least one guarddemon. It had recognized the hob in him, foreseen the danger when Lucrezia tried to use gramarye on him, and provided a diversion.

Whoever heard of a demon capable of that kind of subtle thinking?

A distant clamor of voices reminded him of his peril. He dived for the door, unlocked it, and stepped back behind it just before it flew open and a jabbering crowd of guests and servants poured through. In the pervading gloom, he was able to tag on the end as if he had entered with them. A matching throng rushed in from the far end, and everyone gathered over the remains, clamoring in astonishment. A statue falls over in an empty room?—what an extraordinary omen!

8

As dawn gilded chimneys under a buttermilk sky, Toby strode out to the stable yard, relieved that the party was over and he was free to go. The air was cool and sweet, and even the potent tang of horses was welcome after the cloying palace scents. The buzz in his head came only from lack of sleep, for he had drunk much less than most of the guests. He was carrying the unconscious and partially clad don slung over his shoulder.

The waiting men-at-arms of the escort jeered like seagulls at this evidence of an aristocrat's inability to stay the course, although they expected a man to whore and drink himself senseless on every possible opportunity, because that was what they did themselves whenever they could afford to. Then they began taunting Toby for being able to leave on his own feet, as if this evidenced lack of manhood. He laughed aloud, enjoying their vulgar banter far more than the cynical backstabbing of the gentry he had just left.

The men of the Don Ramon Company were a diverse lot, whose roots spanned the Continent from Portugal to Poland. Some had been born in marble halls and others, like him, in the ditches of poverty. They all shared courage, pride in their own endurance, and a fierce independence that would tolerate neither weaklings in their ranks nor incompetent officers. Among the rights they claimed was that of electing the don's honor guard, and thus to serve in it was a mark of approval greatly prized. There, in the morning chill, illiterate pike-wielding thugs stood elbow to elbow with knights who led entourages of their own. Toby belonged with the thugs, of course.

He heaved the unconscious don aboard the coach as he had once heaved sacks of meal for the miller back in Tyndrum, then glanced around. A man must not arrive at a ball covered in mud and reeking of horse, but that did not mean he had to go home in the same dreadful engine of torture in which he had arrived. He thumped a handy shoulder.

"Facino, I grant you the privilege of holding the condottiere's hand on the journey. Make sure he doesn't choke. I'll see your horse gets back safely."

As a staunch Italian republican, Facino was unimpressed by the Spaniard's impeccable pedigree, and he erupted in lurid protestations that being bounced around in a box with an unconscious drunk was above and beyond the call of duty. His comrades barked more cannonades of laughter.

"I'll give you a medal!" Toby hoisted him bodily into the coach, although he was no lightweight, then closed the door on him. The onlookers laughed louder still, and now even the knights among them were joining in.

Facino's head came out of the window. "A gold one!"

"He didn't tell you where he's going to hang it, Facino!"

"It's the horse that deserves the medal!"

And so on. Chuckling, Toby turned to adjust the stirrup leathers on Facino's mount. He was forestalled—

"Allow me this honor, *comandante!*" The big man with the buttery smile was Baldassare Barrafranca, former lord of Rimini. His career as a condottiere was a catalogue of dismal mediocrity, but he was a capable enough fighter when aimed in the right direction and told when to start. He led his own post of five lances. He was not a man Toby Longdirk would turn his back on in a dark alley.

At which thought, Toby glanced around and caught the eye of the Chevalier D'Anjou. For a fleeting moment he saw slavering jaws, yellow fangs, and slitted wolfish eyes, as if some demonic nightmare was about to leap on him. He blinked, and the illusion had gone—lack of sleep could play strange tricks on a man. The veteran knight was scarred and weather-beaten, with a gray-streaked beard and head habitually canted to favor his right eye, but he was no demon. On the other hand, he could not be described as likable. Toby could not recall ever seeing the crabby old black-guard smile before.

"That is as long as they will go, *comandante*," Barrafranca said, oozing back with a half bow.

"Thank you." Toby put a boot in the stirrup and swung up onto the mare. He nodded to the Chevalier. "Lead the men out, if you please, *squadriere*."

There was a perceptible pause before the yellow teeth showed again. "It is my honor, *comandante*. Guard, mount up!"

The seigneur disliked taking orders from the Scottish bastard. Toby watched the old scoundrel scramble onto his great destrier with help from his squire. Camp tales described him as the last survivor of the French royal house, rightful monarch of several countries. Unlike Barrafranca, he had no cause to blame his misfortunes on Toby—which did not mean he couldn't or wouldn't. He might have been danger-ous if he had not knocked all his brains out years ago.

The procession clattered off along the Via Larga in proper order—six men in pairs, the coach, and a dozen more men behind. Toby was absurdly conspicuous in his party silks, but the others all wore leathers, hel-mets, and breastplates emblazoned with the don's arms of three papillons argent upon gules.

Conversation was impossible in the cramped streets, with carts and pedestrians to be avoided and the clatter of hooves echoing between drab stone walls. He was leaving Florence with what he had come for—three florins a man, twenty thousand men, six months minimum. Three hundred and sixty thousand ducats! What would the good folk back in Strath Fillan say to wee Toby Strangerson earning that kind of money? He would get to keep none of it and the lowly men expected to die for it would see little more. Florence paid a portion in food and fodder, and withheld taxes on all of it. One fifth went to Josep Brusi in Barcelona as return on his investment, another fifth to the don, although he must pay for the artillery out of that. Each man had to provide his own weapons and mounts, or have his pay docked to cover their cost. Toby's share was officially one twentieth, but he always took the last twentieth, which was rarely there to take, because cities were notoriously lax about paying their mercenaries. And there were always unforeseen costs.

His chances of living to enjoy a *soldo* of it were remote anyway. If he had any sense at all, he would catch a ship to Africa and never come back. Longdirk versus the Fiend—why pursue a feud so hopeless? He often wondered about that. He seemed to be too stupid to do anything except fight on.

The company rattled through the Porta Pinti and set off along the Fiesole road, through countryside wakening to spring and a fine day. Escaping thoughts of all the work waiting for him in camp, he spurred forward to join Leonello and Agostino, and listen to their discussion of the relative merits of fat women and thin women, a subject about which he knew absolutely nothing and could never hope to.

9

D'Anjou rode at the head of the line on Oriflamme, who was still his favorite, although the old warhorse was long past his days of glory. So was his master, for that matter. A night dozing on a bale of straw in an overcrowded stable had turned his backbone into a red-hot iron bar. He ought to ask the company hexer to straighten out the kinks for him. The present one was impressively expert and did not demand outrageous fees, but it was a point of honor for an old campaigner not to make such a request until the fighting season opened. He would suffer longer in the name of honor.

Uninvited, another horse settled into place alongside Oriflamme. The Chevalier scowled unwelcome at its rider.

"There were interesting rumors going around last night," the newcomer remarked in heavily accented French. He was Baldassare Barrafranca—a stupid, boorish man of nondescript lineage. He had left the stable for a while during the bodyguard's nightlong vigil and gone off to worm his way into the palace kitchens—making a play for some of the female domestics, no doubt.

"There are always rumors," D'Anjou snapped. "If they reported that the noble High Constable Longdirk shits nothing but nuggets of pure gold, then I must inform you that this is absolute holy truth. He also pisses pure vintage Bordeaux."

Barrafranca chuckled coarsely. "I have better vin-

tage here. Finest Chianti—Monseigneur?" He offered
a wineskin.

"You will withdraw that word." D'Anjou did not
raise his voice, but his tone conveyed mortal threat. He
had shed blood often enough over matters of honor. In
his present station titles were mockery, and he steadfastly refused to acknowledge any hereditary rank.
Knighthood he had earned, so he would remain
merely "Chevalier" until the Fiend was overthrown
and he could return to claim his birthright.

"Of course, messer!" the Italian said hurriedly. "I
have no wish to offend."

"Then I accept your apology and also your wine."
The rotten stuff would rinse the early-morning sour-
ness from his mouth. D'Anjou reached for the wineskin, but the move twisted his back, making him bite
back a gasp of agony. He was not an old man by tally
of years, but the human frame was never meant to be
packed into a steel shell, lifted seven or so feet off the
ground, accelerated to full gallop, and then struck off
again by a wooden beam moving equally fast in the
opposite direction. Two or three such impacts could be
forgotten, but the effects were cumulative. There had
also been crossbow bolts and arquebus balls. Now he
had to cock his head sideways to see clearly, and his
hand would no longer grip a lance as it should be
gripped. To stop and give up, though, was unthinkable.

He drank and wiped his mouth. Italian horse piss!
He thought longingly of the wines of his youth, the
subtle, delicate progeny of vineyards his father had

lovingly planted at various châteaux. Gone, alas! But
what would his father have said to a son of his serving
as common bodyguard to mercenary rabble, spending
the night in a stinking stable while the trash he was
forced to serve hobnobbed in the luxury of a palace?
That he was not worthy of decent wines?

"Tell me the rumors then," he said.

"Well, first, our noble condottiere is to be Captain-
General of Florence."

D'Anjou spat at the weeds. "Did one ever doubt
it? One does not grudge the Spanish boy his success."
Or not very much. The child put on absurd airs, but
give him a lance and a horse and he was magnificent,
worthy of comparison with legendary knights like
Du Guesclin, De Coucy, or Lancelot himself. More
to the point, Don Ramon had a pedigree as long as
D'Anjou's own, a genuinely noble lineage, even if
his family had fallen on hard times in the last few
centuries. "He is a man of courage."

"This is most true. And a man of breeding."

Ha! Baldassare Barrafranca talking about breeding? It was to laugh. He claimed to be marquis of some
tin-pot town in the Romagna, but his grandfather had
stolen the title at sword point, and he himself had lost
it through his own incompetence as a condottiere—
incompetence revealed, amusingly enough, by the cur
Longdirk. Dog eat dog.

It was nice to know that history could throw up a
scrap of justice once in a while. D'Anjou had seen little of it in his life. As a child he had been Louis, but all
his male relatives had borne that name among oth-

ers—uncles, cousins, even his brothers and both his sons—and theirs had been a very large family, spread across Europe. Its head had been an Uncle Louis who sometimes wore a golden hat and sat on a fancy chair in Paris—a most excellent man, cursed by ill fortune. When the King of England succumbed to a mysterious and extremely fatal accident and was succeeded by the juvenile and extremely inexperienced Prince Nevil, King Louis had launched a war against him, which was the correct and time-honored thing to do in the circumstances. It was gravest misfortune that the stripling turned out to be the greatest military genius since Genghis. Louis had lost the war, his throne, his land, and eventually his skin, which Nevil had removed personally to have tanned and made into a jerkin.

The procession was climbing the hill to Fiesole now, winding back and forth. Without risking protest from his back, D'Anjou could inspect the procession and see that all was well. A gap was opening in front of the coach. He slowed his pace a little.

"The don knows how war should be fought," Barrafranca mumbled. He was drunk—but evidently not too drunk, because he added quickly, "But not as you do, of course, messer."

"This is true."

Back in 1511, D'Anjou had girded on armor as so many others had done, kissed his wife and sons good-bye, promised to be home in a month, and ridden off at the head of his knights in support of his liege. He had never seen his estates or his family again. He had never stopped fighting. When France had fallen, he had offered his lance to the King of Burgundy, who was then the Khan's suzerain. When Burgundy fell, Lorraine. After Lorraine, Alsace. He had lost count of the battles, the wounds, the horses killed under him, defeat after defeat after defeat. One by one his knights had died. Without fee or booty or ransoms, the losses could not be made up, and his state had dwindled. He had fought on, motivated only by hatred and a craving for revenge, until at last his troop was down to three lances and he was a mere condottiere, not even fighting against the Fiend, but taking wages to contend with other soldiers of fortune in the hope that one day he could return to the struggle that had consumed his life.

He was the last Louis of them all. Nevil had set out to exterminate the ruling houses of Europe and succeeded admirably. The women who fell into his clutches suffered the same ghastly fate as their brothers, fathers, or husbands. King Pedro of Castile still ruled, but only as the Fiend's vassal. The princes of Kiev and Warsaw survived, as did the Duke of Savoy and some others here and there—those that Nevil had not gotten to yet—but D'Anjou was the last of his house. The cousins, uncles, brothers, sons, wives, sisters, aunts, and daughters had all fallen in battle or been tortured to death to entertain Nevil's court. If the titles they had borne were ever to mean anything again, he would own them all. He was rightful King of France, but he must also be king, prince, duke, count, and everything else more times over than any man in history. Yet he had spent the night in a stable while that Scottish serf fornicated between silken sheets in a palace.

"The don I do not mind," Barrafranca grumbled, still brooding. "That overgrown young blackguard, Longdirk—I cannot understand why the don tolerates his meddling. I am certain they will not make him *comandante* again."

"Of course not! One cannot conceive of repeating such folly. The captains-general elected him last time because they thought he was young enough to be controlled. Look what happened—an atrocity unthinkable! What honor is there in such a victory? It was pure luck that the wind did not change and blow the fire in our direction."

Had D'Anjou known, two years ago in Genoa, that the true leader of the Don Ramon Company was a baseborn outlaw with no formal military training or experience whatsoever, he would have offered his sword elsewhere though he would have starved for it. Starvation had been close at his heels in those days.

"*Sir* Tobias!" he snarled, more to himself than his companion. "Granted he can straighten horseshoes with his bare hands, what does that prove? There was a time when knighthood meant something. Now any roughhousing brawler is given spurs."

"He has always fought the way a demon would!" Barrafranca agreed. "He is crazy! He uses treachery, tactics no honorable man would—" *Belch!* "—countenance!"

One could turn one's head and smile at the olive

trees. D'Anjou took another swig of the wine. "Right from the start. One saw it oneself. His very first *condotta* was with Verona. Venetian gold had bought Tyrolean allies, and the Veronese were so desperate for men that they hired this new, untried Don Ramon Company to guard the northern borders." The Tyroleans, of course, had already signed a *condotta* with the Marquis Baldassare Barrafranca, but it would be too unkind to mention that. "The Tyroleans sent a force south along the shores of Lake Garda, a force far outnumbering the men Longdirk had. It was hopeless! Yet this maniac took it upon himself to give battle, far exceeding his instructions. And his tactics—"

"I am aware—"

"His tactics, I say, were total madness, against all the rules, suicidal. He not only dismounted the cavalry—a mistake becoming distressingly popular these days—but he left the horses and baggage unguarded so he could throw every man into an assault. Cooks, grooms, teamsters, farriers, and similar trash, he armed them all! He had led this untrained, inexperienced rabble on a long march in pitch-darkness, can you believe? It made us weep, we who knew how it should be done. Had the enemy even suspected, there would have been a most terrible massacre, and that would have been the end of the upstart right then. But no. He has demons' own luck. He pounced on the Tyrolean camp in the middle of a moonless night, with no warning. Shameful! It was sheer butchery, hundreds of men murdered in their sleep. Thousands more fled or surrendered, leaving all their arms to the victors. By the terms of the *condotta,* the loot was his, of course."

"Of course," Barrafranca growled. He had been one of the prisoners.

"Oh, it worked," D'Anjou admitted. "Tyrol changed sides, and Verona was ecstatic. The Veronese paid up without complaint, although the *condotta* had lasted less than a month. They wanted to renew it indefinitely, but no, the arrogant barbarian went off in search of richer employers. But it was on the field of Garda that the don knighted him. I saw it. *Sir* Tobias! Sir Turd!

"It is not easy for men of honor to serve under such a man," he added waspishly. How could Barrafranca endure it? The rout at Lake Garda that had made Longdirk's name had blackened his forever. Rather than ransom him, his city had deposed him. "The foreigner upset all the rules by which your condottieri had been operating for so long. I expect one day someone will seek retribution—stick a knife in his ribs, perchance."

"Revenge, messer, is a dish best tasted cold."

"Even a cold dish must lose its flavor if it sits around too long." D'Anjou wondered if the men were listening, but very few of them understood French. They were almost at the camp now. He would shed this obnoxious Italian upstart and take a little rest to ease his back. "What was it you wished to discuss, messer?"

"Mm?" The Italian drank and belched again. "Apparently the *podestà* has received a letter from Naples. An emissary of the Khan has landed there."

The Chevalier straightened suddenly in his saddle and suppressed a gasp of pain. "You jest!"

"No, messer." Barrafranca sounded amused by his companion's shocked reaction. "After so many years, our esteemed overlord has at last noticed that something is amiss in his realm!"

"Did he send an army? I mean, is he sending one?" Tartars were horsemen. If the Golden Horde was going to oppose Nevil and try to recover the lands he had stolen, then it would have to come from the east, by land. But perhaps this was a sign that it was coming! "What good can one emissary do?"

"Spirits know, Chevalier. They said he brings special powers."

"A *darughachi?*" It had been many years since D'Anjou had even thought about the Khanate, that rotted relic of an empire whose claim to rule Europe the Fiend had exposed as utter pigswill. "He has perhaps authority to appoint another suzerain?"

Barrafranca snorted. "Very useful! The Fiend has slaughtered the last four, so—"

"Last five." Three of those five had been relatives of D'Anjou's. Two of them Nevil had taken alive, poor devils. "It will have to be an Italian, because there is no one else left, and a suzerain has always been a red rag to the Fiend. Nothing will make his invasion of Italy more certain."

"His invasion is already certain, yes? And if this

daru . . . emissary . . . does appoint a suzerain, whom will he appoint? In the past the Khan always chose a powerful ruler, yes? But they are all dead now."

Ah! Interesting problem! In Italy—and there was very little else of Europe that Nevil had not conquered—the great powers were the five cities, but Rome was a hierocracy, while Venice and Florence were plutocracies claiming to be democracies. Fredrico of Naples was unthinkable. "The Duke of Milan? This is a choice not to be thought of!"

The Italian laughed. "He can do better than that, Chevalier. A man who knows war as it should be fought, a man who has fought against the Fiend as long as any, a man whose ancestors ruled France when the Khan's were herding goats?"

Again a jerk of surprise sent a stab of pain up D'Anjou's spine, but he barely noticed it. Indeed! Was he not the logical choice? "What are you suggesting?"

"That the emissary ought to be advised of the possibility. A good horseman should be able to reach Naples in a few days, *sì?*"

"I shall consider your advice, messer. I thank you for it." He could almost regret mocking the man, for the proposal had possibilities.

"My pleasure, Chevalier. And when it happens you will give me Longdirk's head in a basket, *sì?*"

D'Anjou chuckled. "I will give it to someone. You may have to wait in line."

"I will settle for his tripes," Barrafranca growled.

10

The camp in the Fiesole highlands was a minor city of leather and linen spilled down a now-muddy slope, a galaxy of many-colored tents, shaped like cones or sheds or loaves. Many of these were very grand pavilions, striped and gleaming in the morning sun, proof of the success the Don Ramon Company had garnered in the two seasons of its existence, but in among their dazzle crouched others more humble—dingy, patched, and decrepit, even some crude shelters of straw to house men who had gambled away their wealth. This bizarre settlement had been home all winter to three thousand men and boys, plus an unknown multitude of women. The treasurer kept sharp tally of the horses, the mules, the oxen, the wagons, the guns, the beans in the commissary, but for some reason no one ever counted the women.

Toby often marveled that he could have started this, but it had all sprung from a single evening's brainstorming in a monastery in northern Spain. As a penniless outlaw he had sown dragons' teeth and then ridden the dragon to fame and honor. It ruled him now. It owned him. Florence depended on messer Longdirk to defend her from the Fiend, but these men trusted him not to squander their lives in the attempt. One slip on his part, and few of them would see the harvest. They were cynical, tough as anvils, and many of them brutal, but they were Longdirk's men and proud of it. As he rode through the camp, he was hailed by lancers, pikemen, arquebusiers, and cannoneers. They were not cheering old Chevalier D'Anjou at his side, the rightful King of France; they were cheering Toby Longdirk, and that was worth far more than all of Pietro Marradi's gilt-edged invitations.

Don Ramon emerged from the coach unaided but unsteady. Framed by auburn tangles, his face had a greenish hue, and the copper mustache that normally twisted up in arrogant horns hung over his mouth like an apron. In only shirt and tights, he seemed almost frail, a slender boy. His unfocused, red-rimmed eyes peered uncertainly at Toby.

"Stand aside!" he muttered.

"You have a duty to perform, senor."

He clutched the coach for support and groaned. "Duty?"

"The *condotta* must be signed today. The Magnificent and I reached agreement on the essentials. You are Captain-General of Florence, senor."

The listeners broke into another cheer, for they had not been paid in weeks. The news would be all over the camp in minutes. That the don was in no state to negotiate with the hardheaded—and undoubtedly cold-sober—Florentine commissioners was very obvious, and there were a million essential details to be settled yet, enough to fill weeks of haggling. But speed was essential, and for all his grandiose illusions, no one had ever accused Don Ramon of lacking courage. An appeal to his sense of duty left him no escape.

"Today it shall be, Constable." He staggered off in the direction of the house. The mercenaries grinned admiringly, but they did not shout vulgar remarks after him as they would have done at Toby. The don was too dangerous to taunt.

Good spirits be with him this day! Fighting was much easier than negotiating. That was why most men preferred it.

The villa had begun life as a humble farmhouse, but now it was a rambling warren of low buildings, stone-walled and red-tiled, set about with vines and olives. The city placed it at the disposal of successive merce-nary captains, and previous tenants had added watch-towers and a crenellated wall, so that it was almost a fortress, but not strong enough to alarm the Florentines.

The domestic functions of the villa were run by madonna Anna, a formidable widow whose iron-gray eyes had seen uncounted soldiers of fortune come and go. She ruled a diverse population of younger women who came and went much faster, and she treated them as servants. Some were legitimate wives of officers of the Company, some were innocents who believed they were about to become wives, and others would nego-tiate with anyone. Toby remained firmly celibate, hav-ing no choice, and Hamish preferred to hunt wild game in the city.

The two of them shared an attic room just large enough to contain a hamper for storage, a bed for Hamish, and seven feet of floor for Toby. It was cluttered with armor and weapons, and he was sure that one night he would be killed in his sleep by an avalanche of Hamish's high-piled books.

He arrived with a bucket of water and his foggy-headed feeling. As he stripped off his finery, he could look down on all of Florence. Seen from this vantage in the Fiesole hills, it was a fairyland of domes and palaces, a cake iced by red tile roofs. The city wall wrapped around it like a cord knotted with towers, and through it flowed the blue Arno, winding on toward Pisa across the fertile plain, between the hills in their olive, vine, and mulberry plumage. It was a jewel among cities, and he was its defender.

Italians had been fighting among themselves for centuries, but they had preserved the traditions of chivalry much longer than most of Europe had, waging war as a stately gavotte of maneuver and siege, where arms rarely clashed and nobody got hurt—certainly nobody of importance, but even the mercenaries' death toll was usually light. The peace treaty would stipulate reasonable ransoms for the prisoners, redistribute a few castles, and allocate some daughters in marriage to show there were no hard feelings. It was fine sport as long as nobody worried about the peasants whose crops were burned and womenfolk raped—and nobody did, certainly nobody of importance.

Fourteen years ago, Nevil had changed the rules by abolishing the rules. No rules, no peace treaties, and winner take all.

To be honest, in Italy it had been Toby Longdirk who introduced the new style of war. Less than three

years ago he had landed at Genoa with Hamish, Don
Ramon, Antonio Diaz, Arnaud Villars, and Karl
Fischart. Even famous condottieri had jumped at the
chance to sign up with these mad foreigners who
would pay a retainer over the winter, when all sensible
employers put their mercenaries out to pasture. The
don was young, true, but he had earned a hero's fame
in the Battle of Toledo. Diaz was an experienced
trainer of infantry. Although Fischart, formerly Baron
Oreste, had a gruesome reputation, he was a hexer of
international renown, and any fighting man wanted a
good hexer at his back. Villars, an obvious scoundrel,
was throwing out handfuls of Josep Brusi's gold,
smooth and yellow as butter.

By spring, when the fighting began, the men of
the Don Ramon Company had discovered that the
methodical Diaz lacked flair and the don had so much
that he qualified as a maniac. They were taking their
orders from a Scottish yokel who had no qualifications
whatsoever—except, as it turned out, a ruthless ability
to bring the enemy to battle on the wrong ground and
beat him.

"You sigh?" asked a soft voice. The intruder in the
doorway was a haggard scarecrow of a man in the
black robe of a penitent, Karl Fischart, formerly Baron
Oreste. He would not have interrupted without good
cause, and good cause must be bad news.

"I was thinking that Florence is the fairest city in
all Europe and I am a fool. Look at it! Isn't it glorious?
Last night I promised to defend it. If I fail, it will be all
gone before winter. Am I completely insane?"

"No, because to die fighting the Fiend is our only hope that some spirit will take pity on our souls. Any other death is ignoble. Faced with paramount evil, the only virtuous course is to die opposing it. We ourselves are so steeped in evil that to survive is evidence of insufficient dedication to the struggle."

So much for rhetorical questions. Toby had no doubts at all about his own sanity and felt no repentance for the deaths he had caused in his military career. Regret yes, but they had been necessary. Fischart was living with memories of the horrors he had committed when he was Nevil's premier hexer. No matter how he went barefoot, ate almost nothing, and mortified his flesh in ingenious ways, nothing would ever console him. Although his face was still round, the flesh on it had melted into bags and dewlaps. Stooped and white-bearded, he seemed to have aged a generation since the day he and Toby had come face-to-face in Barcelona and ended their long feud within the hour. The only evidence remaining of his former evil glory was the collection of jeweled rings on his fingers—plus his tedious habit of wailing his remorse to anyone who would listen.

"What's the bad news today?" Toby splashed water on his face. "Use short words and remember I'm stupid."

"I know you pretend to be. I was deceived once and have been paying for that error ever since and will pay until my death."

"The news?"

"We have been robbed. Gold is missing from the strongbox."

After a moment Toby realized he was staring like a gargoyle, mouth open. "Explain that! You were supposed to have hexed it."

"I am the premier suspect!" The old man wrung his hands in agony. "To fail in so simple a task is evidence that I have betrayed you all."

"Did you take the money?"

"Of course not! You think I would add to my sins by—"

"Then don't rant and wail, be helpful! We're cleaned out?" How much? Two days ago Arnaud had reported two thousand, five hundred, seventy-two florins in hand. Less fifty-seven for flour and eighty-three for fodder—Toby rattled beads on his mental abacus. "There should have been twenty-two hundred and thirty or so florins there!" That was desperation money to keep the Company fed. *Condotta* or not, the *dieci della guerra* might still take weeks to deliver any cash, and it would not be inclined to move faster if the Don Ramon Company sank into debt to the Marradi Bank. Abandoning thoughts of washing, he threw open the hamper and rummaged in it for clothes.

"No, no! You don't understand! Villars insists only one bag is missing, a bag of green leather, one hundred florins. The rest has not been touched, and a purse of the don's is still there, too."

"That's absurd! Who can open the chest, apart from you and Arnaud?"

Fischart's hand rubbing grew more agitated.

"Captain Diaz, Don Ramon, Brother Bartolo, messer Campbell. No one else can even get near it without setting off alarms and being trapped in the adytum. No one except a very skilled hexer."

Toby himself had never even seen the demon-guarded coffer because he never went to the adytum. "Can't you tell?" he asked, balancing on one leg as he pulled hose onto the other. "Don't you know if someone else has used gramarye on it?"

"There are shadows, only shadows. If it was a hexer, he is an incredible adept, better than I."

"Is anyone better than you?"

"No," Fischart admitted glumly.

"What else can it be except a hexer?"

"Nothing."

Morbid and tortured though he was, the old man still had one of the brightest minds in Europe, and it took Toby a moment to catch up with the misery in his crazed eyes.

"Then you will have to test everyone you just named."

The hexer looked ready to weep. "I have. Everyone except the don and Campbell, who isn't back yet but wasn't here when the money was taken. I can find no trace of hexing on them. If one of them took the money, then he was acting voluntarily. He would still have had to use gramarye, of course, but he cannot be under a compulsion."

Needing more time to think, Toby opened the window and tipped out his wash water. Was it possible that the Fiend had managed to hex Fischart himself to spin this tale? No one could be trusted absolutely in this war; but if the baron had been turned, then Toby ought to be helpless already, if not dead. The gold problem made no sense at all. If Arnaud said there had been a theft, there had been a theft. He did not make mistakes. That the Fiend had spies or even potential assassins within the Company went without saying, but why steal one bag of coins and leave the rest? Why should a skilled hexer draw attention to his presence like that? Or possibly *her* presence, he remembered.

"Probably the don took it to spend on some woman. And test him for hexing. I suggest you don't let him know you're doing so." If that failed, then the puzzle would have to wait until Hamish came back. He was the one with brains. "Perhaps you'd better test me as well."

"I can't. I would just find the hob."

Toby grunted. As far as he knew, being possessed saved him from being hexed, which was like not catching measles because one already had tertian fever. "So we have a traitor in camp, who may or may not be one of the people we've been discussing. That really is not surprising, is it? See if you can tighten your wards on the money, and also would you clear Don Ramon's head so he can negotiate the terms of the *condotta* today? There's no time to waste."

For a moment a flash of the old arrogance darkened the adept's face, then he rearranged it like putty into its customary pout. "Even demons draw the line somewhere, but if it will contribute in any way to the overthrow of the Fiend, then of course no task is too humble for me."

"Thank you." Toby pushed his feet into his buskins. He stared at his party clothes on the floor, all rumpled and in need of a wash, and he decided to worry about the fate of Italy first. "The *condotta* has been agreed in principle, so I have a million letters to send." He crouched to see his face in the broken mirror, cursing the great mop of hair he had to comb now. "There was a rumor going around last night that the Khan has sent a *darughachi*. He's said to be in Naples, expected to head north shortly."

The hexer drew in his breath with a hiss. "I suppose fourteen years too late is better than never."

Not necessarily. An emissary with plenipotentiary powers might appoint a suzerain or take overall command himself. Either way, he would certainly ruin all of Toby's carefully laid plans.

"It may be all hogswiggle, because the Magnificent never mentioned it." He would certainly have been one of the first to learn of any emissary, and why would he not confide in his captain-general?

11

Lisa felt guilty for not feeling more guilty. Every step her horse took carried her farther away from Mother, who must be half-insane with worry, yet she kept catching herself actually enjoying this wild adventure, this unreal Arthurian romance into which she had

fallen. Lack of sleep had stuffed her head with bed
socks, and the beautiful Tuscan landscape enclosed
her like a painting—fields, vineyards, olive groves,
red-tiled roofs, geese, goats—all glistening in the
sharp morning light. She must believe that it was real.
She had seen a demon and witnessed Master
Campbell bloodying his sword in her defense.

He was most attentive and excellent company. He
had bought clothes for her from the innkeeper's
daughter and sent one of his men back into Siena to
organize a hunt for the countess. Every now and again
he would peer back along their tracks to where his
other man, Carlo, was trailing a mile or so behind,
keeping a lookout for pursuit. Even Mother had never
gone to quite such lengths, but Lisa was much more
inclined to trust the mercenary's appraisal of danger
than hers.

That did not mean that she trusted him without
reservations. He was not being completely frank with
her. He had motives he was not revealing. There were
questions he would not answer—

"Why did you tell me to keep my kerchief?"

He blinked guilelessly. "When we locate your
mother, we can send it along as proof that we're genuine."

"Then why didn't you give it to Rinaldo to take
back with him?"

"I didn't think of it until he'd gone. Oh, look!
Newborn lambs! Spring!"

Those were not the first lambs they had passed.
Master Campbell was lying. Later she tried again.

"What did you mean about Longdirk using me politically?"

"Taking advantage of you. Demanding ransom, for instance."

That was not what he had meant originally! And the questions he asked were not all innocent, either. He kept trying to find out things about Mother, who was none of his business. As Lisa was riding sidesaddle and he was on the left, she could watch him more easily than he could watch her. She could tell when he was just making conversation and when he was probing. She could also admire his profile, which was acceptably handsome for a knight-errant.

He was good company—witty, intelligent, well read, and very well traveled. Between them they could speak more than a dozen languages, although all they had in common were English and the usual smattering of Latin and Tartar that all well-educated people professed. Nor had they identified a single city they had both visited, for he had traveled mostly in the Fiend's domains, while Mother had always stayed inside territories loyal to the Khan. They shared a love of books. Many of the homes in which she had stayed had possessed books, even if the owners never opened them. Too often, books had been her only companions for months at a time, yet she had never met another genuine book lover. Now the two of them juggled titles and quotations back and forth with mutual glee, arguing what Plato had said in the *Republic* or whether it was worth learning Tuscan just to read Dante.

He admitted to leaving Scotland when he was

fifteen, and later he mentioned this had been in 1519, so he must be about twenty-one now. Most men married younger than that, but she could not ask, and he did not volunteer the information. Despite her best efforts to match his vagueness on personal matters, he was revealing much less than she was. He would talk endlessly about his friend Longdirk:

"Aristocrats despise him because he's not of noble birth, and the crabby old veterans are worse. Some of them still seem to think his success was all just luck, but he calculates everything. He moved us from client to client—Verona, Ravenna, Naples, then Milan, so all the captains-general and *collaterali* got to know him, and when Nevil sent Schweitzer across the border last fall and they needed a *comandante in capo* in a hurry, they elected him because he was the only one they all trusted. He was a neutral, of course. Venetians don't trust Milanese, Milanese don't trust Venetians, and the Florentine captain-general was an idiot."

Lisa soon developed a strong dislike of this vagabond mercenary lord into whose power she was about to be delivered. "Yes, but—"

"The men worship him. He remembers their names, and their horses' names, looks after their comfort, shares out the loot fairly, never spares himself. They're Longdirk's men and proud of it. They swagger and strut like pigeons, and no one queries their right to do so. He's never lost once—siege, skirmish, or set-piece battle."

"But what sort of a person is he? Does he brag and swagger, too? Does he enjoy the killing?"

"Toby?" Hamish grinned. "Brag? He's the only man in Italy who still calls it the Don Ramon Company. He hides behind the don and tugs his fore-lock and runs circles around them all. He certainly doesn't enjoy killing. The only thing he hates more than war is the Fiend, who makes it necessary. He really tries not to shed blood. Take San Leo, for exam-ple. It was supposed to be impregnable. Ha! Two days after the *condotta* was signed, he went up a ladder in the middle of a rainy night with one companion and opened the gates for the Company. By the time the garrison woke up in the morning, the town was ours! That *condotta* only lasted a week."

"Who was the companion?"

"There's Carlo coming now. We can go on—"

"Who was the one companion?"

"It doesn't look like anyone's following you, I mean us. Why are you looking at me like that?"

"At San Leo? Who was the one companion?"

"Me," he admitted grumpily.

"Aha!"

He scowled. "I don't usually do such crazy things. I had to go with him because I'd seen a map of the town, that was all."

Master Campbell was being modest, which was a very odd trait in a man, but might be quite appealing once one got used to it. "Of course," she said. "And no one else ever had? I suppose during the Battle of Trent you sat in your tent the whole time reading a book?"

He shot her a worried look. "Lisa . . . don't!"

"Don't what?"

"Don't start getting ideas about . . . Oh, demons!" He stared straight ahead along the track and said nothing more.

"I was inquiring, Chancellor, what part you played in the Battle of Trent?"

He spoke to the fields. "A very small, very insignificant part. But I did ride in the Great Charge, when Toby led the cavalry against the guns and the demons were loosed. I saw little of it. I was much too busy trying to stay on my horse, and there was fire and smoke and thunder everywhere. Magazines blowing up . . . bodies flying through the air like starlings."

"Monsters?"

"Yes, there were monsters. My horse didn't much like running with dragons. But we had more monsters than they did. Then the Swiss pikemen came in on the right . . . That was awful. Nevil's troops were hexed, so they couldn't surrender."

"So Constable Longdirk does shed blood when he has to! Is it true that he's possessed by a demon?"

"Oh, look! Lambs! Isn't it amazing how early spring comes in Italy? Back in Scotland—"

"Did he really set the forest on fire at Trent?"

Hamish turned to look at her then. His face was grim. "Yes. He had our hexers do it, and that left us open to Schweitzer's demons, so we took heavy losses for a while, but nothing compared to what the fire did to the Fiend's troops later."

"You mean he'll roast an enemy army without a thought but won't dream of using a maiden in distress for political purposes?"

After a brief hesitation, Master Campbell said, "Yes."

12

Given that Italy was a morass of conspiracy and intrigue, it went without saying that there were spies everywhere, using the dark arts of gramarye or just the ears they were born with. Toby tried to make things as hard for them as he could, although he also assumed that anything he said or did would be promptly reported to his enemies or allies or both. He held important meetings in the courtyard, which was enclosed by walls of ancient Roman brick and shadowed by cypresses, fruit trees, and grapevine trellises. It could be entered by a gate from the orchard or a door from the villa itself, but only the hearing of a cat could eavesdrop on what was said there. Even so early in the year, when the vines were bare and the almond blossom had not yet exploded into spring glory, the air was often warm enough to do business out-of-doors. There he passed the day, struggling to recruit an army without actually spending money he did not yet possess.

Seven men defined the Don Ramon Company. The don had ridden off to do verbal battle with Benozzo and the rest of the *dieci,* and Hamish had not yet returned from Siena. Maestro Fischart was also absent, communing with demons in an effort to find the missing gold. The four who met around the mossy stone table that day were Antonio Diaz the marshal,

Arnaud Villars the treasurer, Brother Bartolo the secretary—and High Constable Longdirk, whose duties
were mysterious, even to him, although he knew the
organization would fall apart without him.

"Twenty thousand men," he said. "At the moment
we have . . . ?"

"Three thousand and thirty-three," Arnaud
growled. He was the one the other three thousand and
thirty-two were threatening to hang if they were not
paid soon.

Toby looked inquiringly to the marshal.

"Another four squadrons, no more," Diaz said—
roughly six hundred men or about a hundred helmets.
More men made the Company more difficult to manage efficiently, which was why Arnaud was nodding
agreement, although he and Diaz rarely agreed on
anything. To fulfill his *condotta,* the condottiere must
subcontract other companies.

"Who else is good?" Toby asked, although he had
a clear list in his head already, plus extensive notes
Hamish had left him. Arnaud answered first.

"The Mad Dogs."

"Brucioli's too fond of marching." Diaz's face
never showed his feelings. "They fight well if they get
the chance, though."

"We'll give them the chance," Toby said. "How
about the Red Band?"

The day flew by in argument and discussion, the men
by turns sitting on the wooden stools or pacing around.

Who was good, who unreliable? Who clashed with whom? Why hadn't so-and-so's band been signed up already?

Time and again Toby's mind slid back to the problem of the missing gold. It made no sense. Whoever the mysterious shadow was, why make an impossible mystery out of the crime? Why take one small bag and ignore all the rest? Why take any? Perhaps the unknown spy's purpose was merely to sow distrust. Now no one could feel completely safe or rely on anyone else.

"Fifteen lire a man won't buy many," Diaz was saying. "They all know there'll be no looting, and the cost of everything is going up like a bombard shot. Rosselli is asking a twenty-thousand-ducat signing bonus."

"Can't afford it. He's good but not that good."

How much silver for a man's life? How much gold for his honor? Ignoring gramarye, who might sell out for simple avarice? Any of these three?

Brother Bartolo? The friar was a wine tub of a man, rubicund face perpetually beaming, with only a faint fringe of silver around his tonsure, an Italian edition of Friar Tuck. During a memorable celebration after the Battle of Padua some very drunk young squires had found a steelyard and started laying bets on who weighed more, Longdirk in his battle gear or Bartolo in his gray Franciscan robe. Because those striplings had acquitted themselves like veterans that day, Toby had submitted to the indignity of being weighed. He had lost handily. Enormous Bartolo ran

the secretariat with good humor and unfailing efficiency. Even now, as each decision was reached, he
would poke two fingers in his mouth and emit a whistle louder than a bugle call. A clerk would come running out to hear the details and then run indoors to
write the letter. Soon corrected drafts and fair copies
were piling up, ready to be signed and sealed. Toby
could not imagine life without the fat man to handle
his endless correspondence.

Yet he knew almost nothing of the friar's past.
Don Ramon had hired him to write some letters the
day after reaching Italy, and that timing made it
very hard to see Bartolo as a spy planted on the
Company, because the Company had not even
existed. He evaded his oaths of poverty and chastity
by insisting that his wages be paid to his mistress
and their rapidly increasing family, and a man who
could bend his sworn word like that was not perfectly honest.

Who was? Certainly not Arnaud Villars, with his
enormous black beard, his ferocious dark scowl, his
well-checkered past. The first time Toby had met him,
he had been running a profitable smuggling operation
between Aquitaine and Navarre. After war had ruined
business, they had run into each other in Barcelona—
apparently by chance—and Toby had hired him on the
spot. Without doubt Arnaud skimmed something off
the payroll, so he had no reason to steal openly.
Furthermore, it had been he who reported the loss. As
quartermaster, he was astute enough to stay level with
the Florentine suppliers, as paymaster he ran a per-

sonal army of clerks to keep track of what every man was owed in wages or what he still had to repay on his equipment if the Company had provided it, to assign fodder for his horse and record whose horse it was— and on and on. Toby got headaches even thinking about it. He had known Arnaud longer than anyone in the Company except Hamish. They had fought shoulder to shoulder in Navarre.

But? But why was the leopard curled up on the hearth-rug? Men of action rarely transformed themselves so willingly into quill-pushers. Maybe the old scoundrel was just starting to feel his age.

Diaz? The captain was a true professional, a soft-spoken imperturbable Catalan with a face carved from well-seasoned oak. It was he who had turned the Company into a fighting machine as fine as any in Italy. He recruited, outfitted, drilled, disciplined, and never complained or argued or displayed any facial expression whatsoever. He was a devout man, deeply troubled by the spiritual dangers of his chosen career. The Don Ramon Company would collapse without him. As far as trust went, he ranked right after Hamish Campbell.

Men were never simple. The don, who would die rather than blemish his precious honor, would lie like a horse trader to seduce a pretty girl, promising anything. Maestro Fischart's hatred for the Fiend knew no bounds whatsoever, but he spent his days and nights in the company of demons; he had been enthralled once and might be trapped again. Even Hamish, honest as the hills, was usually either aching from a broken heart or so starry-eyed in love that he blundered into door-posts.

Toby was shocked to realize that the shadows were growing longer already. An arrow took only seconds to flash across a field and end a man's life, but if you counted the year or longer needed to make the bow and the many years required to train the archer, then an arrow was a slow death. Similarly, a war might be settled in a single hard battle. It was preparing for war that took the time.

The don's appointment had become known in the city, and volunteers were reported at the gates. Diaz sent word that they should wait, even knowing that most would turn out to be runaway apprentices lacking even a horse.

They had run out of names at last. Toby arranged the letters in heaps—the good, the bad, the possible, the last resorts. He pulled out four. "Desjardins, if he is still available." According to yesterday's rumors, he had signed on with Naples. "Simonetta, D'Amboise, and della Sizeranne. We need those four."

Three heads nodded.

All four condottieri had wintered near Naples. The fastest mail was the service run by the Marradi Bank, which was efficient—so efficient that a copy of any letter he sent would undoubtedly arrive on the Magnificent's desk before the original left Florence—but message and response would still require at least ten days. If the offers were refused, that meant ten more days lost. A demon ride would be faster, but that option was not available to Toby himself, and he would not call for volunteers. What sort of man would risk his soul for a handful of gold? What sort of man would ask him? The Marradi mail it would have to be.

He threw the letters on the table and sat down to reach for the quill standing in its silver inkwell. "Let's send these ones on their way as soon as possible. Who's next?" Biting his tongue, he began penning his signature . . .

"There is one position you have not mentioned," Diaz said.

Toby looked up sharply, but the marshal's face was as scrutable as mud.

"Who?"

"Il comandante in capo."

"Ah!" He went back to signing the letters.

They were all waiting to tell him he was the logical choice for the supreme command, but that was just loyalty—they would say so if he had a crossbow bolt embedded in his forehead. Was he? Of the thousands of soldiers in Italy, many must know the country better than he did, although he had spent most of the last two years in the saddle, exploring it from the Tyrrhenian Sea to the Adriatic. Almost all would speak the language better, and most would have more experience. Who was he to take the fate of the peninsula on his shoulders? He should not try to judge his own abilities, because no man could be totally impartial about himself. All he knew for certain was that he wanted the job more than he had ever wanted anything in his life. Wasn't that the best possible reason not to get it?

He replaced the pen and looked around the three faces. "Not me. No, it's impossible, never mind why. I accept your support—it's very flattering, and I'm truly touched, but forget me. Who's the next best man for the job? Florence will want to have a candidate, and the captain-general's opinion should carry weight. Who's our man?"

He was a lousy liar. Their surprise turned at once to disbelief. Inevitably the treasurer and the friar looked to the soldier to answer the question.

"There isn't one," Diaz said heavily. "Mezzo's good, but Rome won't ever accept a Neapolitan. Venice can't trust Milan. And so on. If it isn't Florence, it'll have to be an outsider—Girolami of Pisa? Or Barrafranca? The Chevalier?"

After a moment's mutual repugnance, massive subterranean chuckles began to shake Brother Bartolo's soft bulk.

"What's amusing you?" Toby demanded.

The fat man shrugged doughy shoulders. "Last fall I asked messer Campbell why you were moving the Company to winter quarters at Fiesole instead of somewhere warmer. He would not admit that you hoped to succeed the late messer Vespucci as Captain-General of Florence, but he did not quite deny it either, so one night I introduced him to our excellent Chianti wines. Sometime after midnight, we agreed that Nevil must come from the north, so either Milan or Venice will be the first to feel his spite, but those two cities are ancient rivals, and neither will ever trust a *capo* whose first loyalty lies with the other. Temporary deafness when the cry for help went out would be just too much of a temptation!"

Arnaud was leering through the black thatch on his face. Even Diaz looked close to smiling. What matter if they thought it had been Hamish who devised that strategy?

"Furthermore, the admirable Campbell agreed that Milan and Venice can never trust Rome or Naples, because they're too far away and might not get here in time. Florence, though, is right in the middle and is too small to be a threat to any of the other four." The fat man beamed. "Sir Tobias, you do want the golden apple!"

"Of course he does," Arnaud growled. "And he earned it at Trent. He's a foreigner, so he has no local loyalties. He fights in ways the old generals don't understand. And he's the best anyway."

"Swiss won't serve under an Italian," Diaz added. "But they worship a man who once massacred a whole troop of German *landsknechte* single-handed."

Toby scowled. "That we shall not discuss, if you please!" He let a smile emerge. "Yes, I do want it. I want it so bad I wake up sweating. I think the politicians will accept Florence. How do I convince the soldiers to accept *me*?"

"They voted for you last time," Bartolo objected.

"Last time was a panic."

After everyone had observed a moment's polite hesitation, Diaz said, "Call a conclave of the captains-general and *collaterali*—in the don's name of course. Here in the villa: Alfredo from Venice, Mezzo or Gioberti from Naples, Villari from Rome, and from Milan . . . Ercole Abonio, although he'll probably send di Gramasci. When the big boys have accepted, you can invite some of the small fry—Genoa and so on. Wait until you have the Italians behind you before you involve the Swiss or the Tyroleans or the Savoyards."

That was certainly the ram-it-down-their-throats-and-damn-the-cannons approach to be expected from him, but even Hamish had devised no better plan in months of thinking about it.

The friar coughed gently: "?"

Toby raised an eyebrow. "Brother, we have eight elbows on the table and yours are the only *Italian* elbows, so I suppose we may allow you a word or two."

"Condottieri are touchier than prima donnas," Bartolo said sadly. "Every one of them wants to be the loudest rooster in the barnyard, and you are going to *summon* them here to a conclave? You think you're still *capo*, young man?"

"Demons!"

"Upstart foreign stripling! Cocksure, arrogant, little . . . no, perhaps not *little*, but—"

"I've gotten the gist. You're right!"

"Ha!" said Arnaud. "They may think that, but it won't stop them coming. None of them will stay away in case someone else gets chosen. But you don't hold the council here, my lad. Get *Il Volpe* to lend you one of his country houses and leave the rest to me."

Brother Bartolo scowled reprovingly. "Arnaud, is this some evil you learned in your nefarious import-export business?"

The former smuggler donned an expression of virginal innocence, although the effect was spoiled by his ogrish beard. "Evil? No, no! Merely generous hospitality, brother! You fill the house with the finest wine and food, plus many voluptuous, but properly reticent, maidens. You drag your guests out on arduous wild-boar hunts every day, postponing the crucial discussion until after dinner on the last night, when their bodies are limp from exhaustion, their wits are dulled by good cheer, and their hopes are inspired by the vulnerable maidens weeping at the prospect of their departure—believe me, they'll agree to anything to end the meeting and—"

"Impossible!" Don Ramon roared, striding into the courtyard and cutting off the laughter. "Pettifogging money-grubbers! Artisans, merchants, word-splitting advocates and bureaucrats! *Republicans!*" he howled, that being the worst obscenity he knew.

All the men scrambled to their feet. He hurled a bundle of papers onto the table and glared up at Toby with his coppery mustache writhing as it did only when he was close to homicidal. "You told me you had an agreement with Marradi!"

"I certainly thought I had. He made the Ten For War agree."

"Never mind the *dieci!* What about the *podestà?* What about the *gonfalonier della giustizia,* the *buonomini,* the *priori,* the *consiglio del commune,* the *consiglio del popolo,* and the *seven wise monkeys?*" Blue eyes blazed.

"The *who?*"

Eight hands grabbed for the papers, eight eyes scanned them. They were passed around. Demands, restrictions, impossible conditions—matters were much worse than before.

Bewilderment, dismay . . .

"Demons!" Toby said. "Someone explain!"

"Democrats!" howled the don.

Arnaud clawed at his beard with both hands. "I fear so, signore. *Il Volpe* is an autocrat in fact, but officially Florence is still ruled by a hierarchy of officials, committees, and infinitely detailed regulations. The *dieci* will do as he wants, but only when you have met their price." No one knew more about bribery than a smuggler.

Brother Bartolo waggled his chins from side to side in worried disagreement. "Marradi should have foreseen that problem. I wonder if there is worse spite involved? The Fiend must have agents in Florence, spreading poisons. Others certainly do. The cities have been feuding for centuries—that is a hard habit to break." He narrowed his piggy eyes. "And you have enemies of your own, Constable, men jealous of your success."

"The Fiend, yes," Toby protested, "but surely everyone else will set aside petty quarrels . . ." Then he remembered Lucrezia. Was it possible? Did she have enough power to balk him? So quickly? Wishing he had Hamish around to advise him, he looked to the one man who had not spoken. "Marshal?"

"Back in Barcelona," Diaz said with his customary impassivity, "in the *Palau Reial* we had a saying, 'The hand to watch is the hand of the king.'"

"Meaning?" the don barked.

"It means, Captain-General, that in Florence you should never turn your back on the Magnificent. Nothing happens here that he does not approve."

13

Lisa's first view of Florence was from the high ground at the Porta San Piero Gattolino, with Hamish pointing out city landmarks as proudly as if he had built them all himself: the duomo, the various towers, gardens, and palaces. They descended the Via Romana to the Arno and crossed by the teeming Ponte Vecchio, which bore many busy stores, most selling meat and poultry. She admitted she had never seen a city bustle like this one and certainly none as clean, for the streets were paved with stone slabs; they had gutters and raised footpaths along each side. He showed her the Piazza della Signoria, with its astonishing statuary and soaring palaces, then the Old Market, where the noisy crowds were haggling over textiles and leatherwork and pottery set out on booths. She could tell from Carlo's amusement that he was sidetracking to let her see her the sights, but she was in no especial hurry to be turned over to the ominous condottiere Longdirk.

The afternoon was heading for evening, and yet she was not at all weary—possibly because she had enjoyed a wonderful night's sleep. Hamish had stopped at an inn he knew and spared no expense, providing her with a room all to herself, which was an extraordinary extravagance when most travelers slept three or four to a bed.

They left Florence by the Porta Pinti, heading through fertile country toward the hills. Soon he was pointing out their destination, the camp of the Don Ramon Company, bright tents like jewels scattered over the hillside. All too soon her horse was pacing the muddy grass between them, and coarse men were hailing her companions in several languages, hooting at her, making loud comments about the bookworm having done a little looting and so on, very vulgar.

"They are insolent!" she said.

Hamish seemed not at all angry. "I'm sorry they're insulting you, my lady. To me, it's a form of respect. Two years ago they just ignored me. Ever since San Leo, I've been worthy of insult. You should hear them lipping Toby! They don't think much of book learning. I'm not good at the things they regard as important."

"You fought six men and—"

"With a rapier. To them, that's a toy. Battles are fought with pikes or guns or broadswords."

Louts! They were a chilling reminder of the sort of man who *might* have rescued her. And the women were a chilling sight, too—an astonishing number of women. Some might be wives, but most probably weren't. Many carried babies on their backs, and children ran wild everywhere. This raw city of tents was unlike any place she had ever seen, and she dared not think about the future awaiting her if she could not be reunited with her mother.

At the door of a strange complex of buildings, seemingly half fort and half farm, Hamish dismounted and lifted her down. Carlo took charge of the horses, beaming bashfully when she thanked him for his help on the journey. The interior was dim and cool, with tiled floors and tiled ceilings; delicious odors of cooking made her mouth water. There were more women, more children, and more lewd greetings, more laughter.

The women's banter upset Hamish much more than the men's had. Scowling and tight-lipped, he hurried her through the building and out to a small enclosed courtyard, paved with mossy flagstones and partly roofed with trellises for vines. Two men were sitting at a massive stone table. They looked up at the interruption. Then the young one rose.

Hamish had mentioned that Longdirk was big, but he did not seem so at first. When she reached him, she realized that his breadth concealed his height. He was big in all directions. No one could ever describe him as handsome, for his face was all heavy bone— big jaw, brows like gables. Had she seen him in the street without his sword, she would have assumed from the size of his shoulders that he was a blacksmith or a woodcutter—unless she had noticed the penetrating brown eyes, which were appraising her now with worrisome concentration.

Golden hair was rare in Italy, but she had her head covered, and her clothes were nondescript and incon-

spicuous. Yet the giant was either very perceptive or
an excellent guesser; he addressed her in English even
before Hamish spoke.

"Your servant, ma'am." Bow. He moved gracefully for his size. His voice was a rumbling bass.

"I am truly honored to meet the famous Constable
Longdirk." Curtsey.

The other man struggled belatedly to his feet,
looking much like an old beggar, wrinkles and wild
white hair, or perhaps some sort of crazy prophet. His
eyes were certainly mad enough, staring at her. When
Hamish named him as Doctor Fischart, she realized
that this was the erstwhile Baron Oreste, the notorious
hexer. He did not speak, so she ignored him.

She took the stool Hamish indicated and folded
her hands in her lap. He pulled another up alongside
her, comfortingly near, while the adept and condottiere settled themselves on the far side of the table. The
expectant pause began to drag, as if Hamish were at a
loss for words, for it was obviously up to him to speak
first.

Longdirk said, "Perhaps we should order in some
wine in celebration?"

"Celebration of what?" Hamish snapped. "Are
you jumping to conclusions again?" His petulance
surprised her. Was he nervous, too?

The big man grinned. "Not a one. I'm going to be
very interested to hear what the correct conclusions
are. You look like a retriever that's just brought in a
phoenix. You're hiding something, my lad, something
big."

Lisa took a hard look at Master Campbell without detecting any resemblance to a retriever.

"Don't be so vulgar," he said. "Listen. I was minding my own business in Siena on Carnival Night when I chanced upon some bravos molesting a lady. I used my guarddemon to rescue her. Then I introduced myself."

"How astonishing," Longdirk muttered. He flashed Lisa a grin that she found hard not to return. "Then he gave you a long lecture on Egyptian pottery, I presume? Or underwater Gregorian chanting?"

Hamish scowled. "This is serious! I had unwittingly put her in considerable difficulty, because my demon had moved us to another part of town. Having only recently arrived in Siena, she did not know the way back to her residence." (That was a very charitable way of explaining her predicament, Lisa decided.) "Moreover, it was obvious that the thugs had been looking for her specifically, and one of them was certainly a hexer."

The big man's hands closed into fists. "Gonzaga?"

"Probably. He was masked. In the circumstances, Lady Lisa agreed to accompany me back here. I sent word to Landolfo, telling him to try and locate her mother and inform her that her daughter was safe. That's all."

The big man studied him for a moment, then laughed. He had a very big laugh, to match his size. "That's a start. The rest of the camel is still outside the tent, but it'll come. May I inquire your mother's name, my lady?"

"Maud, Countess of Ely," Hamish said. He glanced uneasily at the ugly old hexer. "We must find suitable quarters and a suitable companion for Lady Lisa. Sister Bona, perhaps? A lady's maid, too. I fear her reputation may suffer if this tale gets out."

"I fear more than that," Longdirk growled. "I am at your service, ma'am. Your companion's keeping something from us, I think."

"And from me also, Constable. Is he always so elliptical?"

The condottiere grinned. "He's usually more egg-shaped. It's getting chilly, but let's stay out here a little longer, because it's one place we can't be overheard."

"Whatever you wish," Lisa said. Her hand was entwined with Hamish's, although she did not recall that happening. He had never mentioned anyone called Gonzaga to her.

Longdirk took a hard look at the bizarre old man, who had never taken his mad eyes off her. Longdirk was well aware of that. "Maestro, would you care to comment?"

"Blanche!"

Hamish must have felt her start, and Longdirk certainly noticed it.

"That name means something to you, my lady?"

"No. Nothing at all. I don't know anyone called Blanche. Why should I? Nobody called Blanche."

The hexer's mouth writhed as if chewing something unpleasant. "You have never heard your mother addressed as Blanche?"

"My mother's name is Maud! My father was the

third Earl of Ely and was put to death by the Fiend. Mother fled from England with me many years ago and has traveled extensively."

"I'm sure she has," Longdirk said, his rumbling bass voice sounding surprisingly soft. It was hard to reconcile his gentle manner with the ferocious warrior of the stories, but he was obviously clever, dangerously clever.

Hamish's grip on her hand grew almost painful. "Toby, stop badgering her! She's had a terrible experience and been extremely brave. She must be exhausted after the ride, and she needs some decent quarters and a servant and some proper clothes and—"

"In good time, my friend. Let's talk about Blanche." He turned those cavernous eyes on Lisa again.

She pulled her hand loose from Hamish's grip. Obviously he wanted her out of the way before he discussed whatever it was that needed to be discussed—something everyone but she seemed to have ideas about. Somehow Longdirk had become her ally.

"Perhaps . . ." she said. "I mean, I may have heard Mother addressed as Blanche once or twice. She has used several names in our travels. I don't recall her ever calling herself Blanche, though."

"You are extraordinarily like her," the old baron croaked.

Longdirk folded his big arms, pleased and satisfied. "Tell us a story, Maestro!"

"Can't it wait?" Hamish begged. "She's had a long, tiring journey on top of—"

"It's too serious to wait. Let's get it out."

The old man laid his hands on the table and bowed his head. "My lady . . . I will call you that. I was a scholar at Wittenburg and later Oxford, a man of some repute. One of my pupils was the third and youngest son of the King of England. He was a quiet, studious boy, with no expectations of succeeding to the throne. His ambitions lay more in the field of—"

"Why don't you go straight to the famous Night of the Masked Ball?" Longdirk said.

The old man did not look up. "She does not know as much as you do. Although Nevil wanted to be a scholar, he was still a prince, and princes have dynastic responsibilities. King Edwin made a treaty and backed it up by marrying his youngest son to Princess Blanche of Jutland. She was sixteen, he was eighteen. They had no say in the matter and nothing in common, absolutely nothing. She was a foolish child, caring only for glittering balls and fine clothes, scorning his studies in the spiritual arts as unbecoming to royalty. Nevil sired a child on her, which was his duty, but he had lost his heart to a woman named Valda, a hexer of considerable ability. Valda persuaded him to return to court, and Princess Blanche was packed off to a remote country house to bear his child. Very soon Nevil's two brothers died, and then the king himself."

"Murdered by Valda?" Longdirk asked softly.

"Undoubtedly. Nevil was king, and now Blanche was queen, but she remained at Highcross with her daughter, Princess Elizabeth."

"Who was born when?"

"In 1509—May or thereabouts."

This was unbelievable! Lisa bit her lip and did not look up, although she could feel them all staring at her. Hamish had hold of her hand again and was squeezing it.

"And you?" Longdirk asked.

"I was called to court," the baron said hoarsely, "a summons I dared not refuse. Nevil installed me in the palace and gave me every facility to continue my studies. I saw that Valda was leading him into very dangerous realms of conjuration. I warned him repeatedly, but he was so besotted by her that he would not listen, and undoubtedly she was using gramarye on him. My efforts to break her enchantments failed because she was invoking demons more powerful than any I dared employ. I was certain that she planned to murder Queen Blanche in time. The baby would have died, too—Valda was utterly without scruple. The entire court was terrified of her." He sighed. "Including me. But I did manage to foil a few of her plans, and thus she saw me as her enemy. My influence with Nevil sank even lower."

"The Night of the Masked Ball?" Longdirk persisted.

"Valda had obtained an ancient and famous—infamous—demon by the name of Rhym, immured in a yellow diamond. It was hideously strong, and the conjuration was faulty. Several hexers had perished trying to use it. I begged both of them not to tamper with it, but Valda saw it as the key to her ambitions. With Rhym's power she could rip away the web that I and some others were trying to weave between her and the king. On the Night of the Masked Ball, Valda and Nevil attempted to conjure Rhym and the demon broke free. It took possession of him. How Valda managed to escape, I never dared ask him."

Lisa glanced at Hamish, then looked away quickly. That the Fiend was a demonic husk was a common belief, but this old man was claiming first-hand knowledge. Lisa—Elizabeth? Blanche—Maude? Scurrilous rubbish, surely, and yet it would explain some terrible mysteries.

The old man's voice creaked on. "I was not present, but I was close enough to detect what had happened. I fled from the court at once, not even changing my clothes. I rode alone through the night to Highcross and broke the news to the queen. By dawn she was on a ship bound for France." He raised his head for the first time and met Lisa's horrified stare. "You are very, very like her, child. When you stepped out through that doorway, my heart almost stopped."

"But—"

"Wait!" Longdirk raised a hand. "Finish your own tale, Maestro."

The hexer shrugged, although in the gathering dark his black-robed shoulders were almost invisible. White hair and beard and eyes like caves— "I went back to court to see if there was anything I could do. I had some slight hope that it might have been Valda who had been possessed, you see, although I should have guessed that Rhym was clever enough to make the better choice. Whichever of the two had survived must still know the conjuration, so I had hopes that, with my help, the demon might be immured again."

"You were courageous."

"I was a fool. Rhym enslaved me at once. I served that monster diligently for many, many years, until you released me, and for that I curse you, because I can never be free of the guilt my crimes·have—"

"You bear no guilt, old man, as I tell you every day and as Montserrat told you. Your Highness?"

Longdirk was addressing her with that terrible title! She shook her head violently.

"It fits, Princess," he said. "It fits! No one ever knew what happened to the missing Queen of England. Obviously Nevil would want to destroy her, for that is how demons think, and destroy you also, because you represent some small danger to him. He has wiped out all the royal houses of Europe for much less cause. You are the right age, are you not?"

"It is a sad tale, sir," she muttered, "but nothing to do with me."

Yet her heart was telling her that it must be true, that Mother was not crazy at all with her endless flitting from place to place, staying away from the frontier as the Fiend steadily pushed it south and eastward, depending on friends originally, perhaps, but soon on strangers, loyalists who would shelter her and her child for a few months and then pass her on to others. Until in Siena the pursuers had closed in, two nights ago. Hamish had worked it out and not told her.

"Lisa . . ." he said. "I mean, 'Your Highness.' No,

it isn't 'Your Highness' either, is it? We know that the King of England is a demonic creature, not human. He's legally dead, so you—"

"No, no!" This was worse!

"I'm afraid so—Your Majesty. Your true father died years ago, so you mustn't feel that the Fiend's atrocities have anything to do with you. We know a few of his agents in Italy, men bound to obedience as the baron here once was. We watch them carefully, and when one of them suddenly traveled to Siena, I followed to try and find out what he was up to. I enlisted some men to keep an eye on him. Now I know what he was up to, don't I?"

"Mother? Looking for Mother?"

"Yes, but looking for you even more." His voice sank to a whisper. "You are rightful Queen of England."

It was Longdirk who broke the terrible silence, his voice deep and smooth as a river. "That's not something to worry about today. You're safe here, my lady, but your mother is still in very grave danger. You don't know exactly where the house is? Maestro, what can you do? Can you locate her?"

For what seemed like a very long time the old man stared down at the table and the sparkling jewels adorning his ugly, clawlike fingers. At last he muttered, "No. I don't see any way at all. How close to the girl was Gonzaga?"

"He had his filthy hands on her," Hamish said grimly. "And for that he ought to die several times."

"If he had achieved that much two nights ago, he will surely have found Blanche by now."

"You risked your life to warn her once, old man! So you told us. Are you too old to do it again?"

The hexer looked up sharply, glared at him, then seemed to shrink into his black robe like a frightened turtle. "She knows I was bespelled. Just the sight of me will frighten her to death."

"That would be a merciful end compared to what Nevil would do to her. We must try to rescue her." Hamish slapped the table.

"Oh, must we?" Fischart sprayed spit in his indignation. "Well, it isn't possible. Unless the girl can direct us to the house, we'd need a whole legion of demons to search the city. The tutelary would never allow it."

"Flames! Lisa, I would go if I could do any good. And so would Maestro Fischart, if there was any way. Wouldn't you, Maestro?"

The old man shrugged. "Yes. But there isn't."

Hamish turned to Lisa, and she was shocked to see that he was smirking. "You have that kerchief?"

So now he would deign to tell her what the importance of the scarf was! She fumbled at her neck for it. He took it and spread it out for the others to see—a square of cheap cotton, not silk, ruined by two holes.

"She made a mask for Carnival. Lisa, I am presuming that you did this in your mother's house? Where are the pieces you cut out?"

Apparently he was serious. "On the floor of my room, I suppose. Frieda may have picked them up and burned them by now, or thrown them out with the trash."

Hamish cocked his head at the adept. "Two days

ago? There should be enough residual propinquity for gramarye to locate the part from the whole, shouldn't there?"

"Oh, so now we have another hexer in the Company do we?" The adept was not amused.

Longdirk was, and suppressed a grin.

"Just trying to be helpful." Hamish thought he had been clever, but gramarye was a dangerous business to meddle with.

"If the scraps have been burned, it won't work," Maestro Fischart growled.

"Of course not. But if they're under the bed or out in the gutter?"

"Yes," he admitted, baring his teeth. "But have you any idea what you're asking? Suppose I just provide the demons and let you go alone?" Was that merely anger he was showing, or fear as well?

Hamish shrugged. "Teach me, and I'll try. We must be quick."

"How risky?" Longdirk demanded.

"Very!" Fischart wrung his hands a few times. "Suicide for him if he goes alone. Together we'll have a chance."

This was what Hamish had foreseen all along. This was why he had wanted Lisa out of the way when he spoke to his friends. Demons did terrible things to people—tortured them, maimed them, ate their souls.

"You must not!" she said. "Not if it's dangerous."

"I'm afraid they must," Longdirk told her. "Any risk is worth taking to save your mother from falling into Nevil's hands."

She had not heard him volunteering! "I'll come with you."

"No you won't," Hamish said, with none of the respect due a queen. "I had to work too hard to get you out the first time." He added a smile, but it died young. "Tonight, Baron?"

"Don't call me that. If it's possible. Late . . . preparations . . ." Mumbling, the hexer heaved himself upright as if to leave, but his shoulders stayed bowed. He wrung his hands. "Come to the adytum now, and we'll do a divination. No use trying it if it's hopeless." He was older than she had realized.

"Wait." Longdirk rose also, which was a different matter—he dominated the courtyard. "Hamish, who else knows about Her Majesty?"

"Carlo and Rinaldo know that she's an English lady in distress. But a thousand people saw us ride in together."

The big man nodded. "My lady, we must keep your identity a secret—which is just about impossible in this country. Hamish?"

"You're Mistress Lisa Campbell, my little sister," Hamish retorted, speaking as if reciting something he'd memorized. "In 1519, just before I left Scotland, you were fostered out to our aunt Meg. That's not uncommon for Highland families with too many children. Meg moved to the Continent under circumstances you may decline to discuss. Two years ago she placed you with the Countess of Ely as lady's maid. The countess was visiting relatives in Nice, and when she heard you had a brother in Florence, she decided to visit Italy." He smiled, and she wondered what he was reading on her face. "You don't have to run round the camp telling this tale to everyone. You may never need to use it, but now it's there if you do. We'll work out the rest of the details later." When he was pleased with himself, it showed.

"Yes, sir."

Longdirk said, "Ma'am, you are quite safe here at the moment, but if word gets out that you are the Queen of England, then I don't know what will happen."

"I doubt if anyone would believe it, because I don't." She did not like this oversize warrior. In spite of his gentle manner, he was too much a bull in a pasture, lording over everyone—bulls were slow and quiet until they began pawing the turf. He frightened her, and she was quite convinced that he would *use her politically* if he ever got the chance, no matter what Hamish had said.

She jumped as the condottiere's sword flashed out from its scabbard. He stepped around the end of the table and dropped to one knee. Even then, his eyes were little lower than hers.

"Your Majesty, I cannot admit that you are Queen of Scotland. And my first loyalty is to the Republic of Florence. Excepting those two caveats, I pledge my life and honor in your service as rightful Queen of England." He kissed the blade.

Well! Maybe she had misjudged him. No knight had ever pledged his sword to her before. It must be time for her to wake up and the dream to end, but until it did she could only play her part. She responded with what she hoped was a regal nod. "I am honored to accept your allegiance, Constable Longdirk." She did not rise as the giant strode out, with the hexer shuffling alongside him. When they had gone, she risked a sideways glance at Hamish, not sure whether to grin or stay solemn.

He was watching her with an oddly wistful expression. "I'm sorry."

"It was a bit of a shock." Was that the understatement of the millennium or just of the sixteenth century?

"I wasn't sure, truly I wasn't—not until I saw how the baron stared at you. I didn't know he knew your mother." But he had probably guessed that it was likely. Master Campbell was creepily well informed about almost everything.

"Next time warn me, will you?"

He laughed and clasped her hand in both of his. "Tomorrow I hail you as Sultana of the Turks. Tuesday afternoon you become Empress of Cathay. Believe me, you're safer here with Longdirk than with anyone, truly!"

It was odd to be sitting so close when they were the only people in the courtyard. "Safer with you!" she said, and suddenly she had her arms around him and his arms were around her, crushing her. A bristly cheek brushed hers; her lips turned to his. He was a friend, the only one she had or had ever had, a true, trustworthy friend, and now he was going to leave her and return to Siena, go into danger—

"Oh, demons!" Hamish let go and leapt to his

feet, tripping against his stool and almost overbalancing. "Lisa, we mustn't!"

"Mustn't what?"

"Fall in love! I've been there, Lisa, I know the feeling. We must stop! You're a queen, and I'm a nothing."

"Oh!" she said. Oh, demons!

He should have warned her about that sooner.

14

"This is as close as I want to come," Toby said. "Good luck. Take care."

He was a massive, indeterminate shape in the starlight, but on those words he would have held out a hand to shake. Hoping his own was not too shamefully sweaty on this chilly evening, Hamish reached for it, found it, and endured the familiar forceful squeeze. An owl hooted derisively, sweeping overhead on silent wings.

"I always take care."

"Not so I ever noticed." Longdirk's tone deepened, grew more serious. "Are you sure you want to go through with this? You think Fischart is crazy. Do you want to trust him on a demon ride?"

Sure? The only thing Hamish was sure of was that if he could think of a way out of tonight's escapade, he would cheerfully give up his wisdom teeth to take it— they obviously weren't doing him any good. He'd done his share of roughhousing in the past and even slain some worthy opponents, but he preferred the pen to the sword. Derring-do was not his style.

"I've done demon rides before."

"You've also experienced a broken jaw and being run through with a sword, and you told me those were more fun."

True, but alas, he had promised the lovely Lisa he would tread this measure for her, and the music was about to start. "I didn't say the maestro's crazy. I just said I can't think how anyone else could have taken that gold."

Toby grunted. "You're a stubborn idiot, you know that? A pretty girl smiles at you, and you roll over like a puppy every time."

"I like getting my belly rubbed. We'll be back before dawn." He hoped.

"Good spirits be with you."

They were more likely to be against him tonight, if one included the guardians of Siena. Hamish turned quickly and strode off along the gloomy path toward the ghostly chink of light that marked his destination. Why, why, why had he made that crass remark about belly rubbing? No girl would ever rub Toby's.

Only the adept himself willingly went near the adytum, which crouched like a hunting cat among gloomy cypresses. Some parts were of Roman brick, others of massively thick stonework, all with squinty little window slits, but whatever the building's long history, it had recently been refurbished, and the tiled roof was solid and weatherproof. Even in summer it would stay cool; at midnight in February it had no trouble raising gooseflesh all over Master Hamish Campbell. So did the two horses tethered near the door. He gave them a wide berth.

He clattered the latch instead of knocking, and the hinges screamed like a witness on the rack. The only light inside was a solitary candle on the worktable at the far end, where Maestro Fischart stood, bent over a thick tome. He looked up with a scowl as his visitor approached.

"So the scholar turns hero? Rescuing the girl herself wasn't enough for you. Now you want to rescue her mother as well? Overcome with gratitude, she'll swoon helpless into your manly arms."

"She can swoon into yours all she wants, if you mean the countess. Lisa's enough of an armful for me." Hamish did not care for Maestro Fischart, essential though he was to the Company. He was undoubtedly crazy to some extent, the only question being how much.

Tugging his cloak tighter around him, Hamish looked around for a place to sit. His teeth very much wanted to chatter, and although he could blame the cold for that, chattering did not suit the role of knight-errant. The two spindly chairs bore teetering towers of books, and the plank bed was so piled with scrolls, boxes, anonymous bundles, and old clothes that its owner must be presumed to sleep on the floor. More litter lay on the two ironbound chests that contained the hexer's equipment and accompanied him everywhere he went. Glass vials and alembics cluttered a third, which was larger and stronger, the Company's strongbox.

·

The hexer squawked with derision and slammed the book closed, swirling dust up like smoke from the littered table. "You're mad, boy! You lust after the rightful Queen of England!"

That slash drew blood. Of course any thought of romance with Lisa was unthinkable, but that wasn't keeping Hamish from thinking about it. He'd been in love before, but this time felt different. Didn't every time feel different? Even more different. He had never met a girl like Lisa—haughty, learned, and courageous, and yet witty, naive, and appallingly vulnerable. Two days with her had set his wits so a-spin that the jeer made his temper boil.

"You were never young, were you? That dramatic ride to Highcross you told us about was prompted by nothing more than concern for the public weal? And tonight—hose, doublet, jerkin, cloak? My! What inspired you to discard that stinking robe at last? Want to look presentable to a lady, do you? Renewing an old romance? Playing gentleman? Haven't seen you wear a sword since Spain."

Fischart straightened. "Your ill temper is a sure sign of nervousness. Are you having second thoughts about this madcap escapade?"

Sudden caution. "Should I have second thoughts? What did you learn?"

The earlier divinations had given ambiguous results, and the hexer had promised to make further tests. Augury was always inexact, because no demon or spirit could foresee the future, but a skilled adept could learn whether his personal aspect was in positive or negative mode. Only an idiot would undertake a dangerous venture when the currents were set against him.

Fischart sighed. "The answers were no clearer. If anything less clear." He eyed Hamish for a moment, then dropped his gaze to the table and began shuffling objects around aimlessly. "Shadow. All I find is shadow."

"What shadow? Whose shadow?"

"The thief's. Longdirk tell you about the missing gold?"

"Of course."

"He hid himself with gramarye," the hexer mumbled. "My watchers didn't see him, but they saw his shadow." His hands continued to fidget as if playing a dozen chess games.

"You're sure it was a man's shadow?"

"No, but tonight my aura has that same shadow across it!"

Because it was his own shadow. He had contrived the theft himself for no sane reason. Lots of hexers went crazy. Consort with demons long enough and sooner or later you wouldn't know your armpit from an anthill. Fischart's gnawing guilt made him an obvious candidate for the chaos chorus.

"Across mine, too?"

"No, not yours."

"Then you stay here, and I'll go alone." That was sheer braggadocio. Hamish could not possibly handle the powers required. His new and untried agents in Siena had almost no chance of finding the countess by material means. In fact their bumbling inquiries were more likely to attract the signory's attention and thus drag her farther into danger. If the Fiend's minions had not already located her, the only practical way to find her was with gramarye. Coursing was tricky enough with dogs and with demons would be a roll in a snake pit. So he needed the hexer, and there could be no delay, for the propinquity of the severed kerchief must be fading fast.

"No. I'll come." The old man held out a hand. "Give me back Corte."

Hamish removed his ring. "Why can't I keep it for tonight?"

"Because it is conjured to whip you out of the way of any serious danger. Tonight you have to stay and enjoy it." Fischart dropped the guarddemon in a small casket of ivory and closed the lid. That box was familiar. Toby and the don had worked some real wonders with it once, including saving Hamish's life. He saw several things he recognized in the dust-coated litter on the table, but others were disturbingly strange—a furred hand with too many fingers, a lump of rock crystal containing what looked like golden feathers, a tortoise in a bottle, a basket holding embers that still glowed with worms of red fire and yet did not burn the basket, a small, brownish skull with teeth that were definitely not human . . .

"Have you ever considered becoming a hexer?"

Hamish looked up with an angry retort ready on his lips and was taken aback by the Fischart's pasty smile. The adept's humor was usually mocking, but this time he seemed almost wistful, and something like sincerity might be lurking in the rheumy eyes. That smile and the question were equally disconcerting.

Of course he had. Anyone who enjoyed books and learning as much as he did must at some time consider taking up the spiritual arts, and that was especially true in Italy, for almost every adept in Europe had spent time at the Cardinal College in Rome. Hexers, acolytes serving the spirits in shrines or tutelaries in sanctuaries—almost all were graduates of the College, and so were many of the Khan's shamans. The College would not willingly train a hexer, so only members of religious orders were accepted as students, and only by swearing fearful oaths could anyone join such an order, whatever he or she might do with the learning in later life.

"Too dangerous for me," Hamish said. "I'd rather keep on following Toby around and watching him rattle the world." Besides, the training took years, and its requirements included poverty, chastity, and obedience. Nothing much wrong with poverty or obedience, but chastity was altogether too plentiful already. No wonder adepts went crazy. Who would ever want to become anything like this cobwebby, memory-tortured old mummy?

"I see," said the mummy drily. "I have demonized the horses. Yours is named Westlea."

"It understands English?"

"It understands my English. What you call English is not what the English do. It knows Latin. I have also prepared two rings for you. Lupus will bring you back here the moment you utter the word 'Panoply.'"

"One word? Is that safe?"

The hexer's customary sneer returned. "No. And be warned—I have worded my edicts as carefully as I know how, but Lupus has a sense of humor. If you happen to be clutching a doorframe when you pronounce the word, it may rip your hand off. Or bring the house, too, and drop it on top of you."

"Charming! Is that possible? A house?"

"Perhaps not, but Lupus is an exceptionally powerful demon."

Gulp! *Exceptionally powerful* and a one-word leash? Dangerous! But if gramarye could flash him back here from Siena with one word, why did he have to endure a demon ride to get there? The mummy was waiting for him to ask. Hamish rummaged through his knowledge of gramarye in search of an answer and saw that Lupus could be assigned a specific target for the return—here—but there was no way to define an equally safe destination in Siena. Given any leeway at all, a demon would drop him in fire, open water, a cesspool, anything to cause pain and adversity.

"Tell me about the other one."

"The other is Zangliveri, and you must wear it on your sword hand. If we meet with any trouble, point your blade at it and say, 'Vestige.' The target will be destroyed."

"Destroyed? People, too?"

"Certainly."

The ethics of murder were troubling enough without wondering how the tutelary would react to strangers slaughtering people with gramarye. It might let them get away with killing other strangers, as long as they left its flock alone—or it might not. "You play for high stakes, Maestro."

"There can be no higher stakes than these."

"Is Zangliveri as strong as Lupus?"

"Stronger. You should be able to open paths through stone walls with Zangliveri."

Hamish nodded and cleared his throat, which felt strangely dry, as if he were starting a cold. "Panoply for a fast getaway, Vestige to strike dead."

Fischart stared at him sourly. "You need to practice them again, or may I open the casket now?"

"I think I've got it."

"Good. I'd hate Zangliveri to turn the floor under your feet into an inferno." He opened the box and lifted out two rings of gold. One bore a blue stone, and the other a black. "Zangliveri. And Lupus."

"Pleased to meet you, Your Maleficences." Hamish slid them onto fingers of his right hand. They went on readily enough, then became painfully tight, but that was just the demons playing tricks. A demon would vent its hatred in any evil it could get away with, which might be plenty when it was held by a mere one-word conjuration. "What's the plan?"

Toby defined a plan as "The least likely sequence of events."

Fischart came around the end of the table. "You

ride to Siena, and I follow. We release the steeds, locate Her Maj . . . the countess . . . if we can, and thereafter proceed according to our judgment and the turn of events." He had at least a dozen rings sparkling on his fingers—how many of them had been pre-conjured to react to a single word like Zangliveri and Lupus? The man was a walking powder keg.

Panoply, Hamish thought. *Panoply. Vestige* and *panoply. What are we waiting for?*

The adept wrung his hands. "I am very reluctant to use my skills against innocent men, Master Campbell. I am not as agile as I was, either. So, while I believe I can handle any gramarye Gonzaga is capable of applying against us and can probably distract the tutelary long enough for our purposes, I shall rely on your reflexes and keen eye if we meet with mortal resistance."

It was a nasty shock to realize that the celebrated hexer was as scared as he was. "Fear not!" Hamish proclaimed. "I am dauntless as a cornered rat unless I have time to think. Let's go." He headed for the door. The nauseating knot of apprehension in his belly went with him.

15

Hamish untethered the first demon steed and held its head while Fischart mounted. The brutes looked wrong for horses, acted wrong, smelled wrong, and their hate-filled eyes glowed faintly in the dark. He approached the other carefully, alert for iron-shod hooves and demon teeth that could rip chunks out of a man's flesh, but the hexer must have bound the Westlea demon well, for he was able to mount without trouble. Then he let go the reins and folded his arms. That was a point of honor for a demon rider, because in his terror he might seriously injure the horse's mouth. It was also rank bravado, but only a maniac would attempt this anyway.

"Ready, Maestro?"

"Ready, lad." The hexer's voice was a croak—comforting! "Pivkas, I bid you bear me after Westlea, going unseen."

Hamish wet his lips. "Westlea, I bid you bear me southward, passing east of Florence, going unseen. Go!"

The horse leaped into a place of demons, taking him with it. The first time he had ridden a demon steed, he had screamed for what felt like a solid hour, although in fact he had returned to reality after only a few minutes. Men had been known to go crazy, or faint and fall off, forever lost. One never knew what to expect, except that it would be torment and nightmare. In this case he rode beneath a sky of liquid black, devoid of sun, moon, or stars, and yet there was light of a sort, for the earth was visible from horizon to horizon, barren rock and ash bereft of shadows or color. Buildings were ruined, roofless, and tumbledown. People? There were no people as people, but vague glows writhed here and there like tormented wraiths trying to crawl up out of the soil, wailing appeals as the demon steeds thundered by them. If that was speech they were attempting, it was drowned by the discordant howl of a wind that stirred eye-nipping clouds of dust and once in a while peppered his face with sand. Blasts of feverish heat alternated with skin-freezing cold, both of them bringing rank, repulsive stenches.

He risked a glance behind him and shuddered. All he could see of the hexer was a skeleton astride a skeleton horse. Bones and metal—horseshoes and dagger, boot buckles and coins in a belt pouch. Conversation was impossible in the shrieking wind, but he decided that the old man was coping. His arm bones hung down in front of him, so he must be hanging on to the pommel of his saddle. That seemed like a good idea. Hamish could not see his own saddle, but he could feel it and cling to it. He tried not to look at his own bones or the sword dangling unsupported at his side. The gale tugged at his invisible cloak.

Florence was a ruin and an ancient one, as it might look a hundred years after the Fiend had sacked it, all crumbling walls and hills of rubble. He reminded himself that demons could not prophesy, and it was obvious that a pillar of light marked the sanctuary and lesser glows shone from the many shrines, defying the demonic illusion. To look at them hurt Hamish's eyes. He was not in a state of grace at the moment.

He could not, would not, stand this torment for very long. Coughing at the grit and filth in his mouth, he shouted, "Westlea, I bid you go faster!" A few moments later he repeated the command. Now the demon steed hurtled over the nightmare landscape like a stooping hawk. It crossed the dry bed of the Arno in three or four leaps and raced up the hills beyond. Had the demon world been ruled by the same laws as the world of mankind, it would have left a dust cloud a league long.

The baron was still with him. Either the old mummy was tougher than he looked or he had reinforced himself with some gramarye that he had not offered to Hamish. Either way—

"Westlea, I bid you go faster!"

Now the drum of hooves blended into a roar, like rain. The eldritch scenery rushed by in a blur. Southward he flew over the Chianti Hills, past Impruneta, Greve, and Castellina, retracing his journey of the last two days in a tiny fraction of that time. It just felt longer.

He came at last to a demonized vision of Siena, but the spirits burned there as bright as in Florence and would not take kindly to demons within their domain. Hamish halted Westlea in a field just outside the city wall. Then the air was sweet again, the stars shone above living trees. He bade his steed stand absolutely still and leaped to the ground. He shouted the same command to Pivkas—glad that he had remembered its name—and caught Fischart as he tumbled from the saddle.

A few minutes' rest on the grass, and the old man had recovered enough to start being unpleasant again, berating Hamish for the pace he had set.

"You may enjoy that; I don't," Hamish retorted. "You could have made the cursed thing go more slowly if you wanted. Now get rid of these incarnates before the tutelary blasts all of us!"

Muttering, the hexer clambered to his feet and spoke his commands, immuring the demons back in their jewels. Then the horses were only horses, whinnying with alarm at finding themselves where they had not been before. Hamish tied their reins up out of harm's way, loosened their saddle girths, and left them as a pleasant surprise for some lucky Sienese. His hands had almost stopped shaking. Whatever happened now, the worst of the night was over.

"The scarf," said the hexer. "You hold one end, let me have the other."

Hamish pulled out Lisa's kerchief, felt the maestro grip it also, heard a single guttural word, *Halstuch!* . . . and waited, shuffling from one foot to the other.

"What's happening?"

"El Bayahd's looking for the rest of it."

Searching the whole city? Every cesspit, every slop bucket? And what, pray, were the tutelary and its kindred spirits up to while these intruders disturbed the peace with exhibitions of gr—

The night exploded around him as the demon snatched him away.

16

Silence. Gasp for breath . . .

He stood beside Fischart, with his feet on mud and his nose almost touching the back of a coach.

Beetling eaves showed high overhead against a sky just starting to think about dawn. A horse whinnied shrilly and jangled harness, as if it sensed the demon's passage, but no human voice was raised in alarm. Hooves stamped impatiently, clumping and clopping on stone. A man cursed, making Hamish's hand tighten on the hilt of his sword.

Someone very rich must be arriving or departing, for the carriage was no dainty gig for a jaunt to market but a lumbering shed on wheels that almost filled the roadway and would need a full team of eight. The voice had come from the side, probably a flunky waiting by the footboard. He must have been speaking to someone and there might well be another man holding the horses, possibly a driver on the box as well. Hamish abandoned his hopes that this escapade would involve nothing more vigorous than a tap on a lady's chamber door and a graceful bow as he was presented by her old friend Karl Fischart. Activities more strenuous now seemed imminent.

He leaned around the tall rear wheel to peek along the gap between coach and wall. He saw a bright streak where a house door stood ajar, a protruding footboard directly opposite it, and beyond both of those, two men silhouetted against the glow of lanterns on the front of the carriage. Just standing there waiting for something, but armed, and therefore more than mere grooms and postilions . . . Flames! How many more tending the horses? How many altogether? How much use was Fischart going to be when the trouble started?

"Taking a crappy long time, ain't he?" grumbled one of the two.

In English!

Granted that Italy was overrun with refugees from a dozen lands, common sense screamed that men skulking around long after curfew in Siena speaking English were those same Nevil agents who had tried to abduct Lisa two days ago. A demon had testified that the missing scraps of Lisa's kerchief lay somewhere amid the street garbage, so this must be the countess's residence. Common sense told Hamish to whip out his rapier and unleash demon Zangliveri to even up the odds a little. He tightened his grip on the hilt—

His hand refused to do more. His logic might be wrong. He could not blast men down without more evidence. He squirmed with frustration. He was crazy. Toby would have taken both of them by now, probably with his bare hands, but he was not Toby. Any minute now one of those bravos would decide to take a stroll around the coach and . . .

The house door creaked and brighter light flared up like a sunrise, revealing greasy pavement, footboard, the two guards. They were armed with both sword and dagger and wore no excessive clothing that might hamper their movements. They did not look especially villainous. They looked young and fit and dangerous as hell.

A dark figure ducked out from the door of the house, then raised its lantern and turned to light the way. A woman followed, muffled in a dark cloak.

Her hat concealed her hair, so there was no way to tell if she was Queen Blanche, who in her youth had been called the White Princess, but she was tall enough to stoop for the lintel, and she stumbled awkwardly in doing so. Her arms were behind her, and there was another man right at her back. Abduction?

Of course it was an abduction! *Get on with it!*

Hamish drew his sword and took three steps to poke the man who held the lantern. "Vestige!"

His head jumped from his shoulders in a spray of air and blood. The lantern clattered to the ground with his hand still attached, then the rest of him collapsed into a blood-soaked pile of meat and garments. His head rolled into the gutter. The lantern had already gone out, but there was enough light coming from the doorway to establish that he had been completely dis-assembled. There could not be an intact human body in that heap. Several people screamed, probably including Hamish himself. Certainly his stomach heaved so violently that for a moment he was inca-pable of doing anything. Then a lot of things happened all at once.

Spooked by the blood odor or the demon, the horses reared, screamed, lunged against the collars. A man holding the leaders yelled and fell back. As the rig began to move, another man jumped down from the footboard to join the fray. Shouting, "Blanche! Majesty! It's me, Karl!" Fischart jostled past Hamish, throwing him against the wheel so the hub jarred his elbow and he almost dropped his rapier. The countess was hauled bodily back into the house by her captor. The two bravos flashed out their swords and daggers in an unnerving display of proficiency. Hamish recoiled off the carriage and stumbled over the grue- some stack of flesh that had been the first casualty. Fischart tried to follow the countess into the house, and one of the swordsmen ran him through. He screamed and fell. The door slammed, cutting off the light.

The carriage had departed, so the road was cleared for battle—Hamish Campbell versus no less than four opponents, possibly more. The darkness was on his side, but at least one of the enemy must be Gonzaga, the hexer he had bested two nights before. This time he was not wearing a guarddemon.

Hoping that Fischart was flat on the ground and out of the line of fire, he waved his rapier in the direc- tion of the foe, and said, "Vestige, vestige, vestige!"

He heard the eruption of bursting lungs again. Once? Or twice? The runaway carriage collapsed into a heap of lumber, sending eight horses mad with ter- ror. Its lamps blossomed in golden roses of flaming oil, silhouetting three upright opponents for him, but also revealing him to them. One was waving his hands and chanting, and must be Gonzaga. Fischart was scrambling to his feet, presumably healed of his wound. Shutters were slapping open all along the street.

Two armed men sprang at Hamish. He had Zangliveri demolish the first, but then the second was all over him so that he needed his rapier for parrying and could no longer direct the demon with it. He retreated before a dazzling blur of strokes—cuts and thrusts, blades rattling in a frenzied clitter, clitter, clitter . . . *Spirits!* The man was a leopard! Even the don praised Hamish's fencing now, and as long as he had room to move, his rapier should give him a significant advantage in reach over saber and dagger. So much for theory. He was about to be skinned alive. Parry, parry, parry . . . The dagger would be a sword breaker and must be avoided. Oh, flames! This yokel was faster than Don Ramon himself, superhuman! He had to be using gramarye. *Spirits!*

More light blazed up in the street, making screams resound from every window, for the battle now commanded a sizable audience. Hamish was too engrossed on staying alive to see what was happening, although he could hear Fischart and Gonzaga howling conjurations at each other.

Fortunately, just when wee Hamish Campbell thought he was about to die of terror, he saw an opening. It was briefer than the blink of a hawk's eye, but it let him run his point into Wonderman's forearm. The swordsman yelped and fell back. He did not drop his blade, but pain made him lose his focus just long enough for Hamish to aim the rapier and give the command to Zangliveri. It was a rotten way to treat a fine opponent, but a flesh wound would not have kept him out of action long. Leaping over the collapsed remains, Hamish sprinted back to the battle of hexers.

Gonzaga had summoned his oversized ape-bear

demon with the claws and fangs, while Fischart had countered with a man-sized salamander of coruscating fire, which was the origin of all the lurid lighting. Now the two apparitions were rolling and wrestling about the street, filling the night with bloodcurdling shrieks and a foul sulfurous stench. Only the hexers themselves knew how many demons were involved in that display. Gonzaga was nowhere in sight, which was good, but the lizard seemed to be growing smaller and the furry thing larger and louder, and that was probably bad. Fischart had turned his attention to finding the countess. As Hamish arrived, panting, he hurled a conjuration at the door, which at once shattered into fragments. A tongue of white fire roared out.

It missed Hamish, but only just. He leaped back, wondering if he had lost his eyebrows. It engulfed the old man, who fell to the ground, screaming and writhing as his clothes burned. Hamish glanced helplessly back and forth between that baleful doorway— as dark now as it had been bright earlier—and the dying hexer, whose flesh blazed, charring and reeking horribly of roast meat. He was beyond all help, both mortal and immortal.

Where there's one booby trap there are usually more.

Hamish dived through the door into the house and lived; no wave of fire threw him back. He found himself in a dingy, low-ceilinged room, lit by a single candle, and cramped by half a dozen chairs and a wooden table . . . cupboards and shelves on the walls . . . a closed door that probably led through to stairs and other rooms . . . He saw what he had come for in a corner—the woman in the dark cloak, gagged and tied to a chair. There was no sign of her assailant. He reached her in three steps, sheathing his rapier as he went.

"I come to rescue you, ma'am. Lisa is safe. I know who you—" He felt for his knife to untie her, and it was gone, lost somewhere in the evening's confusion. "Demons! I'm a friend. Will you trust me?"

No nod, no headshake, just eyes rolling in wild terror. He was soaked in blood, and she was beyond rational thought.

What to do? He looked despairingly at the doorway, where the multicolored flashes were fading and the ape's roars completely masked the salamander's dwindling shrieks. Fischart was dead and must be abandoned. Hamish couldn't even take the old man's body back with him, because Gonzaga must be still at large, as well as the accomplice who had tied up the countess.

Where there's one booby trap there are usually more.

This was a worse nightmare than the demon ride, the sort of experience whose memory will waken a man for years afterward, howling in sweat-soaked bedding. With a quick prayer for mercy to the tutelary, he made his choice and leaned over the lady to grip her arms. "Forgive me, ma'am, but we have to get out of here." She was shaking, but so was he. No trap so far.

Lupus. What was the word . . . ?

What was the word?
"Panoply!"
The demon took them away.

17

Having forgotten Fischart's warning that Lupus had a
sense of humor, Hamish expected the chair to go with
them, but the chair stayed behind, and so did the
countess's bonds. She landed on her back in total darkness, and he fell on top of her. Making piteous noises
behind her gag, she struggled and thrashed against his
efforts to restrain her. That was a job fit for Toby, for
she was a large and powerful woman in a frenzy of terror. Even if they were back in the adytum, there would
be things around that could injure her. He wrapped his
arms tight around her and talked comfort in her ear
until she ran out of strength.

"Majesty! Countess! You are among friends. Lisa
is safe. We know who you are—Karl Fischart . . .
Baron Oreste . . . Lisa is here . . . Lisa is safe . . ." His
eyes were adjusting. He could see shards of predawn
light through the slits. It was the adytum. "Let me take
off the gag, ma'am, and I'll escort you to Lisa."

She fell still, if violent shivering could be called
stillness. He released her and felt for the cloth. By
the time he had untied it, and they were both sitting
up, she was weeping. It had been a rough night.
For her, two very rough days. Fourteen very bad
years . . .

"Come, my lady. My name is Hamish Campbell . . ."

And so on. He helped her rise. She staggered, barely capable of walking. The candle had gone out, so the excursion to Siena must have lasted longer than it seemed.

"Lisa? Truly?" She could barely speak, teeth clattering like a forest full of woodpeckers.

"She is here and unharmed. This is Fiesole, just outside Florence. You are quite safe here. We are sworn enemies of the Fiend." Going mostly by memory, he steered her across the room to the door. The cypresses were stains of black against gray, but dawn was coming, the day stretching as it wakened. Birds singing. He talked. She did not seem to hear.

He wondered how he was going to break the awful news to Toby that the Don Ramon Company had lost its hexer. That was almost as bad as losing its cavalry. He was so engrossed in that problem that he did not notice the two figures waiting at the edge of the trees until one of them squealed and came flying. It was Lisa. Toby loped along behind her.

Toby and Lisa? Lisa and Toby? Lisa crashed into an embrace, making predictable noises of, "Mother-MotherMother!" and, "AreYouAllRight?" and "OhWhat'sTheMatter . . . ?" And so on.

Gasping the equally predictable, "LisaOhLisa IsItReallyYou?" the countess staggered and would have fallen if Hamish had not steadied her.

Then he stepped aside, leaving the two of them locked together, weeping.

"Just shock. She's had a very bad time. Don't think she's injured."

Toby said, "You look a little dilapidated yourself. Any of that your own blood?"

"No." He rubbed his face and felt the caked stains. "No. None of it honorably earned, either."

"Rough voyage?" Toby thumped his shoulder.

That was about as far as he ever went in displaying emotion, but there could be exceptions to any rule—he also avoided women as much as he could and private assignations at all costs, yet he had been waiting there on the path with Lisa. Oh, demons! What sort of thoughts were those? There could never be reason to be jealous of poor Toby, not where girls were concerned, and Lisa was forever out of reach for both of them.

"The water was a little choppy." The voyage had been much rougher for some. Hamish was shaking with reaction now, nauseated, thinking all confused. He knew the feelings and had seen them in other men often enough; it was only in books that heroes walked away from battles as if nothing had happened. How many corpses? And Fischart. Oh, spirits!

Before he could find the words, Toby said: "You came back alone?"

"'Fraid so."

"Damn." Longdirk rarely swore and always very quietly. He never lost his temper. Part of that icy self-control he had learned from the saints at Montserrat as the only way to suppress the hob, but he had shown much of it as a child back in the glen. It was absolutely typical of him that now, seeing the Company crippled, his creation perhaps fatally weakened, and all his plans thrown in jeopardy, he said only that one soft word.

Then, "Any doubts? Any hope?"

Hamish shook his head, shivering as he remembered the blackened flesh burning like wax in the gutter. "None. It was treachery."

"What sort of treachery?" Longdirk's voice remained gentle, but there was menace in it.

"The gold thief. I'm sorry, Toby! You asked me, and I was too stupid . . . I should have seen this sooner. The gold was a red herring to distract us. Whoever he was, the intruder was in the adytum to tamper with Fischart's demons—one of them, some of them, I don't know. Not all of them, but when he invoked one in Siena to open a door, it destroyed him." It had not been a booby trap at all. If the door had been booby-trapped, then the countess would have been booby-trapped also, and Hamish would have suffered the same fate as the hexer. Fischart had seen the shadow of his assassin across his path, but the shadow had been there to doctor his demons. "And before that a man stabbed him with a sword. That doesn't happen to hexers . . . I should have guessed!"

"So should Oreste himself." Sigh. "He was a cantankerous, hagridden old blackguard at times, but you could never doubt his loyalty or his hatred of the Fiend. It wasn't your fault, and I'm very happy you made it back safely. Tell me all about it later." He

glanced around at the countess, then inquiringly at
Hamish, who shook his head.

"She didn't see."

"Good. Don't breathe a word to anyone else."

"Aye, aye, sir." Yet Hamish was surprised. It
might be days or weeks before the camp realized that
the hexer was missing, and thus the *condotta* might yet
be signed before the Florentines learned that the
Company had lost one of its major assets, the finest
hexer in Europe, but that seemed very close to cheating—closer than he would have expected Toby to
stray.

"Especially not the don."

"Of course." Hamish would prefer not to be
around if, or when, the haughty, hair-trigger *caballero*
heard the news from somebody else.

"And talking of El Cid," Toby said, "he's nastily
close to his flash point. I know you've had a tough
night, laddie, but can you back him up at the talks this
morning?"

If he could sleep for a week first. "I can try." It
would be a distraction to take his mind off the horrors.
It was also a devil of an imposition on top of a night
without sleep, so it was both flattering and inspiring to
be thought capable—typical Longdirk. He could
always wring more out of a man than there was in
there to start with.

Toby smiled faintly, as if guessing his thoughts.
"Just stun him if he starts killing people. And—"

Lisa interrupted, grabbing his arm to turn him
around. ". . . *great* condottiere, Constable *Sir* Tobias

*Long*dirk, the *hero* of the battle of Trent, the *toast* of
Europe! Constable, my mother, Countess Maud."

Toby bowed over the lady's hand. "Your servant,
ma'am."

"I cannot begin to express my gratitude, Constable."

"I am deeply honored to have been of assistance,
my lady."

Bleary-eyed and thickheaded with fatigue, Hamish
waited to be brought into the conversation, but that
didn't happen. In a few moments Toby offered his arm
to conduct the lady in the direction of the villa, so that
she might be tended and restored by Sister Bona.
Hamish followed, and it was only then that he realized
that affairs were being stage-managed by Lady Lisa.
She moved in close, linking arms. She beamed at him.
In the unreal light of dawn, her eyes shone brighter
than Lucifer, the morning star.

"I think you're wonderful!" she said. "You're so
brave, so clever! You're marvelous! I've never met a
man like you."

Oh, no! No, no, no, no, no, no!

"Lisa!" he croaked—wanting to shout, but whispering in case her mother would overhear. Or Toby.
"Lisa, I told you! You mustn't fall in love with me!"

She gave him a look to melt his bones. "Your
warning came too late. I already did."

After a moment, she added, "Don't you love me?"
menacingly.

He had been a fool to say that word to her. Her
challenge hid a desperate appeal for reassurance, and
the comical bantam belligerence was a mask for terror.

Hers was much more than the uncertainty of a first romance, the insecurity of a child plunging into the world of adulthood, for she was in genuine danger—awful danger—and the destiny that had been revealed to her so abruptly last night would terrify anyone. She needed a champion, a paladin, a hero. She had elected him. She had no one else to turn to if he refused her.

"Lisa, I have never met a woman to compare with you. I would die for you." He saw relief slacken the tensed muscles around her eyes, a hint of satisfaction curl the corners of those breathtaking lips.

"That will not be necessary," she said. "Will you live for me?"

"Till the day I die."

She let the smile blossom. "Say it, then."

Demons! "I love you, Lisa. I love you with all my heart and all my soul, and for all my days to come. I have loved you since the moment I first saw you. I will do anything for you, anything you ask or want, anything at all. I am yours, always. Body and soul, for ever and ever."

She sighed and walked on without speaking, hugging his elbow hard and staring straight ahead.

He'd really done it now.

18

"That's your third yawn in the last furlong," Don Ramon said icily. "How many bawds took your money last night?"

Whether he enjoyed a challenge or just liked to show off his equestrian skills, Don Ramon had collected a herd of the most vicious horses ever to eat the grass of Italy, and that day he was mounted on the worst of them, a monstrous eighteen-hand stallion named Brutus, which his squires were convinced was possessed—they were always threatening to put a blade through its heart. It would kick or bite anything that came within range, so Hamish was having great trouble keeping his dowdy, unassertive palfrey within reasonable distance.

"You wrong me, senor! I spent the hours of darkness doing good works among the deserving poor."

The horns of the copper mustache writhed in contempt. "Spare me your jackdaw Castilian. Your Italian cannot be any worse." His own would never be described as fluent, but that was a problem for other people. "And see you stay alert during the negotiations. How many deserving poor?"

"Four, signore."

"You're lying!"

"All four are less poor, but two remain deserving."

"I may decide to believe that," the knight conceded.

They continued their canter down the hill to Florence. Hamish was dressed as a humble clerk, being careful not to upstage the most successful condottiere in Italy, although that would have been difficult, for his companion was garbed in quasi-royal splendor—silk and sable and cloth of gold. Erratic and capricious in every way, he was especially unpredictable toward Hamish. Usually he considered him as being beneath contempt, like the vast majority of the human race, but he had noted his talents with a rapier and taken infinite pains to teach him the finer points of fencing, he himself being a master trained by de la Naza. Although their backgrounds were vastly different—son of a wilderness schoolmaster and scion of one of the oldest noble houses in Europe— they differed by less than a year in age, and their adulthood had been spent campaigning together. After the sack of Ostra, Don Ramon had presented Hamish with a bagful of priceless medieval manuscripts. Once he had led him off on a wild all-night campaign of drinking and wenching in the slums of Milan and been still in full rampage when Hamish had passed out under the table—or had it been a bed? Twice he would have put him to death had Toby not intervened. Precedents were never reliable where the don was concerned.

"I am minded, Chancellor, to give these motheaten quill-scratchers a lesson in manners. I may even choose to overstate my case a trifle, for the sake of effect. If I decide to do so and you think it would be advantageous to remonstrate with me, then feel free to speak your mind. Provided, of course, that you temper your words with proper respect."

Toby might know what that meant. Hamish did not, and his nerves were still too jangled to play foolish games. "Longdirk told me to stun you if you tried to kill anyone, signore." Wondering what sort of cataclysm that would provoke, he looked up to meet the icy blue eyes.

Briefly they measured him for a coffin. Then the don twirled up his mustache as he did when he was pleased. "Only if I am dissembling. You will not interfere when I am serious."

"*Sì*, signore," Hamish said resignedly.

As they trotted their mounts along the busy morning streets—with Brutus constantly trying to sink his teeth in people and other horses and being consistently thwarted by the don—Hamish saw the soaring dome of the sanctuary straight ahead, and a sudden tug at his heart reminded him that he had survived an exceedingly narrow escape in the night and had also lost a comrade.

"Signore, I most humbly beg a few minutes' grace to visit the *duomo*."

The don's ginger eyebrows soared high, although his stare was shrewd and calculating. "You did have a busy night, didn't you? How many deserving poor, did you say? Very well. You will attend me as soon as possible at the Palace of the Signory."

His surprise was understandable, for tutelaries had little sympathy for soldiers of fortune, men who earned their living by killing. Hamish had not made confession since he arrived in Italy and took up the trade. Nevertheless, times were a-changing. Fighting against the Fiend would never be a sin, and Karl Fischart had died in a noble cause.

Engrossed in rehearsing what he would say, he dismounted outside the *duomo* and allocated the reins to one of the handful of grubby boys disputing for the honor. Normally he found the façade's symphony of white, pink, and green marble fascinating, but today he strode over to the south door without an upward glance. Pigeons and beggars summed him up and ignored him. As he was about to enter, two young men emerged and blocked his path. More of them followed. His mind flashed back to the present, and he fell back a pace, reaching for a sword he had left at the villa.

"One moment, ser," said the nearest. They were fairly typical bravos, finely garbed, arrogant, dangerous, but apparently in this instance merely holding the door for someone, making sure the coast was clear.

"I bid you good morning, ser Campbell."

He looked twice at the grandly dressed lady and twice decided she could not have addressed him. It was only then that he realized that the inconspicuous, somewhat foxy-faced, nonentity at her side was not just another flunky. The bodyguards, the last of whom were now emerging at his back, were there to protect *him*.

Gasp! He bowed low. "I am honored, Your Magnificence!" He almost added, "I did not recognize you," and bit back the words in time.

In truth, though, Pietro Marradi enjoyed being anonymous. He also enjoyed showing off his politician's memory for names and faces—Hamish had been presented to him only once, and that had been many months ago.

"*Duchessa,* may I present ser Campbell, a chancellor in the Don Ramon Company?"

Lucrezia, the notorious hexer? The diminutive lady in the ermine and jewels acknowledged Hamish's protestations of undying loyalty with a nod that implied extreme boredom, but her gaze seemed to sharpen a fraction when her brother added, "Ser Campbell is a close confidant and childhood friend of *comandante* Longdirk." The lowly *ser* was to chide him for not wearing a sword.

"It is hard to imagine messer Longdirk as a child." She did not look notorious.

"Indeed he never was, madonna!" Hamish said boldly. "He sprang fully armed from a Highland bog." That felt moderately witty for spur-of-the-moment.

Lucrezia seemed unimpressed, as if she had already done her duty by a barbarian youth, but Marradi honored the jest with a smile. "Ah! You are a student of the classics?"

"An ignoramus by Italian standards," Hamish protested. "I prefer the moderns, such as your own notable sonnets, Your Magnificence." He quoted a few lines from "The Vine" to show that he could.

Truth makes the deadliest flattery, and Marradi was a celebrated poet. He bowed his head to acknowledge the compliment. "Would you be available to take a cup of wine around the sixth hour, messer Campbell? Some friends will be joining us to witness the unveiling of Maestro Buonarroti's new marble and hear a few sonnets. Bring along a couple of your own favorites to share."

Astonished, Hamish protested his eternal gratitude for such an honor. It was no trivial experience just to be talking to a genuine (if notorious) duchess and the world's richest banker while surrounded by his respectfully waiting bodyguard with half of Florence looking on. To be invited to his salon was an honor half of Florence would kill for. He wondered what his mother would say if she could see him now.

And he wondered if this stroke of good fortune might be turned to advantage. Here, after all, was the hand that held all the strings. If Hamish could wring a few fast concessions out of him, he could turn up at the meeting with a decided edge. Hastily, for Marradi was already turning away, he said, "I came into town, Your Magnificence, to assist Don Ramon in his negotiations with the *dieci*. Time grows desperately short."

He knew instantly that he had erred, but it was a slight tilt of Lucrezia's head that told him. Marradi's expression did not change.

"Indeed it does!" the Magnificent sighed. "The problem lies, of course, with the *podestà,* but I expect you know that." Hamish certainly did not, and gaped like a fish. Before he could comment, the despot added smoothly, "I am told that His Excellency is reluctant to approve anything until the *darughachi* has made his will known."

"The rumors . . . There really is a *darughachi* then?"

"Oh, yes!" The Magnificent seemed politely surprised by his ignorance. "His Highness Prince Sartaq, seventh son of the glorious Ozberg Khan. He brings plenipotentiary powers to suppress the revolt north of the Alps." A shrug, a hint of a smile accompanied that description of the disaster that had engulfed most of Europe for half a generation as a *revolt*. "We expect him to come north, once he has completed his business in Naples and Rome." As a verbal street fighter, Marradi was unmatched—having laid Hamish on the floor, he now applied his boot: "Siena is a delightful town, is it not, ser Campbell? Did you enjoy Carnival?"

Hamish managed a nod, making faint croaking noises. So much for his hopes of wringing anything out of *Il Volpe*.

Marradi sighed and let his face grow doleful. "We were all desolate to hear the tragic news of Maestro Fischart's demise. Do please convey our sympathy to Don Ramon and the constable, won't you?" He strolled away with his sister on his arm and his mastiffs around him, leaving Hamish feeling like something dropped by one of the pigeons.

19

He stumbled into the cool gloom of the *duomo* and waited by the door, planning to allow the Marradi party a few minutes to depart, then scamper like a burning squirrel in search of the don. If the bizarre Castilian learned of Fischart's death from anyone else, he would be most exceeding wroth. If he denied it in public only to discover his subordinates had kept the news from him, he would wax homicidal.

Demons take Toby and his stupid deception! He knew it was impossible to keep a secret in Italy. All the same, granted that the Marradi Bank ran an intelligence network second only to the Venetians', and even factoring gramarye into the problem, there was no obvious way the Magnificent could have heard the news so soon. Did the Siena tutelary correspond with Florence's? Or was this again the hand of the mysterious enemy who had arranged Fischart's death?

The devout of Florence bustled by him, some seeking out booths to make confession, others going forward to pray before the altar. Perhaps some had come just to enjoy the peace and beauty of the great building. The choir was singing, and were he not so preoccupied, he could have lost himself in those intertwining melodies soaring like swallows to the lofty dome. How strange it must be to spend one's life as a musician! Would he be happier if he had nothing more to worry about than producing a pure note or well-shaped phrase—happier than he was helping Toby fight the Fiend? But that thought set him wondering what this vast building would look like in half a year if people like Toby could not stop the Fiend. There would be no singing then.

Time to go. He turned for the door, aware that he would have to admit to the don that he had lied about—

"You have not achieved what you came for, Hamish."

The whisper spun him around. He found himself nose-to-nose with a gaunt, pale-faced youth, a shaven-scalped novice several years his junior. A boy that age must always be judged guilty of mischief until proved innocent, and no doubt the vacant smile and toneless voice of an incarnation could be faked quite easily, but he had spoken in Gaelic.

"Holiness?"

"Do not kneel here. Follow us." The incarnation turned.

"But, Holiness, I have to go and find the don and tell—"

The boy stopped without looking around. "You have more important things to worry about than the wounded pride of Don Ramon."

Hamish twisted in agony. "If I may just go and tell him, Holiness, and then I will come—"

"Follow us." The incarnation stalked off with the hem of its robe swishing around ankles like twigs. It led the way to an empty booth and sat on the bench, fixing its gaze on the wall to Hamish's left and remaining inhumanly still. In the velvet gloom, there was no mistaking the filmy golden glow of the tutelary around it. Hamish knelt on the cushion and gathered up his thoughts.

He spoke at great length, slowly at first and then faster. Once or twice the tutelary demanded more detail or questioned an interpretation. When he thought he had finished, it suggested some things he had omitted, and he added them to his confession. He told everything, but without mentioning that Lisa was rightful Queen of England. That information was irrelevant.

"And what do you want of us?" the spirit asked when he had finished.

He was nonplussed. He had expected a lecture, forgiveness, penance, never that question. "First, I mourn Karl Fischart. Will Siena cherish his soul? I admit I did not like him, but I—"

"Do not concern yourself with him."

Oh! Italian tutelaries seemed to have their own rules. "Then, Holiness, did I do wrong in Siena—when I went to Lisa's rescue and when I returned with Fischart?"

"Your motives were sound," the boy's thin voice said, "but you play a very dangerous game when you consort with demons, Hamish. Had you not relied on gramarye, you would have gone to Siena with a band of strong young men at your back, would you not? Then you might have rescued Lisa without imperiling her soul or yours."

There were a hundred objections to that, such as, supposing the opposition had loosed its own demons against those strong young men? And how would they have found the countess? The tutelary in Siena might have helped the righteous, but who could guarantee that?

"Yes, Holiness." One did not argue with spirits.

Without shifting its gaze, the incarnation held out a hand. Reluctantly Hamish gave it the Lupus and Zangliveri rings and watched them vanish into a belt pouch. A well-trained demon was worth a king's ransom.

"Did you tell Elizabeth you love her?"

"Yes, Holiness."

"How many women have you told that to?"

Squirm! "Two or three."

"How many?"

Hamish dug nails into his palms. "Four or five. But not always. I mean not always seriously. Maybe eight. But not quite like that. It's not the same when a man's, um, in bed with a . . ."

"Or trying to get into her bed," the boy said. "Is that what you want of her?"

"Me? Lisa? No! No! She's a lady, far above my station." He was surprised to realize that this denial was the truth. He had never considered trying to seduce Lisa—not seriously considered. He could have done it on the journey, at the inn. He'd thought about it, decided that there would be no sport in a victory so easy. She was too vulnerable. One glass of wine and some sweet words . . . Even if she was almost past marrying age by Italian standards, she was still only a child emotionally. And she was a queen.

"Do you love her?"

Yes. No. Yes. "Um, if things were different . . . Yes. Yes, I do." Were she not who she was, he might even be giving a thought or two to marriage—if he were not who he was, a penniless adventurer . . . He tried to imagine himself carrying her over a doorstep. She wore flowers in her hair, and she smiled at him.

The prospect was not very terrifying. "Yes, I do." He sighed. Things would have to be very different, though—little things like the history of Europe.

"Hamish," said the tutelary, "all you have confessed is forgiven. These are hard times, and you stand between great dominions in contention. You must be ever vigilant and prepared to make hard choices. If you have time, come and discuss your problems with us before you decide."

"Yes, Holiness. I thank you." Was there to be no penance?

"Your penance is this: You are to guard Lisa with your life."

Hamish stole a glance at the spiritual aura gleaming around the boy and was reassured that this could not be a hoax. "I have never heard of such a penance, Holiness! I will gladly . . ."

Pause. Mm!

"Gladly?" said the tutelary. "With honor? Without asking or accepting the sort of shameful favors a man might demand of a maid? And with your life?"

"It is a fair penance," Hamish admitted. His mouth felt awkwardly dry. It was a demon of a penance! "My resources are limited, Holiness, considering the contending dominions you mention. What foes do I guard against? What foes can I guard against? Nevil?" He laughed uneasily.

"Primarily your accomplice, Longdirk."

"What? I mean . . . *Toby?* But Toby can't . . . Toby *wouldn't!*"

"Wouldn't what?" asked the boy's high voice.

"Rape her? No, even if he did not fear the hob, he is a decent man who does not use his strength unfairly. But exploit her politically? Can you defend her against that, Hamish Campbell?"

He glared at the incarnation, wishing it was human so he could knock its teeth out. "You know who she is, don't you? Did you tell Pietro Marradi that, too? Is this another secret all Italy knows?"

"You are the only man in Florence who knows at the moment. Her safety depends on that secret being kept."

"You're saying Toby won't? That he'll throw Lisa to the hyenas? Why? For some sort of personal gain? I've known him all my life, and I don't believe that. Not for a moment!"

The boy turned his head, and it seemed as if the tutelary looked out of his eyes at Hamish. The illusion was startling, terrifying, and fortunately transient. The blazing intelligence faded back to a blank stare.

"Don't you? The struggle against Nevil is still to come. The contest now is to decide who will lead that struggle. All the princes and powers of Italy are contestants, and Longdirk is one of the leading players."

"But—"

"Hamish, Hamish! You are not the same boy who left Scotland six years ago, are you?"

"Well, no, Holiness. Of course not."

"Longdirk is not the youth who left with you. He has grown and changed. He is not even the young man who came into Italy, for now he knows how good he is. He has won renown. He has discovered ambition,

Hamish, and ambition feeds on success. He wants to be *comandante* again, because he truly believes he has a better chance of stopping Nevil than anyone else does. Do you disagree?"

"No," Hamish agreed sulkily. "But you're wrong about him! He's not a schemer, he's an uppercut-to-the-jaw man. He doesn't deceive people. He plays stupid and lets them deceive themselves."

"Don't argue with us, Campbell," said the spirit. "Do as we command."

20

Toby was trying to come to terms with the hexer's death and what it meant for the Don Ramon Company. As he often did when he needed to think, he sent for Smeòrach and went for a ride. The big spotted gelding was an eager mount and a very good listener. He never argued.

"We'll have to find another," Toby explained as soon as they were out of camp and it was safe to talk. "Rome's full of them, even if the College won't admit it and calls them all adepts."

Smeòrach did not even twitch an ear back to listen. He had a meadow ahead of him, and his simple mind was engrossed in seeing if he could run fast enough to leave the ground altogether.

"In fact, a really good hexer should turn up and volunteer his services right away, shouldn't he? That would show how skilled he is at knowing where he's needed." But no replacement would ever be as good as Karl Fischart, nor as unshakably loyal to the cause.

At that moment a thrush popped out of the hedge. Although it was about one-twenty-thousandth of Smeòrach's size, he decided it was highly dangerous and went sideways so abruptly that he almost dropped Toby in the mud. For a while neither of them had time to worry about hexers. It was an hour or so later, as they were returning to the villa, that the lecture began again.

"The Magnificent won't like it, but we have an agreement. We shook hands. All right, I kissed his, but the principle's the same. No one's going to miss the old man for a couple of weeks, and surely Hamish will get the *condotta* signed by then!"

"Hay!" Smeòrach said loudly. "Water. Oats. A good rubdown. Salt." He spoke in horse, but his meaning was obvious enough. "More oats," he added.

Toby chuckled and patted his neck. "I can always trust you to know what's important."

It was a fine morning. He headed for the courtyard, meaning to summon Diaz and Arnaud for a discussion of the Company's fragile finances. As he ducked his way through bustling, bread-scented kitchens, he was accosted by the formidable madonna Anna, whose customary air of Vesuvian menace was even more marked than usual. She brandished a wooden spoon under his nose, which forced him to straighten up with his head among the dangling copper pans and bundles of onions.

"Condottiere! The English milady! Who is this person? By what right does she rule here?"

If he could have chosen the next problem to be added to his burdens, squabbling women would have been low on the list. How could the fugitive queen have alienated the household in less than three hours? That was certainly not the best way to remain incognito.

"By right of hereditary stupidity, monna, I expect. What has she done to upset you?"

Plenty, apparently, including commandeering messer Longdirk's personal work site. So he stalked outside and found her holding court there, seated on a grand chair with a young woman trimming her nails and Lisa reading to her. The servant looked up in alarm—her name was Isotta, and she was the wife of one of the gunners. Lisa's glance was probably one of amusement, but too brief for him to be sure of. She went on reading, in Latin. The countess ignored him, intent on her daughter. Could she truly be so oblivious of her offense? Anna and the others must have told her whose territory this was.

Toby said, "Leave us, ladies."

The countess looked up and glared. The maid at once bundled up her implements in the cloth on her lap and made haste for the house. Lisa flashed her mother an I-told-you-so glance.

"Perhaps you should step indoors a moment, dear," the countess said grimly.

Lisa closed her book and stalked out with her chin high. Toby remained standing and folded his arms.

In her youth Queen Blanche had been blessed with a fabled beauty. The hard years of flight and exile had not stolen all of it. Her hair was golden, her complexion aristocratically pale, and if the lines at her eyes and mouth could not be denied, her features were still firm. She was a buxom, powerful woman, and her gown was not only too small for her but had been intended as practical wear for some merchant's wife, yet somehow she managed to look like a lady in it, a very frightened lady, a lady bent very close to breaking point.

"Sir Tobias! By what right do you give my daughter orders? You know who she is."

"I do know who she is. I swore to defend her against all foes, and that includes stupidity. Do you want everyone to know who she is?"

Probably no one had addressed Queen Blanche like that since she was a child at her father's court. A hint of true color appeared under the face powder. "You are being offensive!"

"You leave me no choice. We suggested a story to your daughter, a plausible explanation of who she is and who you are and why she is under Hamish Campbell's protection. If I must drop to my knees every time I speak to you, or if you behave as though this camp is your personal estate, then people will gossip. It is almost impossible to keep a secret in this country, my lady. You and your daughter are newsworthy. If you will not be guided by me, then I may as well take you into Florence right away and deliver you to the Marradi Palace. You will be a welcome guest there until the Fiend's agents are ready to kidnap you again."

She had a glare to match the don's, but the effect was spoiled by a tremble in her lower lip. "I am a lady. I cannot behave like the wife of a fish merchant."

"I do not suggest you try. Gentry in exile can retain their self-respect without drawing attention to themselves. We have a marchioness and two baronesses here in the camp. A Bohemian princess and the former Queen of Burgundy reside in Florence. I would present them to you and ask them to give you lessons, but I don't trust the men they are living with. There are many exiled ladies of rank in Italy. Their menfolk did not fare as well, but we have some of those around also. One knight in the Company is the pretender to the throne of France."

"I need no lessons from them or anyone." Her voice was shriller than before. "I have been a fugitive since you were a child, Constable. I have always lived as a lady and expected to be treated as one. Furthermore, I have a duty to rear my daughter in a style appropriate to her rank so she will be competent to take up her inheritance when the Fiend is overthrown. You realize that I have been bereft of my entire wardrobe, all my jewels, my money? What steps are you taking to recover those for me?"

"None, ma'am. Your enemy in Siena was a notable hexer. Any attempt to recover them would lead him to you, and what you recovered would prob-

ably bc poisoned by gramarye. For your own safety
and Lady Lisa's I must ask you to resign yourself to
your losses and just be thankful that you both survived
your terrible experiences unharmed."

She chewed her lip for a moment. He despised
himself as a bully, but he could see no kindness in
lying to her. Her only hope of survival was to face the
brutal realities of her situation. By coming to Italy, she
had left herself without a back door to use when her
husband came in the front.

"I require at least two maids, separate sleeping
chambers for Lisa and myself—with some decent furniture—a wardrobe of suitable garments, and a personal steward. The use of a carriage, postilion, and
footmen two or three times a week. This is an absolute
minimum. Anything less is a flagrant insult to my rank
and person."

To laugh would be unkind. To ask her how Nevil
would treat her if he caught her would be sadistic. She
was a tired and very frightened woman.

"I shall see what can be arranged, ma'am. I had no
warning of your arrival. Sister Bona—"

"Has children! Cohabits with a friar!"

"Can keep her mouth shut."

They traded glares.

Queen Blanche looked away first. "Very well.
Sister Bona?"

"Will assist you, ma'am. I shall have our treasurer
allocate funds for your maintenance. I do believe you
are as safe here as you can be anywhere in Italy.
Chancellor Campbell is currently—"

"Is it true," she inquired in a markedly different tone, "that he is a younger son of the Earl of Argyll?"

Toby wanted to shy like Smeòrach meeting a thrush, but he managed to keep his feet on the ground. Whose invention was this? He hoped it was Lisa's. Doubtless Hamish plied many wiles and stratagems on the battlefield of love, but no man should stoop as low as that.

"Ma'am, please! I told you that secrets are never safe in this country—every leaf whispers to the wind. If the Fiend were to hear that a son of the earl were fighting against him, then his entire family would suffer for it, and perhaps the entire Clan Campbell also."

"Ah, of course!" The countess nodded, apparently convinced. "He is a remarkable young man, isn't he?"

"He is indeed," Toby said with confidence. Was she unusually gullible, or was he gaining some skill at lying? He had not actually lied, of course, merely stated an irrelevant truth.

Evidently it was to be peace for now. She managed a shaky smile. "I admit I am impressed by some of your associates, Sir Tobias. Lisa tells me Baron Oreste is one of them, my old friend."

"He played a major role in your rescue, ma'am, but he has not yet returned from—"

"There he is!" roared the don, striding in through the gate with a dozen men at his heels.

Toby summed them up in a glance. Three of them were the don's personal squires, who would do anything he told them. Four were senior knights, *squadrieri* in the cavalry—Baldassare Barrafranca

and D'Anjou and a couple of other troublemakers—
and they, too, had brought minions to handle dirty
work. Conspicuous among the supporting cast was
the toothless leer of Ippolito Varano, the Company
hangman, a cold-blooded horror who had not yet
had the pleasure of hanging any of its members but
had flogged a few. He and some others were carrying ropes. They spread out as if to come at Toby
from both sides, but by that time, Constable Longdirk had his back to a brick wall, a stool in his left
hand, and his sword in his right. Everyone stopped
to evaluate the situation.

"Good morning, Your Excellencies," he said. "I
do not recall summoning you."

The don's eyes had been crazy enough even
before that remark. "You do not summon me, peasant!"

"That is true, signore. Your companions I can
summon, though, and I can also dismiss. Leave us,
gentlemen."

That was not strictly true, but although Toby had
no real rank, he had considerable standing, and the rest
of the Company would create a substantial fracas if
the don and his toadies dragged him out to the gallows
or whipping post. They would rather do whatever they
intended here in the courtyard. He did not intend to be
hanged this morning.

The countess rose from her grand chair and
walked away, sensible lady. She was doubtless recon-
sidering her favorable opinion of Signor Longdirk's
associates. No one spared her a glance.

"Bind him!" the don roared. "A hundred lashes!" That he was crazy had always been obvious, but until now he had tempered his delusions enough to let reality work around them.

"The first and second men to touch me die," Toby said, and was relieved when no one moved. His sword was two-edged, long as any rapier, and wrought of good Toledo steel, but he was no greased-lightning foils man like Hamish, who might be able to restrict his defense to inflicting minor wounds. He was a slugger and would kill with it. They knew that. "I remind you that we are all bound by the terms of engagement, and any man who breaks them must answer to the whole Company. Only a properly convened court can order me or anyone else flogged. Now, Signor Ramon, will you kindly reveal what has provoked your anger?"

"You deceived me!"

"Never, signore."

"Where is the hexer? Where is Oreste?"

Try to look surprised, dummy . . .

"I do not recall discussing the maestro with you in the last week, so how can I have lied about him? Last night he went to Siena. So far as I know he is still there." Not quite a lie.

"He died there!"

Now try to look disbelieving. He hoped Hamish had not strayed from the agreed story, or he might be about to save his own neck at the cost of putting Hamish's in the noose. "Sad news, if true! Who says so, senor?"

"All Florence knows!"

Not Hamish's doing, then. Toby threw down the stool and sheathed his sword. He felt the wind change as he did so—men shuffled feet and exchanged glances. "Florence is a stew pot of rumors, senor, always. If Maestro Fischart died in Siena last night, how could the news possibly have reached here already? I shall be happy to discuss the matter further with you in private. Kindly dismiss your escort."

Don Ramon turned on his heel. The crowd opened to let him through, then slunk after him. The confrontation was over, but not the trouble. His wretched Castilian pride had suffered, and he was quite clever enough to guess that he was being kept in the dark. It was fortunate that nobility could not duel with the low-born, else he would certainly call Longdirk out and fill him full of holes. For the first time in Toby's experience, the don had lost his temper and made a fool of himself. There was nothing to be done about it now.

Word of the quarrel would be all over Florence within the hour.

21

It was all over the camp in much less time than that, of course. Toby sent for Colin McPhail, who was taciturn and surly and had more brains in his elbow than most men had in their heads, and ordered him to ride like the wind into Florence to find Hamish and warn him of the problem. Then he summoned Diaz and Arnaud for that delayed discussion of the ledgers.

The three of them were still chewing their nails over the account books when the don came striding back into the courtyard. They sprang to their feet, as was expected of them.

"Constable!" The crazy blue eyes sparkled too brightly, but there was no frenzy in them now and no armed mob at his back. Evidently he had adjusted reality to fit his needs. "Rumors are going around Florence that the baron was slain in some sort of spiritual duel in Siena last night."

Diaz and Arnaud must have heard of the morning's argument, for they went very still, looking nowhere.

Toby frowned. "That is bad news. Hamish was worried about him."

The don bared his teeth but held on to his temper. "He did not mention anything to me."

"I ordered him to be discreet. He may have construed my instructions too rigidly. You understand that he returned here yesterday? With his customary efficiency, he had located the abode of the sordid Gonzaga in Siena. When Maestro Fischart heard of this, he decided to go and neutralize the hexer before he achieved his nefarious ends, whatever they might be. Hamish agreed to return to Siena, show the learned adept the house, then come back here. In the instant before he left Siena, he saw a brilliant flash and heard a dreadful sound. He was not sure what this portended. Hence my command that he make no comment until we had confirmation of events."

Who said he couldn't tell lies? The problem was whether his lies would be believed, and the don's scowl was discouraging on that score.

"The rumors speak of a demonic battle, monsters in the streets, dead men and horses, extensive material damage, and also of a dramatic sword fight. The baron was no swordsman."

Toby frowned, which was not difficult, and shrugged, which was, and sweated, which he did not intend to. "Campbell may have withheld some of the details. At times he displays a foolish tendency to excessive modesty."

The don glared, snarled something unintelligible in Castilian, and stalked out of the courtyard.

The remaining three resumed their seats in delicate silence, nobody meeting anyone else's eye. Diaz stabbed a finger at the open ledger.

"Next item," he said. "One hundred shovels, four ducats."

22

On the fifth day of her stay in the villa, Lisa came prancing out . . . was *prancing* a suitable gait for the rightwise born Queen of all England? Perhaps something equally eager but more dignified—*sweeping,* say?

On the fifth day of her stay in the villa, Lady Lisa swept out to the stable yard in the new riding costume of forest green linen she had ordered on her first shopping trip into Florence with Hamish—one of three such outfits, all of which had been delivered last night, together with the fur-trimmed hats and cloaks she had bought on the second day . . . all charged to condottiere Longdirk's credit by Hamish.

There he was, waiting for her with Eachan and Dapple already saddled. She was a little late. Ladies were expected to be late. Sometimes even this late. Hamish tended to be early, which was appropriate behavior for a gentleman, but today he might have been earlier than usual, for he was leaning one arm wearily on Eachen's neck and staring morosely at the mire as if he had taken root. Then he sensed her approach and glanced up, and the flood of joy that then transformed his face was extremely flattering. She would forgive him for being early.

"My lady!" He gazed at her with an awe so overpowering that she would have dismissed it as faked in any other man, but she knew Hamish was always genuine. "You are . . . You are *unbelievably* beautiful in that outfit. Artemis herself." He took her fingers and kissed them. Yesterday, when they had dismounted to rest the horses, she had kissed his lips. He had told her sternly never to do that again. Naturally she had done so again, at once—and was planning to do much the same again today as soon as she got the chance.

Realizing that she had not spoken yet—had, in fact, been smiling at him all this time as witlessly as a stuffed owl—she belatedly said, "Thank you, sir."

"How fares your mother this morning, my lady?" He led the horses over to the mounting block.

"Sleeping. Sister Bona still isn't worried." Lisa would have been quite frantic had this happened in the villa in Savoy, or even in Siena, but here she had advisors, and Sister Bona was a very comforting, competent-seeming sort of person. If the countess wanted to sleep and sleep and sleep, she said, then it would do her no harm. And that was exactly what Mother was doing, all day, all night. It was worrying, but it did allow her daughter time to engage in healthy exercise, such as long rides with Master Campbell. Two a day. Three yesterday.

"She probably has a lot of sleep to catch up on," Hamish said with one of those irresistible smiles that quirked the corners of his mouth into almost-dimples. "Fourteen years."

"That's absurd!" Lisa settled on the saddle and took the reins.

"Not completely. I read once—" He pulled himself up short, grinned at her before she could tease, then swung up nimbly on to Eachen's back. "She probably feels safer here than she has felt in years, so she's catching up on her sleep. Let's make the most of it. Would you like to see the Roman theater?"

"What's on the playbill?"

Hamish's laugh never really started. A large speckled horse came trotting into the yard with the huge and ominous figure of Longdirk on its back, heading for them.

Lisa glanced at her companion, and her heart sank like a rock. "You look like a schoolboy caught playing truant."

"That's exactly what I am."

"Fair morning, my lady," Longdirk said. As always, his face was infuriatingly unreadable.

She nodded without bothering to hide her displeasure.

Hamish just sighed, and said, "Where, when, what, who?"

"I hate to drag you away from important pleasure," the big man told him solemnly, "but it has to be you, and milady can't tag along."

Lisa was shocked at how the day darkened. Being separated from Hamish for very long was unbearable. Did this overgrown barbarian realize the suffering he was causing her?

"Lucas Abonio," he said. "You know his residence? Take every conspicuous precaution to make sure no one sees you entering or leaving."

Hamish opened his mouth, then shut it with a click. "And what furtive message do I whisper to His Excellency?"

Longdirk shrugged. "Tell him about Babylonian chariot racing or that procession of equine oxen that interests you. You'll think of something."

"Italy has not been good for you. You used to be a nice *straightforward* boy." Hamish turned to Lisa, then glanced down at Longdirk's horse as if noticing it for the first time.

"Yes," the big man said. "It is a plot to get you out

of the way. Writhe in jealous rage all you want, but go
and see Abonio."

"Heartless swine," Hamish said sadly. "You'll be
safe with him, dearest, but he doesn't know a Roman
theater from a hole in the ground." Then he made a
brave attempt at a grin and urged Eachen into a canter.

"The Roman theater *is* just a hole in the ground,"
Longdirk said. "Not worth wasting time on. I know
more interesting places to visit."

"I believe I will wait until Master Campbell
returns."

"No you won't. I have something to show you.
Come along."

Thus it was that Lisa found herself being escorted
across the meadows by the condottiere himself that
nippy spring morning, her wishes in the matter having
been totally disregarded. She would have objected
more strongly had she had anything better to do, or if
the Highland gorilla were less intimidating. He scared
her, but she was never going to admit that, even to herself. And she hated the way he ordered Hamish
around, sending him off to Florence like a flunky just
to . . . to what, exactly?

The two of them rode in silence for a while. Then
Longdirk suddenly pointed at the plain below. "The
large dome is the sanctuary, of course. And the tower
beside it is the campanile." He went on to point out the
main landmarks in the city and then those outside—
villages, hills, roads, naming every one and adding

pertinent information. As the trail entered an olive grove he glanced around at her. "You smile, ma'am?"

"Oh, pray forgive me! I was just remembering how you chide Master Campbell for lecturing."

He blinked. "His lectures come out of books. I learned all this on horseback."

"Then you must write a book." That stopped him! "Who is Lucas Abonio?" she inquired, brazenly pressing her advantage.

Peering down from his much greater height, he studied her in silence for a moment, as if she were an errant piece of ordnance. "This must be in confidence."

"Oh, I have no wish to pry, Constable! I should not have presumed to—"

"He is the Milanese ambassador to Florence."

She considered that answer for about four olive trees. "This is a secret?"

"No." The big man's face was less scrutable than some Arabic scrolls she'd found in a castle library once. "No, that is no secret. He's been trying to bribe me to enter the duke's service, and that is no secret either. And Florence is being interminably difficult about giving me the *condotta* we need, but everyone knows that, too."

"Doesn't it want to employ you?"

"I think so. I hope so. Part of the problem is that the present *dieci,* the Ten For War, are due to be replaced on March first, and they're trying to spin out the negotiations so that their successors can share in the bribery."

"Oh. According to Hamish, everything in Florence is run by Pietro Marradi. Why don't you just go and talk to him?"

"I did, my lady. I spent all yesterday morning in his waiting room with a very strange collection of sculptors and poets. I was left until almost the last, and then told he was too busy to see me."

She found that very funny, but she must not let her amusement show. "So today you send Hamish on a secret visit to—"

"No. You can't keep a secret in Florence. The Magnificent will know within minutes that Hamish is visiting Abonio. He won't know why, though."

"But you told Hamish to make—"

"That was just for realism. Marradi will know. And he knows Hamish is my closest confidant."

After several more olive trees had gone by, she said, "I see what Hamish meant when he said you weren't straightforward."

"Does that make me straightbackward? Or bent-forward?" The cavernous brown eyes were as somber as ever. He must be making fun of her.

She was very little wiser an hour or so later, when he led the way into a farmyard, setting dogs to barking and geese into paroxysms of hissing. She had confirmed that she neither liked the big man nor trusted him and found his reputation for ruthlessness entirely credible. Without a word of explanation, he jumped down from his horse.

"What?" she said, looking around in alarm at the low-roofed buildings, half-buried in vegetation like lurking bears.

"Friends of mine. They make some of the finest wine in all Italy." Two ragged-looking urchins came shrieking out from behind a barn, and chickens flapped away in the opposite direction.

Alarmed, she said, "But I do not wish—" and no more, for Longdirk lifted her off the saddle as if she were a child and set her down. Who did he think he was? Or she was?

The boys jumped at him and hugged him in volleys of Italian. He picked them up by their smocks, one in each hand, and swung them high in the air, their howls of glee totally drowning out his efforts to address them. An obese and ancient peasant woman waddled out of the main hovel, wiping hands on apron, jabbering even faster than the children, and smiling to reveal a very sparse set of teeth. She was motherly enough to calm Lisa's worst fears, but not perceptibly the sort of person she cared to befriend. Longdirk set the boys down and introduced Lisa in his limping Italian to madonna Something.

"Do tell her," Lisa said, "how delighted I am to have met her and how much I regret that we cannot stay." The children had noticed Lisa and were gaping openmouthed at her.

Predictably, Longdirk ignored her wishes and led her into the old woman's lair, with the crone following them, nodding and leering. Lisa found herself expected to sit on a tottery stool at a rough

plank table with him beside her. Admittedly the
deeply shadowed kitchen was cozy after the wind,
nor could she could deny that the smell of baking
bread made her mouth water, but there was a baby
screaming somewhere nearby and she had no desire
to indulge in the wine set before her in a cracked
pottery beaker or the curious scraps of food Old
Mother What's-her-name began piling on a platter
between her and Longdirk—cheese and pastries and
dried fruits. The children started stalking these with
nefarious intent, ignoring their grandmother's
efforts to chase them away.

Nevertheless, Lisa's self-appointed escort was
waiting for her to proceed. She took a sip of wine. "Is
this what you meant when you said you had something
to show me?"

"Partly. Do try some of these treats. The white
cheese is good. May I tell monna Agnolella that you
like her wine?"

"Tell her anything you want."

"I'll tell her you can't help your manners, then."

"*My* manners?" Angrily Lisa turned to the crone
and went through a dumb show with the wine—smile,
nod, smack lips. "Does that satisfy you, Sir Toby? I do
hope you're going to eat the food. I can't possibly."
She would have to make an effort, though. Perhaps
she could slip some to the boys or the smelly dogs
around her feet. Why had this annoying man brought
her here? Slumming! It would have been fun with
Hamish, but Longdirk did not know what the word fun
meant. He never smiled.

In response to another of his labored speeches, the old woman bared her gums in a leer even more gruesome than its predecessors, then disappeared into the depths of the house, shooing her wayward brood before her so the visitors could be alone. Mercifully, the baby's yelling stopped.

The pastries were, in fact, delicious. Lisa graciously took a second. "So what exactly am I supposed to be looking at, Constable?"

"Just looking." Longdirk had his back to the solitary window, putting his face in shadow. "I come here quite often. It's a good place to meet people without being disturbed. Or seen. I pay her a few lire for the privilege. Luigi died at Trent, so times are hard for her yet. How old is your mother?"

"I don't see what business that is . . . If you'd listened to Baron Oreste's story, you would know that. She'll be thirty-three next birthday."

"I did listen. Monna Agnolella is the same age."

"Nonsense! You're serious? You mean that baby I heard . . ."

"All of them. Twelve sons. Two of them serve in the Company, following in their father's footsteps. One of them's almost as big as me. Agnolella runs the place with the other ten. Nine, I suppose. The baby won't be much help yet."

Lisa took a drink of wine to mask her dismay, but he had seen it and must be secretly laughing at her reaction.

"Looks about seventy, doesn't she?"

"What have her troubles to do with me, sir? Why

drag me here just to gloat over a . . . a . . . When did she start—eight?"

"Let's see. Niccolò is nineteen—she probably married at thirteen. That's normal. A dozen babies in nineteen years is not unusual, but twelve living is. In a sense she's lucky Luigi died, or she'd have gone on bearing children until one killed her. As to what it means to you . . ." He folded his enormous hands on the table and stared at them. "My lady, I admit that falling into the Fiend's clutches is a very real danger to you and absolutely the worst thing that could happen. But there are other bad things in life that you don't know much about, and one of them is poverty."

"It is most kind of you to take such an interest in my education, Constable, but I do not see why it need concern you."

"Because Hamish is my friend."

"I understand he is of age. He is certainly articulate."

The big man sighed and began to pop morsels of food in his mouth, continuing to speak as he chewed. "He is also very impressionable where . . . women are concerned. Honorable within . . . limits, but very few men are . . . capable of celibacy for long, no matter how solemn their intentions—"

"You speak from experience, I presume?"

He nodded with his mouth full. "Mm." Swallow. "Get Hamish to tell you about his family."

"He already has." Not deliberately, but in passing Hamish had mentioned ghastly things like sleeping six to a room and not having shoes when there was snow on the ground, but he had not seemed to think any of them remarkable. "I still do not see why this concerns you."

"His father was . . . the schoolmaster and . . . rich by local standards." Longdirk had eaten just about everything the old woman had put out. He washed it down with a gulp of wine and reached for the bottle to refill his beaker. "What I'm saying, ma'am, is that any future with you and Hamish in it can only bring misery to both of you. Think on it. You are not stupid, only naive."

"You cannot imagine how relieved I am to hear that."

"Let's find something you will listen to, then." He dropped a small leather packet on the table and fumbled with the catch. "I have a trifle here that is rightfully yours."

"I don't recall losing anything. How long have you had it?"

He glanced up. His eyes glinted very brightly, although his expression was indeterminable against the light. "Six years? More than five." He tipped a shiny pebble out onto the table. "This is an amethyst."

"I've never seen—"

"I know. Just listen for once, will you? As a gem it's worth nothing, pennies at most, but it has other values. The first, to me, is that it was a parting gift from my foster mother, the woman who raised me."

"Your . . . But I couldn't possibly . . ." Was he playing some sort of elaborate joke? "I mean—"

"Listen! She was the village witchwife and more

than a little crazy. She and the hob both. But that isn't what makes this stone special, my lady. The baron didn't tell you everything that happened on the Night of the Masked Ball. You and your mother escaped, but so did Valda, your, er, the king's . . ."

"My father's mistress."

"Accomplice. And Nevil—or the demon Rhym, I should say—hunted her for years and had his minions hunting for her. He put a huge price on her head. That's important, because it's the only confirmation we have of what Valda told me when . . . Yes, me. She turned up years later in Scotland. Where she'd been we don't know, but somehow she'd acquired more demons to replace those she'd lost, and she was looking for a good . . ." He paused as if he had reached a difficult part of his story and tried another tack. "Valda believed that when Rhym possessed your father, your father's soul was displaced in the confusion. That doesn't normally happen in a possession, but remember they were playing with very powerful gramarye. She was convinced that the soul of the mortal Nevil, the real Nevil, had become immured in the yellow diamond that had formerly contained Rhym."

Again Lisa took a drink. Yes, this had to be a joke, in very bad taste.

The condottiere refilled her beaker. "So when Valda reappeared five years ago, she was prepared to redress that misfortune. She wanted to reincarnate your father's soul in a mortal body. She chose me." He was not looking at her now. "An honor I was more than glad to be spared. Things went wrong again. It's a complex story, my lady, but the short of it is that the soul of your real father is now immured in this gem."

Lisa stared in growing horror at the shiny purple crystal. After what seemed a long time, she found her voice. "You can prove that?"

The big man sighed. "I'm very sure. A great tutelary confirmed that there is something in there, something not potent enough to be a demon."

"You mean . . . my . . . my father is imprisoned . . . fifteen years? In there? Is he conscious? Aware? Does he know—"

"I don't know." He shrugged his great shoulders. "Nobody does. In a thousand years of tending mortals, Montserrat had met no precedent. If he can be restored, he may well come back as a raving maniac—and who supplies the living body? But this pebble contains the rightful King of England." Before she could speak, he went on. "There is more. Valda is dead. Hamish killed her."

"*Hamish?* But she was a hexer, an adept . . . Baron Oreste—"

"And Hamish is Hamish. Get him to tell you that story, too. Yes, she was a hexer. Both she and your father knew Rhym's name, the conjuration that was supposed to control the demon."

"It didn't cont—"

"That one time it didn't. Nevertheless, if properly invoked, it may still control Rhym. If your father can be restored to life, he may be able to snare the Fiend with a simple incantation, bottle Rhym up again, and so stop all Europe's suffering with a word of command.

So before you accept this gem, you should be aware that the Fiend will stop at nothing to lay his—"

"Constable, no power in this world will persuade me to touch that amethyst!"

"Your father, my lady—"

"No! No! No! It is yours! Keep it." She would not believe such a tale.

He sighed and nudged the stone back in its case with a meaty finger. "Very well."

"May we go now?" This had not been a very successful outing.

"Yes, if—" He frowned and looked around. "Can you hear something?"

"Flies. Lambs bleating."

He shook his head. "Sounds like drumming."

"The children?"

"Perhaps." Longdirk was unconvinced—puzzled and uneasy, cocking his head as if listening to a distant beat.

Perhaps it was the wine—"Is it true that you are possessed by a demon?"

She flinched at the look in his eyes. It seemed he was not going to answer, but then he said, "How can I be? If I were, I would already have raped you, mutilated you, and tortured you to death. That's what demons do to pretty little girls."

TWO

MARCH

23

The *condotta* was signed where important civic ceremonies were always held—under the high, three-arched loggia adjoining the Piazza della Signoria. The crowds cheered lustily to hail their dashing new Castilian captain-general and his big deputy, who could undoubtedly defeat all the Fiend's horses and all the Fiend's men single-handed with a club. Their betters were of another mind, though.

The new slate of civic officials, especially the *dieci della guerra,* were steamingly furious, because the agreement had been finalized before they took office, cheating them of their just share of the graft. For this they blamed the barbarian giant, who had actually begun striking camp at Fiesole, preparing to move to Milan, and had thus forced messer Benozzo to ride out in haste and agree to initial the terms. Toby had been bluffing, of course, but the big mutt was a mile more devious than he looked and could outwit anyone anytime when he wanted to.

All the two-lire politicos and their wives were now snubbing him as obviously as possibly. If that made the ceremony unpleasant for Toby, it was pure torture for Hamish Campbell. A chancellor was supposed to steer his condottiere safely through the quicksands of Italian politics. That was his job, and to plead that the sands of Florence were quicker than others or that a non-Italian could not understand their constant shifting would be a confession of incompetence. If only someone knowledgeable had written a book on the subject!—someone like that slinky messer Machiavelli who advised the Magnificent, for instance.

However joyously the people of Florence hailed their new defender, the petty leaders were treating Toby more like a foreign conqueror than a guardian who had just sworn to defend them with his life. Most of the sumptuously garbed notables and their almost-as-sumptuously-garbed wives had just stalked by him with noses raised on their way to pay their respects to the captain-general himself before moving across to the Palace of the Signory for the banquet. The don was posturing in his silver helmet, flaunting his baton of office within a circle of fawning admirers. Apparently he had managed to overcome his dislike of taking orders from a rabble of moneylenders and haberdashers. The worst must be over, though. The slow grind of protocol was now about to bring forth the larger parasites.

"The people like you," Hamish muttered.

"What people?" Toby looked down with a grin. Nobody human should be able to smile while being humiliated on this scale, but he was showing that he bore no grudge against Hamish for it, which was typical of him. "If you mean the stolid citizenry of the republic, my lad, then they're still hard at work— weaving, dyeing, or fulling, whatever that is. No, don't bother to explain, I have an appointment later this afternoon. Those out there are the froth."

True. The overdressed spectators in the square were all handpicked Marradi supporters, probably mostly officials of the minor guilds who had no effective influence over the heavyweights of the major guilds, which in turn could do nothing without the Magnificent's approval, but a chancellor was supposed to explain such things to his condottiere, not vice versa.

"Fulling or not, the populace approves of you."

No condottiere in all Italy except Toby cared a fig for any populace. He sighed. "I hope I prove worthy of their trust. Any word on the *darughachi?*"

"Nothing new. His Highness remains in Rome, officially conferring with the cardinals. Unofficially, he is reported to be bedding the entire female population between the ages of thirteen and eighty. He is expected to come north later in the spring, when he has finished."

"It's still spring? Feels like high summer." Toby's face was dewed with sweat under his bronze helmet, for he was in military garb. His doublet and breeches

were so heavily padded with linen that they would
stop a saber or even a pike. They were as elaborately
trimmed as anything the *landsknechte* wore, extrava-
gantly piped and slashed in cerise and vermilion and
peacock blue. With a broadsword at his thigh, he
looked even more huge and dangerous than usual,
dominating the piazza. The notables of Florence might
be snubbing him, but the eyes of their wives and
daughters were nowhere else. When he was leaving
camp this morning, even Lisa had admitted that he
was Mars incarnate.

Which reminded Chancellor Campbell that he
had squandered every lire due him for the next six
months in providing Lisa with an appropriate
wardrobe, and the countess, although her health had
improved until now she was well enough to be a
real thorn in his flesh, was showing no signs of
offering to recompense him for any of it out of the
funds the Company had provided. When the first of
the *condotta* gold arrived and Hamish received his
arrears, he would have to turn it all over to Toby to
start repaying his debts. Oh, women! Oh, ruin! Oh,
Lisa . . .

Oh, spirits! Here came Lucas Abonio with his
half-witted wife on his arm and his two quarter-witted
daughters at his heels. Unlike the snotty Florentine
politicians whose petty noses were out of joint just
because Toby had called their bluff and forced them to
cut short their games at his expense, the Milanese
ambassador had a real grievance against the new
deputy captain-general and against his chancellor, too.

Hamish had gone within an eyelash—a rat's eyelash—of committing Toby to serving the Duke of Milan in return for various castles, fiefdoms, chests of treasure, hands of daughters in marriage, and so on. Abonio had almost certainly informed his ducal master than the deal was made, only to learn later that he had been, um, misinformed.

Now he stumped past the waiting Scots without a glance. His face was even redder and shinier than Toby's. At his heels stalked Jacopo Benozzo, haughtier yet. He had none of Abonio's excuse. Reports of Nevil's preparations were flooding in every day. Hiring a captain-general had been Benozzo's duty, so why had he procrastinated so long? Behind him tottered messer Cecco de' Carisendi, his replacement as chairman of the *dieci*. He was probably too senile to remember who Toby was.

The big hats were coming thick and fast now . . . Guilo and a collection of minor Marradis . . . and still not a glance, not a smile! This could not be their own idea; they would certainly have been primed by the Magnificent. Hamish looked up in alarm to Toby and was silenced by a warning frown: the *podestà!*

Antonio Origo oozed toward them with an elderly, almost emaciated woman on his arm—an aunt, perhaps. Was his wife unwell again? Origo was always greasy, but today he seemed more reminiscent of boiling oil, which might be a mark of displeasure or due simply to the fact that he was grossly overdressed in a jerkin of cloth of gold and a fur-trimmed cloak. Hamish prepared his most obsequious bow. The *podestà* ignored him and almost went right past Toby also. Then he paused, glaring.

"This is highly improper! You can expect to be stripped of your post very shortly. His Highness sent strict instructions that no major decisions were to be taken until he arrived. He will be extremely displeased when he hears the news of your appointment."

Alarmed to note that Toby was wearing his stupid-yokel expression, Hamish braced himself for some outrageous taunt, such as an inquiry as to why the Khan's representative did not boycott the free lunch if he disapproved of the occasion. Origo was having severe troubles of his own. Having ignored their titular overlord the Khan for a couple of centuries, the Florentines heartily disapproved of his reappearance in their lives. Prince Sartaq should not expect a cordial welcome when he arrived, and his flunky the *podestà* must be finding life even more difficult than usual.

But all Toby said was, "I am sure His Highness is well informed about what is happening."

Origo swelled like a bullfrog. "I send dispatches daily!"

"I hardly think he needs your letters, Excellency. Have you not noticed the owl?"

"Owl? What owl? Owls at noon?"

"On that cornice up there. Above the blue washing."

Eyes turned where Toby indicated.

"It can't be real!" Origo bleated shrilly.

Hamish was inclined to agree with him, for once. Owls were almost never seen in daylight. When they did appear, they were invariably mobbed by smaller birds, but that whatever-it-was up there on the roof just sat in full view, ignored by all the pigeons, sparrows, and starlings.

"It flew in an hour ago," Toby said. "I've seen it around quite a lot lately. Can you hear the drum?"

Hamish took a hard look at his big friend. He was flushed and sweating, although not as much as Origo was. Was the glint in his eye mockery or delirium? Smaller men than he could suffer heatstroke in a padded doublet, and it was suffocatingly hot in the loggia.

"Drum?" Origo squeaked. "What drum?"

"A shaman's drum, I suppose. I've heard it several times in the last ten days or so. The owl is usually around when I do."

"You are out of your mind!"

"Whatever Your Excellency commands."

Origo opened and closed his mouth a few times, took another quick glance at that inexplicable owl, and then jerked his skeletal companion forward as he headed for the palazzo and the free lunch.

"You never told me about this!" If Hamish spent less time fluttering around Lisa, he would have more time for his duties.

"There's nothing to tell," Toby said easily. "Tartar gramarye is different from ours, yes? Don't shamans immure spirits in birds or animals?"

"I don't know if immure is the right word. They . . ." Hamish reined in a lecture as he would a flighty horse. "That owl may be a familiar, I suppose."

"I'm sure it is. It makes the hob fidget."

Hamish yelped. "You're not going to lose control of the hob, are you? Not here?" Even a few thunderbolts in this crowded square would lead to a fearful massacre.

"No. It can smell gramarye around, that's all. It isn't worried at the moment. Ears up, lad—here comes Himself."

Having seemingly appeared from nowhere, Pietro Marradi and his train were already only a few paces away. He had Lucrezia on his arm, radiant in lilac silk, osprey plumes, and constellations of rubies. Hamish drew a deep breath at the sight of her. She was easily old enough to be his mother, but he knew he would be carrying a candle for Lucrezia if he were not totally consumed by Lisa at the moment. She had not noticed his existence yet, nor Toby's. She was not going to.

And neither was her brother! Hamish gaped in dismay as The Magnificent and his sister walked right past, heading for the don's admiring circle. So now all Florence knew that the deputy captain-general was out of favor already. Cooperation would drop from minuscule to negative. The money never would appear. Oh, demons! He looked up at Toby, but Toby's face was as inscrutable as the Alps.

"The *darughachi?*" his chancellor suggested, grasping for some rational explanation for this about-face. "If the prince has indicated displeasure, then that might explain why everyone is trying to keep their distance from you."

But if Toby and the don did not carry some sacks

of florins back to camp with them, the Company would riot. Milan was no longer an option—Abonio would never again let Longdirk or his chancellor cross his doorstep. Venice, perhaps? There had to be some rational explanation for this setback.

Obviously someone thought they could deflect Longdirk from his purpose, but that was never possible. Hamish had known him since he was a child, the unholy terror of the glen, goading and tormenting the schoolmaster with a cold-blooded calculation few adults would ever match. Even then he had never spoken a careless word or made a hasty move, as if he was frightened of breaking something with his enormous strength, but that had probably never been the case. The truth was just that Longdirk had an incredible ability to absorb punishment. As a bare-knuckle fighter he had been slow but indestructible, grinding his opponents down to exhaustion, and now he treated the world the same way—Hamish had realized that first in Aquitaine, the second time Toby had provoked Sergeant Mulliez into ordering him flogged. In his own eyes he had scored a victory, although at a cost that would have killed a lesser man. Now he needed Florence to aid him in his battle against the Fiend, so he would use Florence whether it liked him or not. Florence would have no choice in the matter.

"Messer Campbell!"

Marradi himself had shouted and was beckoning. Hamish scurried over to the group, registering trouble writ large on every face in it, including the don's. Marradi seemed close to an explosion.

"Your Magnificence?"

"What is this we hear about you organizing a party at Cafaggiolo?"

For a moment every word of Italian Hamish knew deserted him. He stood there with his mouth open while Latin, French, and Castilian buzzed around his head like wasps. Gaelic, Breton, English, Catalan, French again . . . Italian.

"But, messer . . . Magnificence . . . I was given to understand that Your Magnificence had most graciously placed his, er, your villa of Cafaggiolo at the disposal of the captain-general for three days so that—"

Obviously not.

"No?" Hamish whispered faintly, thinking of all the letters he had sent, all the hours of planning with Arnaud and Bartolo.

"I cannot imagine where you received such a notion. My honored sister has already invited some friends there for that week."

Lucrezia, Hamish observed, was staring over his shoulder—obviously at Toby, who must have followed him, for no one else was so tall—and her face bore an expression of satisfaction such as he had never seen on a woman except in the rapture of lovemaking. The sight was so startling that he again found himself at a loss for words.

It was understood that *Il Volpe* never raised his voice. Except now.

"Well?" he barked.

"Well?" scowled the don, wiggling his baton as if

about to lash out with it. He knew invitations had been sent out in his name.

Hamish's instructions had come from Toby, and Toby had made the arrangements with Marradi himself. Or so he had said. Someone had gone crazy. Or was about to—

"There has been a misunderstanding?" he croaked.

"More a lack of communication," rumbled a deep voice behind his left ear. "It would seem that either my secretary failed to notify yours, Your Magnificence, or yours omitted to inform you of what must have seemed both utterly trivial and self-evidently already known to Your Magnificence, and that is that while we used the name of your villa when inviting certain grandees to the conclave, this was merely a blind to deceive the enemy. It was, indeed, suggested to us by your own illustrious chancellor, messer Niccolò."

After the momentary silence produced by this breathtaking falsehood, Toby continued in the same bland vein. "We are all aware that the Fiend has spies everywhere. He has been known to use demon assassins before now. We plan to meet the guests on the road and conduct them to the true rendezvous—which of course I shall not reveal here. I am confident that this will in no way interfere with the *duchessa*'s festivities, and I deeply regret any distress this misapprehension may have caused, either to Her Grace or Your Magnificent self."

Lucrezia bared her teeth at him in an expression of lethal hatred.

Marradi was less revealing. "What guests?" He looked to the don. "The republic has hired you to defend it against its enemies, signore, not to entertain your friends at its expense. And if you are meddling in political matters, you may find yourself facing serious charges."

Hired? The don would never admit that he was a common employee, subject to restraints. While Hamish was still hoping the loggia would just collapse and kill him quickly, the don laughed.

"Magnificence, the last member of my family to meddle in politics was beheaded by the Visigoths. I instructed messer Longdirk to summon the leading military men from other cities—Venice, Naples, and so on—so that I might hear reports on their respective readiness to take part in the coming campaign. When I have had a chance to appraise the forces and ordnance they have available, I shall instruct them on what more we will require of them. Naturally I shall then inform the *dieci* of the situation and present my recommendations." He twirled up the points on his mustache.

By luck or his eccentric brilliance, he had struck exactly the right gong. The notion of Florence *summoning* the other great powers of Italy to a council rippled through the bystanders like a wave of rapture. He had bewitched them with his own vainglorious delusions.

It must have been many years since anyone so upstaged the Magnificent. Scowling, he offered his arm again to his sister and headed for the palazzo and the banquet. Hamish stared after them, stunned by the detestation he had seen on Lucrezia's face when her plot against Longdirk failed—for no one could seriously believe that she had conflicting plans for the villa. What on earth could the big man have done to provoke such hatred?

24

Lisa had decided to tackle her mother on the subject of Future Plans. She was hard put to believe that she had known Hamish for close to a month now, except when she looked at Mother. Fiesole had done wonders for the old dear. She was gaining health and spirits at an astonishing rate, visibly plumper and glowing with a good cheer Lisa could barely remember seeing in her from the days of her own childhood. She had completely recovered from the weeklong sleeping fit that beset her after she arrived. Unfortunately, in some ways. Then she had been unable to do much about chaperoning her daughter. Now she could, and no young lady wishes to be treated like an imbecilic infant. It was almost three days since Lisa had been properly kissed.

Longdirk and Hamish having ridden into Florence for a meeting, the courtyard was available. It was unquestionably the choicest place to sit and enjoy the glorious spring weather. The countess had ordered her favorite chair carried out to a shady place under the trellis where she could relax in peace while digesting a meal of unladylike heartiness. Her gown was a voluminous

cloud of pale green silk, unadorned but very finely
made, swathing her completely from the neck down.
Her faded golden tresses—even her hair seemed to
have recovered some of its former sparkle—had been
coiled and pinned up, covered with a simple white
bonnet. It was tragic to see a lady of her rank not
adorned with pearls and gems, but she had not
mourned her lost jewels in Lisa's hearing for at least
two weeks.

She welcomed her daughter with a smile verging
on the blissful. "Come and sit by me, dear. Would you
like to read something? How are your Italian lessons
proceeding?" Embroidery lay forgotten on the table
nearby.

"Slowly, I fear." Most of the trouble, although
Lisa was not about to say so, was that her Italian coach
had an abrasive Scottish accent and restricted her studies to poetry with a vocabulary consisting largely of
amore, bella, carina, appassionato, and similar terms.
She brought a stool and set it near. "Mother, it is time
you and I had a serious discussion."

"Oh, no!"

"Oh, yes. What do you mean?"

"Nothing, dearest. I was afraid you meant . . .
never mind. What do you wish to discuss?"

Giving her mother a puzzled glance, Lisa folded
her hands and began. "Every day we hear new rumors
about the huge army the Fiend is gathering."

"Yes, dear."

"Everyone agrees that, having been balked once,
Nevil will make absolutely certain of success this

time. Panic will ensue, as it always does. And there is a limit to how far a coach can travel southward in Italy, you must agree. Consequently, I believe it would be prudent for us to take ship while the going is good." She had not yet discussed this with Hamish, but if he meant a tenth of all the lovely things he whispered in her ear, then he would jump at the chance of escorting the two ladies. He would make a wonderful body-guard and likely much more than that in the near future.

The countess pursed her lips. "And where exactly are we to sail to?"

"Malta," Lisa said. "Or Crete. Malta belongs to the Kingdom of the Two Sicilies and Crete belongs to Venice. I don't like the sound of Egypt or Algeria or any of those Moorish lands."

"Nor I. We should both of us end up on an auction block."

"Mother!" That outrageous remark caused Lisa to lose control of her prepared speech, which threw her off and galloped out of sight. She dithered, at a loss for words.

Worse, her mother seemed not at all repentant. There was a rare gleam in her sapphire eyes. "Nor do I fancy an island. I should feel trapped, confined."

"You mean you are just going to wait until the Fiend arrives?"

"No, I am waiting for the Fiend to be defeated. I believe he is heading for his downfall. I think the scourge will soon be lifted from the back of Europe, and the clouds will lift before a new dawn."

Mothers could make speeches also, however muddled, and reverse previously unquestioned behavior patterns. Lisa stared at her in bewilderment. "What reason can you possibly have for thinking that?" It was an idea at variance with her entire life experience.

Maud smiled serenely at the blue sky twinkling through the olive branches above her. "Nothing goes on forever, dear, although we mortals often forget that and behave as if it will. The demon that possessed your father managed to turn the world upside down, but the world has a habit of rolling back again in its own good time. I am convinced that Rhym has met its match at last."

"Are you referring to that horrible Longdirk?"

Maud flashed a glance of maternal amusement at her daughter. "You don't usually take such dislikes to people, dearest. Yes, I am referring to that truly remarkable young man. I have met kings and dukes and lords aplenty, and at best they were merely stars. Sir Tobias is a rising sun."

"He is a boor! A great ox with no culture or breeding or manners whatsoever."

Her mother took no offense at being so blatantly contradicted. Indeed, she positively smirked. "Not an ox," she murmured. "A doughty warrior, yes. A splendid figure of a man, certainly. His background is undistinguished, I admit, so we must make allowances for his lack of polish, but his accomplishments to date are worthy of note. Think of the truly great shapers of history—Julius Caesar, Genghis, Charlemagne, Alexander the Great. Had you met any one of those men at

Longdirk's age, could you possibly have predicted his future greatness?"

"At twenty-three Alexander had conquered the Persian Empire."

Maud dismissed Alexander with a wave of the hand. "He was born to the purple. All those men I mentioned were of much higher rank than Sir Tobias's."

"There is certainly none lower."

"He has promised that you will take your rightful place on the throne of your ancestors. No, we shall not go to Malta, Lisa. We shall follow the triumphant armies of a Europe reborn as they roll the Fiend back into the darkness, as they reestablish the ancient freedoms under a suzerain rightfully appointed by the glorious Khan. There has never been a female suzerain, of course, but who knows? Since you will be one of the very few monarchs with an undisputed right to—"

"Mother! You are dreaming moonbeams! You are hallucinating!"

"Not very much, dearest. Once the Fiend is exorcised, everything will return to normal very quickly. Wait and see! We must find you a husband."

"Husband?" Lisa's squeal came out at least an octave higher than she had intended. *Hamish! Hamish! Hamish!*

"It is tricky, because there are so few princes left. Ah, Lisa! When you were born I made a list of all the eligible royal bachelors of Europe younger than ten. Of course, I assumed that your father would summon me to court eventually, or at least visit me from time to

time, so we should have other children; I never
guessed you would be the heir. Alas, all those boys—
there were seventeen of them, I recall, although only
five or six were credible contenders—I fear they are
all dead now. You will need a strong man at your side,
dear. England is in a state of ruin and anarchy. All
Europe is in a state of ruin and anarchy!"

Lisa could hardly believe her ears. Maud had
never raved like this before.

"So I may have to wed a mere noble, you mean?
Even, perhaps, a commoner?"

Her mother favored her with a very knowing
smile. "I did say the Fiend had turned the world upside
down, dear, didn't I? Yes, I do believe that I could
even see my way to arranging your marriage with a
commoner. He would, of course, have to be a very *outstanding* and *accomplished* foreigner."

Not Hamish. She didn't mean Hamish. Oh, demons! She couldn't *possibly* mean . . . could she? . . .

"Longdirk? That oaf? You are seriously thinking—"

Lisa sprang to her feet and spoke three words that
she had never spoken before and had heard only
rarely. She was not at all clear what two of them
meant; they just sounded appropriate. Apparently her
mother did not know them at all, for she merely
frowned at the tone.

"Do sit down, dear. You said you wanted a serious
discussion, so a serious discussion you shall have.
Listen carefully. I have given the matter much
thought. If Sir Tobias drives the Fiend's armies back

over the Alps, as I am confident he will, then there is no doubt at all that Europe will rise against the monster and rally to the Khan's banner he bears. He may be a commoner now, my darling, but he will not be one for long under those circumstances. The Khan will—"

"I wouldn't touch Toby Long—"

". . . at least a duke and probably a sovereign prince. He is, of course, greatly smitten with you!"

Lisa almost fell off her stool, having to grab at the edge of the stone table for balance. "He is *what?* Mother, he is the most insulting man I have ever met. He snaps at me, treats me like a child, orders me around. I assure you he likes me no better than I like him, which means utter revulsion. Re*pug*nance!"

Her mother chuckled. "You think so? You should see the way he looks at you. Oh, Lisa, I know longing when I see it, and he craves you mightily. If he seems a little brusque at times, then that is merely because he is struggling to contain his feelings. Realizing how far above his own station you are, he is being careful not to embarrass you by revealing his great affection and desire. His worship must be unspoken and distant. Understand the strain this places on his self-control."

Awrrk!

Lisa drew a very deep breath. "He told me himself that he is celibate because he has no choice in the matter. When I said *ox,* I meant *ox!*"

The countess knew what that word meant, and her fair cheeks colored. "I doubt it very much! If he suffered an injury of that, um, description, then the story

would be general knowledge. Your Master Campbell
has a reputation as a libertine and lecher, but Sir
Tobias's is above reproach."

Oh, worse yet! *Humiliation!* "You have been
making inquiries?"

"Certainly. Women of the lower sort have thrown
themselves in his path and he, er . . ."

"Steps over them?"

"Exactly. Are you quite sure of your own feelings
in the matter, dearest? I have seen how you, in turn,
regard Constable Longdirk when you believe you are
unobserved. He is, of course, a magnificent figure of
manhood, Hercules himself. Any young girl can be
forgiven a certain fascination with such an Atlas."

"Atlas?" Lisa said hoarsely. "Don't you mean
Grendel? That side of beef? Let me tell you, Mother,
that all his stupid posturing as *comandante* is going to
end very shortly. Even Hamish admits that he was
lucky at Trent—that he was only elected commander
because they couldn't agree on anyone else. And now
the Khan has sent one of his sons to rally the opposition, so that problem will not arise again. Prince Sartaq
will appoint a suzerain, and the suzerain will send
Toby Longdirk packing, right back to the Highland
bog he crawled out of in the first place!"

Even those harsh words failed to ruffle her
mother's maniacal serenity. "Will he really? Princes
don't discard warriors who win wars, Lisa, they pro-
mote them. I think," she added, fixing her daughter
with a reproving eye, "that you had better face up to
cold reality, dearest. Everyone is now talking as if

your father is dead, which legally may be true. Under English law an underage heiress becomes a ward in chancery, and Tartar law or Florentine law won't be much different."

Lisa opened and closed her mouth a few times . . . "Or even the laws of chivalry," Blanche continued. "As heir to the throne of England you are a ward of your father's overlord, the Khan, or his suzerain, or perhaps this *darughachi* prince. One of them, certainly. Not the Florentine courts, I hope. Whichever it turns out to be, he will choose a husband for you."

This was ghastly! Even Hamish had never mentioned anything so grim. Talking Mother into something was a matter of persistence and hard work. Tartar princes might be much less malleable. "Mother . . . ?"

"You bring a kingdom as dowry, dear. If the Khan wishes to confer royalty on a commoner, the easiest way is to marry him to a queen, you understand? Now the outstanding military figure in Europe at the moment is Sir Toby. I foresee a great future for Longdirk."

"Foresee anything you like for him as long as you don't include me in it!"

"Lisa, Lisa! Don't deceive yourself. Oftentimes we foolish women fail to understand our own desires. Many a highborn maiden has fallen in love with a man of inferior social station and exaggerated his rough qualities in her own mind to deny the stirrings in her breast. A certain amount of animal sensuality is a virtue in a man, alarming though it may seem to a virgin. I remember how terrified I was when my own parents informed me that they had chosen a man barely older than myself to be my husband. I quite—"

"No! No! No!" Lisa clapped her hands over her ears and fled howling from the courtyard.

25

Although the banquet had lasted late into the night, Toby had been out riding Smeòrach since before dawn. Between times he had slept, but poorly—too many things to do, too much to think about. Drumming had wakened him. He heard drumming often now, and the fact that others did not made it no less real to him. He was convinced that the *darughachi* had set shamans to spy on him, but if the Tartars could do that, then so could the Fiend's hexers. It was past time he found a replacement for Maestro Fischart.

Dusty and bleary-eyed, he strode into the courtyard. Hamish was there already with a pile of reports and correspondence. He looked up and frowned. "Did you come to bed at all?" At times he mothered Toby infuriatingly.

"You were asleep. And still snoring when I left." Toby sat on a stool and enjoyed a long yawn. The one bright note in the morning was that the Company had money again and could hold a pay parade at long last. He leaned his arms on the stone table and scowled at the heap of paper. "What bullguts have you got for me today?" He took a harder look at that face he knew so well and spoke more gently. "What's wrong?"

"Nothing. There's a letter in from—"

"Tell me."

Hamish sighed crossly and laid a pottery paperweight on the heap, although there was no wind. "You tell me what you think of Lisa."

A tiny demon of temptation told Toby to scream at the top of his voice, grab Master Campbell up by the throat, and wave him like a flag. Here they were preparing for a war that would decide the fate of Europe for centuries to come and his chief helper and closest friend—his only friend—was obsessed by an animal fire in his crotch. A fire that could never cook anything. Why couldn't he lust after some two-lire bawd who would drag him into the bushes and quench the blaze for him? Twenty minutes' rollick and he would be the old Hamish again, at least for a day or two.

Lisa? Toby scratched his unshaven jaw. "If you like statuesque blondes, she's one of the greatest beauties you'll ever meet. She has a wit like a whip, a mind like a rapier, and nerves of steel. She is also totally spoiled, completely self-centered, and as devious as an Italian. Not," he added, seeing the storm clouds roiling in Hamish's eyes, "that she can be blamed for all that. It goes with the royal blood. She had a bizarre upbringing, and her mother is nine-sixteenths madder than a March hare. As a king's wife she'd be magnificent, but never as a ruler in her own right. Not for another ten years anyway. I can't imagine her grinding meal or milking the goat. Why do you ask?"

The storm clouds had not dispersed. "Her mother thinks you are in love with her."

Toby said, "Oh, demons!" under his breath.

"You do not deny it?"

"I have told you what I think of her. If I could have dreams, old friend, they might well include a Lisa in them."

"She says you make eyes at her." Hamish bared his teeth. "Her mother is plotting to marry Lisa to *you!* You are going to destroy Nevil's army, reconquer Europe, marry Lisa, and become King of England."

If a ditch-born bastard was a suitable match for the future queen, then why wasn't a schoolmaster's son? Toby was aware that Queen Blanche had taken to smiling at him excessively. He snapped at both her and her daughter as much as he could to keep them away. Apparently that strategy was not working.

"She's even madder than I thought. Marry? I don't dare even smile at a girl, you know that!"

His suffering friend was not convinced. "Are you sure? How long since you lost control of the hob? It didn't escape you even at the Battle of Trent. If you can stay master in a turmoil like that, with gramarye and demons loose, then you can stay master anywhere!"

Toby sighed, shaking his head. "Believe me, it's different. I know." He shuddered, remembered the dozens of innocent people who had died in Mezquiriz. "Remember Jacques, at Montserrat, who tried to be a saint and failed that test? He started with an elementary, not a hob, and yet it became a demon." It had taken most of him with it when it was exorcised, and left a human cabbage. "Have you bedded her yet?"

"No!" Hamish glowered at the papers on the table.

"Do you plan to?"

Without looking up, Hamish mumbled, "You think I couldn't? If I wanted?"

"Sorry. Yes, she's lovely. If I give her sheepdog looks behind her back, then I'm sorry about that, too. I didn't know I was doing it. I probably ogle lots of women—didn't you tell me once that that was why men's heads could turn?" Briefly Toby considered ordering his chancellor to report to the camp brothel, but discretion prevailed. His troubles were too serious to cure that way. "Old friends should not squabble over a prize that neither of them can ever hope to win."

He ought to be more sympathetic. Things were easier for him, who was forever denied love. Time had dulled the pain of Jeanne and that terrible night in Mezquiriz, and yet he still dreamed of her sometimes. He wakened weeping.

"It does seem irrational." Hamish was too upset to smile. "It's the thought that she's going to have to marry someone, and probably very soon. Demons, Toby, I'm crazy about her! I've never felt like this about a woman, never. At times I want to burst out laughing, yelling, 'Lisa loves me!' so the whole world can know. And then I remember that some man is going to drag her off to bed to breed a pack of royal brats, and I want to kill myself. It's driving me insane! I can't eat or sleep or think straight." He pounded his fists on the table.

Man chooses woman, woman accepts man, society forbids the match—it happened all the time, but that made it no less tragic.

"Flea farts! You slept like a millstone last night. You're also doing the work of three men and managing to squire Lisa at the same time. Let's get started here. What have . . ." A flash of movement on the roof of the villa . . .

"What?" Hamish looked where Toby was looking.

"My keeper is back."

Hamish's eyes grew almost as wide as the owl's. It was a white owl, a large one, staring fixedly at them. "It's the same one. Can you hear drumming now?"

"No. Can you?"

"No."

This was new. Drumming with no owl, yes, but never owl without drumming.

Before Hamish could comment further, Don Ramon de Nuñez y Pardo came striding out of the villa with a couple of squires at his heels. He paused long enough to wave them away before advancing on the table like a stalking leopard. What would he say to tales of invisible drummers? He probably heard them all the time, and bugles, too. Toby and Hamish rose and bowed.

He sat down without inviting them to. He was even more resplendent than usual in a dazzling new military doublet that Toby had not seen before; he had his silver helmet on his head and carried his captain-general's baton. Although his blue eyes shone inhumanly bright, he did not seem especially mad this morning, neither angry nor crazy. Time would tell.

"I want an explanation for that scene yesterday! You told me that Marradi had put his villa at your disposal."

Toby met his glare squarely. "He did, senor. I suspect his sister bears me a grudge, and the problem is of her devising."

"The word in Florence is that the *duchessa* has sworn to have your hide for a rug and certain other parts of you as paperweights."

"I have done nothing to provoke her enmity."

"Obviously doing nothing was the trouble. Demons have no fury like a woman scorned, Constable." The don's smirk implied that he had not made the same mistake and his information had been collected firsthand, which was certainly possible.

Hamish was scrabbling in his papers. "A note arrived from *Il Volpe* this morning, Captain-General. He apologizes for the misunderstanding. The meeting may proceed at Cafaggiolo as planned."

All very fine, but a private apology would not begin to undo the damage of that very public snub.

"Typical republican stupidity!" said the don. "Never apologize, under any circumstances."

Hamish had not finished. "There is also a note from *podestà* Origo. He says that the prince has absolutely forbidden any meetings until he arrives in Florence. He does not say when that will be."

"Sometimes republicans don't seem so bad," Toby remarked glumly. "Does the idiot think the war will wait on his pleasure?"

After a tense silence, the don said, "Who was coming?"

Toby had been trying to keep the don and the proposed meeting well apart, but he could not refuse his nominal superior information when he asked for it, especially after the brilliant save the man had improvised in the loggia yesterday. He passed the question to Hamish.

"There was a letter in last night from Rome. The College will send Captain-General Villari. That's everyone we invited! Ercole Abonio from Milan— and he's bringing di Gramasci of the Black Lances. The Stiletto from Venice. Mezzo will come if his health improves; otherwise he'll send Gioberti or Desjardins."

The don raised aristocratic eyebrows. "Mezzo?"

"Paride Mezzo, *collaterale* of the Kingdom of the Two Sicilies." No one but Hamish ever bothered to use that formal name for Naples. He just liked the sound of it. "We were about to invite the small guns: Verona, Bologna, Genoa—"

"Bah! They don't matter. They do what Milan and Venice and Florence tell them, and those three have no choice but to cooperate."

"They have some very competent soldiers," Toby protested.

"We do not need advice." From the don, that *we* was a remarkable concession, unless he had just taken to classifying himself as royalty. "The keys are Naples and Rome—Naples because it has the men, and Rome because it has the hierocracy for hexers. It also has to let the Neapolitans march through. Get those two into the coalition, and we may have a chance. At least we'll bloody the foe. The Swiss?"

"We can try. They're as biddable as cats."

"I assume that the real purpose of the orgy was to get you elected *comandante?*"

"Would be nice," Toby admitted. "But I do want to discuss strategy. We need to plan how to resist the invasion. We can't know *where* until we know which way Nevil's coming."

"Make up your mind, Constable. If you want to be elected *jefe,* then you bring in every little town that can field a pikeman. They'll all vote for you because Florence is less of a threat than any of the other four, but they'll never agree on anything else. If you need to decide whose crops are going to get burned, then you leave them out, all of them." Whatever illusions Don Ramon pursued, he was never stupid. He had a much better grasp of politics than he normally cared to admit.

"Another thing we must talk about is gramarye," Toby said. "We don't have a single hexer, and I've heard that the College is being absurdly uncooperative. If all the senior condottieri unite to appeal to Rome, then perhaps the hierocracy will bend a little."

"What need have you of hexers if you have one good shaman?"

Toby had registered Hamish's slack-jawed astonishment a split second before that new voice at his
back spun him around.

A bizarre figure came limping across the courtyard toward them. It was short and completely
enveloped in a floating costume of many colors and
many parts—panels and swatches in green and brown
and gray, bedecked with ribbons and lace, beads and
embroidery, bunches of feathers and wisps of grass, a
design that was either completely random or fraught
with great meaning. Some parts of it looked new, others were grubby and worn by many years of use. The
dainty, pointed chin suggested a woman, but she might
be a young girl, or even a boy. Her hair and the upper
part of her face were hidden by a blindfold and an
elaborate headdress. Around her neck hung a drum as
large as a meal sieve, which she steadied against her
hip with one small brown hand.

Obviously she had just come out of the villa, but
how had she passed the guards in there? How had she
even entered the camp unchallenged? The hob was not
reacting as it did to gramarye. Was this one of the
camp brats playing a joke?

To his credit, the don remained on his stool. A
slight narrowing of his eyes was the only sign of tension as he crossed his legs and leaned back to rest his
elbows on the table. "And who might you be?"

She smiled, revealing a perfect set of sparkling
white teeth. "Are you not in need of a hexer?" Her
voice had a singsong accent and a curious huskiness.
"And are you not all faithful children of His Splendor

the Khan, who has sent his son to direct you? Who doubts that the illustrious prince has sent his personal shaman to be your guide and protector against the demons of the foe?"

Toby did, but he bowed. Hamish just glowered.

The don frowned. "A battlefield is not a fit place for a woman!"

"Who is it a fit place for?"

For a moment he bristled at such heresy, then twirled up his mustache, which was usually a sign of amusement. He rose gracefully and bowed. "Don Ramon de Nuñez y Pardo at your service, madonna."

"And I am Toby Longdirk."

"Who does not know you? Am I not Sorghaghtani? And is not Chabi my eyes, who found you?" The shaman raised an arm, and the great white owl floated down to settle on it, then shuffled sideways until it stood on her shoulder. The shaman was not just a boy playing pranks.

The don had not been aware of the owl.

Hamish said, "How do we know that you are sent by the prince and not the Fiend?"

"Are you not still breathing?" Chuckling, Sorghaghtani perched on a stool and arranged her drum on her lap. She ran fingertips over the skin, raising barely audible tremors like distant gunfire. Her hands and the visible part of her face had a brownish olive cast that was not European. Inside those extraordinary hodgepodge draperies she might be young or old, but there could not be very much of her. She was brazenly sure of herself and her owl—nothing else was provable at the moment. "Is your imp distressed by my presence, Little One?"

Toby assumed she was speaking to him, as the owl was staring in his direction. "No. Do you keep a spirit immured in your pet?"

"Who is the pet and who the keeper? Is it wise of you to arrange your council and not include the illustrious Neguder?"

"I have never heard of anyone called Neguder." Toby was starting to believe he was holding this conversation with the bird and not the woman. She was inhumanly motionless, except for the resonant tremor of her fingers on the drum and the movement of her lips as she spoke.

"Who else would be military advisor to the splendid prince?"

"Is he competent?" barked the don.

The owl turned its head in his direction. "Competent?" the shaman shrilled. "Who asks if a Tartar general is competent?"

"I do. Is he?"

"How could he be, when all preferment in the army is based on birth, when the Horde has not fought a war in two centuries, when all the skills of the steppes are forgotten and the swords rusted? Who would trust a man who drinks himself to stupidity every night?"

The don looked ready to eat his mustache. "Then why should I invite him to anything?"

"Will you defy the express command of illustrious Prince Sartaq, noble son of Ozberg Khan, your exalted liege lord?"

"Show me this command!"

"Can you not wait and ask him yourself?"

"Why," snapped the don, "do you always answer questions with questions?"

"Does it annoy you?"

"Yes it does."

The woman smiled.

Hamish leaned across the table, peering at her blindfold to see if it was genuine. "Why should we trust you? How do we know you are not sent by the enemy? Or are just a fake? How old are you?" He was seriously annoyed

"Will you believe in me when I give you such boils on your backside that you cannot sit down?"

"Do that, and I'll wring your bird's neck and make it into soup. Why are you blindfolded?"

"If Chabi must be my eyes, will not the noon sun be too bright for her?"

"Well, yes, but . . ." Hamish straightened up. Frowning, he fell silent as he tried to puzzle out what that answer-question implied. At least the shaman had taken his mind off Lisa.

26

They might be violent by nature, but soldiers of fortune were rarely monsters. The men of the Don Ramon Company were as concerned for the welfare of their souls as most other men, as heedful of the guidance of good spirits, and as abhorrent of demons' mindless evil. They were reasonably devout—but only reasonably. They would have as soon trusted their opponents not to use gramarye against them as they would have gone into battle wearing paper helmets. Only gramarye could fight gramarye, so the death of the company hexer had been the cause of much foreboding. If Longdirk tried to lead them to war before he found a credible replacement for the late Karl Fischart, he would march alone. Could they accept a woman? Even more unlikely, could they accept a shaman, whose style of conjuration would be so unfamiliar to them?

Could he? It was to be expected that the Tartar prince would show interest in the victor of Trent, but for Sartaq to assign his personal shaman to one of the smaller mercenary companies out of all the dozens in Italy was a gift horse with a very large mouth indeed. Was Sorghaghtani what she said she was? Whom did she serve? Hamish did not want to trust her, although he could not explain how he would test any adept for hidden loyalties. Toby was prepared to accept her because the hob seemed to. Either she was a hexer of such enormous power that she could blind the hob, or else she meant no harm. If he vouched for her, Hamish would go along, and the don probably would. How about the rest of the Company?

Sorghaghtani herself asked that question before he did. She also inquired why he did not invite all the officers to meet her at sunset in the courtyard and why he did not show her to her quarters in the meantime.

Since Fischart's death, the adytum held no spiritual threat to disturb the hob. Toby could go there now and had even inspected it a few days previously with the idea of turning it into a gunpowder store, eventually deciding it was too close to the villa. He conducted the little shaman there. She seemed pleased with the building and asked why he did not leave her to get on with her work.

He walked by it a few times during the day and each time heard her drum throbbing away inside as if she were performing some sort of shamanistic spring cleaning, but the hob paid no attention. Twice he tapped on the door to ask if she needed food and neither time was there any answer, but when he went to fetch her at sunset, she came out to meet him with her drum slung around her neck, all ready to go. An instant later the owl swooped down to settle on her shoulder.

"Do you need food, madonna?"

"Who? Why give me titles? If my mother called me Sorghaghtani, is that not good enough for you? Who can quest in the spirit world with a full stomach?" She hobbled off along the path. She was blindfolded, although the light would not bother her owl now. He could not tell whether her awkward gait meant that she was old or just badly shod. For all he knew, there was an adolescent inside that grotesque costume.

He caught up with her, staying on the non-owl side. "Have you cleansed the adytum of evil influences, Sorghaghtani, the shadow Oreste mentioned?"

"Have you sharpened the pikes, Little One?"

"You would rather I did not ask you questions?"

"Is not one of us enough?"

He could not tell if she was being humorous, since her face was hidden—he was so much taller than she that he could not even see the owl's goggle-eyed stare. He tried again. "I have assembled the officers. Will you tell me what you propose to do?"

"Why cannot you wait and see?"

"Do you ever say anything that is not a question?"

"Why do you ask?"

Toby sighed. "I'm beginning to wonder."

She chuckled, and that was an improvement.

"I have seen your owl many times in the last few weeks, and heard a drum. Was that you?"

"Who else?"

"Why were you spying on me?"

"Was I spying or just trying to find you?"

"I assume when you answer like that . . . I mean, I take that answer to mean that you were trying to find me."

"Do you?"

This was becoming more than a little irritating. "Warn me what you plan tonight, Sorghaghtani, because the hob—my imp as you call it—will not tolerate gramarye."

"Have I vexed it yet, Little One? Would it behave so well if I were a danger to you? How much will it do your bidding?"

"I try not to let it do anything. If I do, it will soon learn to bypass my controls and then overpower me.

The tutelary at Montserrat warned me of that many times. Let sleeping demons lie."

The shaman chortled. "Tutelaries? You always believe tutelaries? Why do you carry it so strangely in your heart?"

"I do not carry it willingly at all. It cannot be exorcised, for we have grown too much together."

"Think you I cannot see that? Will not both become one soon?"

"Not soon. In many years perhaps, and I can only hope that then I will be the one who survives."

She did not offer her opinion of his chances.

Even before the horrors of Trent, Toby Longdirk had seen more manifestations of gramarye than most men, but not all of it had been violent and destructive. In the days before he learned to suppress its antics, the hob had often played tricks around him—often embarrassing, as when he found pretty things collecting in his pockets, sometimes deadly, but once in a while very convenient, almost as if it could think and were trying to please. So he knew gramarye, and yet Sorghaghtani's séance that evening was unlike anything he had ever witnessed before. It was subtle and stunningly effective, and the hob never stirred.

The courtyard was deeply shadowed, lit by a willowy moon in the pink dusk and the gleam of a few candles inside the villa itself. After the long-awaited payday, not all the officers of the Company were available to attend a council or competent to

understand what was happening if they did, but the
don had collected at least a score of them, perhaps
thirty. They stood in small groups around the edges,
under the trellises, staying well back, as if frightened the new hexer would turn them into goats to
demonstrate her skills.

Toby presented Sorghaghtani, personal shaman to
His Highness Prince Sartaq. He mentioned how honored and fortunate the Don Ramon Company was to
have acquired such a hexer. The resulting silence
might have come straight out of one of the age-old
Etruscan tombs that were being excavated around
Tuscany. Unless these men could be convinced, they
would not persuade the rank and file.

"Are you always so mud-headed?" Sorghaghtani
demanded shrilly. "What must I show you? Will you
give me your hand, Little One, and stand at my back
lest I fall off?"

Clutching his fingers in a powerful grip, she
scrambled up on a stool and then the stone table itself.
Evidently she could move as nimbly as a child when
she wanted to, and his estimate of her age plummeted.
She sat down cross-legged, gave the owl a wrist to
step onto, and raised it overhead. Chabi spread her
wings and floated away into the night. Sorghaghtani
squirmed a few times as if to make herself comfortable on the hard tabletop, then settled the drum on her
lap. "Do they understand that they must not speak, lest
they anger the spirits?"

Of course they did not, so Toby passed the word.
He stood ready behind the shaman and waited to see

what she could do to convince this case-hardened crew of mercenaries.

For a long time she just drummed, but no one protested or made jokes or tried to leave. The rhythms were hypnotic and also restless, seeming to sing back and forth to their own echoes, although normally there were no echoes in the courtyard. To and fro, in and out, the sound went, surging and falling, then stopped abruptly, leaving a silence taut enough to raise the hair on a man's neck. The shaman sat hunched over her drum, motionless. When she spoke, the voice that rang out was female, but not hers.

"Mario! I, Angelica, speak. I need you. The mare foals tonight."

In the far corner, Mario Chairmontesi cried out.

Then another voice came from Sorghaghtani's throat, and this time Toby knew it, although he had not heard it for almost three years. "Ramon! Francisca am I. The new casa is ready, but servants . . . oh, to find servants!"

Wherever the don was standing in the courtyard, he did not comment, or if he did, the sound was lost in another voice: "Martin, my child! Hilda. So tall you are, so strong! Hilda with Ehingen am."

At that, Toby really did feel the hairs on his neck prickle, for Ehingen could only be a spirit or tutelary, so the woman who had spoken was dead. But he had no time to wonder what Martin Grossman was thinking before another spoke, and another, faster and jostling, as if the voices were struggling to take their turn in the shaman's mouth—not wives or lovers, only

mothers, and more than half of them naming the spirit
that now cherished them. Most spoke in Italian, but
others used German or French or Spanish. Some, like
Hilda, spoke as if to children. One just wailed inco-
herently, perhaps a wraith with no tutelary to care for
it. One said plaintively, "You never knew me." The
audience was reacting. Men tried to answer, or ask
questions, or call back those who had spoken and
fallen silent. Others tried to hush them as they waited
for their own message. Some merely howled. Many
wept as the significance sank in, and the weeping was
infectious.

Barely audible through the rising hubbub, the last
voice of all spoke very softly in the lilt of Gaelic.
"Meg, Tobias. You do not remember, but I am with
you. Proud I am." He had expected Granny Nan . . .

With him? None of the others had said that. Oh,
spirits! No, no! Never in the years he had been possessed by the hob had he considered that it had been,
in its witless, blundering, indifferent fashion, the nearest thing Tyndrum had to a tutelary. Only to the hob
could the souls of the dead in Strath Fillan appeal for
succor. So had it cherished them? All of them or some
of them? When the hob left its haunt and went on its
travels in Toby Longdirk, did it in some sense take
them with it? He had no time to think of the implications, for the séance was over, and Sorghaghtani toppled backward into his arms.

She weighed nothing. He stood and cradled her as
he would a child while his mind scrambled to recall
every nuance of those faint words. *You do not remem-*

ber . . . Of course not, for Meg Campbell had died giving birth to a bastard rape-child, and she had been only a child herself. All around the courtyard, the officers of the Don Ramon Company were shuffling toward the exit—going alone, not in groups, not speaking. But a lot of them seemed to be weeping, and Toby realized that his own cheeks were wet, and his throat ached. Meg Campbell, the mother he had never known . . .

The shaman mumbled and began to stir. She had proved her skills. She had turned a score of intractable mercenary veterans into sniveling children.

27

Lucrezia Marradi had two brothers. The elder, Pietro—poet, patron of the arts, head of the family bank, and, hence, head of the family—in his spare time ran city and state as a family fief. The younger was illegitimate, but bastardy mattered little in Italy, and he had followed a notable career in spiritualism, rising rapidly in the College until he was one of the senior cardinals, perhaps a future Holy Father. Early in March, Ricciardo Cardinal Marradi paid a visit to his native city, of which he was officially arch-acolyte.

Relieved that he would not have to send Hamish to Rome, Toby wrote asking for a meeting at His Eminence's convenience. He took the precaution of routing the request through the Magnificent. He waited, with growing concern. He asked again. He took the matter to Benozzo's successor, Cecco de' Carisendi, but the old man seemed unable to comprehend the seriousness of the problem—there was very little he did comprehend. It was on the tenth and final day of the cardinal's visitation that the captain-general and his deputy were summoned to the Marradi Palace to meet him. Toby took Hamish along.

He had been hoping and expecting that the meeting would be private, but they were shown into a busy antechamber, teeming with the usual crowd of sycophants and supplicants, and there they were left a long time. The snub itself was disturbing, both because it would soon become common knowledge in Florence and because anyone could guess why the captain-general needed to call upon the cardinal. Even when they were led through into the next high-ceilinged, overdecorated hall, they had not done with waiting. In the center the great man was holding court within about a score of people—mostly acolytes, male and female, but also four or five members of his family, including his brother and sister—and they were all just standing there having a loudly jolly chat, punctuated by much laughter. Clerks and stewards wandered around to no clear purpose.

The don was not noted for his patience. Cooling his heels always made his head hotter, and already he was muttering Castilian things under his breath. Eventually a chancellor arrived to confirm the visitors' identities, as if silver helmets were two-a-penny in Florence. Another wait. Then three of the courtiers kissed the cardinal's ring and departed. Everyone else remained, but now it seemed that the visitors were to have their audience.

Not so. The chancellor led forward a couple of very elderly female acolytes, tottering on canes.

"I see," the don announced loudly, "that I am too young to be trusted with important concerns. I prefer to do my aging elsewhere." He spun on his heel and strode out.

Hamish and Toby exchanged glances that included equal parts of relief and despair. No one else was reacting at all, but that did not mean that the insult had not been noted. It probably cost them another twenty minutes, but eventually they were judged to have suffered enough. Then they were led forward and graciously permitted to kiss the ring. Among the spectators, Lucrezia and the Magnificent watched in silence. Lucrezia was smiling.

Ricciardo Marradi was a plump, satisfied, and yet enigmatic man in his mid-thirties, five years younger than his brother. The Lombardy redness of his hair clashed horribly with his scarlet robes and biretta. His features were paradoxical—a sharp nose and small mouth flanked by brown eyes wide with babyish innocence, set in a soft pink complexion. He wore his power like steel armor, yet his voice was high-pitched and petulant.

"How may we aid your cause, Tobias? You understand that we are about to take our leave and cannot spare you long."

"The matter concerns the safety of the city, Your Eminence, indeed its very survival."

"Surely, then, it should be brought to us by Captain-General Signor Ramon de Nuñez?"

Years of practice let Toby restrain his temper. "Yes, it should, Your Eminence. I hoped it would be. But it seems that I shall have to suffice." For a moment he thought he was going to be dismissed unheard, but then the arch-acolyte gestured with a pudgy hand.

"Be brief." Accepting a sheaf of papers from a secretary beside him, His Eminence began to flip through them.

"Reports from the north tell of the Fiend preparing to bring his hordes across the Alps, Your Eminence. We expect him within a month or two at most. The brave men of Italy will resist his evil, but flesh and blood and courage are no match for gramarye. Nevil is a demon incarnate and fights with demons. It has long been suspected that he has refrained from trying to add Italy to his dominions only because he fears the righteous powers of the Cardinal College. I come to ask for the spiritual aid that the defenders—"

"Rest assured, my son," the cardinal twittered, barely glancing up from the documents, "that the Holy Father and members of the College will continue to pray without surcease for the defeat of the Fiend whether or not he invades Italy. We regularly remind all acolytes of the Galilean Order in all shrines and sanctuaries everywhere to petition the spirits they serve for assistance against the evil. Our esteemed Captain-General Villari has been told to save no expense to defend the holy city itself."

"Are not these the same precautions you took before France was conquered, when Austria was overrun, while the rest of Europe was ravaged by the monster? I am sure I speak not only for the armies of Florence but for all—"

"You may be sure of that." Marradi thrust the documents back at the secretary, approving them with a nod. "But we are not. If, as I fear, Tobias, you are about to ask the College itself to engage in gramarye, you should remember that the Holy Father and his predecessors for more than a thousand years have refused to countenance the use of demons under any circumstances whatsoever. The Galilean enjoined us to serve, worship, and educate the holy spirits within their natural domains. To abduct and torture them into demons is contrary to all that is virtuous. Fighting evil with more evil must always be self-defeating. Our shield must be love and goodness our sword."

Were this meeting the confidential and intimate parley Toby had requested, he would now agree wholeheartedly and mention that the Don Ramon Company was in dire need of a good healer, as battles were not necessarily fought within easy reach of a sanctuary. In other words, he would ask for a hexer. The cardinal, if he were reasonable, would refuse sadly and later arrange for one to appear. But this cardinal was not being reasonable and did not deserve to be treated reasonably.

"That was not how Rome escaped conquest by the Tartars in 1248, Your Eminence."

The onlookers flinched. No one contradicted an

arch-acolyte in public, let alone a cardinal. Marradi's smooth pinkness turned a fraction pinker. He pursed his little mouth

"You were there, I suppose?" he squeaked.

Toby could boom. "No, but I am here, in Florence, in your city, which I have sworn to defend with my life. Why are you not willing to assist its people in their hour of need? For all of that thousand years you mentioned, the College has waged war on hexers, and rightly so. It has invariably confiscated any immured demon it could lay its hands on, and it is public knowledge that all of those hundreds, nay thousands, of—"

"Public knowledge is worthless knowledge, my son. Those jewels and the demons they contain are taken to Rome to be destroyed, not hoarded in some secret cellar as you imply." His Eminence gibbered the words, sprayed them. "Even if we did control a legion of demons, to use it for the furtherance of evil would—"

"Is self-defense evil? If we use them only for that?"

"I have told you. Those demons do not exist."

"Then if you will not take pity on the men who will die because of your stubbornness, will you not save the tutelaries and spirits? Do you deny that whenever Nevil takes a city he turns its spirits into demons to serve his cause and thus continues to increase his power while you and others like you close your eyes to the suffering and—"

"Insolence! Blasphemy! Chancellor, remove this man and his companion from our presence!"

Toby turned on his heel and walked out.

Hamish stalked at his side, growling low in his throat. As they clattered down the broad staircase, he said, "Did ye see yon Lucrezia? Smirking and panting like a bitch in heat."

"I'm sure she enjoyed the performance," Toby said tightly, "but I don't think she wrote the music. There's another hand behind all this."

"Whose?"

"The shadow who arranged Fischart's death. There's a traitor in the Company."

28

Never since the Tartar conquest of Europe almost three hundred years earlier had a member of the Khan's immediate family visited Florence, and no expense was spared to honor the *darughachi.* The ceremonies would begin at the city gate on the Roman road, the Porta Gattolini, where bands played and banners flew above elaborate staging, where all the rich and powerful came to see and be seen, even those not required to participate. An honor guard lined both sides of the road out for more than a mile. Marshal Diaz had threatened to flog any man who did not meet his standards of perfection, be he cavalry *squadriere,* infantry commander, or Constable Longdirk himself. Growly old Antonio was probably capable of trying it, too, but the threat was not necessary. The entire Don Ramon Company was determined to upstage the

Florentine *provisionati,* so sunlight blazed off helmets
and breastplates, off shields and pikes and swords, off
buttons and harness buckles buffed like silver. Even
the horses looked polished. Toby had taken care that
he would not be found wanting. At his post close to the
gate, he flashed and sweltered in full armor like the
rest.

The Company had begun deploying before dawn.
Great carriages of the rich started rumbling out not
long after, then the commonality emerged from the
city like a noisy tide to roil over the fields, churning up
the young wheat. They danced, picnicked, and generally enjoyed a sunny holiday. Hucksters and pick-
pockets plied their trades.

By noon the bands had given up, the honor guard
was losing its glitter, and everyone was becoming
grumpy. It was midafternoon before the long procession was seen winding in over the hills. It took almost
another hour for the van of the Sienese escort to reach
the first of the honor guard, and even then the end of
the baggage train was still not in sight. The music
began again, and maidens strewed flowers on the road
before the prince's steed. Cannons boomed, startling
the horses. Some ambitious souls began to cheer,
although that did not last long in the heat.

All this was only preparatory, for the main events
would take place in the city, in the Palace of the
Signory. But before the speeches and masques, before
ceremonies in the piazza and services in the sanctuary—before anything else at all—the city leaders must
make the Tartar ritual of obeisance, which was so

ancient that it had been conveniently forgotten in Tuscany centuries ago. Nevertheless, it was required now, however much republican blood might boil.

A herald proclaimed the name and rank of the Khan's official deputy, the despised Antonio Origo. The *podestà* advanced on foot, bowing seven times. Then he had to kneel and touch his face to the ground, rise to his knees, and kiss the prince's boot. Later, when Sartaq sat enthroned in the palace, there would be formal oaths of allegiance, with each participant lifting the royal foot and placing it on his own head, but that could not conveniently be done when he was on horseback. Even this ritual was more difficult now than it had been in ancient times, for where the prince's world-conquering ancestors had ridden shaggy little Mongolian ponies, he sat astride a long-legged Arabian stallion, and the dumpy messer Origo had considerable trouble reaching his lips to the boot without lifting his knees off the ground. Muffled sounds of amusement could be heard from the distant ranks of citizenry. Even the notables around Toby shimmered a little. As Origo rose and backed away, bowing seven more times as required, his face was observed to be redder than the rich wines of the Chianti Hills. Truly, the lot of a *podestà* in Florence was never easy.

Sartaq seemed younger than Toby had expected, although those unfamiliar Asiatic features were hard to judge. Under a towering, many-colored and many-layered hat, his complexion was the same olive-brown shade as Sorghaghtani's, plump and unlined, with a

thin black mustache curving down almost to his jaw-
line. He was short, probably stocky, although little of
his shape showed through the grandiose robes of
bejeweled and emblazoned silk—not for him the simple furs and leathers of his horseborne steppe ancestors. He looked very bored, but possibly he was
merely wearied by a long ride on a hot day.

None of the twenty or so glorious-garbed courtiers
behind him seemed likely to be the military attaché
Neguder. They were all elderly and could be assumed
to have been sent along to keep the young prince in
line.

All the innumerable priors and other dignitaries of
Florence had now to be proclaimed by the heralds and
then follow Origo's footsteps over the crushed flowers. Pietro Marradi was not there, because formally he
was only a private citizen. He was also too much of a
realist to feel slighted by the omission, although all the
lesser politicians, while denouncing the ceremony as
barbaric and antiquated and humiliating, had been
ready to riot if they were excluded.

The military were to come next, starting with the
captain-general. Don Ramon might well be the haugh-
tiest man in Italy, but an abasement that shocked
republicans was no problem for him. He understood
the rights of rank. He probably believed that he was
entitled to much the same sort of veneration himself—
after all, he could trace his lineage back six or seven
centuries farther than the prince could, for the Khan's
line had been undistinguished before it produced the
great Genghis. He strode forward cheerfully, a limber,

athletic contrast to the stodgy, overfed burghers who had preceded him. He was the first to perform the obeisance with grace.

Then the captain of the city's own troops, the *provisionati,* but no one put any stock in *him.* Toby was next. He braced himself . . .

"His Royal Highness," bellowed the herald, "the Duke of Anjou, knight of the Order of the Golden Sword, companion of the Crystal Star, Sieur de la Loire, seigneur of Anjou, of Beaupréau, of Les Herbiers, of—"

Toby had swayed slightly on the balls of his feet, but he regained his balance without giving onlookers the satisfaction of seeing him flail his arms. His immediate companions were hissing in astonishment as the catalogue of seigniories rolled on and on.

And on . . .

". . . of Sablé-sur-Sarthe, of Aiffres, Viscount Chateauroux, Baron Bonneval, castellan of La Roche-sur-Yon."

The old scoundrel had never admitted to any of those honors before. Even now, he was obviously laying claim only to the titles he had possessed *before* the war, before Nevil turned his family into dog food. Since then he had inherited a third of Europe.

The catalogue ended, the rangy old mercenary limped forward to greet the prince. Granted that D'Anjou himself had probably instigated this royal recognition, who had worked him into Toby's spot in the ceremony? It was universally assumed that the main purpose of the *darughachi*'s journey west was to choose the next suzerain. If blood was what mattered, then D'Anjou must be the logical choice, but there was certainly no chance of D'Anjou then appointing Toby Longdirk *comandante*.

That crashing noise was the sound of plans collapsing.

D'Anjou rose and retreated, bowing. The herald proclaimed Baldassare Barrafranca, certainly one of the most incompetent fighters ever to sign a *condotta* and pretender to one of the least justifiable hereditary titles. Obviously Toby Longdirk was not going to be called forward at all. He supposed he should be feeling anger, but his inner calm remained unruffled, almost as if he had expected this; the hob slept on.

"They did it again!" said an irate whisper at his elbow. Even Hamish was polished up like a silver wine jug today, but now his face was scarlet with wrath. He was speaking out of the corner of his mouth, of course, as all attention was supposed to be on the ceremony taking place in the road.

"Did what?"

"Insulted you! Deliberate public humiliation!" He managed to spit the words without moving his lips, quite a feat.

"You mean I'm supposed to feel slighted because I'm not allowed to kiss a man's boot?"

Hamish glanced sideways at him. "Don't snarl at me, messer Longdirk! What Lucrezia does isn't my fault. I got your name as far up the list as was humanly possible."

"I'm not snarling."

"Well, you should be! Tell me why *Il Volpe* lets his sister interfere like this! She's doing everything she can to make your job harder. Nevil will hear of this. His spies will tell him."

"Lucrezia is a formidable signora." Toby had not identified her among the massed beauties in the ladies' stands. But she would be there, watching him to enjoy his reaction. "If she's the puppet master, she's doing a remarkable job, but she isn't really hurting me. I don't care about the prizes she keeps snatching from me. Bowing and scraping folderol! No, I'm sure the Magnificent knows his sister well enough not to let her meddle in policy. Someone else has turned him against me, and it must be a traitor, someone working for the Fiend. That worries me a lot more than a woman's spite."

The pattern was repeated when the procession reached the palace. Toby was not at all surprised to discover that he had been struck off the list of dignitaries to make obeisance before the throne. This omission was clearly intended to be another snub, but he could not feel hurt by it. The opportunity to place another man's foot on his head seemed a very questionable honor.

After that he rode back to Fiesole with the rest of the Company, skipping the inevitable banquet without finding out what little treats had been planned for him there.

29

"The *duchessa* was very disappointed that you missed the banquet last night," Don Ramon remarked airily. On that splendid spring morning, he and Toby were leading a group of senior officers into Florence to wait upon General Neguder. He looked astonishingly pert for a man who had partied all night—which he must have done, because he had not returned to Fiesole until well after dawn.

There was no justice. Toby, who had gone to bed at a respectable hour like a dutiful little boy, felt bleary-eyed and bedraggled. The life of a penniless outlaw had been much simpler than that of a condottiere.

"I bet she was."

"Mustn't disappoint influential ladies."

"I am sure you did not, signore."

The don smirked and twirled up his mustache. "I believe we gave satisfaction." He was riding the devil-horse Brutus, which kept trying to bite Smeòrach. Both Toby and Smeòrach were growing very short of patience. Toby had surreptitiously slid his boot out of his stirrup and was waiting for the next provocation.

"What did darling Lucrezia have planned for me—gunpowder in the soup?"

"I believe vipers in the pasta. What's wrong with your mount?"

"I'm not sure." Smeòrach was trudging down the hill like a cart horse, not at all his usual high-spirited self. Possibly he had been infected by his rider's glum mood. Toby gave him an affectionate pat. "I think I'm neglecting him. The big dolt isn't getting enough exercise."

"Not enough? If you want my—"

At that moment Brutus aimed another nip at Smeòrach. Toby's spur slammed into Brutus's flank, and at once the don had an unexpected fight on his hands. It was several minutes before order was restored and the procession could continue down the trail. The don had probably not witnessed that low blow, but he was already glowering suspiciously at his companion and would find the wound when he dismounted. Some of the sycophants following would have noticed and would tattle to him later. Which reminded Toby of the worst of the nightmares that had troubled his sleep.

"Are you prepared to accept the Chevalier as suzerain, Captain-General?"

The don shot him an astonished glance, then exploded into laughter.

"You don't think D'Anjou will be appointed suzerain?"

"No, I don't, because I know who will be."

And now he wasn't going to tell—so there!

The hall to which the noble condottiere and his men were conducted was neither the largest not the grandest in the Palace of the Signory, but it was large enough and grand enough to dazzle any native of a poor, drab land like Scotland. Its walls and ceiling blazed with gilt moldings and vivid frescoes of glorious battles from the war-smeared history of Florence. Only a greasy layer of smoke stain from innumerable years of candles marred the brilliance.

Here the visitors were required to stand for a considerable time, long enough to make them feel less important than the roaming bluebottles. Eventually a herald hurried in and ordered them to kneel for the entrance of His Splendor General Neguder, military aide to the Illustrious Prince Sartaq, Swift Sword of the Khan, High Warrior of the Golden Horde, and so on. Later a trumpet brayed outside. Still later, it brayed again. And in due course the great man did waddle in with a train of attendants almost as splendidly arrayed as himself. The visitors, having been properly instructed, pressed their faces to the floor and squinted out of the corners of their eyes.

He was elderly, tall for a Tartar, and wide for a man of any race. Even flowing silks could not disguise the bulge of that belly. He took the throne with obvious relief, leaned back, and probably closed his eyes—it was impossible to be certain, because his eyes were tiny slits in the blubber of his face. His followers took the chairs arrayed to right and left of him. The visitors were left where they were, noses on an evil-smelling carpet reeking of generations of boots.

The herald said something inaudible, probably in Tartar.

The general then delivered a speech. Officially he delivered a speech. In practice one of his aged flunkies read it for him, remaining seated while doing so. Its meaning, if it ever had any, was gutted by the man's gruesome accent and skinned by Toby's inadequate command of Italian, but the shreds of meat remaining seemed to consist mainly of a review of great victories won by the Golden Horde in ancient times and the lessons to be learned from them. The tactics mentioned were rarely suitable for Italian terrain. There was no mention of firearms. There was no hint that the Khanate was prepared to support resistance in Italy with a strike at Nevil from the east, across Hungary.

The speech lasted about two hours. Toby wondered if a first snore would be a capital offense, or if he might be allowed a second. Not that the meeting was not educational. Nay, it was most exceeding instructive! Ever since Nevil's rampage began, the Khan's loyal subjects in Europe had been appealing to him for assistance. The lack of response had been a mystery much discussed, but it was a mystery no longer, not to Toby. These men were imposters. The once-invincible Golden Horde, whose ancestors had conquered all the world from Spain to Cathay, was a legend now. It had no more substance than a bubble on a stream.

In their time the Khans had ruled well, imposing peace on a very quarrelsome continent—more or less peace, and at a price, for the suzerains had been tax collectors before they were anything else. They had always managed to pocket a lionish share of whatever they gathered, but much of the gold had flowed east to Sarois.

With that insight came another. If the Khanate was only a mirage, then why was Toby Longdirk crouched on a rug being bored to distraction? Answer: Because power worked on men's minds, and the Khan's almost illusory power was still enough to make the Florentines serve his son's will. If Toby stood up now and tried to walk out, Florence would bring him to heel. He would be beheaded at best. So even the last reflections of glory could dazzle. These mummified incompetents were still in charge, and their orders would be obeyed until it was too late. All Toby's carefully nurtured plans would crumble to dust, and Nevil would take Italy without working up a sweat.

Hearing a faint moan to his left, he unobtrusively turned his head. The old Chevalier was beside him, his face twisted in agony.

"Trouble, signore?" Toby murmured.

"Cramps!" came the whispered response.

"Be grateful that they keep you awake."

The old scoundrel just scowled, a man without humor.

At last, thank good spirits, the speech ended. Now, perhaps, the mercenaries would be presented to the acclaimed General Neguder and could ask a few penetrating questions about his strategy and intentions. Alas, not so. A herald shook the noble warrior awake. He rose and shuffled out, followed by all his entourage. The audience was over.

The visitors scrambled to their feet and jigged up and down to restore circulation. Don Ramon—to Toby's delight—was deep purple with fury.

"What of Prince Sartaq, senor? Is he any more, um, impressive?"

The don gnashed some teeth. "His Highness is a worthy scion of his exalted forebears."

Splendid! They were going to need all of those they could get.

30

The Khan's son was an entertaining novelty at first, but his stallion interests quickly alarmed all mothers and husbands of young Florentine women. A week of Sartaq was enough to start them whispering that it must be time for the illustrious prince to go on and visit Milan. He must see Venice. Why not Padua? Verona was especially lovely in the spring. Anywhere. The city of flowers fidgeted, but the Magnificent tightened his grip and the complaints remained no more than complaints.

Rumors—never in short supply in Italy—were excessively, superfluently abundant and contradictory. Everyone anyone had ever heard of was going to be appointed suzerain, but the prince had decided to lead the armies of Italy in person, that he was going to flee the peninsula long before there was any chance of the Fiend arriving and catching him there. Also, Nevil's armies were massing to cross Mount Cenis Pass, Brenner Pass, and Simplon Pass, and to enter Italy by the coast road through Savoy. Choose the truth you preferred.

Toby Longdirk, the supposed defender of the city, was no wiser than anyone else. His petitions were

ignored, his plans frustrated. He was shut out of the
inner councils, if there were any, and the don now
seemed less certain of what was being planned, if anything was. If Lucrezia was his source, she might not be
as well informed as he had thought. Although he normally bragged openly of his conquests, he was almost
discreet in his talk of the *duchessa*. She must be dangerous indeed if she frightened him.

Toby had a formidable lady of his own to handle.
One rather typical afternoon was made worse by a
stormy interview with Countess Maud, alias Blanche,
Queen Mother of England.

By noon the air was stifling. He could find little com-
pensation in the knowledge that the trellis vines would
provide better shade later in the spring. Later in the
spring he might be far away or even dead. He would
be ready to break off and take a siesta if he could only
convince himself that he had done any good at all so
far.

He had wasted more than an hour repeating a
familiar argument with Alberto Calvalcante, master
of gunnery in the Company. Calvalcante had conceded that transporting guns in carts was an untidy
and inefficient business. Yes, the noble constable's
idea of building a permanent but transportable
mount so that a cannon or bombard could be hauled
to the battlefield and be ready to fire in minutes
instead of hours or days, was an appealing notion.
But, he insisted mulishly, such a carriage would fly

apart at the first shot unless it was built of enormous balks of timber, so it would require as many oxen to haul it as all the carts it replaced. The recoil would drive it back into its own lines. The wheels would fall off. On muddy roads—and most roads were muddy most of the time—it would sink right out of sight. Toby had managed to answer all the objections except one, which was that a gun had to be aimed. That was achieved now by building a trough for it to lie in pointing at the target, which was almost invariably a city under siege. This fancy carriage of his, the gunner said, would require a mechanism to change the elevation of the barrel, and Maestro Calvalcante would never believe that such a contraption could be built strong enough not to fly apart after a couple of shots.

Toby was baffled but not convinced. In the last twenty years or so, armorers had perfected ways of casting bronze cannons far stronger than the old ones built from iron strips, and yet the military had found no better way of moving them around. Doubtless Nevil would bring many guns with him and use them to batter down city walls. Florence was a big target and stayed where it was. The attackers would not be so obliging.

After Calvalcante came Marshal Diaz, to present half a dozen minor condottieri who had signed up to enjoy the Florentine gold and serve under the celebrated *comandante* Longdirk. All of them were foreign refugees except one, a crusty peasant farmer from Romagna who led two lances composed entirely of his

own sons, aged sixteen to twenty-three. Diaz swore
they were as tough a gang of warriors as he had ever
met, and Toby promised to come and meet them all in
the next day or two. He refrained from asking how
many mothers they shared.

Even Diaz, that stolid, imperturbable Catalan,
was becoming frayed and harassed these days. The
Company had expanded past the seven thousand
mark, with no end in sight. There were too few large
bands left to enlist as associates, and the small ones
had to be included under the don's banner; it was the
lesser of the two administrative evils. In theory, Toby
could now field more than seventeen hundred helmets
for Florence, half of them in the Don Ramon
Company itself, but theories never won wars. Men
did, good men. D'Amboise, Simonetta, and della
Sizeranne had all accepted his invitation and were
marching north with their troops. When they arrived,
he would have to warn them that he was out of favor
in Florence. He was certain that none of them would
choose to serve under the don.

As Antonio and his recruits departed, Chancellor
Campbell arrived with Brother Bartolo and Sorghaghtani—plus, of course, Chabi, who swirled down
from the sky and flattered Toby by choosing his shoulder to perch on. She gave the back of his doublet a
token of her affection, too. These were the Company's
Intelligence Arm, but their subdued manner as they
settled round the table told him that they had no significant news to report.

"Well?" Toby demanded. "It is almost April. The

roads are dry in the north. The passes are open. Which way is he coming?"

Hamish grimaced, making his narrow features seem almost wolfish. "I don't know! As of five days ago, there was still utter, absolute, outright nothing. I'm sorry, Toby. Demons, I'm sorry! I'm doing everything I can!"

"You expect me to shoot you? If you don't know, you don't know."

Hamish had posted agents at the mouth of every Alpine pass to talk with travelers. Doubtless they reported what they had learned as promptly as they could, but all of them were stationed at least five days away from Florence and some even farther. The first word to arrive might be a report that Nevil's army was already entering Italy.

Hamish sighed. "You want a guess, I'll give you a guess. It's going to be the Brenner again."

"Well, we know that country. Why the Brenner?"

"Because traders are going north and almost none are coming south. Either there's a dragon eating them in there, or Nevil's shut off the north end of the pass. And the only reason to do that is to hide an army."

"Or weather," Bartolo remarked gently. The friar's face was still as round as a full moon, but it had lost much of its old jollity. "Bad roads in Austria, floods on the Danube. And the Tyroleans may not be cooperating." Tyrol had been horribly mauled by Schweitzer. The survivors could not stop another army, but they could tear up the road and throw down bridges.

"So what have you learned?" Hamish demanded grumpily. "Tell me where Nevil's mustering, and I'll tell you what passes he'll come by. What about the Swiss?"

The fat man spread his fat hands in a sort of shrug. "My correspondents north of the Alps report no massing of troops. Either Nevil has decided to wait until later in the year, or he is masking his movements with gramarye."

Toby looked to the inscrutable shaman. He wondered how the girl—he had concluded that she was little more than a child—how she managed not to cook inside that monstrous heap of cloth. Every day she rearranged the beads and lace and replaced some of the dangling vegetation. She moved panels of cloth around, too. It was a strange way to change one's clothes, but she was the strangest person he had ever met.

"Well, Sorghaghtani? Can the Fiend hide a whole army?"

"How many demons does he have? Is there anything you cannot do if you have enough demons?"

"Are you telling me I have to plan on fighting an invisible army?"

"Even if he can hide from the friar's clerks, how can he hide from spirits, Little One? Can he hide from Chabi, who sees all?"

"Do you keep watch on the passes?"

"You think an owl can fly so far?"

He was adjusting to her maddening speech, in that it now annoyed him only about half the time. This was one of the times, but she obviously meant that the Alps were beyond her range.

"Maestro Fischart once spoke of putting a demon watch on the passes."

"Who will give me the demons?" she snapped. "Even if he did leave a casket full of them in the adytum, what are their names, mm? Who will tell me that?"

Toby shook his head. However skilled Sorghaghtani was, she could not compare with the baron for raw power. She was now very popular with the men, because she would accept no fees for healing and could cure the Spanish Pox just by playing her drum. Tutelaries assigned severe penances for the pox. Her evening consultations always drew long lineups outside the adytum.

"And the Swiss?" Hamish asked again.

This time the friar's shrug was even larger, a huge heaving of meat. "Like the Tyroleans, they will harass the Fiend as much as they can but cannot hope to deny him passage."

Toby growled in frustration. "Will they join in the battles, though? Will they even come to the conclave?"

This time Brother Bartolo just shrugged.

The prince had belatedly given permission for the conclave to proceed, beginning on the first of April. Arrangements were Arnaud Villars's responsibility, and before Toby had read a third of the papers Hamish and Bartolo had left for him, in stormed Arnaud in a typical frenzy, tearing his beard. It was amazing how that furry jungle survived his continual tantrums.

"Money!" he roared. The *dieci* were already behind in payments. That was to be expected. Veteran mercenaries were surprised when their pay wasn't in arrears.

"Prices!" he howled. Horses were going for more than five hundred florins. The cost of wheat, of barley, of wine . . .

"The conclave!" he screamed. The *darughachi* had invited every knight and archer and man-at-arms in all Italy. The villa would not hold them, there was no place to feed them, and the Company was expected to pay for everything . . .

Toby listened sympathetically because being a scratching post was part of his job. The big Gascon was merely venting his frustration on a target he could not damage instead of taking out his feelings on his subordinates. The last time this happened had been two days ago, and then Toby had assured his treasurer of his continuing support and confidence and reliance. This time, for a change, he waited until the fires had died down a little and then laughed. Arnaud fell silent and began turning purple.

"Pardon me, old friend! I've seen you worked up too often. Oftentimes I've talked you out of strangling people—haven't I?"

"Certainly not! Well, maybe. Once or twice."

"More than that. You always tell me that the world is about to end, and you always solve the problems on your own. Always! Now, what are you going to do this time?"

Glowering, Arnaud began to list the measures he was planning to take, such as moving tents to Cafaggiolo for sleeping quarters. He had hardly begun when—

"Ah, there you are, Constable Longdirk!" The countess swished into the courtyard in a haze of russet-and-purple silk.

The men exchanged fraught glances, then rose and bowed low.

"I need a word with you, Sir Tobias—alone?" That aloneness would not exclude Lisa, of course, who had come scowling along at her mother's heel in a yellowy green robe and was illuminating the courtyard like a goddess.

Realizing that he was gawking at her, Toby swung his attention back to her awesome mother. "Pray speak freely, my lady. Treasurer Villars understands no English."

He registered his folly as soon as the words were out, for the countess had had dealings with Arnaud, and he, being a Gascon, spoke better English than Toby did. Fortunately, he never did so from choice, and the countess's failure to react showed that he must have forced her to converse in French. She dismissed him from consideration.

"Constable . . ." She did not presume to sit, so everyone remained standing, but she was displaying an uncharacteristic lack of confidence. "Constable, tell me how you expect . . . how you see events unfolding in the next few months."

"Months? I cannot see months, my lady. I expect the Fiend's armies to invade Italy within two or three weeks. Armies loyal to the Khan will oppose him and, hopefully, will deal with Nevil as we dealt with his flunky Schweitzer."

The lady was not pleased. She squeezed her lips together. "Under whose leadership?"

Her daughter was not pleased either. So they had learned just how bad relations now were between Toby and his employer, the republic of Florence, but why was Lisa not smirking her royal smirk at his downfall?

"That is for Prince Sartaq to determine, ma'am."

Blanche hesitated, as if about to ask him what his chances were, but then she changed her mind. "Victory is by no means certain, is it?"

"No, my lady. Nor is it impossible." What was she up to and why didn't she get on with it?

"I fear for my daughter's safety in the event of a defeat, Constable."

Ah! "And your own, ma'am, of course."

She sighed the sort of sigh that would have felled a royal court in her youth. "I am little concerned with my own fate, Sir Tobias. After so many years of flight, one wearies of the chase. But Lisa still has many years of life to look forward to, and I do not wish to leave her at risk. In the light of what you have said, I believe that we should withdraw to the island of Malta until the danger is past and you have won your great victory."

"Probably a wise decision under the circumstances," Toby murmured politely. What the lady was not saying—or had not said yet, at least—was that she was now penniless and had run out of friends to prevail upon. That would come.

She acknowledged his concession with a nod. "Then would you be so kind, Constable, as to have your staff make the necessary arrangements?" She indicated Arnaud with a fluttery gesture. "I plan on leaving as soon as possible."

Doubtless. So did all the thousands of panic-stricken refugees already packed into every port in the peninsula. Ships were rarer than sea monsters.

"I shall instruct messer Villars accordingly, ma'am. It may take him some time to find a suitable vessel, you understand."

The countess smiled as if about to terminate the interview, then remembered another detail. A moment before she spoke, Toby guessed what was coming. That was not just dislike in Lisa's eyes, although there was certainly enough of that. It was tension. And Blanche had it, too, although she was hiding it better. There was something between them that they were not revealing.

"My own staff was left behind in Siena, Sir Tobias, as you know. In particular, I feel the need for a steward, a majordomo. I have my eye on one of your chancellors, Master Campbell. He was of some assistance to both my daughter and myself in Siena, and I am favorably impressed with his qualities. We understand he has an indenture of some sort with the Don Ramon Company. May I prevail upon you to consider

transferring this contract to my name, Constable? As a
favor to the future Queen of England?"

She wanted to buy Hamish? Toby drew in a long,
slow breath. Lisa was as taut as a bowstring, and he
would wager that there had been a very stormy
scene—several scenes, possibly a whole stage play—
between mother and daughter before a compromise
had been hammered out. Hamish was the price of
Lisa's cooperation. Not *buying* him, though. Blanche
expected him to *give* her Hamish. He did not know
whether to bellow with laughter or keep the game
going until Arnaud exploded, which might not be very
long at all.

"It is true, my lady, that everyone in the company
has put his name or made his mark on a scroll, but in
the case of senior personnel like Chancellor Campbell,
that is only because our clients insist on formal
records. I would not dream of holding him against his
will. If he wishes to enter your service, either perma-
nently or temporarily, I will never stand in his way."
So much for Master Hamish, who must have been the
one to tell Lisa about the contract and who had, therefore, almost certainly been using it as an excuse to
avoid making a commitment.

Meanwhile Lisa was having great difficulty in
suppressing a leer of joy and triumph, and her mother
was less pleased. So Lady Lisa thought she could talk
Hamish into anything, and the countess was not as
stupid as she pretended.

"Messer Arnaud?" Toby turned to Villars but was
careful to avoid meeting his eye. "Kindly book pas-

sage to Malta for Their Ladyships and a small party of attendants. Charge it to the casa."

"*Sì*, messer."

"You are most kind, Constable!" The lady offered her hand to be kissed and paraded solemnly out of the yard, with Lisa floating blissfully at her back.

"How much priority do I assign to that last instruction, Your Magnificence?" Arnaud inquired acidly.

"Don't move a finger on it," Toby growled, staring after the disappearing visitors. "Spin her all the tales you like, but do nothing."

Lisa was far too valuable a card to be allowed to float around loose. At least, he hoped that was his motive. He hated the idea that he might no longer trust Hamish.

THREE

APRIL

31

The Marradi villa at Cafaggiolo was more of a
palace than a family farm, but its formal gardens
blended into fields, vineyards, and olive groves; it
grew herbs and vegetables and raised some of the
finest livestock in Italy. The greatest artists of Europe
had decorated its halls. Now Toby had unwittingly
turned it into a barnyard. An intimate meeting of a few
had exploded into a conference of hundreds. It seemed
as if every city and town north of Sicily had sent its
captain-general or *collaterale,* then backed him up
with most of its signory, either because the politicians
did not trust him or just because they wanted the honor
of being guests of the Marradi. All these cavalcades of
dignitaries had brought trains of attendants and
guards. The Tartars were going to come later, perhaps
even the prince himself, if they could lure him away
from his romantic pursuits.

The villa had space for only a tenth, nay a fiftieth,

of this multitude. They overflowed into the stables and outhouses, they set up camps in the fields and orchards, they filled up the nearby village and colonized the hills. When hunger bit, they were sure to start looting. Even before he reached the gates that first morning, Toby sent a squire galloping back to Fiesole to summon a hundred more lances to help keep order. Arnaud went with him to organize more provisions.

Making excuses was not in Toby's nature, but again and again during those terrible three days he found himself repeating, "I did not plan this!" The men he really wanted to see had all come—the top military leaders of Italy, all men he respected even if some of them he could not like, and he was proud that he could now regard himself as one of them. So he had invited them to a conclave and landed them in a bear baiting.

Even as he was trying to reach the main door with Hamish and half a dozen others at his heels, pushing his way up the steps through a yabbering, screaming, hand-waving mob of soldiers and civilians, he saw a face he knew looming over the throng and changed direction to reach it. Ercole Abonio, the Duke of Milan's *collaterale,* was a gruff, rawboned man, almost as tall as Toby himself, more than twice his age. Lombard ancestors had bequeathed him red hair and fighting skills second to none, but he was also a true knight in the finest traditions of chivalry, as if all that was honorable in his bloodlines had come to him, and all that was tawdry and larcenous had gone to his brother, the ambassador. Ercole had taught Toby much of what he knew, and yet at Trent he had steadfastly refused to accept the supreme command, pleading Toby's case instead of his own on the grounds of ill health. He had then fought like a maniac, being wounded twice and having three horses killed under him. There was no one that Toby admired more than the big Milanese, and the quirk of amusement that lit up the man's craggy face was a knife twisted in his heart.

As the two full-sized warriors were clearing a path toward each other through the shrubbery of stunted clerics and burghers, Toby realized that Ercole's companion was Giovanni Alfredo, Captain-General of Venice. That made a difference. Alfredo was not a personal friend, so this cozy little meeting of the three military powers of the north was going to be business, and it was also going to be conducted in the presence of their respective followers and a riot of onlookers. One careless word might overturn many apple carts.

Then Ercole was within reach and could grab Toby in a ferocious bear hug, roaring out his delight at their meeting. Toby gave as good as he got; they exchanged massive shoulder thumps as they parted. He turned to offer a more restrained greeting to Alfredo, who was already shaking hands with Hamish. They were cast from the same mold, those two—slim, dark, and quick of eye—and not far apart in age, either. Alfredo had been the unquestioned rising star of the younger condottieri until Toby had come on the scene. On paper he was still ahead, for he

was captain-general of a richer, greater city than
Florence, but he was ambitious and would not be satisfied to fight for others all his life. His brilliance at
maneuvering around his opponents to turn up on their
flanks or in their rear had earned him the name of
Stiletto. He was reputed to have similar skill at politics, which many soldiers of fortune did not. Present
company included!

Then the formalities were over, all the underlings
acknowledged—

"I had not anticipated quite so many fellow
guests," Ercole remarked. His expression was
superbly innocent, but his eyes were twinkling.

"I did not plan this," Toby protested—for the first
time, but knowing it would not be the last. "I don't
know where they all came from." The entrance to the
villa was now plugged solid by this meeting of the
three warriors, their followers having packed in close
around them to hear the exchange. Onlookers were
openly eavesdropping on the outskirts.

"You should have learned by now, Sir Tobias,"
Alfredo said, "how rare a thing in Italy is a secret
meeting." The glint in his dark eyes spelled satisfaction. He would not be human if he did not resent this
brash foreigner who had upstaged him at Trent and
was now looking very foolish.

"I should have known." Toby sighed. "Especially
I should have known if you did, for you have only to
deal with Venetian politics, whereas I am faced with
the Florentine variety, which are so much more . . . er,
how do you say 'Byzantine' in Italian?"

"Milanese," Alfredo countered.

Ercole and his Milanese were not afraid to join in the laughter, but the Venetians at Alfredo's back remained carefully wooden-faced, recognizing that the joke was really directed at the Most Serene Republic and frightened they might be thought to be enjoying it. Venice was notoriously more Byzantine than Byzantium had ever been. Soldiers of fortune might be allies this year and next year enemies, but as professionals they bore no grudges. They all shared a healthy contempt for civilian rulers, whether they be the merchants of Venice and Florence, the aristocrats in Milan and Naples, or the acolytes of Rome. They would bleed or even die for those men's gold if they had to, but only courage and fighting skill would buy their admiration.

"Possibly in the next day or two we can arrange a private chat apart from the main meetings," Toby suggested.

"If a secret meeting is rare, one from which politicians are excluded is like the phoenix." Stiletto's eyes conveyed warning. Venice was always suspicious of its condottieri and had been known to chop off their heads. So, of course, had Florence. If those limp-eyed flunkies behind him had been sent along to keep an eye on him, who was keeping an eye on Toby?

"My dear brother is around here somewhere," Ercole remarked, including himself in this unstated brotherhood of the sword against the poison pen. "But I am more worried by the real foe. How many spies do you suppose the Fiend has sown in this conference?"

The three men exchanged grimaces as if they had all heard footsteps walking on their tombs. Alfredo smiled thinly. "Perhaps that's where everybody came from, messer Longdirk?"

32

Fiesole was a dull, dull place without Hamish. Lisa had her lady's maid for company—Beritola knew some wonderfully scandalous stories but not much else—and Sister Bona could be entertaining when she was not occupied being dam to her litter of children. All the other women had duties and interests that left them no time for frivolities such as conversation. There were men, some of them mildly amusing at times, but men just reminded her of Hamish and increased her misery. And of course there was Mother, who was admittedly much more endurable than she had been a few weeks ago. She had mellowed so much that she sometimes laughed now and would talk of her childhood and marriage—astonishing!

But the villa was dull. Life itself was dull without Hamish. Every moment they shared was as precious as rubies because they both knew their idyll could not last. The war would come; Maud would drag Lisa off to some safe refuge. Hamish refused to commit himself on what he would do then, but what could life hold for them but more agony? Their love was doomed. She had offered many times to renounce her royal heritage and marry him, and he would not hear of it. Men were stupid!

As she trotted her horse back to the villa on the second day of Hamish's absence, with her escort following, she was disturbed to see a large and impressive carriage standing at the door. Real glass in the windows, gilded moldings and bright enamels—a very splendid vehicle indeed, and the eight matched grays in the traces must be worth a king's ransom. Half a dozen saddle horses were being held by two men in blue-and-yellow livery. She ought to know that livery. Hamish had pointed it out to her in the city. Who had come calling with an escort of six men-at-arms?

A crowd had gathered at a respectful distance to stare—soldiers, women, children. With so many of the senior men in the Company currently absent, she did not doubt for a moment that this ominous intrusion concerned her. A strange knot was tightening in her insides, palms damp, heart pounding. Hamish! She needed Hamish, but he was leagues away at that fatuous conclave he admitted wasn't going to achieve anything. Even Longdirk, she decided. She would not mind at all seeing that overgrown lout planted near the coach, because he always got his own way, and so far he had provided her with admirable protection and hospitality, even if he was a merciless butcher and his manners would shock a rookery.

Her approach had been noted. Down the steps came Mother and several other people—saturnine Marshall Diaz, madonna Anna, and three others not recognizable. Behind them strode the six guards, glittering bright and dangerous.

She could not avoid the encounter. When faced with the inevitable, pretend it's what you want. That was what Hamish said when she warned him she was going to have to kiss him again. Or he would insist that no true lady would kiss a man of her own volition, and he would not allow it. In either case he would then crush her in his arms and preempt her kiss with one of his own, long and lingering and passionate. How dare he be missing when she needed him!

She reined in behind the coach and jumped down from the saddle before there could be any nonsense about bringing stepladders. She shook her skirts out, straightened her bonnet, and walked around the vehicle to face the group now waiting for her. One look at Mother's face was enough to confirm her worst fears.

Maud held out a hand to her. Lisa moved quickly to take it before anyone else could notice how it was shaking.

"We have company?"

"Elizabeth . . ." Her mother's voice was a croak. Her eyes were as round as a trout's. "We are honored by a visit from Her Grace, the dowager Duchess of Ferrara . . ."

Lisa had never met a duchess before and to be greeted by this first one with a full court curtsey, skirts right down in the mud, was shocking. Ferrara? Hamish had mentioned that name. She was petite, face rather childish, hair bright red but apparently natural, magnificently arrayed in a gown of deep blue satin with a daring décolletage and padded epaulettes. Its slashed sleeves displayed golden lining, and at least a hundred pearls adorned it. There were another fifty on her *balzo* cap. A duchess did not go down in the mud like that to anyone less than a queen. The bag was now catless, obviously.

"Please do rise, Your Grace."

Who had betrayed them?

"And, er, His Magnificence, um, messer Marradi, her brother," Maud said.

Ugh! Lisa felt as if she had just fallen off a horse. Backward. Now she realized. This insignificant middle-aged man in drab brown doublet *kneeling* to her was the Magnificent, despot of Florence! His sister was the notorious Lucrezia Marradi. Hamish had told some stories about her that had made Lisa's hair stand up, or try to. Beritola had told others that curled it.

"Oh, please rise, Your Magnificence."

Maud did not present the third visitor, an elderly, portly man, but his threadbare garb and the way he lingered in the background indicated that he was of no importance. And Marshal Diaz would be no help. He always looked as if he had been carved out of oak. Today he had been cast in bronze.

She did not attempt Italian. Mother had been speaking French.

"Your Grace, Your Magnificence—I am most honored to meet you, although you catch me at an unfortunate moment. Dishabille! Had I known in advance of your coming, I should of course have been most

delighted to enjoy, er, share your visit. I have heard so
much about . . . I mean next time . . ." It was not going
to work.

"You poor child!" said the duchess. "How can
you have endured this horrible place? Tonight you will
sleep in silken sheets on a swansdown bed, as a queen
should." Her smile would melt a portcullis.

"But . . ." But she was about to be taken away and
locked up, and she would never be allowed to see
Hamish again. She turned to glare at her mother. Why
had she admitted her identity after denying it for so
long? Had Lisa been here, she would have stiffened her
backbone for her. Deny it! They could prove nothing!

"I have accepted Her Grace's invitation, Lisa."

"Well, I have not! Go if you wish, Mother. I will
stay here. I am the guest of Constable Longdirk, and it
would be most discourteous of me to leave when he
himself is absent, and without thank—"

The notorious Lucrezia laughed most gaily.
"Longdirk? I don't think that overgrown brute will
cause—"

"Be silent," the Magnificent said sharply, stopping her instantly. He turned a pair of alarmingly sharp
eyes on Lisa. "Your Majesty, we learned of your presence here and your identity only this morning, and we
came at once. What we have learned, others will. I
confess that our interest has now made this inevitable,
but it would have happened anyway. You are no
longer—"

"Learned how?" Lisa demanded. "From whom?"
She was digging nails into her palms, desperately try-

ing to dream up some valid defense, some way of staying here until Hamish returned.

"From a source I trust too much to reveal, madonna." He was amused by her resistance and barely managing to pretend otherwise. He gestured at the third member of the group, the elderly fat man. "For many years messer Minutolo was my family's agent in London. He was present at your parents' wedding, and we brought him along to confirm your mother's identity, so we should not cause trouble or distress to anyone if our information was false."

Marshal Diaz took up the cudgel. "My lady, His Magnificence also brought a warrant from the signoria. The Don Ramon Company is in their employ, my lady. I shall inform Constable Longdirk immediately of what has transpired, but in the meantime I respectfully counsel you to be guided by Her Grace and His Magnificence."

Stupid, stolid, stagnant Diaz! He should have been an acolyte, not a mercenary! The footman and postilion had opened the coach door and dropped the steps. The guards had closed in around the group.

"Come, dear." Maud laid a hand on her arm.

"Where are we going?"

"My house is at your disposal, Majesty," Marradi said.

She had seen that gloomy pile. Hamish had pointed it out to her. It looked like a fortress. "My clothes—"

Lucrezia laughed. "You will have all the clothes you can stand to try on, child, garments more suitable for a palace, I daresay."

"My maid! Beritola?"

"We can send for her if you wish, but I can give you a dozen better."

Reluctantly—oh, so reluctantly!—Lisa let her mother urge her toward the coach. Hamish would rescue her! No. Disloyal though it seemed, she did not believe that. The only person she could imagine who might be able to rescue her from the Marradi's clutches was Toby Longdirk.

Unless he had been the one to betray her.

33

The conclave was a disaster. Hour by hour it became more obvious that the cities would never agree, and the Khan's intervention had only made things worse, because Sartaq knew nothing, his advisors were incompetent, and every one of them wanted to meddle. Nevil would be receiving very encouraging reports from his agents.

The agony was that it should have worked. The men Toby had invited had all come: Giovanni Alfredo, Ercole Abonio, Bruno Villari from Rome—whose only good quality was that he fought like three rabid badgers—and from Naples, Egano Gioberti, Jules Desjardins, and even Paride Mezzo, the *collaterale,* who had ridden all the way in agony, knowing he was dying but anxious to do his duty to the end. All for nothing! Even the Swiss had responded. On the second day Beltramo di Nerbona rode in at the head of a delegation from no less than ten of the thirteen cantons, which was an astonishing show of cooperation. They left before dawn. They knew a lost cause when they saw one.

At first Toby assumed that the senior delegates would be able to meet privately together, ignoring all the hangers-on and political parasites, but even that proved to be impossible. Every man had a spy or two at his shoulder put there by his own government, quite apart from the dozen or so others assigned to him by other states—at times the gramarye in the air made the hob itch so much that Toby could hardly think. Hundreds of minor condottieri and would-be condottieri swarmed like mosquitoes, all trying to gain promotion by signing on with one of the major states or larger companies, while the Tartar officials and innumerable Italian politicians just kept getting in the way. It was a madhouse, worse than juggling beehives.

The meetings and conferences were all held in public. No one knew who was supposed to be included, so everyone turned up rather than insult the Khan's representatives. Neguder was brought all the way from Florence in a litter and carried back again three days later, having not sobered up once. He slept on a throne as his interpreter read his speech again, the same speech he had given in Florence, while all the senior soldiers in Italy and half the second-string politicians crouched with their noses on the floor.

On the second day there was almost a riot. Nevil would certainly be told about the two cardinals who turned up and were very nearly hanged on a tree by enraged mercenaries. The Don Ramon Company was far from alone in being short of hexers, but the College remained obdurate. Rome's own Captain-General Villari admitted that he lacked adequate spiritual protection and did not intend to move his forces far from the walls of the Eternal City itself.

Sartaq arrived about noon on that last day. He had sent no warning, so the sight of the long procession trotting up the slope to the villa with pennants flying and armor flashing threw the whole conference into panic. Fortunately Toby was one of the first to notice, and with Hamish's help he organized a makeshift guard of honor on the steps—military leaders on one side, politicians on the other. There was barely even time to argue about precedence. One portly *priore* did try to move closer to the top, but after Toby picked him up and carried him back down to where Hamish had put him there was no more trouble.

The grand parade halted; the prince dismounted. One of the Tartar courtiers had emerged from the villa to gabble hasty instructions. As Sartaq reached the start of the honor guard, everyone knelt and touched his face to the ground. Because Florence was hosting the conclave, Hamish had put the don at the top of the steps, with old Cecco de' Carisendi opposite him. Toby crouched beside the don for what seemed like a very long time as the prince paced up the steps, and he was hard put to contain a rising tide of anger. He could almost dream of giving in to his frustration and letting the hob go on a rampage, blasting and smiting everything in sight. All his work was being wasted, his efforts balked. Surely there had never been a more useless council of war in the history of war itself! Men who ought to be preparing for a terrible struggle were being humiliated to honor a stripling foreigner whose only qualification was that he claimed to be descended from some notable butchers three hundred years ago. The *darughachi* who had been sent to save Italy was destroying it, and Italy was letting it happen.

Temptation itched like nettle rash. The Don Ramon Company controlled the villa and would follow Longdirk's orders. He could put the prince under arrest and declare Italy free of the Khan's hegemony. At best the states would unite in the face of the Fiend's threat. At worst his coup would divide them worse than before and make Nevil's task easier. Republics like Florence might split wide open. Sartaq's Tartar bodyguard would certainly resist, and some of the delegations might side with them, so the bloodshed would start immediately.

It was an impossible dream. However bad the *darughachi*'s leadership might be, it could not be replaced now. That was another mystery of power—it was almost indestructible.

The royal riding boots came to a halt in front of his nose; he heard a brief exchange in Tartar. Then the prince went indoors, and the honor guard could rise and hastily brush dust off their knees and hands before bowing to Sartaq's entourage as it came up the stairs after him. The drab, unimpressive figure in front was the Magnificent himself, Pietro Marradi.

He acknowledged them all with a small bow, a smile, and almost invariably a name—right, left, right, left . . . Once or twice he turned his ear to a chancellor at his back, who would whisper a name he had forgotten, and no doubt he had been provided with lists of all the more important guests, but it was still a masterly performance. His smile turned toward Toby—and vanished.

Toby paused halfway out of his bow, then straightened up more slowly. "Your Magnificence?"

"Messer Longdirk!" It was understood that *Il Volpe* never lost his composure and would continue to smile politely under any circumstances. But he had displayed anger in the piazza three weeks ago, and he was making no effort to hide it now. "You presume far, messer, when you keep secrets from me!"

"Me, Your Magnificence? Secrets?" What was going on now? Toby could think of nothing he had withheld that was of any significance. Bartolo submitted all the required reports to the *dieci*. "I can only assure—"

"Very significant secrets!"

"I cannot imagine to what Your Magnificence refers." Nor could he imagine why he had to be humiliated with this accusation before such an audience.

"Indeed?" Marradi sneered. "Does the name *Blanche* mean nothing to you?"

It felt like a punch in the kidneys. "What has hap-

pened?" Was Lisa in danger? Where was Hamish? . . .
don't let Hamish do anything rash . . . Lisa!

His shock had shown on his face. The Magnificent smiled grimly at this evidence of guilt.

"What has happened is that your private conspiracy has been uncovered, messer. Fortunately the lady in question and her daughter have now been escorted to quarters fitting to their rank, where they will be much less at risk than in a camp full of mercenary rabble."

Demons! Lisa was in no immediate danger if she had been kidnapped by Marradi himself. For a moment Toby could think of nothing more except the scores of ears and eyes around them. Nevil must certainly have agents here in the villa, and would guess who Blanche was. Hamish. Was Hamish within earshot? How to keep Hamish out of trouble? He found his tongue.

"Your Magnificence, if we must discuss a lady, surely we can do so in private?" Betrayed! Who could have revealed the countess's true identity?

The Magnificent was seething. "There is no need to discuss the lady, messer. She and her daughter are quite safe now. What we shall need to discuss is your conduct in concealing them from us when your obvious duty was otherwise." The Magnificent stalked past the don and on into the villa.

Toby looked around anxiously for Hamish.

"How very extraordinary!" Villari remarked. "Do you always let him talk to you like that, Constable?"

Toby resisted an impulse to flatten the odious little man. Villari was a competent fighter when he had no choice in the matter. So was a rat.

The don snorted and charged to his deputy's defense. "He is only a moneylender—what do you expect? Which bawd is he pursuing, Constable?" The copper mustache curled in a smile; the mad blue eyes were raging.

"Not the one he thinks he is, signore. I fear there has been a most unfortunate mistake."

If that disclaimer convinced anyone at all, it was no one in Italy. The audience grinned from ear to ear, a hundred ears, one enormous multiple grin all the way around them, a forest of teeth.

"Perhaps it was you who mistook the name, messer Scotsman," Villari suggested loudly. "You may have misheard because her thighs were over your ears."

Pounding him into the ground would be too good for him. And there was Hamish in the background, staring at Toby with eyes like open wounds and white cheekbones showing through his tan as if it were varnish. Think of something, quickly, think of some reason to keep Hamish busy so he could not vault on Eachan and spur like a maniac to Florence. "Chancellor!" At least now there was no need to worry that Hamish might vanish in the night with Lisa and her mother en route to Malta. But, oh, Lisa! She was lost now. The great monster Politics had wrapped its tentacles around her, and she would never escape. A nightingale caught in a net. A sunbeam lost in fog. She had been under his protection. Whatever would they do to her? Hamish arrived.

"Lists?" Toby babbled. "You have some lists we have to go over. The seating for the banquet. Guard roster . . ."

Hamish looked at him as if he had taken leave of his senses, which perhaps he had. "They will have to wait." He switched to Gaelic. "Have you gone deaf? They are calling all senior military personnel to wait on the prince."

"Er, what?" He had not been listening . . .

"A council. Sober up, Toby!"

"Demons! You mean it's actually going to happen?"

"Of course." Hamish took him by his elbow, as if he were a child or a tottering geriatric and guided him into the villa, walking with the tide. "This way. But for spirits' sake keep your back to the wall."

Not only was Sartaq going to confer with the military, he had graciously stipulated that the meeting would be held in western fashion—meaning upright, not kneeling. As Toby strode into the hall and saw the senior condottieri and *collaterale* standing before the throne, he felt a flutter of hope for the first time in weeks. It wavered when he realized that they were far from alone, and more people were flooding in behind him. Did Sartaq truly intend to discuss strategy in public? The politicians were much in evidence already— Marradi and a group of Florentines, the Venetian commissioners, the Neapolitan ambassador, who was King Fredrico's bastard son. Seeing Ercole Abonio towering over the throng, Toby began pushing in his direction, and none too gently, but before he arrived at his destination he heard a chancellor thump his staff on the floor and had to stop where he was. The crowd hushed expectantly.

In happier times the brilliantly decorated hall must have been the site of fine banquets. The usual tables and benches had been removed for the conclave and replaced by a single chair of state. Even so, the prince's bodyguards had to push a path through the crowd for him. He advanced to the throne, but instead of sitting he just turned and stood in front of it, looking over the assembly, acknowledging the bows with a solemn nod. He was clad in Italian costume of tights, shirt, tunic, and a short cloak, all of somber browns and greens that had probably been carefully chosen to suit his coloring. He was short, but there was more than padding spreading the shoulders of his doublet, and his legs were impressive. It was the first time Toby had seen him at close quarters. He did not look like an idiot. His eyes were quick. Younger sons of Oriental potentates were traditionally sequestered at puberty with unlimited opportunities for debauchery so that they would rot their brains, ruin their health, and never become a threat to the succession. Sartaq did not look as if that had happened to him, but he was the product of a decayed system, so perhaps he had just never learned to think for himself.

His gaze came to rest on Toby. Toby stared right back. The men in front of him sidled out of the way, dissipating like morning dew.

"You are the one called Longdirk?"

Toby bowed. "Your Highness's most humble servant."

"You were in charge at the Battle of Trent." The accent was strange, but his Italian was better than Toby's, spoken without hesitation.

"I had that honor, Your Magnificence."

"If you were in command of all my father's armies in Italy now, what would you do to deal with the Fiend's invasion?"

The obvious answer began, "I would call a secret and intimate conclave of the leading soldiers . . ." But that was what he had done when the problem had been winning agreement between the five major states. Now the problem was different. The prince could command obedience.

The second most obvious answer began, "I certainly would not announce my plans with half the population taking notes." But that would be lèse-majesté and disaster.

Toby stepped forward, clear of the crowd. "Your Highness, we know that the traitor is mustering armies and moving them south. We assume, and must assume, that he plans to bring them over the Alps, but we do not yet know which pass or passes he will choose. Roughly, he can come by the Brenner Pass, which will lead him through Trent and Verona and pose an immediate threat to Venice." Let the spies test their memories on this—there was nothing in it that Nevil did not know already. "He may come by one of the central passes, such as the St. Gotthard, but the

established route uses boats to traverse Lake Como
and is not practicable for a great army. The western
passes—"

"I have seen the maps, Constable. I asked what
you would do."

Sweat! This was either his chance to win the
post he craved or some horrible trap, and the fact
that he had been given no warning made the trap
explanation the more likely. He knew exactly what
he would do if he were *comandante*. He was not
going to reveal it here. He bowed again. "I crave
Your Highness's pardon. In brief, I would prepare to
relieve either Milan or Venice. The Fiend must protect his supply lines, or we can starve his army by
wasting the country around him. He dare not leave
Milan and Venice as threats in his rear. He might risk
bypassing one of them, but never both. He must lay
siege to one or the other, and that will be our chance
to bring him to battle."

The prince rubbed his wispy mustache with a
knuckle. "I did not ask for a lecture on the traitor's
problems, messer. I asked for answers to mine. What
will you do *now*—today and days following—if I
reappoint you *comandante?*"

"Your Highness, the Fiend undoubtedly has spies
in this hall."

"You refuse to answer my question?"

Sweat, sweat, sweat! "Signore . . . I would order
the states to put their armies on twenty-four hours'
notice to march. I would provision a rallying point at a
suitable location." It would be at Piacenza, of course,

north of the Apennines. All roads led to Piacenza, and Nevil must cross the Po there.

The hall was very quiet.

"You would do no more than that?" the boy demanded incredulously. "How long will it take King Fredrico's troops to march from Naples to this camp you have prepared for them, 'north of the Apennines?'"

"About a month, Your Highness."

"So you will allow the Fiend a clear month to lay waste my father's dominions! To loot and ravage unhindered. You hope that Milan or Venice can hold out against a siege for a month before you even muster your army to come to their aid?"

Of course not! It would take Nevil longer to bring his full strength over the Alps, so the other armies could be there to meet him. Meanwhile—

"We have heard you, messer," the prince said, silencing him with a wave of his fingers. "We have listened to youth. Now let us hear what age and experience can tell us. Monseigneur D'Anjou?"

Toby fell back a few steps and almost knocked over whoever was behind him, conscious of a chilling certainty that this charade had been planned in advance down to the last detail. In his darkest moments, he had feared that the haggard old French aristocrat now hobbling forward might be appointed suzerain. Making him *comandante* would be even worse.

D'Anjou had not been taken by surprise. He bowed low and spoke in French, but flatly, as if by rote. "Most Exalted Highness, there are only four or five passes by which the traitor Nevil can reasonably enter Italy. Another three or four are possible but unlikely. If you honor me with supreme command of our glorious Khan's armies in Italy, then of course I shall at once prepare to contest those passes. Why should we let him in without a fight?—to loot and ravage unhindered, as you so aptly put it a moment ago. I should also move all cavalry available to the plains of the Po, so that we may use their mobility to concentrate them against the Invader when he comes. I should order the Neapolitan and Roman forces to begin advancing north at once." The Chevalier bowed again. Then he flashed a predatory smile across at Toby, who had managed to catch only the gist of the speech.

He had made out enough to know that it was rubbish. When Nevil came, his army would be huge. He would bring it over several passes at the same time, so to contest its passage would be a criminal waste of men, serving no real purpose. To put all the Khan's forces in the field now, before there was even a threat, would produce problems in provisioning so bad that the plains of the Po might be looted and ravaged by their own defenders before the war even reached them. And the talk of cavalry just meant that D'Anjou had no faith in, or understanding of, infantry. He still thought a charge of mounted knights could settle anything.

The prince smiled approvingly—better an incompetent aristocrat, rightful King of France, than a peasant bastard from the barbarian ends of the world, however lucky the kid might have been last year.

"Chevalier, you are a man of courage and vision." He raised his head to scan the spectators. "Know you all that by virtue of the power invested in me by my beloved and puissant father, His Illustrious Majesty Ozberg Khan, I hereby appoint and name Louis, Duke of Anjou, supreme commander of all military forces in our father's dominions in Italy and charge him to take all necessary measures to repel the traitor Nevil. We likewise order all the said forces to obey his commands and all states and powers and dominions to cooperate with him in every way."

A moment's silence was followed by a ragged cheer.

The prince seated himself on the throne. The Chevalier advanced and knelt, obviously to perform the ceremony of obeisance. Toby's stomach churned. Disregarding all rules of protocol and courtesy to princes, he spun around and shoved his way through the crowd, heading for the door.

Since joining the Don Ramon Company, D'Anjou had never lost a battle. In the eleven years before that, he had never won one.

34

In the field where the Company's mounts were picketed, Hamish was already saddling up Eachan, intent on heading back to Florence to locate Lisa. Toby fetched Smeòrach and joined him. He received a quizzical glance.

"Running away? Not like you."

Toby hauled on Smeòrach's girth a little harder than necessary. "Nothing more for me to do here."

"Stand still, lummox!" That remark was addressed to Eachan. "How can Sartaq expect D'Anjou to defend anything more valuable than a wheelbarrow?"

"Possibly because he's a degenerate, pampered, royal moron."

About to mount, Hamish paused and frowned as he did when he had a juicy puzzle to gnaw on. "Even so, there's something wrong, you know? D'Anjou's only qualification for anything is his royal blood. Militarily he's laughable. Logically, he should have been appointed suzerain and told to leave the fighting to you. That would have worked. There's something going on I can't see."

Toby snorted. "It's called stupidity. It's the national pastime."

"No. It's as if . . . You don't suppose Sartaq's actually working for the Fiend, do you?"

The thought was tempting. "It would explain a lot, wouldn't it? But they whipped him into the sanctuary smartly when he arrived. The spirit would have blown a bugle if he was a traitor. Now let's get out of here before our esteemed captain-general finds me."

The don would be incensed that his deputy had been insulted, appalled at the thought of serving under a commander so incompetent, and yet hopelessly trapped by his loyalty to the Khan and his conviction that aristocrats were invariably superior beings. Conflicts enough to unhinge the sanest of men would drive him into a gibbering frenzy. Let somebody else handle him this time.

"Do you feel," Hamish asked, as they rode off along the road, "that this conclave has achieved anything at all?"

Toby thought for a moment. There had to be some use in anything. "Yes. I think future historians will use it to date the fall of Italy."

They spoke very little. Hamish was calm but understandably bitter at the cruel blow fate had dealt him. Toby had only clammy comfort to offer. He mentioned the bereavements he had known—Granny Nan, Jeanne, friends in the Company—and of how all wounds must heal in time. But that was sometime, this was now.

"You always knew it could not be," he said. "You never expected to share her throne in Greenwich Palace. Could you have endured watching her washing clothes in the burn?"

Hamish gave him a sour look. "Do you think she wouldn't wash shirts for me, or I wouldn't dig fields for her? If the Don Ramon Company ever pays me what it owes me, I'll have enough to buy a farm, and farmers can afford servants. Or I could go back to Barcelona and work for Josep Brusi. He offered me as much to wield a pen as you pay me to risk my hide. I

should have put Lisa on a horse and ridden off into the
night. I should have taken her where the Fiend would
never find us."

After a long silence, Toby said, "Yes, you probably should have."

He wondered what he would have done, had he
been in Hamish's place. Had he been like other men.

They did not turn aside to Fiesole, but went on to
Florence and the Marradi Palace. Even Hamish, who
had made a point of befriending all the Magnificent's
gatekeepers, could not gain admission that evening.
He learned only that two golden-haired foreign ladies
had arrived the day before and were staying on as
guests. It was encouraging that their identity had not
yet become public knowledge, but this could not be
long delayed after Marradi's display of temper at
Cafaggiolo.

They rode back to the villa to break the bad news
and reassure Diaz that he had made the correct decision when he surrendered Lisa and her mother to the
Magnificent. Then there was nothing else to do except
clean up and eat and go on with the rest of their lives.

35

"We call this the portrait gallery," Lucrezia said. "At
the far end you will find some very imaginative
impressions of what my forebears wished their fore-

bears had looked like. At this end the art is more pleasing and probably more plausible. This one, for instance—Orpheus calming the waves. By Ruffolo."

Lisa said, "Charming."

"You prefer Apollo driving his chariot?"

"Bizarre."

The duchess eyed her guest thoughtfully, as might a hangman or taxidermist. "How about this one, Sisyphus rolling the boulder?"

"It is quite realistic." After an entire day in the Marradi palace, Lisa had not been tamed yet. She had a lot of fight left in her, although it was not likely to do her much good.

"The naked man or just the boulder?"

"Boulders are dull; they don't do anything. The man reminds me somewhat of High Constable Longdirk."

However well the courtesies were being observed, Lisa was a prisoner and the little smiling duchess her jailer. The Marradi Palace was a treasure-house of gorgeous things, but it was also a trap, a web shining in sunshine, and Lucrezia was the spider, the smiling spider. All of Lisa's struggles merely amused her. The one exception was Longdirk. He was the one topic that could cut through the woman's insufferable smugness. Any reference to the condottiere riled Lucrezia excessively. The man did have some uses, therefore, if he could bring a flush to Lucrezia's cheek and a flash to her eye.

As now. "I think you are indulging in wishful thinking, monna!"

Lisa attempted what she hoped was a cryptic, wouldn't-you-like-to-know smile. "About the calves, I mean. Have you never noticed those great bulges in Toby's hose? When he walks they run like rabbits up and down—"

"Come and sit here, Lisa." Mother had noticed the battle in progress. She was huddled on one of the gold-silk sofas as if she were freezing to death, although the gallery was hot and stuffy. She had aged twenty years since leaving Fiesole the previous day. Having spent her adult life staying one jump ahead of the hounds, she was convinced—as she had explained to Lisa fifty times in the night—that as soon as the two of them were identified in public the Fiend would catch them. Now it was about to happen.

Lisa ignored her. She turned her back on the Sisyphus anatomy lesson. "And what happens now, Your Grace?"

"Do please call me Lucrezia, Your Majesty."

Lisa smiled and waited.

Lucrezia smiled right back at her. "Now? Now we have a private little dinner party, just six of us. Tomorrow or the day after, there will be a banquet so the signory can welcome Queen Elizabeth of England and Queen Mother Blanche to fair Florence." Queen Mother Blanche moaned in the background, but the duchess ignored her. "You must excuse my brother for keeping you waiting like this. They only just got back from Cafaggiolo."

So the conclave was over. Longdirk would have returned to Fiesole and learned that his guests had been abducted—or rather that his prisoners had been stolen, because Lisa had no doubts that she had been just as much a prisoner in the villa as she was here. A prison with Hamish in it had much more appeal, though. Could even Longdirk do anything against the Magnificent? Did he want to? Had the goods been stolen or sold?

"Do tell me what happened at Cafaggiolo. I know that Constable Longdirk held few hopes of the conclave."

Lucrezia's smile had *triumph* all through it like the gold thread in her gown. "Then he would not have been surprised. Disappointed, yes, of course. The prince has appointed a *comandante in capo,* and it is not Longdirk."

Hamish had made no secret of the fact that Toby had wanted that title, but evidently he had not bought it with Lisa, which was encouraging. "I do hope Florence does not feel slighted. And who is the new champion?"

"You will meet him shortly."

"Oh. And who else?" Lisa realized she might be facing a long evening.

Lucrezia's smile confirmed that supposition. "Just the prince. You can ask him yourself why he did not choose your lover to be *comandante.*"

"My who?"

Another catlike smile. "So it *was* wishful thinking!"

"If there is any wishful thinking, it is more on his part than mine." Lisa would not admit that she and

Longdirk detested each other, snarling like cats every time their paths crossed. But she was in retreat now, like an outclassed fencer, and Lucrezia's rapier was flashing, drawing blood with every stroke—

"Then he will not be further disappointed when he learns of your betrothal?"

Squeak! "My *what?*"

"Dear child, what do you expect? The royal houses of Europe have been decimated and must be rebuilt. You have a lifetime's work ahead of you."

"You make me sound like a broodmare!" Lisa very nearly stamped her foot.

The duchess shrugged. "Call it what you will, I am sure the *darughachi* will want to br— will have plans for your early marriage. You can ask him that, too."

"I have no dowry!"

"You bring all England as your dowry, child." Oh, how Lucrezia was enjoying herself! Now it was Lisa who was outranked.

"Not very easy to collect."

"An interesting challenge. You are prime marriage material. The greatest houses in Europe would accept such a bride, even in normal times. Now, if necessary, you can be used to confer royalty on some man of lesser rank."

The footmen stationed outside the door opened it and bowed in the Magnificent, who in turn bowed to Lisa and then her mother.

"Your Majesties, my house continues to be honored by your presence. I trust that your comfort lacks nothing?"

Insignificant, unimpressive, he was yet a dangerously clever, foxy man. Lisa did not trust him even as far as she trusted Longdirk, which was no distance, but she had to admit that Marradi was charming, with manners sweet as honey. And Lucrezia was enemy enough for now.

"I feel I have been invited to stay in Olympus, Your Magnificence! Everyone has been most kind." Lisa heard her mother babble something similar.

He frowned and turned to his sister. "Is madonna Elizabeth dressed as becomes her rank? Could you not have—"

"We tried!" Lucrezia said. "She chose the style and fabric herself. Her coiffure, also. I offered to lend her pearls and jewels. She prefers to dress like this." Like a clerk's daughter, said the smile.

Her brother shrugged. "Then we honor your decision, monna. In truth, the lily needs no gilding."

That was very annoying of him, because Lisa had been trying to establish some independence by insisting on the simplest possible dress. Now he had turned her defiance into a virtue. Before she could comment, the door opened again. She braced herself for new battles.

Two men. The young one with the slanty eyes, squidgy nose, and stringy mustache must be the prince. Any son of the Khan took precedence over her and would do so even if she had been crowned queen in the sanctuary at Westminster. She sank into a full curtsey.

"Elizabeth! By the spirits, rise, rise!" Sartaq

stretched out both hands to her. "Messer Marradi was raving so about your beauty that my thought was he was exaggerating. Reticent he was."

She rose and returned his smile as well as she could. "Your Highness is most gracious." Not exactly. He was shorter than she was. He had bad teeth and those slit eyes—even Longdirk's battlement features were better-looking. She also knew he already had two wives, and if he decided to add her to his collection, then no one in all Europe could stop him. Smile!

She expected him to release her and turn to receive Mother, who was waiting to be told to rise—it was a grim sign that she now ranked behind her own daughter. But the prince let go only Lisa's left hand and turned the other way, to the third man.

The third man was the ancient Chevalier D'Anjou, and suddenly she knew he was the new *comandante*. Hamish never had a good word to say about him. His nose had been shattered so often that he had almost no nose left. He stood as if his back hurt and held his head cocked sideways as he leered at her with a mouth that had lost most of its teeth. He had a grizzled beard, damp near his mouth. He made even Sartaq seem handsome.

The prince laughed. "*Duchessa?* Advise me. Your western etiquette for me makes a puzzle. Do I present the Queen of England to the King of France or the other way?"

36

Toby had gone to bed just after the sun did, expecting to sleep well for a change—he had done his best, and events were out of his hands now. When he realized he was awake the angle of moonbeams from the window told him it was not yet midnight. For a while he lay and cursed, certain he would not go back to sleep. He began to worry about Sorghaghtani. She had not been in the adytum, and no one could recall seeing her for two or three days. Unlike Sartaq, she was a problem he could do something about. He sat up and reached for his shirt.

"Where are you going?" Hamish was lying on his back with his arms under his head, alert and brooding.

"For a walk."

"Why don't you sleep? You've been yawning for weeks."

"I'm not very good at giving up."

"You've never tried. It's time you learned how."

Toby stuffed his feet in his hose and rose to pull them on, crouching to avoid banging his head on the rafters. "I'll try. Go to sleep."

Hamish sighed and closed his eyes and said nothing more.

The hob raised no hackles when he approached the adytum. He tapped and tried the door; it opened. The tinderbox was still in the nook where Fischart had kept it. He lit a candle, and its dancing light confirmed that there was no one there.

He walked around the big room without finding

anything to tell him where Sorghaghtani had gone or when she had left. Indeed, he saw almost nothing to indicate that she had ever been there, except that the place was tidier than it had been in Fischart's time. In his torment of guilt the hexer had slept on the floor and used his bed for storage. Sorghie had covered it with straw and a blanket. Otherwise, the little shaman might never have existed. The water jar was empty.

Toby blew out the candle, replaced it where he had found it, and went for a walk in the moonlight.

He found no answers in the night. It was doubtful that Don Ramon would ever put the Company under D'Anjou's orders, and Ercole would certainly not cooperate. He might ask his duke to contribute a few lances, no more. In Florence the signory would doubtless pay lip service to the new order as long as Sartaq remained in the city, but the moment he left it would be business as usual, which was Florence first and everybody else nowhere. No, any army the new *comandante* raised would fly apart at the first sign of trouble. He would fail.

Toby Longdirk had already failed.

It was not far short of dawn when he was summoned. He was giving Smeòrach a rubdown by moonlight in the stable yard when a white ghost swooped over his head and cried, "Hoo!" An instant later she came again, this time lower so that he felt the wind of her passing. He had no doubt that it was Chabi. "Hoo! Hoo! Hoo!"

He opened the stable door and slapped
Smeòrach's rump. "Go to bed, big fellow!" With a
snort the gelding lumbered inside, heading for his
stall. Toby took off at a run, with the owl plunging and
swooping over his head as if pleading for haste. Even
when he reached the narrow path through the
cypresses, she stayed with him. He thumped on the
door and hauled it open at the same time, but pulled it
shut behind him before the owl could follow, knowing
Sorghaghtani rarely allowed Chabi inside.

"Sorghaghtani? Sorghaghtani! Sorghie?"

The cypresses were shadowing all the windows,
but something had changed in the darkness. His hands
shook as he fumbled with the tinderbox. Fortunately
the first spark caught, and he breathed it up into a
flame for the candle. The darkness lifted then, showing her sprawled on her side in the middle of the floor,
one arm stretched out as if trying to reach her drum,
which lay just beyond her fingers. Her headdress had
fallen off, her dress was ripped in several places.

Setting the candle on the floor for safety, he lifted
her and carried her over to the bed, marveling once
again at how little she weighed. He could see no
injuries except a few faint scratches on her face, arms,
and one of her tiny breasts. There was no blood anywhere, and her breathing sounded peaceful. Her lips
were crusted and her tongue swollen. Water? He
would have to leave her and run for water, for the jar
had been empty. It was worth a second look, though,
so he took a second look and was relieved to see that
he had been mistaken the first time. There was a small

amount left in the bottom. He filled a beaker and took it to her.

All the time, he was saying, "Sorghie! Sorghie!"

He wet a finger and laved her lips. Her tongue moved. He sat beside her, raised her up, held the beaker to her mouth. "Sorghie! Sorghie! Wake up, Sorghie! It's Toby." Her straight black hair was crudely hacked short, like a boy's, and she smelled of fresh hay. She was even younger than he had guessed and might have been pretty had she not been horribly mutilated. Where her eyelids should be there was only white scar tissue, hideous and sunken, apparently burns. Tongue moved, lips moved, and in a moment she swallowed.

"You'll be all right," he said, over and over, although he had not the slightest idea what was wrong. Her injuries—the scratches and ripped clothes—might have come from falling into a gorse bush, but he wondered if she had dropped through some cypress trees. It made no sense, it just seemed to fit. If evil men had maltreated her, they would have done much worse. The loss of her sight, whether atrocity or accident, had happened years ago.

"Toby?" The single word was both a croak and a whisper, but very welcome.

"Yes. What do you need?" He was still supporting her in the crook of his arm.

She did not answer for a while. Then her tiny hands pulled her dress closed over her miniature breasts. "Were you looking?"

"Yes. Very pretty."

She smiled at that. "Why do you not open the door so I can see?"

"I'll have to lay you down."

She struggled feebly. "Cannot I sit?"

He eased her back so she could lean against the headboard, then went and opened the door. Chabi came in with a rush, circled the room, and soared up to a rafter. Toby scooped up the fallen hat and blindfold and went back to kneel beside the bed and offer them to the shaman. "Feeling better?"

She hastened to cover her ruined eyes, but he took the chance to run fingers through her hair. Short though it was, it was thick, and its coarseness made it heavy and somehow sensuous. She smiled at him.

"Why do you look so worried?" She was flattered by his concern.

"Are you not my friend? Should I not then be worried?"

"Are you learning bad habits from me, answering questions with questions?"

"Probably. But since we are friends, will you not tell me the truth now? The prince did not send you. He's never heard of you, has he?"

She shook her head, apparently looking down at her knees.

"Then where did you come from?"

Her tiny hand tried to close on his huge one and settled for squeezing one finger. "How well do you know the Caucasus, Little One?"

"Only that it . . . er, they . . . they are very far away." He could ask Hamish. "How did you come?"

"When I arrived, was I not limping?"

"You walked? How long did it take you? Who sent you?"

She seemed willing to tell him her story now, but her inability to speak anything other than questions made the process difficult. As far as he could tell, she had walked for the best part of two years to reach Florence—or to reach him, for it seemed that he had been her goal. She must have set out about the time he arrived in Italy to become a soldier of fortune, and she had certainly been only a child then. Why? Because the spirits had called her, of course. Hamish had mentioned that shamans were always called; the spirits gave them no choice. Of her family or what had happened to her eyes she did not speak, and he did not ask.

"You must rest now," he said. "But one more question. Tonight you traveled in the spirit world. What did you find there?"

Her mouth twisted as if in pain. Her voice dropped to a whisper. "Know you anthills, Little Boy? Myriads and myriads of ants? By a lake, do you see?" She moaned and swayed. He sat on the edge of the bed again and held her. She leaned into his bulk, seeking comfort. "You know Lemanus and the Mount of Jove, Little One?"

"No."

She made a sound like a sob. "What else can we do? Am I not trying my best?"

"You are doing your best, and it is more than enough. I know who will tell me of those names. Now you must sleep, Sorghie. Will you eat first? Drink more?"

"Drink?" she murmured, and he gave her the beaker to sip again. He kissed her cheek and stood up.

She demanded her drum and insisted she wanted nothing more. When he opened the door to leave, Chabi hurtled by him and vanished into the dawn. He sprinted for the villa and returned with water, and bread, and oil, but she was already asleep, clutching the drum and sucking her thumb like a child.

Hamish lay on his pallet in exactly the same position as before, head on arms, snoring like a water mill. He was going to have horrible pins and needles. Toby poked him.

"Hamish! The Mount of Jove—where is it? Hamish, wake up! Lemanus! Where is the Mount of Jove? And a lake. Lake Garda? Como? Maggiore?"

He grunted a series of, "Who? What?" noises. His eyes opened, wavering. He tried to move an arm and grimaced.

"Where is the Mount of Jove?" Toby shouted.

"Uh? What's the matter?" Hamish brought his eyes into focus like an archer aiming an arrow. "Toby? What time is it? Demons, my shoulders! Go roll in the honey pits."

"Answer me! Where is the Mount of Jove? And Lemanus?"

"Mount of Jove is the pass of Gran San Bernardo.

And the road goes by Lacus Lemanus, Lake Geneva. Why the Latin? *Why are you asking?*"

Toby sank back on his haunches with a sigh. "Because that's how he's coming—the Fiend. He's on his way." It was to be Turin and Milan.

37

Before the city roosters fell silent, Toby was in Florence, beating on doors. The don, the Chevalier, the Magnificent, Prince Sartaq, even doddery old Carisendi, chairman of the Ten—he tried to warn all of them that the Fiend was on his way. Not one of them would believe that any shaman or hexer could see as far as the Great Saint Bernard Pass, let alone Lake Geneva. They all seemed much more interested in the grand public reception that was to be held for the young Queen of England.

When it was duly held, three days later, it was a very elaborate affair indeed. No one actually said that it might be the last one ever to be held in the Palace of the Signory, but that implication overhung it like a rain cloud heading for a picnic. The don wore his silver helmet and was almost ignored. Every flunky and officeholder and his wife crammed into the banquet hall, and most of them delivered speeches. All the rest of Florence turned out just to catch a glimpse of the two English queens arriving in their coach and then to shed a tear over their dramatic and tragic tale—and perhaps also to savor a *frisson* of dread that with the terrible Fiend poised to invade Italy at any moment here were his wife and daughter in the flesh. It was a stunning civic triumph, and it took all day.

Captain-General Don Ramon and his deputy had been standing in a packed and suffocatingly stuffy hall for almost two hours before they even caught a glimpse of the guests of honor, to whom in due course they would have a chance to pay their respects. Blanche looked like a well-decorated corpse, or a puppet on strings. Lisa was . . . was Lisa. Someone with exquisite taste had robed her in torrents of pale blue silk and sprinkled jewels all over her, and any man would have cheerfully fallen at her feet. Knowing her as he did, Toby could tell that she was nervous and upset, but she was hiding it with an aplomb far beyond her years, smiling, acknowledging, thanking. She was displaying a truly royal grace he had not seen in her before—was that an inherited trait she had never bothered to reveal, or was she just enjoying being the center of attention? This was not the spoiled, self-centered brat he had known for the last two months. She was barely a woman, still some days short of sixteen, and yet her aura filled the hall. Had Hamish been present, he would have died of longing.

The don, never patient, was fretful but would control his temper because he was waiting on royalty. Mostly he passed the time accepting adulation from lesser folk brought into his proximity by the slow shuffle of the line as it wound snakelike about the hall, but once he turned to Toby and demanded:

"Have you established yet who betrayed our guests?"

Until the scene at Cafaggiolo, he had believed like everyone else that Lisa was Hamish's sister. Toby had expected him to raise a tempest over that deception, but this was the first time he had mentioned the subject.

"No, senor. When I do, I will break every bone in his body."

Don Ramon smiled. "Let me know in advance. I shall enjoy watching."

"*Sì*, senor. Do you wish me to save you a rib or two?"

"No. I would not hinder you in any way." After a moment he added, "But I was constantly amazed that we were able to keep the secret as long as we did."

To which the only possible reply was, "*Sì*, senor."

Eventually protocol delivered them to the royal guests—the two queens and Sartaq, who was acting as host, liege lord of the city. When the presentation was over there would be time for only a couple of quick sentences. Toby had been agonizing over what he would say to Lisa, but even when he was bowing to the prince he had not decided.

Sartaq looked extremely pleased with himself. "Constable!" He dropped his voice to a whisper, and spoke—surprisingly—in English. "We leave out Scotland after all!"

"Your Highness?"

"Not wanting to hurt your feelings!" With a chuckle and a twinkle that seemed almost a wink, the Khan's son turned to the next in line.

Toby managed not to say, "After what you did to me at Cafaggiolo you are worried about my feelings, you young idiot?"

His family was hopelessly inbred, of course, given to congenital insanity.

Now Lisa! She acknowledged Toby's bow with a nod, but her royal composure wavered as she glanced at the line behind him—looking for Hamish and not finding him.

Toby blurted out the message, still wondering if it was a cruelty in the circumstances. "He said to tell you he will never forget."

"Tell him . . ." She swallowed hard. "Tell him to try. We shall never forget your kindness, Sir Tobias. Do you know who . . . ?"

"No, ma'am. When I find out, I will kill him for you."

"Kill him again for Hamish," Lisa said bitterly.

Then he had to move on.

Queen Blanche gave him a skeletal smile. "You tried, Constable. Whatever happens it will not be your fault."

He mumbled some suitable reply. It would be his fault, of course. Had he wanted, he could have put Blanche and her daughter on a ship to Malta. He wondered why he had not. Could his reluctance to lose Hamish have been the whole reason?

The finale of the ceremony saw Lisa doing homage to the darughachi for England, Wales, Ireland,

Aquitaine, and a few assorted other possessions of the
English crown. Nevil had long since been branded
traitor and declared deposed, of course, but this was
the first time the Khanate had recognized a successor.
The palace rang with cheers, which were undoubtedly
mostly for the lovely madonna Elizabeth. No man
would have received such an ovation.

So Sartaq had not been entirely joking about
Scotland, although Toby was certain that whatever the
reason it had been left off the list, his personal feelings
had not been involved. He was not even sure who his
rightful king was since Fergan had been caught and
murdered. He made a mental note to ask Hamish when
he returned to the villa.

"You know," the don remarked quietly, twirling
his mustache, "Nevil is certain to hear of this. It should
feel as good as fleas in his armor."

"I'm glad I don't have to break the news to him,"
Toby agreed. The only silver lining he could see in it
all was that Lisa must now be under Sartaq's protection. He would be ringed with defenses against demon
attacks, and he certainly would not hang around Italy
if the Fiend seemed likely to overrun it.

38

The following morning, couriers arrived with news
that the Fiend's horde had been sighted in the pass. His
advance scouts had come down into the plains two
days after Sorghaghtani's questing, and this was duly

reported a few days later in Florence. D'Anjou's grand
plan was ashes already. Toby could take no joy of that.
He had predicted a month. It would be April, blood on
the lilacs. Had he been put in charge, he would have
moved faster, but he still would not have had time to
organize a united defense. The delays caused by
Sartaq's meddling had made disaster inevitable. Nevil
would be in Naples before the end of June.

The Chevalier summoned all the armies of Italy to
muster at Piacenza, then rode north to take charge. The
Fiend's forces poured into Savoy. The duke and his
family fled Turin, which seemed certain to be the first
target.

Next came word that a second army, even larger,
was crossing the Brenner Pass and menacing Trent,
the city Toby had saved the previous fall. That news
made him grind his teeth in frustration, for had he
been able to establish a base at Piacenza as he had
wanted, he would have been able to strike at the two
columns separately, before they could unite.
Meanwhile he worked day and night preparing the
army of Florence to ride out. The Don Ramon
Company was ready, but too many of the other units
were still in a state of muddle. He set the eighth as the
day of departure.

On the seventh he and the don were summoned to
a meeting of the *dieci*. Doddering old Cecco de'
Carisendi, who usually gave the impression that he
might have been someone of note in the silk weavers'
guild early in the previous century, was that day surprisingly clear spoken and effectual. He stood erect

with his nine fellow councillors at his back in the gloomy, paneled chamber, and he minced no words. There would be no march north. The army of Florence was to remain in Florence.

The don roared like an artillery barrage. Wars were not won by defense, he declared. This was cowardice, betrayal, and folly. The Fiend would like nothing better. After he had repeated everything twice, he fell silent, glaring. He had not quite threatened to take the Company north anyway, but he was obviously considering it. All eyes turned to Toby.

"Am I correct in assuming that His Highness has left the city?" He tried not to let the question sound like a sneer.

Carisendi shook his head and blinked his bleary eyes. "No, indeed, messer. I saw the prince not an hour ago. He is preparing a . . . He has no plans to leave Florence yet."

That was a surprise, if true. "And he approves of this action?"

"That is not your concern, Constable. Under the *condotta,* you are bound by the directives of the *dieci della guerra.*"

"I am well aware of this. Why do you buy a guard dog and then chain it?"

Ten hapless burghers twitched and fidgeted; they scratched and shuffled their feet, and few of them could meet his eye. They all knew that what they were demanding was wrong. He wondered who was twisting their cords—the Magnificent? or Sartaq? or perhaps it was the Fiend himself.

"You must understand," Carisendi bleated, "that the forces of Rome and Naples have not yet made their way north. Florence cannot denude herself of defenders while two great armies are due to pass through Tuscany. Once they have gone by, then the matter will be reviewed. Your advice will be solicited at that time, Captain-General; yours also, of course, Constable."

That was never. Bruno Villari had repeated loud and often that unless the College provided more spiritual protection—meaning hexers well supplied with demons—he would refuse to move his men out of sight of the city walls. Conversely, while Rome retained its potential for attack, King Fredrico would not strip Naples' defenses. Nobody was coming north.

"You can expect a large influx of refugees, Your Magnificence," Toby said. "I haven't heard any news today, but I imagine Trent and Turin have both burned by now. Verona will fall tomorrow or the day after. If Nevil sees no sign of organized opposition, he may even tackle Venice and Milan at the same time before—"

"I have not finished issuing you your instructions, messer. Effective immediately, you are to post guards on all gates to prevent any mass exodus."

"So we are not your defenders? We are jailers?"

The chairman scowled. "Certainly not. You will allow people to pass freely, but not carry away their household possessions. Trade must continue, but panic could be extremely deleterious. And henceforth you will concentrate all your energies on preparing Florence to withstand a siege."

Somehow even this ultimate stupidity was not a surprise. "Florence cannot withstand a siege. Your walls are two hundred years old, and while they may have been adequate when they were built, cannons have made them obsolete. The Fiend will set up his artillery on the hill of San Miniato and blast you to fragments."

"We have cannons!"

"But they cannot throw a shot high enough to reach the hilltop."

The *dieci* exchanged shocked glances.

"Cannot you extend the walls to include the hill?" Carisendi asked weakly.

"I can try," Toby said. If the citizens were to be held in the city at sword point, they would be happier being kept busy building walls. "The timing will be very tight, but if Milan manages to hold out for a month or so, the Fiend won't get here before the middle or end of June."

The old man sighed. "Take whatever steps you can, messer. Your written instructions will be delivered by noon." He looked very frail as he returned the two mercenaries' bows.

Side by side they marched across to the door.

"Absolute insanity!" the don barked, even before he was outside the chamber. "This is what we get for prostituting our honor to a stinking gang of dyers and weavers!"

For once Toby was inclined to agree with him. He

had signed the *condotta*, so he was bound to obey orders. In the past he had always contracted to perform a specific deed and retained some freedom to choose how he would do it. He had not seen that Florence's terms were different. Too late now, for he could not march away in a snit, leaving the city with no defenders.

No cities had ever successfully resisted the Fiend—they surrendered or they fell. Unlike the great Genghis, Nevil rarely showed mercy to those who submitted to him, because the demon in him enjoyed the cruelty too much. Even if he left one of his two armies in the north, the other could crush the defenses in a matter of days. He had too many demons, too many guns, too many men.

The only hope was another appeal to the Cardinal College. If it would supply the hexers needed, if it would send Villars north, if Naples would then cooperate, if there was enough time . . . then Toby might be able to organize a line of defense in the Apennines. Milan and perhaps Venice were lost now, and all the lesser cities of the Po Valley, but it was still just possible that the war could be kept away from Florence.

As the two mercenaries crossed the antechamber, Hamish stepped into their path and one glance at his face was enough.

Toby said, "I bet my bad news is worse than your bad news."

"I doubt that." Hamish never smiled now.

"Tell us!" the don snapped.

"The prince has appointed a suzerain. The edict has just been proclaimed."

"It's a tie," Toby said. "We all know what the Fiend does to suzerains. Who is the lucky man?"

Hamish pulled a face as if the words had a foul taste. "The King of England."

His listeners exchanged perplexed glances.

"No, Hamish. The king of England is the one we're fighting. You've got your flags mixed up."

"Pietro Marradi, the Magnificent. As of this morning he is suzerain of the Khan in Europe. He's going to marry Lisa, and then he will be officially recognized as King of England." It was the wedding, not the appointment, that was sickening Hamish.

Toby's first thought was that Sartaq had made a very shrewd choice—an amazing choice! He had done the unthinkable, appointed a commoner, but Marradi's infinite political skill was just what the Khanate needed if it was ever to outmaneuver the Fiend. Even if he was more than twice Lisa's age, he was still young enough to take a second wife. She was marrying the richest man in Europe . . .

His second thought came just as the don put it into words: "I wonder what the Fiend will think of this?"

39

It was done. The ink stain on her finger was evidence enough to damn her. She, Blanche, dowager Queen of England, had signed the contract betrothing her royal

daughter to an Italian banker. Would future generations scorn her and heap curses on her head, or would
they praise the brilliance of her acumen as madonna
Lucrezia predicted? Would they laud Prince Sartaq as
brilliant strategist or condemn him as merciless
tyrant? A bully, certainly. Had she listened to Lisa, the
pair of them would even now be locked up in a dungeon in the palace of justice, indicted for defying a
direct order from the Khan's *darughachi*. He had not
been bluffing, she was certain.

The verdict of history not yet being available,
Blanche was pacing the chamber she shared with Lisa,
back and forth, to and fro, hither and yon. It was a spa-
cious and elegant room, but it had not been designed
for pacing and was cluttered with chairs, chests,
wardrobes, and dressing tables. Lisa had hurled herself bodily into the feather mattress and, as far as it
was possible to *slam* curtains, had slammed the curtains behind her. Periodically muffled signs of sobbing
came through the heavy material. Blanche had rea-
soned, pleaded, and remonstrated, to no avail. All Lisa
would say was that she was going to kill herself at the
first opportunity.

"Kill me first," Blanche said miserably, and
received no reply. After all these years . . . For a while,
a little while, a brief two precious months while she
had been Longdirk's guest at the villa, the nightmares
had stopped. After all these years! For some reason
she had trusted that large young man as she had trusted
no one since the demon ate her husband, and her sleep
had been untroubled. And now it was all back—nights

of torment, hands shaking, stomach writhing at the sight of food. Now she was known. She was exposed, like the nightmare where all her clothes fell off in the middle of a busy street. She was trapped, like the nightmare of the cage and the rising tide. Now—today—she had, just maybe, found a new way out. She had betrothed her daughter to one of the richest men in the world, who was now one of the most powerful, the Khan's suzerain. He would not let his young wife and his mother-in-law fall into the Fiend's talons, would he?

The record of suzerains' survival was not very encouraging, but their families had done somewhat better. The nightmare of the skinning knife was perhaps the worst of all. What choice had she had? None. Sartaq was overlord, and Lisa was his ward. It was no more than courtesy on his part to ask Blanche's consent.

A scarcely audible tap on the door barely preceded its opening, and in strode the duchess of Ferrara, magnificently attired in scarlet and emeralds. Perhaps no one so petite could be described as striding, but her habitual no-nonsense air was even more marked than usual. She eyed the anonymous bed curtains, then looked inquiringly to Blanche.

"She is still a little upset, Your Grace."

Lucrezia shrugged her elegant little shoulders. "You can see why our Florentine laws leave marriage entirely to parental judgment. When I threw tantrums as a child, I was birched. My husbands were all amused by the scars. I should have thought Her

Majesty was a little old for that, but I can certainly arrange to have it done now if you wish, monna."

"Oh, no!" Blanche said hurriedly. "I am sure that once the shock wears off she will be restored to her usual self." Was Lisa's usual self adequate for the present situation?

"Well, by all means let us give her another five minutes." The duchess settled on a chair, arranging her skirts. "My brother is a patient man, but even he cannot tolerate a wife who throws hysterics. I know he chastised Filomena a few times when they were first married. Now his friends are pouring in and will naturally wish to congratulate the future bride."

"Just a few minutes." Blanche wanted to sit down also, but her body refused. She took a few more paces, turned, paced again . . . Like the nightmare of the snakes . . .

"I cannot see," said the duchess, "how we can possibly have everything ready by the end of the month. Normally it takes two years to arrange a Marradi wedding. Lisa? Are you likely to be bleeding around the thirtieth?"

There was no reply.

Lucrezia looked to Blanche, who felt herself blush.

"I believe that date will be acceptable." Lisa was quite right—this wonderfully delicate, suave, *civilized* duchess was also a ruthless and callous bitch. Her brother, Blanche's future son-in-law, was known as the Fox, and vixens were vicious.

"Lisa, dear," Lucrezia said, raising her voice to address the four-poster, "you realize that you are making a terrible fuss to avoid something that you will be absolutely begging your husband for once you have tried it?"

The bed uttered an audible wail.

A ruthless, callous, and *vulgar* bitch.

Lucrezia tutted in annoyance. "By her age I had experienced two husbands and several lovers. There wasn't anything about men I didn't know. Is she really a virgin?"

"Certainly!" Blanche had gone so far as to ask, and Lisa never lied to her.

"Amazing!" Lucrezia studied the bed curtains with amusement. "So her previous romances have all been pure and platonic?"

"What previous romances? This is slander, madonna!"

"You are *not* going to tell me that a woman of Lisa's age has had *no* male friends whatsoever?" Lucrezia's smile flowed into a simper. "Have you not noticed how frequently she mentions Constable Longdirk?"

"Oh. Well, she is young, and he is an impressive figure of a man."

"Only if your taste runs to blacksmiths and quarry workers. So there was a, shall we say, friendship between them? Nothing improper, of course, but a . . . an *interest?*"

Cornered as in the nightmare of the giant cat, Blanche conceded the possibility. "If you imply no more than that, well, yes I do believe that Lisa and Constable Longdirk were, um, attracted to each other."

Lisa uttered a wordless howl of protest from behind the curtains.

Lucrezia laughed. "Stubborn, isn't she? I do hope you explained the impossibility of such a match?"

Blanche nodded, although she recalled that she had once brought up the subject with Lisa, and it had not seemed so impossible then.

"And what were Longdirk's feelings?"

"He behaved perfectly. But you could see by the way he looked at her that he was . . . drawn."

Lucrezia sighed and smiled again. "So tragic a tale! We must give some thought to the guest list. Normally the families . . . I do hope, madonna, that you are not planning to invite your husband!" She trilled a laugh.

"Of course not!" Vulgar, ruthless, callous, and *heartless* bitch.

"Perhaps some of the English exiles," the duchess said, "to balance the parties. Let us decide tomorrow." She rose. "Come out now, Lisa, and prepare to meet the visitors, or I'll have you dragged out."

Like the nightmare of the sealed tomb.

40

Toby had little time to worry about Hamish's broken heart or Lisa's sword-point marriage. He had a year's work to do and only days to do it in—days and nights, for he never seemed to sleep now.

The most urgent need was to enclose the hill of San Miniato within the city walls. He tossed the problem to Hamish, telling him it would help him forget his lust for another man's betrothed. Whether this was true or not, Hamish went to work with his usual zeal.

The don looked like the next most trouble. The *dieci*'s written instructions forbade both him and Toby to leave the city, but he never read the edict, and Toby forgot to mention that clause. He sent the captain-general off with a hundred lances to scout the roads through the Apennines. The Company itself had to be brought into the city, a move that raised rumbles of mutiny because the only thing less popular than storming a city was being trapped inside one during a siege. Fortunately there were many green areas within the walls to pitch tents.

Those were all obvious problems. A thousand lesser matters swarmed like midges—livestock and fodder, setting up guns, tearing down every building and uprooting every tree and shrub within a mile of the walls, stockpiling human food and fuel, hanging chains across the river, organizing hospitals and fire-fighting, establishing a new *casa*, drilling the citizenry—a clerk or wool carder could drop a rock off a battlement as well as a knight could. Days went by in a blur of questions, demands, and protests. He made each decision in turn and went on to the next. There were many evenings when he could not remember having been off his feet since dawn.

Antonio Diaz, for example, looming out of the morning confusion and raising his voice almost to a shout: "Another five hundred!" Toby had never seen him so agitated.

"Another five hundred what?"

"Gone!"

It took a few questions to establish that the cavalry was absconding, vanishing into the night, but it was going by squadrons, not just deserting in a rabble. The don had not been seen since he went off to the north. There was a connection there somewhere. The don would never run away from battle, but he would prefer to pick his own ground.

"Fewer mouths to feed," Toby said. "The only use we're going to have for cavalry is as a source of steak. Let's just keep this under our helmets."

"We can't draw pay for units we can't locate!"

"What good will gold do the Florentines when the Fiend arrives?"

Diaz harrumphed and stalked away in outrage. The poor man had too many morals for his own good.

Behind all this surface frenzy, the war continued along its own relentless track, always a few days ahead of the news so that every report had to be extrapolated: "If they were there then, they must be about here now . . ." The vast tide of refugees Toby had feared did not appear, because most people just dived into the nearest town and slammed the gates, hoping the war would go elsewhere.

Turin had burned. Trent had burned. He had predicted both of those. There had been a minor battle outside Turin, and the Chevalier had been wounded, but no one knew how badly.

Milan and Verona ought to be next, but after the middle of the month the picture shimmered and steadied again like a reflection on a pool. Nevil had not laid siege to Milan. He had not turned aside to Venice. He was not even trying to link up his two columns—he did not need to, because no serious opposition had taken the field against him. His western army was apparently heading for Genoa. The eastern force had bypassed Verona, headed straight south to the Po, and then halted to build a bridge where there had never been one before.

Toby found Hamish on the hill of San Miniato bellowing at a work gang who had unloaded a wagonload of stone in the wrong place. He was using half a dozen languages, but his meaning was quite clear.

Toby thumped a hand on his shoulder. "This isn't going to work, my lad. You don't have time to finish the wall, and half a wall is as much use as half a head. Pay them off and send them home to their wives."

Hamish gave him a hard stare. "News?"

"Bad news. Nevil is still busy building his bridge. Work is going very slowly. His western column has bypassed Genoa."

"This is absolutely crazy! Has he lost his mind?"

"No," Toby said. "He's defined his objectives."

It was amusing to watch the gears turning, the rising incredulity as Hamish worked it out. "The western army is heading down the coast at a forced march?"

"Looks like it. And when it reaches Lucca, it will turn inland. By that time, of course, the eastern army will have crossed the Po and sacked Bologna. I estimate he'll be here by the first week of May."

Hamish grimaced as if he were being racked. "We've got to get Lisa out of the city!"

"Oh, that would not be courteous," Toby said sourly. "She's the reason her daddy's coming to call."

There was little satisfaction in being right. The only surprise in those waning days of April was that the Tartars stayed on in the city, with Sartaq making himself visible, delivering speeches, and generally behaving as a prince should, usually in the company of the new suzerain and his future bride. The Florentines drew comfort from their leaders' courage and resolution, not dreaming that their city had become the Fiend's primary objective. There was no word of Don Ramon and the Company cavalry, but the *dieci* never asked why he had disobeyed orders.

Under the best conditions, seven leagues a day would grind down the toughest, best-trained army very quickly. Nevil was famous for forced marches that left a trail of dead men and horses by the roadside. When his western army reached Lucca and turned aside to advance up the Arno, he struck with the eastern force down the old Roman road through the Apennines. Toby had been wrong on only one detail—

the Fiend did not destroy Bologna. In his haste to close the trap around Florence, he left it intact.

The Chevalier was reported to have died of his wounds in Milan, but he had never been relevant. Sartaq made no move to replace him.

As the last day of April dawned, Toby came limping back to Giovanni's inn, which now acted as the Company's *casa*. From long habit he shared a room with Hamish, and let him have the bed. He himself seemed to have no time for sleep at all anymore. He had been up all night and most of the previous night, supervising the final preparations. As he stripped and began organizing a shave, he was so tired that the world would not stay in focus.

Hamish duly sat up and rubbed his eyes. "I've seen you before somewhere, haven't I?"

"Not recently. Do you happen to remember my name? It seems to have slipped my mind."

"Genghis Caesar." Hamish yawned, stretched, scratched, and reached for his shirt. "Don't throw away that water. Anything happen in the night?"

"Half a dozen scouts disappeared. Got too close and were eaten by demons, I expect. He'll be here before noon." Razor in hand, Toby turned to peer at his friend. "As of half an hour ago, the Siena road is still open. Nevil's trying to cut it; he's got a column of light cavalry heading across country to San Gimignano. He thinks they're masked by gramarye, but Sorghie found them. They're not there yet, so why don't you go while the going's good? I'm sure Sartaq will make a break for it and take Lisa with him."

Hamish leaned back on his elbows and studied his friend with a curious expression. "Do you think I'd do that?"

"No. But I wish you would."

"Well I won't. And I don't think Sartaq will, either. Or Marradi. You've got the people convinced that Florence can hold out indefinitely. You're the famous Longdirk, who's never been beaten. Everyone's persuaded you have something up your sleeve, that Naples and Milan and the others are marching to the rescue."

Nauseated, Toby went back to shaving. "I never told anyone that! It's Sartaq, spirits forgive him! Keeping up morale is one thing, but holding people here for no real purpose when the city is doomed—that's criminal!"

"Have you said that to anyone but me?" Hamish pulled on his hose.

"Of course not. It would cause a panic. But I don't tell lies, either." He couldn't if he tried. His face would never deceive a blind horse.

Hamish chuckled. "Doomed, you say?"

"Doomed. I don't lie to you, friend."

"Toby!" Hamish had to be very excited for his voice to squeak like that. "Be serious! You do have something up your sleeve, don't you? It's the amethyst, isn't it? You've learned Rhym's true name!"

Toby forced himself to turn and look him in the eye. "No. No true name. Nothing up my sleeve. I swear."

Dawning belief made Hamish's lips curl back in horror. "You must have! I've never known you to obey stupid orders before!"

"I'd never promised to obey them before. This time I did. I have no choice." Toby went back to shaving, having to stare at that failure peering at him out of the mirror.

"Toby!" Even squeakier. "We've been friends for years. *You can trust me!*"

"I do trust you. Hamish, I swear I have no secret plans. I can see no way out of this. Nevil is going to sack Florence. We are going to die. That is the honest truth, upon my soul. I'd prefer you didn't tell anyone else, please."

After a moment's silence, Hamish said, "I won't breathe a word until after the wedding."

Toby almost chopped off his nose. "*That's* still on?" He had forgotten. This must be the last day of April.

"Yes, it's still on. And we're both invited."

"Well!" Toby said. "Why not?"

41

Toby Longdirk was a military genius, but he had some curious limitations. For weeks he had been striding around Florence, organizing the defenses to resist a siege, grinning all the time as if this were tremendous fun, laughing away fears, winking knowingly when asked what was going to happen. Then he professed surprise that people trusted him to work a miracle! He had complained to Hamish a thousand times that he was a lousy liar, when in fact his face was less scrutable than a badly eroded Etruscan terra-cotta funeral monument.

But he did have something up his sleeve. He *must* have something up his sleeve! Hamish could not believe otherwise.

Now he insisted that Lisa's wedding had to be a diversion, a decoy. The Marradis, he said, having made grandiose preparations for a royal marriage and convinced the whole city that it would go ahead as planned, would vanish before the first guests arrived. Sartaq would flee with them, and it was just to be hoped that they would have the grace to take Lisa and her mother and not abandon them to the Fiend's ghastly spite.

Hamish disagreed adamantly. He had been prying, as was his wont, and although all his efforts had failed to win him a single word with Lisa, he was personally convinced that the Magnificent was going to do exactly what he said he would do— marry Lisa and remain in Florence. Prince Sartaq was not going to sneak out any back doors either. Nor were the *priori*. The truth was that all those men were just as much under Longdirk's spell as the lowliest weaver. If *comandante* Longdirk was not worried, then neither were they. Toby had an astonishing air of permanence, an indestructibility that inspired absolute faith. The Fiend's armies were closing in on the town—by nightfall they would have it in their grip—and Pietro Marradi was going to get married regardless.

Hamish was not going to miss the wedding. This would be his last chance ever to speak to Lisa, probably his last chance ever to see her. The Fiend and all his horrors were not going to stop that.

"You'd better catch some sleep," he said. "You look as if you haven't shut your eyes in days. You're out on your feet."

Toby shrugged. "I'll sleep some other year. Food and then duty—but if nothing goes horribly wrong, I'll come to the wedding, I promise."

After they had eaten, they went their separate ways.

Just before noon, the Fiend's army came to Florence with bugles and drumbeats, dust and glitter, men and horses streaming down from the hills. Fiesole was burning, and the city gates had been closed. Another column of dust to the west showed where the army from Lucca was hastening up the Arno to join in the siege. The mood in the streets was one of shock and denial. No one had expected this, or not so soon. Even Hamish, who had been privy to all the intelligence reports, had trouble believing that it was really happening.

When he went back to the inn to change, he found Toby there already, having another shave. If he opened his eyes wide he would bleed to death, but apparently he intended to keep his promise.

What could be more reassuring to the citizens than seeing their betters whooping up a celebration and ignoring the nonsense outside the walls?

Nothing provoked Italians to ostentation like a wedding. Weddings were political and had very little to do with love or procreation. A marriage was a treaty with an exchange of hostages, and the two families involved were honor-bound to squander money to insanity. In this case the bride's family had no money at all, so the groom's must spend enough for both. Thus it was that, while Nevil's armies gathered like hyenas around Florence, inside the walls the inhabitants held carnival, gala, fiesta, and revelry. Bands played in the piazzas, floats displaying classical themes were dragged through the streets, wine flowed from fountains. The crowds outside the Marradi Palace were being regaled with free wine, food, and music—small wonder they cheered themselves hoarse when condottiere Longdirk arrived in his carriage. They would have cheered the Fiend himself.

Within the grim-faced block, Hamish found a less exuberant mood. Oh, the bunting and decorations were breathtaking, the women's gowns astounding, their jewels celestial, and the orchestra Elysian. No conceivable extravagance had been overlooked. Each guest on entering was presented with a medallion displaying the Marradi arms impaled with the

lion rampant of England, all set in gems. Other rich
gifts would undoubtedly be distributed several times
during the course of the celebration, and the meal
would include twenty or more courses, each with its
own wine. A hundred artists had labored on grotesque conceits around the courtyard, heraldic animals and mythological beasts taller than a man.

All the same, the attendance was small, perhaps
forty, and most of the revelers were the innermost of
the innermost circle, the Marradi family en masse.
They knew that all was not well. They were going to
deny it for a few hours, but they must know that the
next party they attended might be hosted by the Fiend,
who had gruesome ways of entertaining important
captives. Their jollity had a brittle ring to it.

Lisa? Hamish peered anxiously around the courtyard, but there was as yet no sign of the bride or her
mother.

The Magnificent welcomed each arriving guest
with smiles and laughter, and for once he was dressed
as a dandy in multicolored splendor. Give him his due,
he did not look forty. That did not mean he looked
young enough to marry Lisa. He greeted Toby as
"comandante," then smiled as if that had been a slip
of the tongue. "We are especially overjoyed by your
noble presence, for it confirms that you have already
taken all the steps necessary to secure the safety of the
city."

Toby's Italian still made the natives wince, but it
no longer reduced them to tears. "I left everyone
enough work to keep them busy for an hour or two,

Your Magnificence. You will excuse my rudeness if duty calls me away before the end of the festivities?"

Sartaq was close to upstaging Marradi, garbed like a peacock and chattering in urgent Italian, hands swooping like summer swallows. His mustache had disappeared some weeks ago, so only his eyes and the color of his skin seemed in any way alien. Judging by the pride of lionesses around him, he was still making husbands nervous.

And Lucrezia of course. She triumphed over her years and, in the absence of Lisa, was a clear first in the courtyard for beauty. Toby bowed low to kiss her fingers. She did not wait to acknowledge Hamish at his side before flashing her spite like a rapier.

"Welcome, Sir Tobias. It is kind of you to put aside your personal sorrows and join our celebration."

Toby's puzzled expression made him seem close to half-witted. "Sorrows, madonna? My only sorrow is that it is so long since I have had the pleasure of looking upon your glorious self."

The funny thing was that the great lummox genuinely thought he didn't know how to handle women. Most of them fell on their knees as he went by, and he could knock the rest over with a smile.

Lucrezia was not quite so easy, though. She smiled disbelievingly. "I confess that the lady still speaks of you often, but I'm sure she will grow out of that once she has a husband to comfort her."

Hamish quelled a murderous impulse. Toby just smiled blandly.

"Not even a rightful-born queen could ask for a

nobler husband than your magnificent brother, *duchessa*." His eyes were innocent as owls'.

A puzzled frown disturbed the baby smoothness of Lucrezia's brow. "And you must just learn to live with a broken heart!"

"You shattered it the first day we met, madonna."

Then it happened. A trumpet brayed. Sartaq, having left the courtyard unseen, made a grand return entrance, escorting Lisa and her mother. By cruel chance, the door they used was right where Lucrezia and the two mercenaries were standing and partially blocked by an enormous phoenix of fabric and paper. Lisa came around the beast and face-to-face with Hamish. She halted so suddenly that the prince stumbled and her mother almost ran into her.

He dreamed of her every night and thought of her from dawn till dusk. He knew every eyelash, the two tiny moles by her lips, the little fleck of silver in her right eye, and yet in a month he had forgotten how beautiful she was. In her wedding gown she was unbelievably, epically gorgeous. The famous Marradi rubies burned at her throat like arterial blood.

They stared at each other for an age, a blink, a thousand years, a trice.

"Oh, madonna!" he said. "Will you topple the towers of Troy again?"

"Master Campbell . . ." Then she was walking on with the prince and her mother, and the moment had ended.

As Hamish returned to reality he realized that the Duchess of Ferrara was staring at him with a look that made his whole body cringe. "You?" she said, and the flames in her regard might be disbelief or incipient murder or both.

Toby was laughing! "Of course him! You didn't think she hankered after me, did you, monna? Great clumsy me?"

No! Hamish thought. *No, Toby! Whatever you do, don't ever laugh at Lucrezia Marradi! Better to poke your finger in a lion's eye.*

But the damage, whatever it might be, was already done.

42

Toby was seated between young Guilo Marradi and one of the token English guests, Sir John Whitemouth, who had been knighted on the field of Rioz by Lisa's great-grandfather. He was certainly the deafest man north of Sicily, and his conversational skills were further restricted by a total lack of teeth. Hamish was at the far end of the long table, while Sartaq held place of honor in the center. The bridegroom had a chair at the ladies' table, with his back to the men's.

Lisa in white shone with an ethereal beauty like pearls or moonlight, which was accentuated by the blood fire of her rubies. She was putting on a fine performance, chattering glibly with her neighbors—Marradi across the table, her mother and Lucrezia flanking her—as if she had been married a dozen times. Blanche looked as if she had died of some wasting sickness and found her smiles in the charnel house. Lucrezia kept staring at Toby and glancing away quickly every time he noticed, so he was certainly not back in her good books, if she had any.

The two long, white-damasked tables were separated by a gap wide enough for the double line of servants who paraded in with every course. The meal began with wine, antipasto, and speeches. The first orations had been assigned to junior Marradis. Guilo went second and did a workmanlike job, invoking so many classical authorities to bless the union that Toby understood barely a word of it. Important people would speak later. An orchestra tuned up and began. He swallowed a yawn and an olive and turned to bellow something trivial in Whitemouth's ancient ear.

Course followed course, armies of footmen parading in to place a golden bowl in front of each diner simultaneously. Toby had met this conceit before at banquets and considered it needlessly embarrassing, because it forced everyone to eat roughly the same amount. With his appetite, he preferred the standard custom where each diner ladled out whatever he needed from a common dish onto a trencher of hard bread. Gold tableware made the food cold before it even arrived, and he could not wipe his fingers on it.

Whitemouth passed him the goblet, a servant filled it with wine, he drained it, and passed the goblet on to Guilo. In a little while it came around again. Servants removed one course, offered washing water and towels for sticky hands, brought another. After the carp, each guest was presented with an enameled rose; after the capon, a silver inkstand bearing the entwined insignia of the bride and groom.

Then a steward brought in a splendid golden chalice inset with jewels and paraded it along each table in turn. The Magnificent filled it with wine and carried it across to the men's table to present to the prince. Sartaq rose and drank while the company applauded.

A few moments later Marradi performed the same ceremony with another goblet, this time giving it to his bride. After the roast swan, all the guests were presented with fur-trimmed cloaks. And so it went: food, wine, speeches, gifts, and music, followed by more food, wine, speeches, gifts, and music. Toby wondered how large a sack he would have to carry away with him and what he would do with the stuff.

Tomorrow the war.

The marriage was not forgotten. A nervous notary read out the betrothal agreement, and the couple acknowledged that they had confirmed their intentions before the tutelary in the sanctuary. An hour or so later the marriage contract was read and then signed, with the prince standing in for Lisa's father. Toby was glad he could not see Hamish.

Lucrezia was still lobbing calculating glares in his direction. He should not have laughed at her. Had her misapprehension been encouraged by Lisa? A girl who could tell her mother that Hamish was the son of an earl was capable of just about anything.

He would really enjoy eight hours' solid sleep. A tiled floor like this one would do.

More toasts, more costly goblets.

More food, wine, speeches, gifts.

Sir John, who drank better than he could eat, launched into a long, damp dissertation on the evils of guns and how they had ruined warfare. His English was less intelligible than Guilo's Italian.

Then came a brief ceremony in which the groom placed a ring on Lisa's finger. Oh, poor Hamish!

"Is that the end?" Toby asked. "Are they married now?" He ought to be out on the battlements watching the disaster unfold, except that he had already done everything he possibly could.

"Not quite," Guilo said. "We see them to the chamber door. As soon it shuts, they're considered married."

"Seems a little hasty. He'll need at least fifteen minutes at his age."

Guilo had been drinking heavily. He found that remark so hilarious that he had a coughing fit, and then had to whisper the joke to his other neighbor. While it was going on down the table, he turned back to Toby to explain how the bride and groom would complete the ceremonies by visiting the sanctuary next morning as husband and wife. In this case, that would be when the prince would recognize Cousin Pietro as King of England, Ireland, and other barbarous places.

Assuming Nevil's ghouls had not broken through the gates by then.

Toby fidgeted, wondering how the war was going. The sun no longer shone into the courtyard.

Servants removed the canopies over the tables. He should return to duty, although there was no reasonable chance that Nevil would be in a position to attack before tomorrow at the earliest. Sartaq would undoubtedly speak at some point in the evening. He should wait for that.

Another glittering goblet was paraded along the tables. Who was going to be the lucky one this time? Marradi took the goblet, filled it, and rose to his feet. He was pinker than usual, but so was everyone after all the food and wine. "Your Highness, my lords . . ."

Obviously it was to be Toby himself. He gritted his teeth, wondering what he could possibly say in his response. A few words of thanks were customary, but they would want more than that from him. What was there to say—that he was sorry? That they had entrusted their city to the wrong man? That he would have tried to do better next time but there wasn't going to be a next time? Try to lay the blame on Marradi himself and the Khan's son?

Now the Magnificent walked across, but he did not at once give Toby the goblet. Smiling, he looked around to include the ladies, then spoke to the men. "This is an unusual announcement at a wedding, friends, but in this case a very appropriate one. You all know that the Chevalier D'Anjou was wounded in battle and is now reported to have died, although that has not been confirmed. In his place, with the permission and enthusiastic agreement of His Highness, in my capacity of suzerain for His Majesty Ozberg Khan the Glorious, I name Sir Tobias Longdirk *comandante in capo* of all loyal armies in Italy, and charge him to drive the rebel forces from the land!"

What a good idea! It came three months too late, though.

Loud applause. One or two of the men were drunk enough to cheer. Toby rose and leaned across the table to accept the gift. It was heavier than he expected, his fingers were still greasy from the lamb ragout . . . or perhaps he felt a prickle of warning from the hob. Whatever the reason, he dropped the cup. It hit the board between him and Marradi and exploded rich red wine all over the Magnificent. He fell back with a cry of anger.

Somebody screamed very shrilly.

Marradi wiped his eyes with a sleeve, waving his other hand for a towel as servants came running to assist. He dropped his arms and gaped incredulously at Toby . . . slid limply to his knees . . . toppled face-down . . . and lay there, motionless.

Many people screamed then. Guilo and even old Whitemouth leaped to their feet, knocking over their stools in their haste to get as far as possible from the scarlet stains on the white cloth. Prince Sartaq vaulted nimbly over the table and was the first to reach the corpse. He knelt to see, but he did not touch it. Several Tartar guards came roaring into the courtyard, with two shamans at their backs. Screaming, shouting, and hysteria.

Toby said nothing, did nothing. That was more than poison. That wine had been hexed. That was supposed to be him lying there.

"Silence!" Sartaq was on his feet, and his bellow echoed over the tumult. Despite his youth, his voice had a royal resonance that compelled respect. He pointed at the women, who were all on their feet by now. "Which of you screamed first? *Who was it?*"

In the icy moment of horror while the accusation gelled, all faces turned to face one face.

"Lucrezia!" Lisa shouted, backing away.

"Lucrezia!" said another.

Lucrezia shrank as if she were arching her back like a cat. She raised a clawed hand to her mouth, gabbled a command, and was gone, vanished as she had vanished when the statue fell on the night of the Carnival Ball. More screams. Women swooned. Men rushed around the ends of the tables to reach them and comfort them. The shamans began thumping their drums, either exorcising the poison or trying to locate the culprit. An ashen-faced Hamish had his arms around the widow, who was clinging to him fiercely and sobbing on his chest. That was not going to reduce the scandal any.

The Magnificent was dead. Florence had no ruler.

The suzerain was dead.

The Fiend was outside the walls.

"Longdirk!" Sartaq roared.

"Your Highness?"

"Did you mean to do that?"

"No, Your Grace. I didn't know. It slipped through my fingers." Was that true? Had he been incredibly lucky or had the hob saved him?

The prince stared very hard at him, as if trying to

read his thoughts. "Very well. Your appointment stands, *comandante*. Go and attend to your duties. Go and save the city."

Where had this vibrant royal leader come from? Why hadn't he appeared months ago, when there had still been *time* to save the city?

Hamish was still consoling Lisa.

Toby bowed and hurried from the courtyard.

43

He commandeered a Marradi horse and galloped through streets darkened by evening shadows but still breathlessly hot. An ominous hush had settled over Florence. The revelers had dispersed—many to the sanctuary to pray, no doubt, and others to the walls or bell towers to watch the Fiend's armies digging in. The shock of the Magnificent's death was still to come.

In the stable yard he hit the ground running, yelling for Smeòrach to be made ready even as he dived through the low door into the inn itself. Brother Bartolo was holding court there at a table littered with papers and several abacuses; clerks and pages were streaming in and out the front door like ants provisioning their nest. "Report!" Toby roared, and went up the stairs at a rush, which risked breaking an ankle or stunning himself on the beams, but he made it to the top safely and ran along the gallery, hauling off his doublet. Shirt and hose followed it as soon as he was in his room; he grabbed up the fighting garments he had left there ready: shirt, breeches, padded jerkin.

Floorboards creaked outside, then Bartolo's great bulk filled the doorway. His normally rubicund face was pale as parchment.

"Well?" Toby demanded, stamping his feet into riding boots.

"Two hundred and three thousand. Still coming."

"From Lucca, too? Well, they won't be much good for a few days." Nevil's fondness for exhausting his armies with inhuman marches would betray him sooner or later—but not this time, because there was no enemy to oppose him. "You can stop counting now. Did you organize the bell towers?"

"We have reliable watchers in every campanile, and a sharp-eyed youngster as well. If they try any sort of sneak attack anywhere, the nearest bells will start ringing. The guards on the walls have been told how to use the bells to call for help."

"Good work. Put the criers into the streets right away—I've been appointed *comandante in capo*."

The friar beamed. "Well, that is certainly the best—"

Toby buckled on his sword. "And the Magnificent is dead."

Bartolo's gurgle of horror was a fair warning of how Florentines would react. Florence without a Marradi to run it was unthinkable, and there was no obvious heir ready to take over.

"What? How?"

"Murdered. Announce my appointment first!"

Toby squeezed around him to reach the door. "Keep the other thing under your"—he ran along the gallery—"cowl!" He avalanched down the stairs. Clerks scattered out of his way like chickens.

He rode first to the Porta al Prato, near the stadium, which was an obvious site for an attack and close to where he guessed the army from Lucca would have pitched camp. The myriad campfires starting to shine in the gathering dusk showed him that his instincts had been correct. Nor was he alone in his inferences, for there he found Antonio Diaz.

The Catalan was haggard with exhaustion, but his dogged confidence had inspired his troops. The cheers with which they greeted Toby were both gratifying and appalling, so he did not know whether to weep or clap his hands over his ears and scream. Instead of doing either, he made a rousing speech from Smeòrach's back. What lies he told hardly mattered, because he kept twisting his head around to speak to everyone, and also his horse was very restless, clattering hooves on the cobbles all the time. Besides, his accent was so bad that no one would be able to catch much of what he said, but they cheered him again anyway, even louder. It was bad enough that he was condemning most of these men to die, but far worse that he must deceive them into thinking their deaths would serve some useful purpose.

Before leaving, he drew Diaz aside. "San Miniato is going to kill us. We'll have to sortie at dawn, before they're ready to open fire. Spike the guns at worst, drag them into town at best."

The Catalan nodded resignedly. "I know. And I know they'll be waiting for us to try just that. You want me to lead it?"

"Please. I'll join you if I can."

"No. You're too valuable."

"I have never felt more worthless," Toby said, but he knew there was truth in what Diaz was saying. A commander who threw his life away on a suicidal mission at the opening of the battle was not serving his cause. He ordered Diaz to get some sleep and rode away, despising himself from the bottom of his heart.

That was only the beginning. The night became a repeating nightmare of torch-lit faces. He circled around the city walls, crossing and recrossing the Arno, inspecting, approving, encouraging. Everywhere he found men of the Don Ramon Company and the Florentine militia together—gnarled veterans husbanding their strength for the morrow in among peach-faced apprentices shivering with excitement. All of them seemed glad to see him, cheering and jesting. Not even the crabbiest old trooper showed doubts or threw angry questions at him: Why have you locked us up here to die? What difference can we make? How will anyone benefit from our deaths? No one asked. He would have had no answers if they had. They all stood a little straighter when he left.

The Fiend had bridged the river both upstream and downstream from the city, just beyond cannon range. That was a very efficient piece of work, considering how long he had taken to span the Po, and the forces that had crossed already had completely surrounded the city. Lisa would not escape to Siena. Nor would Toby Longdirk, although he had never intended to try.

He found Arnaud Villars making his own tour of inspection, checking on stocks of arrows and missiles and powder and shot and grappling hooks and all the other thousands of items that might be needed at dawn. Toby ordered him to get some sleep. The attack might not come for days yet.

He even ran into desiccated Alberto Calvalcante the gunner, working on a few last adjustments to some of the defenders' cannons. He, too, looked as if he had not slept in weeks.

"You were right, Sir Tobias," he growled. "They do have guns on wheels, what I said were impossible. Saw them being dragged up to San Miniato. Don't know they'll work good, of course," he added grumpily.

"I knew it ought to be possible, and I'd heard the Fiend emplaced his artillery very quickly at Trent. Did you see how they do it?"

"Lugs, messer! They cast the cannon with a lug on each side of the barrel to make a pivot."

So then the guns could be tilted to the correct elevation and wouldn't blow themselves out of the mobile cradles. Simple! "Can you melt down all our cannon and recast them by dawn?"

Calvalcante spat. "Certainly, but those lazy carpenters can't make me the carriages I'd need." The listeners laughed, which was good, and Toby—feeling like a parrot now—told him to get some sleep.

He rode off to the next tower, the next gate, the next cluster of men around a lantern or brazier, the next lying speech telling them to hold firm if they were attacked, that help would come. Dying in battle was not such a terrible death, but dying with so many lies on his conscience was going to be. Strange that there was no sign of the don anywhere! Toby had expected him to return before the siege began, but perhaps the man just wanted to die in the open. A charge of a few hundred lances against tens of thousands might appeal to him as a worthy death.

The night was breathless and steaming hot. Eventually he realized that he had worn himself out, and his poor horse, too. If he went back to the inn, could he take his own advice and enjoy a few hours' sleep? More likely he would just toss and worry, but he turned Smeòrach in that direction, or as close to it as he could, for he was in the old Roman quarter, with its grid of narrow ways. A shutter opened above him.

"Sir Tobias?" It sounded like a child, but it might be a woman.

He reined in and peered up at the window, seeing only the faintest blur of a face. "I am, but how did you know?"

"The spirit wants you. Go to the sanctuary."

Ah! He could deceive the men of a thousand lances, but never the tutelary. His crimes had caught up with him.

"I will. May it send you good rest in return for this
service."

He turned Smeòrach again and nudged him into a
weary trot.

FOUR

MAY

44

As he had expected, the sanctuary was busy. Even the streets outside were full of aimless people, as if Florence had been smitten with a plague of insomnia. He had dismounted and loosened the girths before one of the inevitable horse urchins appeared to hold his reins.

"Business is good tonight?" he asked.

"*Sì,* messer!" The lad tried to grin, and it became a yawn.

"His name is Smeòrach. He won't cause you trouble." He thought of adding, "And if I don't come back before dawn, he is yours," but of course no one would believe the boy. "He needs water."

He walked stiffly over to the door, feeling a huge load of fatigue settling on his shoulders. When the attack came, it would come from so many directions at once that he would be as bewildered as anyone. From then on there would be no central command, only terror and bloody struggle. He would have little more to do than try to die as bravely as other men. He had done everything he could do, and it would not be nearly enough.

The interior was a vast darkness, packed with unseen humanity, many of them singing along with the choir that stood before the altar at the end of the long nave. That was where the candles burned, illuminating the altar and the incarnation on the throne—which was a small child at the moment. The heady odor of incense could not hide the reek of too many people, suffocating heat, the palpable oppression of dread. Alas, poor Florence, doomed to join the ghostly ranks of cities Nevil had razed. Weep for her!

Men did not normally visit the sanctuary wearing swords and carrying steel helmets. He began to edge his way forward, trying not to frighten people or disturb their singing. Finding he was making little progress, he stopped, and quietly said, "Help?"

The elderly man in front of him turned around. "Is it not about time you asked our help?" He was stooped and toothless and ragged; he did not smell very pleasant, but the air around him had taken on a pearly shimmer.

"I have been busy, Holiness."

"We are well aware of what you have been doing. Come with us."

When the incarnation led him, the crowd parted unasked, people moving out of the way without realizing that they were doing so. They first went forward, toward the altar, and then over to one side. Above them the great dome soared unseen. Toby's guide halted at an insignificant door near the north entrance.

"Go up, Tobias, all the way to the top. We shall meet you again there."

He bowed, but the old man was already just an old man again, looking around in surprise. Toby began to climb the stairs.

It was a long climb for a man in full battle gear, and the night was sweltering. He was puffing hard when he emerged on the gallery around the lantern at the top of the great dome, fifty spans above the ground. Another incarnation was waiting there for him, an elderly woman. In the darkness, she was an indistinct, humped little shape.

The view was awe-inspiring. He could overlook everything—the dark and silent streets far below, the blank no-man's-land beyond the walls, and the whole valley of the Arno, which twinkled with myriad camp-fires as if half the stars of heaven had fallen. The cooks were already preparing breakfast so the troops could fight on full stomachs. Probably the guns would be ready by dawn to begin the brutal business of battering down the walls. It was surprising that the Fiend's demons had not begun their attack already.

He had never failed to take a city that defied him, nor had he ever shown mercy to the inhabitants.

"What are your plans, Captain-General?" asked

the tutelary. "The damage so far has been serious but
not unendurable. Tell me of the Allied forces that will
arrive to lift the siege."

"Allies?" Toby laughed bitterly. "Milan's army is
guarding Milan, Rome's guards Rome, Venice's
Venice. They would not listen. They would not cooperate. Nevil will pluck them one by one. We are but the
first."

"So this failure is as serious as it looks?"

Did the spirit expect him to deny the obvious?

"I see no hope at all. The fault is mine, and I
accept the blame." He would not plead for mercy
when he did not deserve it. He would not even beg for
a quick death, for that would be too great a favor when
everyone knew how the Fiend would treat the citizens
after he took the city. Whatever form of execution the
Florentines might decree for Toby Longdirk would be
infinitely more merciful than anything the Fiend
would do to him if he caught him. "I shall be surprised
if the city lasts beyond sunset, Holiness."

The eastern sky was perceptibly lighter than the
rest. Traitors were traditionally executed at dawn, but
if the failed captain-general was to be subjected to
some pretense of a trial, he would apparently live
through this dawn and die another day. He wished the
tutelary would just throw him in a cell and let him
sleep, although that might mean he would fall into the
Fiend's hands. It would be better to die on the battlements. Meanwhile, the responsibility was still his, so
he ought to be down there on the walls, inspecting the
sentries, guarding against one of Nevil's sneak dawn

attacks like the Bloody Sunrise that had destroyed
Nuremberg.

The incarnation had fallen silent, staring out
motionless at the night as if the tutelary had gone away
on other business and forgotten to summon the woman
back to inhabit her own body. Toby paced restlessly off
along the gallery, half-wishing the darkness would fade
so he could see the enemy's deployments; wishing
much more that it would never lift, that this one night
would go on for ever and ever, preserving fair Florence
in a bubble of time, a butterfly in amber eternally safe
from the forces now poised to destroy her.

When he returned to his starting point, the woman
had disappeared. The tutelary had made no farewells,
pronounced no sentence, granted no forgiveness. He
still did not know why it had summoned him to this
aerie in the middle of the night, and he could not guess
what he was supposed to do next—report to a dungeon
in the palace of justice, or go off and lead the defense
of the city through an endless day of fire and blood?
The one option closed to him was sleep.

Puzzled and irritated, he walked around again.
The eight ribs of the octagonal dome and the eight corners of the lantern joined across the gallery in stone
arches. He counted them as he walked and at eight
concluded he was now alone. There was no one else
there—no one human, for a blur of white in the darkness and a breeze in his hair became an owl settling on
his shoulder. Startled, he jumped. Then he reached up
to stroke a finger over her downy breast. She made her
odd little purring noise.

"Chabi! I'm glad you're back. I was afraid the Fiend's archers would get you." The Fiend's demons would be a greater threat. They must be all around the city now, like his army, and they would know she was more than merely owl.

A faint golden glow in the nearest arch heralded the return of the incarnation, apparently following him around the lantern. Why would a tutelary play childish tricks? "We hope you recognize the honor she pays you," said the tuneless voice. "For a shaman's familiar to befriend anyone else is close to a miracle."

"As long as she doesn't sick up a dead mouse in my ear, I don't mind her."

"Have you made progress, Holiness?" asked Sorghaghtani's voice from his other side. Where had she come from? She did not seem winded as if she had climbed all those interminable stairs. He was glad she was safe, too. Safe for the moment, at least. She was even smaller than the woman.

"None," the tutelary answered. "He has forgotten."

"Forgotten what?" Toby snapped. What were these two plotting? Shaman and tutelary? What an unholy combination! Or a too-holy combination! He had never considered this pair as likely partners, and the idea disturbed him.

"If you remembered you would not need to ask, Tobias. Why did the Fiend come to Florence? Why did he not start with Milan or Venice?"

"Isn't that obvious? Because of Blanche. Having the suzerain here must have tempted him, Nevil's wife and daughter even more so, but I suspect he could have ignored them if they had kept their heads down. Even when they were paraded around in public and Lisa was hailed as a queen, he might not have done very much. But when Blanche had the audacity to marry her daughter to the suzerain and name England as her dowry . . . even a demon can only stand so much."

45

It was almost dawn. Horizon showed all around the world, the stars were folding their tents, birds flitted over the rooftops of Florence, and roosters screeched in the yards far below him. Chabi sat contentedly on his left shoulder. He could see the incarnation clearly now—wrinkles and wisps of white hair dangling from under her headcloth, the back humped by a lifetime of toil. On his other side cryptic little Sorghaghtani sat cross-legged on the platform, all muffled in draperies, beads, and tufts of herbs. The camps of the foe were too far off for him to discern, but the bugles must be sounding there.

"What is to be done?" Sorghaghtani demanded angrily. "Can we not help him break the binding?"

"We must try," the tutelary answered. "For him to fail at the last minute would be tragedy for all Italy. But the dangers are extreme."

"Is he not a strong man, able to withstand what must break most others?"

"Undoubtedly, but even for him the shock may be mortal."

"Will you two stop that!" Toby roared, glaring from one to the other. "If you are going to put me to death, Holiness, then go ahead and do it. Otherwise, throw me in a cell where I can get some sleep. Or, best of all, let me go down there and die beside the men who trusted me, the men I have betrayed. But stop discussing me as if I'm a colicky horse!"

They ignored him.

"Great Spirit, will you not explain his error to him?"

"He cannot believe us, and there is no time. The forces are poised, and the word must be given before the sun rises. Sorghaghtani, daughter, bid Chabi take him to the spirit world and show him the truth."

The little shaman uttered a cry as shrill as a bat's. "Nay, Holiness, do you know what you ask? Is he not untrained? What has he done that you would destroy him so horribly?"

"Tobias, if you could save the city by laying down your life, what would be your choice?"

His knuckles were white on the railing. "Do you have to ask?"

"You have to answer."

"Take my life, then. Will it be quick?"

"No, and it may be a shameful death, but we have no more time. Send him, Sorghaghtani, send him."

The shaman's fingers awoke a gentle rumble from the drum on her lap.

"No!" Toby protested. "The hob! Do not rouse the hob!"

"It is time to rouse the hob," said the tutelary.

The beat became a muffled thunder, and then a roar of blood in his ears. A weight of worlds crushed him down. He folded to his knees and bowed even smaller, feeling as if he were shrinking under a merciless load—tiny and smaller still, no larger than Chabi. He spread his arms, for he could move nothing else, and his arms raised him. He soared, and Chabi went with him, together borne on the imperative of the drumming. The dome rocked and spun and vanished away in the wind. Like an autumn leaf he rode the tempest, spinning through shapes and shades of madness, lights, and colors no mortal eye could see. Chabi was with him.

At last he sank. The rushing slowed and tumult faded, leaving him in the stillness of a moonlit glade. The drumming was a distant background, a pulse in the world, a voice chanting far off. Deer slept in the long grass and thorny shrubs, does mostly prone, fawns curled small. The stag was on his feet, antlers held proud aloft as he stared at the newcomer, although if he could see Toby, it was more than Toby could. He had no sense of being there, neither in his own body nor any other. But the stag knew him and saw him, and there was sorrow in the great liquid eyes.

"You call from afar, shaman," the stag said, "very far from the worlds of the ancestors." He twitched his black nose inquiringly, seeking the missing scent. "We are not a fighting people. The wolf drives us in winter, and we must run."

Toby could not speak, but drumming spoke for him, and the stag seemed not to mind. It turned its magnificent head to look eastward. "Many have cried in distress to the fathers, but always they wanted us to fight for them, and we are not a fighting people. Thus say the ancestors to us: 'You shall not enter their battles. They must turn the pack themselves.'"

The beat lamented, then changed, growing more agitated, urgent. Forest shifted and blurred and reformed as walls of stone. Moonlight puddled silver on floorboards under narrow windows, its reflected rays sketching in the inner darkness a massive bed of finely carved woods and thick brocade. Through a gap in the draperies showed the slender whiteness of a girl asleep.

The herd had gone, leaving only the stag, and he looked to the west, sinews straining in his mighty neck as he supported the weight of his rack. "Your song is different. You ask us not to fight, but to run, and this we can do. Behold, I answer your call! I will go before the pack and run for you, shaman."

The drum's pulse rose in triumph, and the stag himself changed——fur melting, flesh flowing—until what stood before the moonlit windows was a young man, stocky and muscular, and yet his thick shoulders still bore the stag's head and antlers. A cloth tied loosely around his now-human loins was probably not normal wear but something taken up in a hurry. He looked to the north. "Show me the way. I am yours to command."

Still Toby could not reply, and again the voice of the drum answered for him, its beat slowing to a somber throb, a dirge, a funeral march, full of menace. The stag-man understood, for his shoulders sagged. He turned to the south, and his voice rose in complaint, a voice growing more and more familiar, just as the walls and the windows were aching at the edges of memory.

"You ask too much, shaman! To flee before the hunters is no shame when one is not sprung from a fighting people. But not to run, or to run in circles, or to cower in a hollow and watch the pack close, ah, but you ask too much!" His antlers were visibly melting and drooping. "Think you because I will not fight that I have no honor? That I forget the ancestors?" The wilted antlers hung over his chest like ropes; and all his pride was shame. He laid his human hands on the window ledge and belled a great note of despair to the starlit night and the sea. "This is what you do to me, shaman! I will have recompense. You will suffer for this."

Castel Capuano! It was Castel Capuano!

"I will suffer," Toby said aloud, and the scene shattered in a cacophony of drums.

He sprawled on the gallery with his arms outspread and the stonework cold under his face. "No!" he said. "No, no, no! I do not remember."

"More, Sorghaghtani!" said the toneless voice of the tutelary. "He will recover and thank you for it, or he will not return to reproach you. Even madness will be better than failure."

Again the drumming swept him up and whirled him into the spirit world.

46

A forest at sunset. He stood naked before a huge and ancient oak, staring up at a hole in the trunk and a squirrel that sat on the edge of the hole, gibbering at him as the rumble of the drum faded into the distance like a passing storm.

"Go away, go away!" the squirrel chattered. It was a very red little squirrel, and it wrapped its bushy tail around itself and peered down at him with eyes like angry bright beads. "Go, go, go! Go now! Go away! They are mine."

"I only want to borrow them," Toby said.

"No! No! No! No! They are mine. They are ours, not yours, shaman. Go! Go away! Mine! Mine! Mine!"

"I will bring them back." He reached up to the hole and tried to push the squirrel aside. It bit his finger. He cried out at the pain and snatched his hand away to suck the wound. He could taste the blood.

The squirrel danced in fury now on the edge of the hole, jabbering, "Mine! Mine! Mine!," and "Ours! Ours! Ours!," and sometimes, "Go away! Go away!" It lashed its shiny tail around like a feather duster.

"I need them just for a little while. I will bring them back." He reached up to grab the brute. It ran up the trunk out of reach, clinging to the bark with its claws.

"There is nothing there, shaman. The hole is empty."

"Then you won't mind if I look?" He stretched as high as he could and felt inside the hole with his right hand. The squirrel jumped on his wrist and bit it. As he grabbed for it with his left hand, it dived into the hole, and suddenly he had both hands in the hole and they were caught there. He was trapped. Inevitably, the ground sank away under his toes then, leaving him hanging by his wrists. The tree bark was harsh and spiky against his skin. He knew what was going to happen now. This was Sergeant Mulliez's whipping post again.

The squirrel bit on his fingers a few times, then poked its head out between his hands to smile at him. "You must promise to bring them back!"

"I promise," he said.

The lash crashed across his shoulders and he gasped, but it was not quite a scream. He had made no sound before on the whipping post, and he would not now.

"Promise more faithfully!" sneered the squirrel. It was redder than ever, red as the blood he could feel streaming down his back.

"I promise!"

Crash! This time he had been ready for it.

"You are still lying. Swear, shaman!"

"I swear!"

Crash!

Someone was screaming.

"Stop that, Sorghie!" he said. "You won't get around me that way."

The roughness on his hands and face was stone-work again. He was leaning against the wall with his arms over his head, still in his armor and soaked in sweat, not blood. His helmet had fallen off. He dropped his arms and turned around, but he continued to lean against the wall, for his legs were trembling. The shaman sat at his feet, doubled over her drum.

"Will nothing convince you?" she wailed.

"Not this. None of it makes any sense to me."

"Again!" commanded the tutelary. "This must be the last time. No matter what it does to him, leave him there until he stops struggling."

Toby started to say, "I've never admitted defeat in my life," but they didn't give him time to get the words out.

47

He sat in darkness, a warm and cozy darkness smelling of loam and animal fur. He was listening to a tantaliz-ingly familiar voice. It spoke in Italian, but slowly and clearly, a soft voice with steely undertones:

". . . problem is trust. After so many centuries of disunity, cooperation is foreign to us. Even when we face a common foe, we cannot combine because no state can ever trust another. Alliances change too fast." The shape emerging from the darkness was not human. Human eyes were closer together and did not glow with that yellow light.

"Trent was a miracle, but it was a very brief miracle. One day's cooperation—yes, even Italians can agree for a single day when the enemy is in sight. But more than that . . ." The speaker sighed and smiled, animal teeth showing close below the eyes. "As soon as the sun sets we start conspiring again. To let another's army march across your *contado* is hard. To put your forces under another's command is almost unthinkable. To send them off to guard another city and leave your own vulnerable—that is an impossible concession."

The light creeping into the scene had the bluish tinge of daylight. The speaker was a fox, a very large red fox.

"Then we must plan accordingly," said another voice, one that Toby did not recognize. Nor could he see the speaker. "One day's cooperation, no marching through others' territory, no putting your forces under a stranger's command, no leaving your home city unguarded."

"If you can devise a strategy that satisfies all those conditions, then you are indeed a military genius." The fox was melting, shifting. The cave, too, was changing.

"It may be possible to come close, Your Magnificence."

Il Volpe pricked up his ears. "Indeed? How close?"

"Close enough, because no one makes alliances with the Fiend. You can trust your oldest enemy before you trust him."

"Some have tried." It . . . he . . . was becoming human, at least below the neck. The surroundings were beginning to look more like a room than a fox's earth, too, smelling less of loam and musk, more of polish, printer's ink, leather bindings, and wine.

"And lived to repent it, but not much longer. First, territory. Obviously someone will have to make a concession so that the separate states may bring their forces together. But this will not be a problem once the Fiend has already invaded, will it, messer? Any state will welcome its neighbors in if they come to drive Nevil away."

Who was this Unknown? He was using almost exactly the same words Toby himself had used many times. He was certainly no Italian.

The fox sipped from a stemmed goblet. "They may not agree so before it happens, but do continue."

"Command, then. You said yourself, that command can be relinquished for one day. It happened at Trent, it can happen again."

"One day?" The fox smiled. "That might be negotiable."

"Leaving the city unguarded—would you settle for sending your army out as long as it remained between you and the foe?"

The fox laughed. "You bargain with a gentle touch, messer! Tell me your plan." When did foxes ever concede anything? He was human from the neck down now, a fox-headed man covered with a red pelt, sitting back at his ease in a silk-upholstered chair. The earth was fast becoming a room, Pietro Marradi's little private office, which was a nook barely big enough for two, three at the most. It was lit by daylight but still dull, as if seen through smoked glass.

This was a distorted memory. The only time Toby had seen this room had been the morning when Marradi had summoned him in from Fiesole and announced that it was time to negotiate the *condotta*— meaning that all the sparring between Don Ramon and the *dieci* that had gone before was of no importance and the matter would now be settled by the principals, messer Marradi and messer Longdirk, man to man. Which is what they had proceeded to do. At the Carnival Ball that evening, the Magnificent had forced the *dieci* to accept the terms, then the next morning he had gone back on his word.

But it was a false memory. Sorghaghtani was weaving lies. Marradi had never had a fox's head, and Toby had never made the absurd promises the Unknown was making. This imposter with the barbaric accent must be the mysterious Shadow, the source of all the trouble, the one who had turned Marradi against Toby, tampered with Maestro Fischart's demons so that he died, betrayed Lisa—and even stolen that missing bag of gold.

"The Fiend must strike at Italy," the Unknown said, "can we doubt it? He rules his dominions by terror and cruelty, continually stamping out dissent. He cannot tolerate another defeat, for if he ever starts to seem vulnerable, all Europe will explode under his feet. He will come in the spring, and he will bring the hugest army he can raise. If he makes those mistakes, I can break him."

The fox narrowed its eyes suspiciously. "How? Why is size a mistake?" His fur was starting to look like clothes.

"Because a great army eats greatly and is clumsy to maneuver. If he waits for the harvest, my plan may not work, but if he comes in the spring, then he must either bring his provisions with him, which will slow his advance, or else guard his supply lines. Nevil likes to move very fast. He also tends to overextend himself. He has not been caught out yet, but one day he will be. Our strategy must be to encourage his overconfidence, draw him onward, lengthen those lines, lure him into a trap."

"And what will be the bait in this trap?"

"Florence, messer."

Toby wanted to scream and could not. He wanted to shout *Stop! Stop!* He tried to yell a warning: *Stop, because whoever he is, you are being tricked.* But he uttered no sound at all. Marradi remained unaware of the hidden watcher in his future. Even so, he was not pleased at the prospect being offered.

"You presume far, *comandante!* You expect me to stake out my city as a sacrificial lamb?"

"I see no other way of dealing with the threat, Your Magnificence. The Fiend will send his thousands and hundreds of thousands pouring over the Alps. He will devastate the north—Turin, Milan, Venice,

Parma, Verona, and all the rest. You will be over-whelmed by starving refugees; he will follow slaver-ing at their backs. Even if Rome and Naples try to come to your assistance, by then the roads will be full of refugees, the northern powers will have been destroyed, the price of food will be—"

"Stop, stop! You give me waking nightmares. Why Florence?"

"Geography, messer. We must tempt Nevil south *before* he sacks Milan or Venice, or very many of the smaller cities. He may bleed off some troops to guard his supply lines, which will help us, but the main point is that when he throws his siege works around Florence, he will be between the four great powers. Milan, Venice, Rome, and Naples can move in. The jaws of the trap close here."

The fox smiled skeptically and lifted the goblet to his muzzle. "I believe the beginning. I approve of the ending. It is the middle I distrust. What lure can you dangle to attract a demon?"

"Several things," said the Unknown. "I have already presumed to make a few preliminary arrange-ments."

"Oh, you have, have you?" Skepticism became open suspicion. "What arrangements?"

"In confidence, Magnificence?"

"You have my word."

"Well . . ." The Unknown hesitated. "After Trent, the Khan wrote to congratulate me. I wrote back and asked him to appoint you suzerain."

Marradi almost leaped from his chair in horror.

"You what?" Lips curled back from the carnivore teeth.

Lies! Lies!

"You know how Nevil feels about suzerains?"

"I certainly do! He pickles their heads in jars of brine."

."He must catch them first. So if there is a new suzerain in Florence, he will be very tempted. And there is myself. I do not wish to sound immodest, but I have been a nuisance to him for longer than anyone, and at Trent I did nothing to win his affections."

Who was this demon-spawned fraud, this imposter with his glib falsehoods? Obviously Marradi thought he was speaking with Toby himself.

Now he stared at the Unknown with deadly intent. "I cannot imagine what he would do to you if he took you alive, messer. You would truly stay in the city while the Fiend closed in to besiege it?"

"I will. Throw me in jail if you don't trust me. I also have something he wants very much, the only thing he fears, a certain gem. He knows I have it. I also had the audacity to suggest to the Khan that he send a personal envoy. If he complies, then Florence will contain your noble self as suzerain, me, the amethyst, plus the Khan's envoy. If your Magnificence can think of any additional bait, then we should add it to the hook."

Lisa! Poor Lisa walked into this conspiracy that very night. It was Lisa and Blanche who brought the Fiend to Florence.

The fox steepled his fingers, seeming unconvinced. "You really think this will tempt him south, leaving enemy strongholds in his rear? I am no soldier, messer, but even I would not make that mistake."

"The deception will have to be carefully staged," the imposter conceded. "We must lull him into over-confidence. For example, he is well aware that Maestro Fischart, formerly Baron Oreste, is the most skilled hexer in all Europe. To him, in truth, belongs the credit for the victory at Trent."

"He did what you told him to, you mean?"

"What I asked, yes, but he achieved it. The mae-stro and I are devising a fatal accident for him. If we can somehow convince the Fiend that his old teacher has perished, he will be much less inclined to suspect treachery."

"How often do skilled hexers meet with fatal accidents?"

"Rarely, alas. It will take some thought."

But Hamish's encounter with Gonzaga in Siena had created a wonderful opportunity to fake a disas-ter—except that this Shadow, this Unknown, this imposter, had made it into a real one! Double cross. Triple cross!

"Speaking of gramarye, Your Magnificence," the villain continued, "may I have leave to appeal to your distinguished brother, His Eminence the cardinal? No amount of strategy and courage will save us if we can-not field adequate demon power."

The fox snarled. "I have discussed this with him already, believe me! He admits that the Holy Father is being very difficult. He . . . my brother, I mean . . . will be here in about a month. Will that be soon enough?"

"I fear the matter is too urgent to delay, messer. I have ways of making brief visits to Rome, if you could arrange a meeting place for us. It would have to be in the middle of the night, I am afraid."

Ha! Wrong! The real Toby Longdirk could not go on demon rides because the hob wouldn't tolerate gramarye.

Marradi clicked his fox teeth in amusement. "Indeed, messer? You would travel by gramarye to a meeting with a cardinal of the College? I admire your audacity, if not your judgment. Certainly I can write and ask him to grant you an audience. Whether he will and whether he will then cooperate, I do not know. He was much easier to handle when he was small and I could thump his ears. Since he gained his red hat, he has developed an unfortunate independence of mind."

The Unknown chuckled politely, as one does at the jokes of the great. "Your Magnificence is most gracious."

"And you are extraordinarily devious! I thought only Italians were capable of such chicanery. But I find it hard to believe that Nevil will willingly walk into your trap." *Toby did not. It was a wonderful plan. He wished he had thought of it.* "The Fiend, messer Longdirk, is not stupid, and he knows now that you are not."

"He knows, also, Your Magnificence, that I am only a penniless soldier of fortune. I would cheerfully disappear altogether, but that would be suspicious in itself. It seems to me that we should announce the generous terms for a *condotta* that you have granted me here this morning, and attempt to hammer together a union of the states, because that is what he will expect us to do. Then everything must appear to fall apart like a puffball—which is what we fear it will do. You will make it known that I am in disgrace, that you are over-ruling me. Block my efforts. Insult me in public. Nevil has spies everywhere. He will hear of all this and dis-count me."

"It will make you look like a fool!"

The Unknown laughed. "My feelings do not mat-ter! I am not a prickly aristocrat like Don Ramon. I am not even, with respect, a burgher who must watch what his creditors think of his solvency. I have no fam-ily or close friends to suffer from my disgrace. The men of the Company know I can fight, and that is all they care about. I am a bastard peasant, the lowest of the low. Shame me all you will. In a worthy cause I can endure a few slights."

Easy for him to say, whoever he was! It was Toby himself who had suffered those months of humiliation and frustration, and apparently all that time Marradi had believed that he wanted *such treatment?*

The fox scratched the side of his muzzle. "You impress me with this offer, messer Tobias. I know of no other condottiere in all Italy who would submit to such an arrangement, and Nevil will never suspect that you are submitting to it voluntarily. I will not give you my unconditional acceptance now, but let us proceed with the *condotta,* for we must do that in any case. I shall write to my so-eminent brother on your behalf, while you go ahead and arrange that unfortunate accident to Maestro Fischart. If you can make that appear convincing, and if the College will arm you with the gramarye you need, then I may even agree to tie a noose around my city's neck as you request. Secrecy, above all, will be essential. Who else knows of this plot of yours?"

"Only Oreste and yourself, messer. The Khan knows I want to set a trap, but none of the details. His Eminence the cardinal will have to be told, and eventually the senior military leaders, men like Ercole Abonio and the various captains-general. Less than a dozen, I hope."

Unexpectedly, the fox chuckled. He rubbed his human hands and ran a long red tongue over his chops. "This is a wicked game you plan, *comandante!* I confess I enjoy such sport, and I am delighted to have misjudged you—as I hope the Fiend will misjudge you—for I confess I suspected your success at Trent was merely a fluke. Forgive me if I ask this, though. I have years of practice at such intrigue, but you strike me as a man more inclined to use his fists than his tongue. I shall keep your secret, I promise you, but are you sure that you can?"

"You mean, can I tell lies with a straight face?"

"I am afraid that skill will be an essential ingredient." The fox showed sharp teeth in a smile.

"No, I cannot. But I told you I have ways of traveling to Rome, messer. I can also invoke gramarye to prevent myself from giving the game away. I can even prevent myself from thinking about it or remembering it when I do not need to."

"This is dangerous, surely?"

"Life is dangerous, messer. The worst I risk is that I will completely forget the strategy someday when I need to remember it. If you ever think that has happened, Your Magnificence, then you will have to take me aside and remind—"

Toby screamed.

Out! Out! Sorghie, get me out of this!

48

He reeled to his feet and stared out at a world made glorious by morning—the broad valley of the Arno brilliant green under the ethereal light of Tuscany, the lumpy hills in their rich garb of olive trees and mulberries, misty peaks beyond rolling off to infinity. He scowled at the disfiguring camps of the enemy ringing the city just out of cannon shot. Already the eastern sky was almost too bright to look upon, heralding the sun. The Allied armies were waiting under their masking gramarye. He had told everyone he would give them the signal before sunup—Ercole, Alfredo, all of them! If he did not appear in time, they would assume that something had gone awry and start withdrawing. Then all chance of a victory would be lost, the great surprise attack would become a panic retreat, disaster.

"You have remembered!" the tutelary said, and there was a sound very much like joy in the normally dead voice.

"Little One, it worked?" Sorghaghtani cried.

"It worked!" He bent to take up his helmet and put it on his head, then he lifted her into the air as he straightened. He kissed her and set her down. "Thank you! Holiness, thank you, also. Excuse me. I must be about my business."

He vaulted over the railing into the sky.

By rights he should have bounced three or four times down the steepening curve of the redbrick dome and ended as a disgusting mess on the roof of the nave. He didn't. At about the time he ought to have made his third impact, his boots hit the flag-stones of the piazza a couple of spans away from Smeòrach, who jerked his head up and rolled his eyes, but who was well used by now to his owner's peculiar abilities. Several early-bird passersby jumped and peered in alarm, unwilling to believe what they had seen. The genuine early birds, the sparrows and pigeons, were less gullible and exploded upward in a wild flapping.

The boy had removed the saddle and laid it on the ground so he could sleep on it, with the reins tied around his wrist. Smeòrach's hard tug wakened him; he sat up, bleary-eyed. "Oh, messer, I am sorry . . ."

"You did well!" Toby said, untying the knot. "I don't have time for the saddle. Keep it. It's yours. And this." He dropped a gold coin, which rang on the stone. It was one of the last of the bagful he had stolen from the Company coffers to use as expense money on his secret journeys.

He vaulted on to Smeòrach's back, and Chabi set-

tled on his arm in another whirring of wings. He tried
to shake her off. "You think I'm going hawking? Be
off! This is not safe for you!"

"Who is safe today?" she asked in Sorghaghtani's
voice.

He had no time to argue with an owl. Hoping he
could leave her behind, he kicked in his heels and sent
Smeòrach bounding forward. The spectators saw the
big spotted gelding take off across the piazza like an
arrow, but after a very few strides horse, rider, and owl
became smoky, transparent, then vanished altogether.
The hoofbeats, some later asserted, could be heard for
a few moments after that. Most of the good folk fled
screaming into the sanctuary and were comforted by
the spirit.

From Toby's viewpoint, and possibly Smeòrach's, they plunged into a faintly luminescent fog
devoid of landmarks or scenery. Iron shoes rang on an
endless shiny plain like a dark lake, and their reflection raced along below them.

"Hoo?" the owl screeched, digging talons into the
padding on his arm. "Where is this?"

"Are you Chabi or Sorghaghtani?"

"Who? Do I look like Sorghaghtani? Do I sound
like Chabi? What part of the spirit world is this?"

"No part, so far as I know. I call it the Unplace." He
had settled on this as the least distracting dreamscape
for his ghostly excursions—not properly demon rides,
because Smeòrach was not demonized. Smeòrach was
probably not necessary at all, but he was company, and
his presence reassured the people Toby journeyed to

meet in the real world. Better a demonized horse than a demonized commander.

He patted Smeòrach's neck. "Faster, lad, faster!" Their speed had nothing to do with him, of course, but the big oaf didn't understand Gaelic anyway. He seemed to enjoy the exercise on the endless flat surface.

"How can you stand it without a drum?" asked the owl-shaman. "How long must we stay?"

"I never know." Even the hob could not move him instantaneously. "I only hope I haven't left it too late."

Busily using claws and beak, she worked her way up his arm to his shoulder. "What went wrong, Little One?"

"I blundered. I think I was just too tired." He had ridden round to all the Allied camps the previous night, returning to Florence just before dawn to do a day's work before he went off to attend Lisa's wedding. As always he had closed off what he thought of as his hob memories, so that he would not need to tell lies to anyone, but in his haste and weariness he must have barred the door too well. He had failed to remember his other existence when he needed to.

Chabi turned her head around, scanning the Unplace. Sometimes she seemed to make complete revolutions with her neck, but that couldn't be right. "How long have you been coming here?"

"You are Sorghie, aren't you?"

"Who? Why don't you answer my question?"

"Who asks? Since just after Trent. In the middle of the battle, Nevil sent demons after me, and I fought them off. Not only demons, though—a couple of arrows seemed to veer away from me, and once I was charging straight at a cannon and their match went out when they tried to fire it. Later, when I had time to think, I decided I'd been using the hob's powers, but the hob hadn't gone on a rampage. Neither of us has gone insane since, so far as I can tell. The Fillan hob and I are pretty much one and the same now."

"Did you not tell us that you feared you would turn into a demon incarnate if that happened?" The familiar sounded annoyed, although Sorghie must have realized she was dealing with two separate Tobys, and the daytime version did not know the moonlight version existed.

"I do. It's my worst nightmare, but if this will help overthrow Nevil, I am willing to take the risk. I try not to use gramarye except when I must." He sighed. "Sometimes it just happens, like a blink happens if something comes too close to your eyes." Or like repelling Lucrezia's advances by dropping a statue across her path, or putting Hamish to sleep so he wouldn't notice the midnight comings and goings.

Smeòrach was flagging, and Toby resisted the urge to drive the big fellow faster. They would arrive when they arrived. Sometimes a jaunt from Florence to Fiesole took longer than a trek to Naples or Milan or Venice. The first time he had ventured on a nightmare ride like this had been his journey to Rome for the secret audience with Ricciardo Cardinal Marradi.

"In this horrible place, why are you laughing, Little One?"

"Who are you calling a Little One, chicken? I was remembering that fight I had with a squirrel in your spirit world, Sorghie dear. I just realized what memory you almost awoke."

His Eminence had stipulated that the meeting be held at Tivoli, in the hills east of the Eternal City, where he had a summer villa, but this was not summer, and Toby emerged from the Unplace into a chilly drizzle. He had not thought to bring a cloak. Obviously he had much to learn about his new abilities.

The Magnificent had given him directions beginning at the bridge, meaning he must first find the bridge in pitch-darkness without falling into the gorge. Just how he managed that he could not have explained, nor even how he followed the trail once he had located it, but eventually he rode up to the gates bearing the Marradi arms. He was well aware that he was mud-spattered and soaked, reeking of wet horse and wet man, and he towered four or five hands taller than the wizened old doorkeeper who answered his knock, but this ancient showed no sign of surprise or alarm at the mysterious night visitor. Having admitted him in complete silence and barred the door again, he took up his lantern and led the way through a building that seemed much more a mansion than a villa. The wan light flickered on marble and gilt, hinting at riches crouching in the shadows. By the time he was ushered into the great man's presence, Toby had almost stopped dripping a muddy trail for the servants to clean up.

The cardinal had obviously been napping over a book in a comfortable chair. He roused himself and strutted forward like a robin, offering his ring to be kissed, but holding it low enough to leave no doubt that Toby was expected to kneel first. So he knelt and was left shivering on his knees on a very cold marble floor while his host wandered back to stand in front of the hearth. The doorkeeper, having added a few more logs to the fire, had withdrawn, still silent, and no one had mentioned warm spiced wine. No one had said anything about hospitality for Smeòrach, either, but of course he was assumed to be demonized.

"State your case," the cardinal said. "You are wasting our time unless you have something new to say."

The noble acolyte was small, pudgy, and chinless in his grandiose red robes; and for his manners he deserved to be kicked very hard from Sicily to the Alps.

"I have defeated the Fiend in battle, Your Eminence. That is new. No other man can say as much."

The cardinal shrugged. "You bested one of his underlings, not Nevil himself. You did so by using gramarye, which decent men do not touch. Last week your arch-hexer died a deservedly horrible death in Siena, so now you come crawling to the . . . no?"

"With respect, Your Eminence, Baron Oreste remains in excellent health."

The little man scowled. "Carry on, then."

After that cool beginning, the audience waxed

even frostier. His Eminence conceded that the College might possess a few immured demons that had not yet been destroyed, but not that it kept any great horde of them in the crypts of Rome. Even if some could be found and their names determined, the Holy Father was adamant that the College could never allow them to be used, nay not even to defend Italy from the Fiend. That would be a great evil.

Oreste believed that the College used its vast cache of confiscated demons to defend Rome itself. That, he had said, was why the cardinal had insisted on meeting Toby at Tivoli, because any attempt to ride a demonized horse closer to the city would be very quickly fatal. He also suspected that the present Holy Father was senile and the College was badly divided on the question of how far it could bend its principles in order to resist the Fiend.

"If the gramarye were to be strictly limited to defense?" Toby asked. His knees ached, and the cold of his wet tunic had soaked through to his bones.

The cardinal sniffed. "And what is defense, pray? A bowman shoots at you so you wipe out an entire army and call it defense? I see no point in continuing this conversation."

"I am trying to save your native city from total destruction, Your Eminence."

"It sounds to me as if you are exposing it to totally unnecessary risk. I can't imagine why my brother would waste a moment contemplating the wild plot you suggest. The Holy Father would be incensed if he heard that I was even discussing the use of gramarye.

It is an evil that has perverted many fine adepts into hexers and so damned them."

"With respect, Your Eminence, the baron believes that he can find volunteers to handle the demons according to his instructions. They would not be jeopardizing their souls with forbidden knowledge."

The cardinal considered that offer, pouting. It was the first time he had hesitated. Oreste thought the arrangement would appeal to the College because it could more easily deny involvement if it supplied only the immured demons and not the adepts to handle them.

"I doubt that that is possible."

"Maestro Fischart will be more than willing to attend Your Eminence to explain how he can arrange this."

Marradi shook his dewlaps in refusal. "I had as soon turn my villa into a public brothel as consort with anyone so notorious. The solution is of very doubtful morality. Granted that war requires taking risks, these volunteers of his, by their innocence and ignorance, would be placed in grave danger from the very demons they expected to control."

It seemed that nothing would work. The cause was hopeless, and Toby was becoming increasingly worried about Smeòrach, shivering outside in the rain. He had only one last desperate plea left in his bag.

"If the use of the demons were strictly limited, Your Eminence? The heart of my plan is that the Allies encircle Nevil without his knowing. With sufficient gramarye, their armies could be concealed from his view until the trap had been closed. If this is evil, surely it is no more evil than resisting his invasion by the use of cold steel or black powder?"

The adept gathered his scarlet robes more tightly over his little paunch as he thought about that. "What guarantees would you give that the demons be used for that purpose only?" he asked suspiciously.

A gleam of hope flickered. "Any guarantees Your Eminence requires."

Heavy lids drooped over the fishy eyes. "And if I require you to pledge your life on it?" the cardinal asked softly.

"I will pledge."

"You will swear?"

"I will swear."

The little man's voice grew quieter yet. "Would you submit to a stronger charge than that?"

So much for the doctrine that the College never indulged in gramarye. Toby doubted that the hob would allow him to be hexed with a lethal conjuration, but if he breathed a word about the hob to this pompous little parasite, he would find himself with an iron blade through his heart in very short order.

"Anything Your Eminence requires." He hoped that the hob, if it did rebel, would begin by frying Ricciardo Cardinal Marradi in batter.

"Mm." The arch-acolyte seemed almost disappointed. "I shall discuss this proposal with my colleagues. Return in four days at the same hour, and I will let you know then of Their Eminences' decision. If it is favorable, I may even have some material for you to transport to your hexer, Fischart. I warn you that you will be the one pledged for their proper use and safe return."

The College, or some powerful faction within the College, did accept the agreement. Even more surprising, the hob did not object to the binding, and Toby had returned from his second trip to Tivoli carrying the squirrel's horde, a sack of jewels so heavy that even he could barely lift it single-handed.

49

Without warning the mists wavered, and the hoof-beats lost their odd metallic note. Trees came into view, at first like wraiths and then more distinct. A wall, a gate . . . reality returned at the wooded uphill edge of the muddy, disfigured slope where the Don Ramon Company had camped for half a year.

Smeòrach rarely made a fuss entering the Un-place, but coming out of it was another matter. There were dangers in the real world, in this case shrubbery, walls, many men on horses, and a foul reek of burning. He brayed, bucked, and kicked up his heels. Toby was no Don Ramon. He was an adequate horseman at best, and he had no saddle. He hit the real world with a crack that blew all the air out of his lungs. Chabi went in search of a tree. Demons! That was not exactly a dignified way to begin a war. His linen armor had saved him from serious hurt, but he needed a moment to let the sky and branches stop spinning.

A banner bearing the winged lion of Venice came into view, being carried by a puzzled-looking young *gonfalonier* on a white horse. A knight in full armor on an armored destrier appeared beside him.

"Hawking with an owl?" inquired the mocking tones of Captain-General Alfredo. "In daylight? How many mice today, messer?"

Ignoring the scorn for the moment, Toby sat up and took stock. The villa had been sacked the previous morning—he had seen the smoke then, and now he could smell it and view the charred remains. But the Fiend's troops had moved on, and in the night Alfredo's had come, the army of Venice that had been treading on Nevil's heels all the way from Bologna. The wood was full of knights and their warhorses, and there would be companies of infantry behind them. This was a small host compared to Nevil's multitude, although it included men of Padua, Verona, Ferrara, and many humbler towns. Even villages and hamlets had sent their youth to Florence to fight the Fiend.

To his left, the dozen or so hooded figures in white robes were Maestro Fischart and his hexers. Downslope, Smeòrach was still playing the fool, and no one had dared to go after him because they all thought he was demonized. Toby put two fingers in his mouth and whistled. The first edge of the sun blazed on the horizon, but there was still time, for Fiesole was very high. Dawn would come later down on the plain, where Florence glowed pink in the morning light, with no sign of war yet. Two hundred thousand men—it was a shock to realize that Nevil himself must be down there, too. For the first time in his life, Toby Longdirk was within reach of his implacable foe.

The Fiend had walked into his trap. That felt very good.

Feeling ready to face Stiletto's mockery, he scrambled to his feet. "Good day to you, Captain-General. Last night the *darughachi* appointed me *comandante* of the armies of Italy."

A careful smile appeared under Alfredo's visor. "Officially at last? Congratulations! Well earned. And what orders have you for us today, Your Excellency?" As if he did not know.

"Just one, messer." Toby pointed to the enemy. *"Kill!"*

Alfredo's grin became more convincing. He raised his silver baton in salute. "It shall be done, *comandante*. Drummer, sound the Prepare to Advance!"

Toby turned to give Smeòrach a pat, then heaved himself onto the big oaf's sweat-slick back. Chabi wheeled down to his shoulder as he rode over to the waiting hexers. Volunteers they all were, officially, and he had not asked where Fischart had found them, but he was confident that most of them were skilled adepts, so he had already bent his oath to the cardinal very badly. He intended to break it into tiny fragments shortly. Four of the thirteen were women, and two of the others seemed barely more than boys. Most were keeping their hands out of sight inside their sleeves, but he knew that their fingers were weighted with rings, and they had chains of assorted gems hung around their necks under their robes. With this huge spiritual artillery they had concealed an army of more than fifty thousand from the Fiend's demons.

Fischart hurried forward to meet him, white robe swirling around his ankles. For once the grim old man was smiling, if that wolflike snarl could be called a smile. Nothing in his world mattered except fighting the Fiend, and he was about to inflict on that monster the worst shock he had ever had.

"Success!" he shouted as he approached. "We did it! Not a sign of alarm. No gramarye yet."

Drums were beating, bugles sounding, as the army of Venice prepared to move out down the hill.

"Magnificent! My congratulations to your associates. Lift the shield when the sun is one fingerswidth above the hills."

"The men won't be in contact with the enemy by then."

"You heard my order. Use no more gramarye until battle is joined or the enemy looses his demons."

Still panting from his run, the hexer scowled up at him. "You are hiding things from me!"

"I am *comandante*. I'll hide anything I want from anyone." Including, reasonably enough, himself. "I don't explain orders on battlefields, Maestro. I trust you to obey and do your best." He saluted the line of hexers, wheeled Smeòrach, and urged him forward into the Unplace.

❏   ❏   ❏

After the morning light, the Unplace seemed like a fog at midnight. Smeòrach's trotting hooves rang in a steady refrain.

"How do you know where you are going without a guide?" asked Sorghie's voice.

"I don't know. Don't know how I know, I mean. I seem to be my own familiar."

"And what secrets are you keeping from the man in the white robe?"

"The same ones I am keeping from you."

His helmet saved him from suffering a bitten ear at that point. Instead, the owl leaned under the brim and nipped his nose, which was no improvement.

"Stop that!"

"Will you tell me now, or must I hurt you more?"

"Well. It's a long story," he said. He did not know what the truth of it was. The cardinal had no reason except personal spite to want him dead. The hob probably would not have tolerated a real death hex. Enchantments on people faded quickly, and it was more than two months since his second trip to Tivoli—although Marradi might have renewed the gramarye when he was in Florence in March.

Before he had to answer, Smeòrach left the Unplace, trotting out of the mists onto green pasture. This time Toby calmed him and kept him under control, although he could no more have explained how he did it than he understood his own navigation. It seemed his wishes were commands now.

They were on the north bank of the Arno, a league or so downstream from Nevil's invading army—less

than a league, for he could make out individual tents in
the Fiend's camp. But vision could be deceptive here,
for when he looked around, he was only a bowshot
away from another army, already advancing at a slow
march to the beat of a drum, and obviously the enemy
had not seen it, nor the camp behind it. He turned
Smeòrach and cantered to meet the vanguard. His
appearance had coincided with the moment when the
first sliver of the sun's disk peeked over the ridge, and
a great cheer went up to greet him.

Wonderful, wonderful sight! This was to be
Longdirk's day even if it killed him, as it might do very
shortly. Here was an army larger than the one he had
led at Trent, yet still merely a quarter of the forces he
was now sending into battle. Even if he lost, he would
be remembered for having achieved one of the greatest
surprises in military history, while if he won . . . Time
enough to think about that when he did.

He was surprised that Ercole had put his cavalry
squadrons on the right and the infantry marching in six
battles on the left. He would have placed the men-at-
arms on the other wing, so the river would protect
their flank, but doubtless the old warrior had his reasons. Out in front rumbled the *carroccio,* a flat-
bottomed, rectangular cart, garishly painted and
drawn by two armored oxen. Traditionally the hexers
rode in this absurd battle wagon, but it was also a
mobile headquarters and a symbol of sovereignty. The
finest troops in the army would guard the *carroccio*
and perish to the last man around it if need be. Above
it floated the serpent banner of Milan.

There were other banners in the background—Savoy and Genoa, Pisa and Lucca, others, too. All the ancient rivalries had been set aside, and for that Toby could claim no credit. Well, perhaps a little bit. They had rallied to the standard he had raised.

Ercole Abonio was riding forward to meet him, accompanied by a knight whose surcoat bore the blazon of the Black Lances and who must therefore be di Gramasci. Two of the finest military leaders in Europe roared a welcome as soon as they were within earshot. In the far distance, cannons rumbled a reply. He glanced around, but it was too soon to discern smoke. He hoped it signified only Florence's defenders warning off an attack, not the battery on San Miniato opening fire on the city.

"I was getting worried!" Ercole shouted.

"I couldn't find a clean shirt!"

He halted, and they reined in on either side of him, eyeing the owl on his shoulder with surprise and noting the curious absence of a saddle, but the terror-thrill of upcoming battle was making them beam like children under their raised visors. On closer inspection their faces also showed the wear and tear of the long forced march, although less on the condottiere's, for he was the younger. Abonio had visibly aged since the conclave at Cafaggiolo, a month ago. No matter, Nevil's army had come farther and would be even wearier.

"You're late," the old *collaterale* said. "Trouble?"

"No trouble." The *comandante* just forgot what he was doing, that was all. "That's a truly dainty army you gentlemen have brought. Why don't you go and do something useful with it now?"

"We await only your word, Sir Tobiaso." Di Gramasci was not normally pompous. Did even these seasoned veterans suffer from battle nerves?

"Then here it is: Destroy the enemy! Have your hexers drop their shielding when the *carroccio* reaches that tree. Tell them to do nothing more until the fighting starts. That's important."

The two men exchanged puzzled glances, but did not argue.

Di Gramasci raised his baton in salute. "As you command, signore!"

But Ercole hesitated. "Forgive me if I ask one last time, lad. Must it still be no quarter?"

He was a good man, Abonio, an honorable soldier who had been loyal to his cousin the duke all his adult life. This savage new warfare was foreign to him, hard to take. Even Toby's heart twisted at the thought of the orders he had given, the suffering he must now cause. The two of them had argued this through most of the night at one of their secret midnight meetings in Milan, but Toby's view had prevailed in the end and must prevail now.

"You know what quarter the Fiend gives. Your orders are to show no mercy whatsoever. Announce that any man doing so is to be shot. Let the burden be on my soul."

He turned Smeòrach away and rode off into the Unplace.

❑   ❑   ❑

The mists had hardly swallowed them before Chabi asked, "Why must there be no quarter?"

"Because it must." Did she think he could not feel pity? She did not see the visions he saw, of thousands and tens of thousands of Nevil's troops surviving as lordless fugitives, starving outlaws, rabid dog packs overrunning Italy. There was no way to imprison so many, no money nor organization to escort them back to their own lands.

"Why is it important that the hexers do nothing before the fighting starts?"

"Because it is." What had he forgotten, or overlooked? If the cardinal's hex killed him soon, as it well might, could the alliance forge ahead to victory without him?

After a moment the shaman—or her familiar, or perhaps it was both of them—tried again. "Why did you suffer when we took you into the spirit world? Where did the pain come from?"

"An old memory." Perhaps he should have designated a deputy to take over if he fell, but it would probably have been a fruitless exercise. The coming carnage would be so confused and catastrophic that each of the six armies in the coalition would have to fend for itself. With the Magnificent dead, Sartaq would try to take more power into his own hands. He might even succeed, for he was a very shrewd and devious young . . .

Talons digging into his jerkin, the owl flapped her wings and screeched, much too close to his ear, even with the steel helmet between them. "Why do you not trust me? Did I not help you find your lost self? Where would you be now, who would you be without my help? What would have happened to your war?"

Women! And birds, for that matter. But Sorghaghtani did have a claim on him today.

"The demons the hexers are using were loaned to me by the College. I swore a solemn oath that they would be used only to make the armies invisible while they were assembling. They are not to be used for any other purpose, not even to heal wounded. I agreed to this because I had to, but I did not tell Maestro Fischart of the terms, so he has prepared his minions to take part in the battle."

Smeòrach's hooves rang in the silence for what seemed like a long time before the owl said, "You will break your solemn oath?"

"It has been broken. I have no way to stop the hexers now, and they would not obey me if I tried. You think they would stand by and watch Nevil's demons destroy living men? Or watch men bleed to death when they can be healed? That is a greater evil."

Chabi shifted feet on his shoulder. "Does the College not know this?"

"Yes, but the cardinal who provided the demons probably did so without proper authority. His crime can remain a secret only if I limit their use as he required. But I am not going to, so he will be exposed, and important people will discover that *he* broke *his* oath."

"How does that explain the orders you gave? Why should it matter if your oath is seen to be broken now or in a little while from now?"

Before he could think of suitable words to explain about the death hex, Smeòrach trotted out into sunlight. Now they were on the hills south of the city, on the downstream side, not half a league from the Porta San Giorgio, and the cannon fire was an almost continuous rumble. As far as he could see, all the smoke was rising from the gun towers on the walls of Florence, so it was still defensive fire. Nothing showed yet on the crest of San Miniato.

The Roman contingent was small but so well supported by its own hexer auxiliaries that Villari had dared to pitch camp almost on top of the enemy. Whatever his personal faults, the abrasive captain-general was a fighting cock. He had not waited for Toby's signal. His infantry was advancing with band playing, and his cavalry was already down in among the Fiend's baggage train, silencing a ragged rattle of arquebus fire. The cats were out of the bag, and Toby could wish he was back on the dome of the sanctuary hearing the excited screams of the Florentines as their deliverance poured into view from all directions.

Or in the fight, even better.

It would be even nicer to hear what King Nevil was saying at the moment. He had arranged his whole gigantic army facing inward to assault Florence and now had the impossible problem of turning it inside out to face an attack from the rear while it was already under fire. He would not panic, but his mortal minions must be in chaos already.

The Romans had shared their camp with lesser bands from Siena and Perugia, and the lion rampant banner of Florence still fluttered over Don Ramon and his cavalry. He probably would not have restrained himself more than another few minutes, but he did not have to. The ground trembled as he brought the monstrous armored Brutus galloping across the field to meet Toby. Excitement flashed in his blue eyes as bright as dawn on his shining armor.

"*Comandante!* At last!" He ignored the owl.

"Senor! All is as planned, except that the guns are on wheels. If they manage to turn them on you before you get there, you will be in grave danger."

The don's brief scowl brightened. "But then when we take them, we can turn them on the Fiend!"

"I hope you do. I ordered the sortie to aid you, and it will include cannoneers. Good luck, Captain-General."

"San Miniato is yours, *comandante!*" Don Ramon wheeled the great warhorse and cantered back to his command.

That left only the big Neapolitan contingent two hills over. Poor Paride Mezzo had stayed home, sending word that he would be less trouble to everyone if he died in his own bed, and the king had appointed Desjardins captain-general. That pugnacious warrior would almost certainly be on his way to join the battle by now, but he should still be given the signal promised. Toby kicked Smeòrach into a canter that took him back into the Unplace.

There was a sixth force in the Allied army, but it was far away . . .

"Why are you laughing, Little One?"

"Did I laugh? I was remembering the Swiss contingent arriving at the conclave, that's all. I hadn't taken old Beltramo into my confidence at that point. When I told him he was not welcome, the expression on his face was most wonderful to behold!" The crusty old soldier had worked miracles to wring agreement out of the cantons and hammer together the combined delegation, but when he arrived unexpectedly at Cafaggiolo, Toby's first reaction had been less than tactful. Of course the situation had been clarified at that night's secret session—shielded from spies by Maestro Fischart—and the Swiss had enthusiastically agreed to join the deception. They had stormed off in feigned disgust the next morning, and undoubtedly Nevil's agents had informed him that he need not fear Swiss intervention. So today his lines of communication and the garrisons he had left to hold the Alpine passes would be chewed to rags. If he did manage to pull his forces loose from the Florentine trap, he would find the door locked behind him and no way home.

"So you have won?" asked the owl.

"Won? *Won?* No! Not yet. We've hardly started. We're still badly outnumbered, and Nevil has beaten long odds before now. But if the don can seize the guns on the hill, then Florence is safe. If the Milanese and the Neapolitans can take the Fiend's bridges, we'll have cut his army in half. In an hour or so we'll know the shape of the battle and who needs help. Why do you only speak in the Unplace?"

"Is this not part of the spirit world?"

Somewhere a demon was loosed. The hex struck. Toby screamed and fell off Smeòrach's back.

50

Lisa awoke with her mother having hysterics beside her left ear because guns were firing and that meant the Fiend was coming to get them. Possibly so, but a screaming panic seemed an entirely inappropriate reaction, at least when there was no sturdy Hamish around to apply the treatment of choice. Grabbing Blanche by the shoulders, she administered a thorough shaking. Had this treatment not worked, she would probably have worked up to face-slapping, but that proved unnecessary. Silence fell.

There were cannons firing, and that was scary. "Let us get dressed," she said, "and go down and find out what's happening." She scrambled out of bed and rang for help, although she suspected it might not appear. "Come, Mother!"

There was only room in her life for so many emergencies, and she had not finished dealing with yesterday's yet. Was she or was she not married? The contract had been publicly signed and sealed, which ought to mean *yes she was*. But the, um, private parts of the arrangement had not been completed, and probably that meant *no she wasn't*. She rummaged through a chest in search of fresh linen.

"I hope we can find out today," she said as she tossed her findings in her mother's direction, "whether

I am a guest in this place—and if so who our host is—
or if I own it."

"I just hope it doesn't get burned down before
sundown," Blanche retorted, struggling to dress herself without the assistance she had enjoyed all her life.
The guns were growing louder.

Had any Queen of England ever been tortured to
death by her own father?

Presentable, if not quite as well groomed as was their
wont, they descended the great staircase hand in hand
and were greeted by a low bow from Prince Sartaq,
who was wearing riding boots and had just handed his
cloak off to an attendant. His two villainous-looking
shamans and half a dozen of his Tartar guards skulked
in the background.

"Greetings, ladies! I trust you rested well after
yesterday's harrowing experiences?"

"What news?" Blanche demanded.

His smiles made his eyes disappear altogether.
"Good news! Excellent news. The Fiend has been
dealt such a blow as he never dreamed of. Come, let us
together break our fast, and I will tell you all about this
miracle."

Lisa was still not sure whether she liked the Khan's
son or not. She had been prejudiced against him by
Hamish, who had foamed at the mouth when
denouncing the prince's meddling. An idiot, he had

said—a libertine who wantoned with loose women
when he should be attending to business, a procrasti-
nating popinjay who claimed the right to make all the
decisions and then refused to make them or made
stupid ones, and so on, with other complaints fortunately being expressed in languages she did not comprehend. Now she had lived in the same palace as
Sartaq for almost a month, and he did not seem so con-
temptible. He had insisted they adopt the royal habit of
addressing each other as "cousin" to avoid awkward
considerations of precedence. He could be witty and
even charming once you got used to his horse-
stepped-on-it face. From the neck down he was
impressive. Although Mother had mumbled some
embarrassed warnings, and the chambermaids had
told very scandalous stories, he had behaved like a
perfect gentleman to Lisa. Despite his lack of years, he
had more self-esteem than a peacock and could bran-
dish his father's authority like a battle-ax when he
chose. He had taken charge of the whole palace after
Pietro's death and evidently still retained it.

Now he commandeered a minor dining room and
demanded fast service. While waiting for results, he
explained: "The Fiend has fallen into a brilliantly
planned trap. Yesterday he brought his two armies
together at Florence. This morning he was taken by
surprise when *comandante* Longdirk attacked. The
battle still rages, but I am confident that Nevil is
doomed to a major defeat."

"Praise to the spirits!" Blanche cried, dramati-
cally clasping hands under her chin.

"So the big man really is a military genius?" Lisa inquired uneasily. "Did he burn any forests this time?"

Sartaq glanced at her inscrutably. "No, Cousin, but he conceived one of the greatest deceptions in the history of warfare, and then managed to pull it off. With a certain amount of assistance, I add in all modesty. Let us sit here, Aunt. We have still found no trace of Lucrezia the wicked. Perchance we never shall. No one knows who will succeed to leadership of the family and city. I expect the cardinal will make the final decision. This need no longer concern us, for Florence has served its purpose."

As soon as food had been laid out, he shooed the servants away. "I shall myself wait upon you, ladies," he declared, "for I have secrets to impart unheard. Red wine or white?"

When he had poured wine for everyone, he settled on the other side of the table. "A toast! I am confident that the threat to Italy is over. Nevil has met his match at last." He raised his goblet in salute. "To his fall and destruction!"

"To the fall and destruction of Rhym." Blanche had recovered much of her color, although she was not yet about to smile at anything.

"Ah, true! Forgive me. If your unfortunate husband can be restored, then we shall all applaud that outcome. However . . ." Seemingly quite unabashed by his slip, he looked thoughtfully at Lisa.

She dropped her eyes and noticed the basket of rolls in front of her. One day she had told Pietro how much she had enjoyed the French-style rolls she had met in Savoy, and they had appeared on every table since, fresh baked. She would not pretend she had ever loved him, but he had been a considerate host and a generous fiancé. She had grown accustomed to the prospect of being married to him, comfortable with it. He had not deserved that shameful death. She knew she might yet do a great deal worse in the husband market than Pietro Marradi.

The prince was still appraising her like a dealer at a horse fair.

"Am I now a widow, Cousin?"

Sartaq chuckled. "You mean can you claim a share of the Marradi fortune? I doubt it very much. Even if there is a way for a woman to own property in this city, which I doubt, and if you can hire a skilled advocate to take your case, which I doubt even more, to expect any Florentine court to rule in your favor would be optimism verging on fatuity. Whatever gifts the Magnificent gave you will still be yours, I expect, and you can probably extract a generous settlement if you just promise to go away and stay away, so you are a wealthy woman by most standards. Without even counting your claim to England, I mean."

"But it is my claim to England that is chained around my ankle, isn't it?"

"Lisa!"

"It's true, Mother. There are men dying out there, so let us not play games in here. You are already wondering who to marry me off to, aren't you, Cousin?"

The prince acknowledged her argument with an

amused nod and reached into the fruit bowl. "Not exactly."

"You've already decided?" Her heart sank. No, it dived under the table and tried to creep out of the room unnoticed.

"The choice is very limited." He popped a date in his mouth. "Fair lady, I would most eagerly marry you myself. That solution creates new problems, though, because I gave my father and certain significant brothers my most solemn oath that I would neither name myself suzerain nor otherwise attempt to seize power. This condition they insisted on before they would approve my meddling in the affairs of Europe. It is written into my accreditation, and I am fairly sure they also hexed me so that I will drop dead or my head will fall off if I break my word. Trust"—he turned his face to spit out the pit—"is not a prominent trait in my family.

"The situation let me explain, Cousin. My mother was my honored father's third wife, one of those chosen for political reasons, and of his sons I am seventh born. I am not sure how many of us there were at last count, but enough for any reputable purpose. In recent centuries it has become customary for the succession to pass to the Khan's eldest son by his principal wife. Eldest surviving, that is, for mortality has always been fairly high among the leading candidates to rule the Golden Horde. Nevertheless a run of six misfortunes—accidents, sudden fevers, or suicides—is not reasonably to be expected. I seemed foredoomed to limit my interests to falconry and camel racing."

Lisa had not heard him discuss himself or the royal family before. She was not at all sure she wanted to. "You are being cynical."

His slit eyes narrowed in what might have been a smile. "I enjoy the chance to speak freely, Cousin. In Sarois these remarks would be suicidal, even within the family. Especially within the family. Where was I? Oh, yes. We have known for many generations that the Horde is not what it was. The descendants of fanatic steppe warriors have become fat cattle, indolent and timorous, who will one day be conquered and enslaved just as our ancestors enslaved the known world. Nor were we at all surprised to see Europe rise up against our rule. Our claim to overlordship has been largely a fiction for at least a century, although we did provide a useful service by maintaining the balance of power. If any ruler grew too powerful, the Khanate would assign the suzerainship to whomever seemed most likely to bleed him back to health, but such dominion must ultimately rest on the power to enforce it, and Nevil exposed our bluff for all the world to see. We regretfully concluded that our hegemony had ended.

"A confession: In my youth, being somewhat ambitious—within the limits of my loyalty to my dear Brother Kublai, of course—I always harbored a secret dream of striking some dramatic blow to bring the rebel lands back into the fold, and even had hope that such a demonstration of martial prowess might win me advancement."

Lisa raised a skeptical eyebrow.

"That and a couple of murders," Sartaq agreed, helping himself to a pastry.

"Including Prince Kublai's?"

"Especially Kublai's, definitely. When news came that Nevil had finally lost a battle, I ventured to write and congratulate the young unknown who had achieved this feat. In my father's name I wrote. He replied, a most interesting message. Over the previous dozen years, appeals have poured into Sarois by the hundred, all of them saying, in effect, 'Send help! Come and fight for us! Send men, guns, horses.' This one was different. It said, 'I can defeat Nevil, but it would be advantageous if Your Majesty would send an envoy.' He did not say very clearly why or how, and he admitted that the man in question should be expendable." He chuckled. "My brothers were all in favor of sending me. Especially Kublai. So here I am."

The general direction of this conversation was highly unsatisfying! Not Longdirk? Surely not marry Longdirk! Lisa's fingers were systematically crumbling a roll to dust. "I did not realize you came to Italy to assist Sir Tobias."

He noted her tone and paused. "I have just explained that my intention was to use him. Why are you surprised?"

"Well . . ." she said. Not Longdirk! He must not marry her to Longdirk! "Do please understand that he never discussed such matters in my presence, but the general chitchat around the camp was that he found your actions to be somewhat at cross-purposes with his own."

Sartaq did not take offense. Indeed, he chuckled and refilled his goblet. "If that was the worst you heard, then I failed utterly. My first encounter with that human bull came a few nights after my arrival in Naples. He turned up at Castel Capuano in the middle of the night and won admittance to my bedchamber—which was a hair-raising achievement in itself. Having dragged me from my bed, as it were, he explained to me just how he intended to set a trap for King Nevil. You understand, I had come on this wild escapade in the hope of winning renown? Longdirk wanted me for bait. He was setting a trap, right here in Florence, and needed every minnow he could find on his hooks, with the Khan's son as an especially juicy morsel. He also—"

"And a Queen of England as another?"

Sartaq sighed and reached for more dates. He was watching her reaction, though. "I am afraid so, Cousin. He told me that the Fiend's wife and daughter had fallen into his hands two days earlier, quite unexpectedly, and when the time was ripe, he would . . . dangle you before the bull, I think was how he put it. He used some curious Spanish imagery."

"How can this be?" Blanche demanded, her fingers fidgeting nervously on the cloth. "I admit I was not at my best then, but I am sure Constable Longdirk was never absent from the villa long enough to make a journey to Naples."

"He did not travel by lawful means, Aunt."

"It is true, then, that he is possessed by a demon?" Lisa asked. Perhaps she would get a straight answer at last.

Sartaq heaved his big shoulders in a shrug. "He is possessed by something, certainly. It does not seem to be a demon, not a true demon, or perhaps not yet a demon, but he wields powers honest men do not."

"Oh, no!" Blanche said. "We were in the clutches of an incarnate?" She eyed Lisa in alarm, as if wondering what damage she might have overlooked. "You say it was he who revealed our identities?"

It must be. Sartaq had arranged this entire conversation just so he could make that indictment.

"Absolutely," he said regretfully. "He told the Magnificent and me about you early on. Toby planned everything, including your betrothal to Marradi. He persuaded me to name Marradi suzerain, he told Marradi to let slip your existence by deliberate accident during the conclave, when we could be certain Nevil had spies in place. And so on. He brewed his plans with gramarye in secret and in public faked a monstrous disorder."

"But . . ." Blanche protested. "When the Magnificent named him *comandante* last night at the wedding, I was watching his face, and I am certain he was taken by surprise."

"No, dear Aunt," Sartaq said with exaggerated patience. "He had ordered the Magnificent to do that. He had ordered me to approve it. He is an incredible actor. At Cafaggiolo I had to play court fool by naming the incompetent D'Anjou to the post—absolute idiocy! It was all Longdirk's idea, and he had given me detailed instructions on the matter the previous night, yet when I made the announcement he turned

scarlet with anger, as if he had been taken completely
by surprise.

"You see now why I so disliked his proposal when
he explained it at Castel Capuano? I had come west
hoping to be a hero. I could just accept the notion of
being bait, for there is a certain cachet in offering
one's breast to the sword. But he also required me to
play the fool, to act as an incompetent. The more we
could make it seem that my intervention had tangled
the traces, the more likely Nevil was to swallow the
lure. Very few people knew what was happening."

Hamish had not been one of them! That was
something to hold on to in all this terrible litany of
deception and betrayal. Hamish had been honest. He
would not have tolerated Longdirk's treachery.

"This churl . . ." The prince's bantering tone was
wearing thin. "The first thing the nursery eunuchs
taught me was to recite my ancestry back fourteen
generations to Genghis, yet this baseborn serf cast
himself in the role of Savior and me as Lord High
Bungler! I could hear my brothers' laughter already.
When it comes, it will be audible all the way from
Sarois."

"But you did cooperate?" Blanche said. "You
went along with his deception?"

Sartaq spat out another date pit. "I had no choice,
Aunt. There was no other plan in sight, and I was certainly not capable of organizing one. When I asked
people—King Fredrico, the cardinals, condottieri,
anyone—who would make the best *comandante,* the
only name I ever heard was Longdirk. He had

ensnared me with that single letter, months before. I
had to cooperate or slink home with my ears down. I
confess that the opportunities he gave me to slight him
in public have been the most enjoyable parts of my
visit."

He chewed for a moment, then said with a reluctant smile, "There is something almost noble in the
way he endured it. By day, we spat in his beard. By
night, when we met, he would thank us! Small wonder
that Nevil discounted him."

"And you will force me to marry this snake,
Cousin? This churl, this betrayer, this demon incarnate?"

Sartaq turned to Lisa, looking startled.

"Forgive me. I express myself poorly in this language. I am aware that your heart draws you to this
man, but—"

"With respect, Cousin, it does nothing of the sort!
Far from it! Disregard any such rumor."

"Oh?" He laughed. "Then this is easier. What I
am trying to tell you is that the last man in Europe I
will let you marry is Toby Longdirk. He has worked
wonders. He may even destroy Nevil completely
before this day is out. But is he an improvement?
Where does his loyalty lie? I do not know. Nor do I
know if he planned this, but because we excluded him
from all the ceremonies, he has never performed the
ritual of obeisance! Not even when he was appointed
comandante yesterday."

Lisa gasped, and a moment later her mother
gulped.

"Are you telling us, Cousin, that Longdirk deliberately murdered my husband to avoid having to swear allegiance to the Khan?"

Sartaq shrugged and drew his knife to cut a slice of meat from the cold lamb. "I don't think so." He seemed reluctant to make that admission. "We had not planned to include the obeisance in the middle of the wedding. My advisors believe that the murder was aimed at Longdirk, and his spiritual defenses deflected it. But it is worrisome. If this battle goes Longdirk's way, as I expect it will, then there will be no stopping him. Don't be surprised if his men turn up at the door to take you into, um . . . 'protective custody' is the usual expression, I believe."

51

He could see nothing. He could hear. He could smell sweat, taste blood, and he most certainly could feel.

The drum beat its slow refrain—*tap*—pause—*tap*—and after each *tap* the cat-o'-nine-tails crashed against his back, and the whole world exploded in fire. He was back on Mulliez's whipping post, hanging by his wrists, being beaten to bloody shreds.

tap—pause—*"Neuf!"*

But this was wrong. He could not think because of—

crash!—

—the pain, but this could not be happening. This was gramarye and—

tap—pause—*"Dix!"*

he ought to be able to deal with it, if he could just find—

crash!—

—oh, demons!—the answer. This was not real. This was gramarye. Hex.

tap—pause—*"Onze!"*

—the cardinal! Hob! Help! Sorghie!—

crash!—

—oh, spirits! Help me, Sorghie! I've never called for help in my—

tap—pause—*"Douze!"*

—life before, but I need you, need you, need you . . .

In a dark sky on a dark field a white owl swoops low and, snatching up its quarry, is gone on wings of silence . . .

He had his clothes on. There was no blood in his mouth or on his back. He was lying on rough ground with his head in Sorghaghtani's lap, and she was sobbing hysterically, weeping without tears. Sunlight through branches dappled the sky.

"Sorghie! Sorghie?"

She gasped, barely able to breathe. "Little One?"

"It's all right, Sorghie. Thank you, oh, thank you!" He found her hand and squeezed it. Trees, early-morning sky, a few birds singing . . . No sign of Chabi. "How did you get here?"

"Did you not need me?"

"I needed someone, yes!" He would probably have managed without her, eventually, but the sooner the better in that sort of trap. Marradi! That nasty, small-minded—

She choked a few times. Her absurd shaman hat lay discarded on the grass, and sunlight glinted highlights in her thick black hair. Her eyes were still bandaged. "What happened, Little One?"

"A very spiteful man, that's all." Ricciardo Cardinal Accursed Marradi.

"He was going to kill you?"

Toby heaved himself up to a sitting position. His head swam a bit, but he was basically unharmed. One day, when he had time, he would try to work out what had happened. "Maybe. I don't think so. I think he laid a death hex on me so he could tell his friends he had, but he knew I had some gramarye and could break it." No way to be sure, though. He wasn't even sure he could have broken it without Sorghie's help. It had been a close call.

"You broke your oath now?"

"Let's go and see." The sun was still very low through the trees, but that distant rumble was the mudded-up sound of guns and thousands of hooves, war cries and dying screams, drums and bugles—the noise of battle that could inspire a man to wild killer frenzy and simultaneously make him want to crawl under a bush and hide. It could not have been going on very long yet. He rearranged himself to rise, and somehow the movement put his face closer to hers, and then it was quite natural to take her in his arms and kiss her.

She was as tiny as a doll. She returned the kiss eagerly, moaning with delight, seeming willing to let it go on forever, child trying to become instant woman. He wanted to crush her and certainly could if he tried, while her embrace was barely perceptible through his armored jerkin.

Breaking loose was surprisingly difficult. "Oh, Sorghie! That cannot be."

She buried her face in his neck, snuffling like a puppy. "We helped, didn't we?"

"You didn't just help. Without you and Chabi it would have been impossible. I would not have remembered to give the signal, and the armies would not have attacked."

"Our walk was not for nothing then?"

"No." He kissed her again. He did not fear the hob with Sorghie. She was so tiny in his arms that his body was not taking her seriously. Given time, though . . . He eased his lips away from hers. She smiled and also sighed.

"All over?"

"Yes, I'm afraid so. Come along."

Smeòrach had tangled his reins in a bush not far off and was resolutely trying to eat with the bit still in his mouth, which would just plain ruin his digestion. Toby climbed aboard and pulled the blind shaman up beside him. Then he rode off into the Unplace.

Only two reserve battles of infantry remained near the Neapolitan camp. Voices were raised in alarm when the unknown horse materialized nearby, but a glance showed him that the war was not here, and he did not linger.

Smeòrach's hooves clattered on paving, and he neighed in alarm to find himself in the crowded street outside Giovanni's Inn. But this was home at the moment. It had oats. He neighed again, more hopefully. Other horses and even some people neighed back at him, alarmed at his mysterious materialization.

"Toby!" Hamish came plowing through the crowd like a mad bull. "Where have you been? Do you know what's happening out there?"

Toby lifted Sorghaghtani and more or less dropped her into Hamish's arms, then slid off Smeòrach's back. A wagonload of fatigue seemed to land on his shoulders, making his knees tremble. Hamish was never going to forgive him for keeping him in the dark so long.

"More or less. Is Diaz ready at the Porta San Miniato?"

"He says you were babbling about a suicide sortie."

"Well, it shouldn't be suicide now. The don's about to take the hill. Round up all the reserves we've got and get them over to Porta San Miniato to help. Tell Diaz he'll need . . . No, look after these two, and I'll tell him." Thrusting Sorghie at Hamish with one hand and the reins with the other, Toby turned and ran.

He had never tried the Unplace on foot before. The shiny surface was oddly bouncy and yet slippery, the mists more menacing, but in a few moments he returned to reality just inside the Porta San Miniato. Even from the street he could see that there was a battle in progress on the hill as the don tried to seize the guns and the Fiend's troops defended them. Diaz already had the gate open and was leading the infantry out at the double. Toby squeezed into the column and went with them, laughing at his neighbors' astonishment, shouting encouragement and promises that the Fiend was heading for defeat. Once outside the walls, he stepped aside and surveyed the scene. Things seemed to be going well, as was to be expected with the don and Antonio in charge. He could leave it to them, and the army of Florence would win its share of the battle.

A riderless horse came galloping down the slope in terror. It was not one of the armored chargers the knights rode, but its trappings were too grand for the nags that archers and pikemen rode to the field. Most likely it was an infantry officer's mount. It responded to his whistle—accompanied by some of this strange unconscious gramarye he could call upon now—and he sprang onto its back, not even waiting to lengthen the stirrups.

"Onward, Orphan!" he said, and rode into the Unplace.

52

Nevil had moved much less than half his forces across the Arno, so the battle would be decided on the north bank, where he had the advantage of numbers. Toby headed downstream again, to Ercole and his Milanese.

Set-piece encounters might last all day or several days while the opposing commanders maneuvered and countermaneuvered, and some condottieri were notorious for never coming to grips at all. Toby had broken the rules yet again by involving almost all of the forces right from the start, and furthermore most of the men and horses on both sides had just completed prolonged forced marches. The battle of the Field of Florence was likely to be brief, with one side or the other collapsing from exhaustion.

He emerged from the Unplace close behind the Milanese *carroccio,* which had come to a halt. No one even noticed him. The whole army had come to a halt, infantry and cavalry alike drawn up in battle order, cheering and roaring approval as the famous Genoese and Pisan crossbowmen poured arrows into the plunging chaos of the Fiend's forces. His infantry had been advancing to assault the city walls; his cavalry had apparently been caught napping or at breakfast, still in quarters. Now knights were struggling to don armor, squires were trying to saddle up horses, about thirty thousand noncombatants were milling around in panic, and the men-at-arms were fighting their way through the camp to face the threat from their rear—while all the time that deadly hail fell from the sky.

The archers would run out of ammunition very soon at the rate they were going, but the terrain here was flat and open, perfect for the cavalry charge Ercole was about to launch. The effort to imagine what would happen when that hit the massed disorder was enough to raise Toby's flesh in goose bumps. Obviously this part of the battle was proceeding satisfactorily, meaning there was going to be a massacre. With a shudder, he rode back into the Unplace.

Next port of call must be the upstream north bank, where Alfredo's Venetians were seriously outnumbered, but Orphan was not Smeòrach. Disapproving of the ringing mirrored surface, the pearly mists, and the looming darkness behind them, he was skittish and unruly, more inclined to go sideways than forward. Toby was so intent on controlling his mount that it took him a moment to realize that they were not alone. Something was tracking them, several somethings. The hob knew them better than he did—dark, low shapes bounding along, closing rapidly. He kicked Orphan into a gallop. Idiot! He should have remembered the Fiend's enormous stable of demons. He had been detected.

At least six of them. He sensed fangs and claws, giant nightmare weasels with eyes glowing green. Orphan had seen them, too, and needed no encouragement now, but his best turn of speed was not going to be enough. The monsters were closing in, claws skittering on the shiny dreamscape.

Spirits! How did one get out of the Unplace in a hurry? Even if he knew some way to jump back to reality, he might land himself in the middle of Nevil's army. Time was unrelated to distance, so changing his destination now might merely prolong his danger. Orphan was going flat out and had already worked up a fine lather, his eyes wide with terror, yet still the monsters drew closer—coming in on the left, where Toby could not get at them with his sword, even if a blade would be any use against discarnate demons. Or perhaps they were trying to drive him to the right. Right, left, front, or back all seemed exactly the same here, but he strongly suspected that once he let them choose the direction they could also choose the destination and force him to emerge where they wanted him to emerge, which might be right in front of Nevil himself.

Water! If the shiny surface were water, it ought to hinder those low-slung horrors more than it would hamper Orphan. He called for water. Orphan's hooves began throwing up splashes, and the surface rippled wildly. Deeper, make it deeper, up to Orphan's knees . . . Now the weasel-things were floundering, splashing, slowing down. But water had its own dangers. It continued to grow deeper of its own accord, and he could not stop it. Orphan broke out of his gallop, to a canter, then a trot, and the dark tide was washing at Toby's boots. The weasels had vanished. Something else was raising ripples behind him and drawing closer on his left. Water had not been a good idea. If he did not reach Fiesole soon, he wasn't going to reach it at all.

A spinning ball of flame soared in out of the mists

ahead and plunged into the water barely a span from his left foot. Something huge and dark reared up, burst into flames, and screamed. Orphan plunged forward in terror. Another ball of flame, then more, all hurtling overhead to smite the unseen pursuers. When he glanced back, he saw six pillars of fire roaring in the water, boiling up columns of steam.

Orphan stumbled out of the Unplace onto grass, and came to a shivering halt, frozen by gramarye, with his eyes wildly rolling.

"That was excessively stupid, even for you!" Maestro Fischart had to shout over the shrieking wind that was thrashing his white robe around. The dozen or so adepts gathered behind him were similarly being roiled and buffeted, staggering as the gusts changed direction. The sky overhead loomed low, black clouds hiding the sun, but the storm was local, confined to the area between Fiesole and the river.

"What's happening?" Toby demanded. He had no time for recrimination or even thanks. The nightmares he would enjoy later, when he had leisure. And he could see what was happening. Alfredo's initial attack had been repulsed. Now his Venetians were being driven back toward Fiesole by sheer weight of numbers. He had dismounted his cavalry, making the knights fight on foot, two men to a lance. Nevil had done the same, but he had three times the numbers, and his advantage in standard infantry might be even more than that. The speed with which his forces here had rallied from their surprise suggested that Nevil himself was in charge of this sector.

"We're holding him in demons," Fischart shouted. "But we need more helmets." Lightning flashed overhead, thunder boomed painfully close.

"I'll see what I can do." In the end, all battles came down to the basics of steel and flesh.

"Wait! You need a guard." The hexer turned to his remaining supporters and shouted orders.

Toby did not wait. They could catch him. He urged Orphan forward, feeling the calming enchantment lift at his order. But he dipped only briefly through the Unplace, emerging alongside Alfredo, where he sat his horse with half a dozen officers and mounted squires around him. They were surveying the battle, and the faces showing under their raised visors were grim.

Toby gave them a big smile. "Stiletto! Are you enjoying this fine morning?"

Alfredo's return grin was strained. "It's good exercise! You want to bring some friends to join the party? We can make room for more."

"I'll round some up. How long can you hang on here?"

If the Venetian captain-general shrugged, his steel breastplate hid the gesture. "An hour at most. Fifteen minutes would be healthier."

"Don't go away!" Toby vanished.

Now the Unplace was populated. He rode within an escort. There seemed to be at least a score of them, but they were shadowy and indistinct, mostly mounted knights with their visors down, riding in silence on either side of him. Some of them—or perhaps all of them some of the time—had other shapes: centaurs with lion heads, dragon monsters with wings above their backs, even giant scorpions. He paid no attention. He had seen demons before, and what they looked like was immaterial. All that mattered was that they were conjured to defend him.

He crossed the river to join up with the Neapolitan forces, and there he found himself in a full cavalry charge, riding alongside Jules Desjardins, the captain-general. That was no place for a man without a lance and a complete suit of steel mail, but he had a few seconds before the thundering line met its approaching counterpart. He bellowed over the din.

"Captain-General! It's me, Longdirk."

The steel-clad figure showed no reaction, but that was hardly surprising. His hands were fully occupied with lance and reins. He could not move his helm, and he had very little lateral vision inside it. His opinion of Toby's timing for a chat was best left to the imagination.

"We need to reinforce Alfredo," Toby yelled. "I'm going to take Gioberti." The two lines of cavalry were closing fast. He had to leave or die.

He left.

Egano Gioberti was Desjardins's deputy. Busily regrouping two battles of infantry, preparing for a second assault, he looked up in astonishment as Orphan emerged from empty air beside him and shuddered to a halt. Toby barked orders: The Fiend's bridge was still standing, and if Gioberti could seize that, then he could start moving troops over the river to relieve the

Venetians. He might not get very many across, and they
might be slaughtered when he did, but he would at least
distract the Fiend and relieve pressure on Alfredo.
Gioberti was an experienced condottiere. He understood at once and began shouting orders of his own.

Florence was out of danger because its own army had
taken the summit of San Miniato hill. Now the don
was expertly supervising the hunting down and butchery of survivors and at the same time redirecting the
guns to fire at the Fiend's forces. They were at the
extreme limit of range, but a few balls bouncing along
into their backs ought to distract them a little, enough
to make Desjardins's work easier.

    Master of Gunnery Calvalcante was there, too,
chortling over the newfangled cannons. Nobody
needed Toby's help. He left them all to it.

That left Bruno Villars and the Romans. The fight in
the southwest was almost over, and Villars had
enhanced even his reputation. Perhaps if he were a
more pleasant person, he would not be so demons-
take-it good at fighting. He had driven the Fiend's
forces into the angle between the river and the city
wall and was slaughtering them. Revolted by the sight,
although it was what he had ordered, Toby went on
without stopping.

                    ❏   ❏   ❏

Ercole Abonio again . . .

A score of the Milanese knights were standing around, or sitting on the ground, recovering from their exertions while squires fussed around them, tending them and their horses. One or two were being tended by medics. The old *collaterale* had removed his helmet and was seated on a low stone wall. His face was still flushed from the heat inside his armor; he had a wineskin in his hands. There was blood all over his surcoat, and his thinning salt-and-pepper hair was streaked by sweat, but he grinned when he saw who had arrived.

Toby leaned down from the saddle. "Can you spare a mouthful?"

"Only if you're sure you've earned it." He passed over the wineskin. A boyish squire came running with another.

"That isn't your blood, is it?"

"Isn't even human, I'm afraid. Horse."

Toby took a drink and surveyed the field. The makeshift bridge was a smoking ruin, but since the Allies were obviously winning on both banks on this downstream side, that was not overly serious. Now he could appreciate why Ercole had stationed his infantry on the left. Having broken the opposition with his archers and cavalry, he had deployed the foot soldiers to close off any possible retreat to the hills. Like Villars, he had pinned the Fiend's forces between the river and the city wall. He just had not reached the butchery part yet, and there was a lot of arquebus firing going on.

"How is the struggle going elsewhere, *comandante?*" asked a sweat-soaked face from inside a helm, a young knight Toby did not know.

"Very well on the left bank. Upstream, the Venetians are in serious trouble. Ercole? Can you—"

The old warrior brightened. "Certainly! Luigi, Giovanni—help me up. We can leave the infantry to clean up here, Tobias. If I take the cavalry around, will that be enough?"

Toby almost laughed aloud with relief. "You'd probably be enough all by yourself, you old scoundrel. Yes! By all means. But be as quick as you can."

Ercole opened his mouth and pealed like a thunderstorm over the noise of battle: "Fresh horses! Drummer, sound the Prepare to Advance!"

Toby went off to tell Alfredo that relief was on its way.

The Fiend's Brenner Pass army was pressing Alfredo hard when Abonio brought the Milanese knights around the city to attack on its left. Shortly after that, Gioberti fell on its rear. The Venetians took new heart and counterattacked. Even so, the fighting continued to rage under the howling demonic storm clouds. It seemed incredible that men could continue to fight for so long without dropping dead of exhaustion. Toby lost all track of time. More than once he found himself in the lines, fighting alongside Tyroleans, then mercenaries wearing Neapolitan insignia, finally Venetians. Later he discovered blood on his sword and had very little memory of how it got there. (The legends that grew up later had him fighting in a hundred places all over the battlefield, rallying defeated troops with rousing speeches, leading charges, slaying famous warriors in single combat, but the truth had to be much less that that.) Three times he was attacked by demons, but each time his demonic bodyguards drove off the assault.

The end came suddenly, when a fiery apparition in the shape of a phoenix swirled up from the knoll where Nevil's standard flew and sped away to the north. Everywhere Allied troops raised a mighty cheer, knowing that the Fiend himself had quit the field with his attendant demons. Then Maestro Fischart and his assistants were able to break the enemy forces' spiritual bindings. Their resistance collapsed at once; they threw down their weapons and fell on their knees.

"No Quarter" was the order of the day, and most of the officers made efforts to enforce it. They failed. With few exceptions, Italian rank and file flatly refused to slaughter their defeated opponents. This minor mutiny had begun even before Nevil departed, and it spread rapidly over the entire battlefield, in a strange and spontaneous demonstration of mercy. If the invaders groveled convincingly and were willing to swear loyalty to Toby Longdirk, then their lives were spared. No one knew where that second condition came from, but possibly it was simply the most obvious way to dispose of the problem. No right-thinking Italian wanted his city to undertake the expense of maintaining a defeated army, but equally he did not want any of its neighbors to own it either, so he decided to give it to that young foreigner everyone seemed to trust. Let the *comandante* take it far away.

By the end of the day, the nightmare Toby had foreseen had come true, and almost seventy thousand of Nevil's troops were still alive. What he had not foreseen was that they had all sworn allegiance to him. They were all going to want to eat.

53

The continual booms and rattling of gunfire were apparently mere celebration. All the bells of Florence had been ringing for hours, while bonfires blazed in the night, and drunken mobs teemed through the streets. Even within the Marradi Palace, the few servants still around were unsteady on their feet and inclined to leer at their betters in ways that would not normally be tolerated. No family members were in evidence. Sartaq had advised Lisa and her mother to remain in their room and keep the door locked. Whether he was doing the same, they did not know, but he at least had a bodyguard and a couple of tame shamans around to look after him. The Fiend's defeat, in other words, was turning out to be little less frightening than his success might have been. It was after midnight when Lisa, supperless but exhausted, decided she might as well go to bed. Before she could say so, a thunderous knocking on the door almost sent her mother back into hysterics.

Lisa bent to shout through the keyhole. "Who's there?"

A blurred male voice said something about a *lettera*.

Even she could understand that word. "Um, *sotto il porta!*"

Not understanding her Italian, he just pushed the letter under the door and went away. It was brief, written in a poor hand.

> Sir Toby will wate upon thir magesttys within ye our.

He must have written it himself.

Blanche, reading over her shoulder, uttered a squeak like a pierced cat. "He's coming to get you!"

"Nonsense, Mother. I'm too young for . . ." Her voice wavered into silence. "Oh, Mother!"

The two of them fell into each other's arms.

To the victor belongs the loot. King Longdirk the First.

The summons did not come for at least two hours, far beyond the limit of time even two royal ladies could spend making each other ready for an important audience. The street racket remained as raucous as ever, but when the tap on the door came, it was more courteous than before.

"Who's there?"

"Colin McPhail, Your Majesty."

Ah! Half of Lisa shuddered in horror at the real-
ization that Longdirk really had come for her, and the
other half acknowledged that she knew Colin McPhail
and he was a decent young man. She unlocked the
door.

McPhail had a Marradi flunky with him as a guide, but
also half a dozen pikemen, which seemed an excessive
bodyguard for a journey downstairs in a palace.
Perhaps he knew more than she did. By the time they
reached the top of the staircase, Lisa was grateful for
their support, or at least for the lanterns they carried.
The great mansion was dark and deserted, even the
street noises barely penetrating its walls. Statuary
loomed like guardian spirits, the pictures were mysterious splodges—although she noted that the ones she
liked best by daylight were still the most interesting in
near darkness. She wondered if Pietro's wraith
haunted his ancestral home, and quickly decided that
he had not been evil, and the tutelary would cherish
his soul. Lucrezia was another matter altogether.
Where had she gone?

The hall was a cube of black emptiness whose
lower surface was sprinkled with a few candle flames
like fallen stars. At least a score of men were standing
in the middle, but the buzz of conversation ceased as
she approached. She recognized Guilo Marradi, and
Sartaq, and Longdirk by his size, but almost no one

else. Most of the men were soldiers—all swords, boots, armored jerkins, steel helmets.

Sartaq stepped forward. She curtseyed.

"Rise, Cousin," he croaked in his harsh accent, "and Aunt, too. I am happy to tell you that *comandante* Longdirk has just been reporting how he destroyed the Fiend's army, as instructed. Hence I have the pleasure to assure you that your royal persons are no longer in peril. Italy is saved."

Lisa curtseyed to him again, not to Longdirk. "That is indeed wonderful news, Your Highness. Sir Tobias is large, but I assume he had some assistance?"

"Indeed he had. Allow me to present: first *comandante* Longdirk, the hero of the day. You know Captain-General Don Ramon . . ."

As each man in turn stepped forward and bowed, she noticed that the two shamans were standing in the gloom at the edge of the group, but so also was Maestro Fischart, who was supposed to have died in Siena. So Longdirk's gramarye probably outweighed Sartaq's, and the prince was certainly outmatched in sheer muscle and steel if all these mercenaries were on Longdirk's side.

Then she saw Hamish in the background and forgot everything else. He was standing behind a small table that bore a gold candlestick, so his face was lit from below, making his expression eerie and hard to discern, but he was certainly staring very hard at her, and she was hard put not to stare back instead of going through the necessary absurdities of acknowledging the soldiers' bows. *Oh, Hamish, don't just stand there!*

*Take me away from all this madness. Drag me onto
your horse and ride for the hills.*

When the stupid rigmarole was ended, she was
left standing between Sartaq and her mother and could
no longer deny to herself that she would not be here if
she were not the subject of the meeting. Marriage?
Couldn't it wait until tomorrow? Even in the dancing,
uncertain candlelight she could tell that everyone there
was exhausted. Longdirk looked the worst, as if he
were close to unconscious on his feet. Servants were
doing something at the far end of the hall, laying out a
meal, perhaps.

"So what exactly is your proposal, *comandante?*"
Sartaq said. "Start at the beginning again, for we are
all very tired. Start, in fact, by explaining why the matter cannot wait a few days and must be discussed in
the middle of the night."

The big man squared his shoulders with a visible
effort, as if he carried an ox on them. "Logistics, Your
Highness. We have sixty thousand prisoners or more
outside the city and Allied armies three times that size.
Tuscany will be eaten to the roots if we wait. Nevil
must not be given time to raise another army. We must
start moving out right away."

"Orders," said a quiet voice from the wings. A
few heads turned to scowl at Hamish, who was the
prompter.

"Yes, orders," Longdirk mumbled. "Orders.
Someone has to be able to give the necessary orders,
and I have fulfilled the mandate . . ." His voice tailed
away.   .

"Two hundred thousand bodies," Sartaq said. "You need a few days to bury those . . . But carry on."

Longdirk seemed to sway. He turned his head. "Chancellor?"

Hamish spoke from where he stood. "These noble knights, Your Highness, your officers, petition you to appoint *comandante* Longdirk to the post of suzerain, replacing the deeply lamented Pietro Marradi." Hamish paused. Lisa thought he drew a deep breath. "Subject to your gracious consent to this appointment and to confirm his status, he humbly petitions the hand in marriage of your ward, Elizabeth, lawful born Queen of England and diverse other realms."

She managed not to shudder too visibly, but shudder she did. So Longdirk wanted her as a trophy of war, did he? And England, too. Not a bad prize for a ditch-born Highland bastard. He was having a good day.

Sartaq let the silence lengthen. Clearly this delegation was by way of being a mutiny. The Khan's armies were encamped all around Florence and their leaders had just given him an ultimatum. He was hunting for a way out. Lisa did not think he was going to find one.

"And you expect me to make this decision now, on the spot?"

"There is a movement afoot . . ." said a younger man. "It would not be seemly, but the danger is . . . The men are already hailing him as suzerain, Your Highness."

Pause. Then another man remarked to no one in

particular, "And the liberated troops have all sworn allegiance to him personally."

This time the pause was ominous. One of the other mercenaries spoke up, a man almost as big as Longdirk, although older.

"Would it not be an appropriate and generous gesture to complete a day so magnificent, Your Highness?"

"I think this is tomorrow already, messer Abonio," Sartaq grumbled. "And we like to decide for ourselves when to demonstrate our generosity." Lisa thought he might turn his head and ask her what she thought of the match, but he didn't. Nobody *cared* what she thought of the match, nobody except Hamish, and he was a field mouse in a pride of lions. "If I approve this appointment, *comandante,* I presume you will make the usual obeisance and pledge loyalty to the Khan?"

Longdirk blinked as if his eyes would not stay open. "Is there an option? I thought obeisance was obligatory."

"So it is," Sartaq said thoughtfully. "And you will do homage for the realm of England?"

"Chancellor?"

This time Hamish left the table he was guarding and walked closer to the center. "Your Highness, English common law permits an heiress to do homage for her estate, as Queen Elizabeth already hās, to Your Grace in your personification as the *darughachi* of His Majesty Ozberg Khan. The proposed marriage contract specifies that she will appoint her husband King

Consort but will retain in her person and sole right all honors of England, Wales, Ireland, et cetera. As dowry, she brings to her husband merely a quitclaim of any rights professed by her forebears to the throne of Scotland, plus a grant of certain lands within the Duchy of Lancaster providing an income of—"

"Spare us the jackdaw chatter," Sartaq growled. "I require that he do homage for the throne of England, whether it is the throne matrimonial or not. And he will do homage as suzerain also."

"That requires no change in the marriage contract," Hamish said. "Sir Toby, you have no objections?"

"Hmm?" Longdirk seemed to focus one eye at a time, like a bird. "Objections? No objections."

Sartaq muttered something under his breath. "Aunt, it seems that we shall have to concede."

"I don't suppose," Blanche squeaked, going shrill as she always did at moments of stress, "that anyone could think of asking my daughter's opinion in this matter?"

"Ah, your quaint western customs," Sartaq said. "Very well. Cousin?"

Lisa looked in despair to Hamish.

Hamish had started back to the table. He glanced around briefly—and nodded to her, very urgently: *Say yes!* Then he turned his head again quickly, and continued as if that had never happened.

"Your High . . ." She stammered, unsure of what she had seen, unable to believe he would betray her now.

Again he glanced around and signaled, *Yes! Say yes!*

Was no one true to her? She heard her own voice respond. "I shall be obedient to Your Highness's wishes."

Sartaq shrugged. "Very well. Let us set the date and—"

"We have the marriage contract here," Hamish said. "The notary has advised us that the betrothal may be waived."

"Time is short, Your Highness," boomed the big Abonio man. "Sir Toby will have to lead his troops north in a day or two at the latest. Naturally he is impatient, yes? Seeing the bride, can any of us blame him?" The other men guffawed crudely.

This was obscene! Betrothed and married in ten minutes? Lisa wanted to scream a protest, but Hamish had taken up position behind his little table again and was definitely signaling to her. Beside the single candlestick stood an inkwell with a quill in it.

"If I am to be married at a gallop, then by all means let us get it over with!" Lisa declared, and swept across the floor to Hamish. She hoped he would explain.

His eyes gleamed inhumanly bright, reflecting the dancing flame. On the table, between candle and inkwell lay several pages of vellum covered in minute, cramped, handwriting. "If Your Majesty would just sign here. And here . . . Don't say a word," he added in a whisper, not moving his lips. "Trust me."

Tears made the vellum swim into a blur. Trust him? What was he going to do—abduct her from her husband's bed in the nick of time?

"Sign here!" Hamish insisted.

Lisa took up the quill and signed her name. Twice, three times. A tear splashed on the vellum.

"Now, Your Highness," he said loudly, "as *de jure* guardian, and the bride's mother as—Oops!" Clumsy Hamish had knocked over the candlestick. He stamped on it before it could damage the priceless Cathay rug. "Sign, er, here, Your Highness . . ."

So the contract was signed—Lisa and Longdirk, the prince and her mother, Guilo and Hamish as witnesses.

"The Magnificent Guilo," Hamish announced loudly, "has most generously provided a wedding breakfast—if Your Honors would come this way."

Longdirk offered Lisa his arm to walk half the length of the room. The prince and Blanche and the mercenaries trailed after.

"You smiled at your last wedding," her husband said. He had been riding and fighting all day in the hot Tuscan sun. Horse and man and gunpowder and worse. How very romantic!

"I liked my last bridegroom."

"He had money, but he was very small."

"You have none and are far too big."

"I think we are in for a very interesting married life."

"I don't."

They reached the table the servants had spread,

and the grinning guests hastily lined up to congratulate the happy couple. There were no chairs or stools. This was to be a wedding feast on the hoof. Legal rape was what this was, and yet Hamish had told her to submit, to acquiesce. Had she misjudged even Hamish? Had he betrayed her to trick her into marriage with his longtime friend?

Yesterday the banquet and then, *whoops!* the groom just died, wait a minute, here's another, carry on where we left off . . .

Longdirk offered her a goblet of wine. She noticed again that he was almost out on his feet. Whatever else her wedding night might offer, romance was not on the playbill.

54

The wedding feast lasted seven or eight minutes, while the mercenary leaders bowed to her, offered leering congratulations, and thumped her husband on the back. And made crass remarks.

Such as: "Are you sure you're capable of this tonight, Big One?"

Longdirk responded vaguely: "Capable of what?" or "I'm told it isn't difficult."

She was very hungry and managed to snatch a mouthful or two before she found herself on her husband's arm being escorted out of the hall by all the guests, carrying lanterns. Hamish was leading the way. Hamish, Hamish! Had she misjudged Hamish?

What had he meant by those cryptic words and mysterious glances . . . ?

"Magnificent Guilo," Longdirk mumbled, "been kind, enough, put a room at our, our, er . . . Sorry. Not usual sparkling self."

The wedding ended, she recalled, when the bride and groom withdrew behind closed doors.

"I am curious," she said. "Did you murder my last bridegroom?"

"Hope not. Couldn't have pulled off the fraud without him."

"Another thing I always like to know about my husbands. Are you possessed by a demon?"

They walked up ten or twelve steps before he answered. "Two days ago would have said no."

"That's not quite the comfort I was hoping for. Now you say yes?"

"Now not quite so sure." He stumbled and recovered.

"When did you last sleep?"

"Don' 'member. Weeks."

"Well, you can have a nice, long, quiet night tonight."

At the end of a corridor she had not visited before, Hamish opened a door. There was a very large four-poster bed in it, a table with some refreshments, chairs and chests, another door leading perhaps to a dressing room. There was more crude humor. The door closed. There was silence. She had been left with one candle and one useless husband. She slid the bolt.

Longdirk walked across to the bed and laid a shoulder against the nearest post. He leaned, arms dangling limply, and the whole great bed creaked in alarm.

"Demons!" he muttered. "I . . . have . . . never . . . so tired. In my life."

Lisa fought for a grip on her temper. This was her second marriage in two days. Her first husband had been murdered in front of her eyes, her second was a physical wreck, and she was chained for the rest of her days to a lowborn bastard serf she despised and detested.

She had done nothing to deserve this!

"I am not going to undress you. You stink. Take your boots off and lie down. And stay away from me until you're respectable."

He peered around the post at her, struggling to make his eyes focus. "You compre . . . comp . . . un'ershtand . . . have just witnessed one of the great sleight of hands of all times?"

Carrying the candle, Lisa went across to inspect the other room. There was nothing in it whatsoever, just bare floor. She came back out again and closed the door. Longdirk was still on his feet, but barely so, propped up by the bed.

"'S Hamish," he mumbled. "Mashermind the whole think."

"If you're not going to go to bed, will you please turn your back while I undress? I am not accustomed to an audience."

"Should hope . . . hope not. Have to keep

secret. 'S part of the deal, understand? Not even your mother."

No, she did not understand. He did not smell of wine—everything else but not wine—so he must be just stupefied by fatigue. If she blew out the candle, he might fall down and go to sleep on the floor. She was tired. She wanted to sleep, and if she had to be married, then she would rather deal with the implications tomorrow.

Now he had twisted farther round, wrapped on the post like a gigantic vine, and he was peering blearily at the outer door. "Who lockit?"

"What?"

"'Snot right!" the new suzerain announced. He pointed a finger.

The bolt slid aside.

Lisa choked back a scream. Gramarye!

"'S betterer!" he announced, and yawned ferociously. "Can't wait," he mumbled. "Congratulations, Queenie. Wish you ever' happiness." He straightened up with a huge effort and staggered over to the other door.

"That doesn't go anywhere," she said.

Ignoring her, he went in and closed it behind him.

She waited for him to emerge.

The outer door clicked shut, making her spin around.

"Hamish!"

He slid the bolt again, laid down his lantern, crossed the room, gathered her into his arms, and choked off her protests by putting her mouth to other uses. Her ribs creaked in his embrace, her back would break, his body was hard against hers; it was like being roped to a tree trunk. The world spun madly. Lips and tongues. She pawed at the back of his head as if to make him kiss harder yet.

"Married!" she muttered when he let her speak. "Mustn't! I'm a married woman. Must not! Oh, Hamish, Hamish!" If he let go, she would fall in a heap. If he didn't, she would weep in his arms.

He pulled his head back so they were nose-to-nose instead of mouth-to-mouth. "You didn't look!" he said in delight.

"Look at what?"

He was too close to see properly, but why was he grinning like that? "Look at what you were signing, you muffin! I didn't knock over the candle until . . . You didn't look, did you?"

"Don't you dare laugh at me!" she shouted. "Why are you laughing? My husband's in there, and he'll be out again in a—"

"No, he won't. No, he isn't."

He kissed her again, even longer. She melted. He squeezed harder. She melted more. Oh, *Hamish!*

"Oh, Hamish!"

"Toby doesn't need a bed. He always sleeps on the floor. And he's not your husband anyway. You didn't read the contract, you silly duckling. You didn't watch who signed where!"

She was trying to kiss him again, but he turned his face away until the importance of what he had said sank in.

"Urk?"

". . . except in public. You must not tell anyone, ever,

promise? It won't be easy. He needs your public persona, but he can't marry you, Lisa, because the hob, his demon . . . Well, he can't." Apparently Hamish meant this, for his face was all earnest angles and sharp planes.

"He only wants me so he can claim to be King of England!"

Hamish snorted, still holding her so tight she could barely breathe. "That's what I meant."

"Isn't that *using* me, politically? What you said he never would do?"

"You want to be my wife or not?"

"Yes, but—"

When he released her mouth the next time, she mumbled, "Will Longdirk make obeisance to the prince tomorrow?"

"I doubt it. If he does, he won't mean it. He's going to pack Sartaq off back to Sarois very promptly. He's been useful, but we don't need him anymore."

"So I'm not the only one he uses? And you?" She refused another kiss, struggling to see Hamish's eyes when he answered.

"Yes, me. He used me, too. But he offers fair payment. You made Toby King of England tonight, darling, but he's going to make you Queen of Europe before winter. When you have children, make sure they look like you."

"What?" That was too much too soon. "Queen of Europe? But . . . But . . . *Who did I marry tonight?*"

"I'll show you who!"

With an unexpected move, Hamish tumbled them onto the bed together.

REALITY CHECK

There has never be anything quite like Renaissance Italy, and nothing I could make up would ever match it. Until now this series has admitted no historical characters later than 1241, but alert readers may have noticed a couple of notable Florentines managed to get themselves mentioned. They would both have been around town at the time, two stars in a galaxy of geniuses.

Longdirk's world is lagging a little behind ours. Mobile cannon were introduced into Italy by Charles VIII of France in 1494. Improvements in firearms soon made armored knights obsolete. The age of the great condottieri, which had begun with the (largely English) White Company in the mid-fourteenth century, ended with the death of Giovanni of the Black Bands in 1526.

In 1527 Florence drove out the Medici family for the third time. This was a serious error, because Pope Clement VII was a Medici, and he arranged for the Spanish army to bring the rebellious city to heel. The siege began in 1528 and lasted a year before starvation forced Florence to surrender. The man who extended the walls to enclose the hill of San Miniato was an engineer named Michelangelo Buonarroti; he also dabbled in sculpture, painting, architecture, and poetry.

Pietro Marradi is loosely based on Lorenzo de' Medici (who was not distinguished as Lorenzo the Magnificent until long after his death in 1492). Lucrezia is based not on Lucrezia Borgia, but on her public image. Personally I do not believe she had any part in the numerous poisonings attributed to her brother Cesare and their father Pope Alexander VI, nor that she bore an illegitimate child by either of them. Her daddy, however . . . They just don't make popes like him anymore.

TIME LINE

1241–44:
Ogedai Khan's Mongols overran Western Europe, incorporating it into the Khanate of the Golden Horde.

1246:
England conquered.

1500:
England's King Edwin II was at war with France. The Scots rose in revolt under Malcolm V and were brutally defeated at Leethoul. Malcolm died with two of his three sons. So also did Kenneth Campbell, Laird of Fillan. Typical of Edwin's savage vengeance (known as the Taming) was the abuse of six local women by the garrison imposed on Lochy Castle in Strath Fillan.

1501:
(7 Sept.) Meg Campbell died giving birth to Toby Strangerson.

1510:
Edwin died. His successor, Nevil, dabbling in gramarye, became possessed by the demon Rhym, and his own soul was immured in a

gemstone. His mistress and fellow hexer, Valda, fled the country. So did Queen Blanche and her baby daughter.

1511:

France attacked England's Continental possessions. Rhym (still known to the world as Nevil) won the war and was crowned King of France. The Scots rose in revolt and were trounced at the battle of Norford Bridge. King Fergan was captured, exhibited in a cage, and carried off to captivity in London. A puppet governor was installed, Eric MacLachlan. Nevil set out to conquer the rest of Europe.

1519:

Demon Sword. Lady Valda came seeking a body to hold the soul of Nevil, but was destroyed by her own demons. Toby was possessed by the Fillan hob. Narrowly escaping capture by Baron Oreste, one of Nevil's hexers, he sailed off with his friend Hamish Campbell and adopted the name of Longdirk. They were shipwrecked in Brittany by the hob's mischief.

1520–21:

Oreste pursued Longdirk and Hamish, narrowly missing them several times. The fugitives gained varied on-the-job experience in numerous occupations, being conscripted on separate occasions into armies on both sides in the continuing war. While members of the smuggler band led by Arnaud Villars, they escaped from Nevil-controlled Aquitaine across the border into Navarre.

1522:

In the village of Mezquiriz in Navarre, Longdirk's first romance ended in disaster. Nevil—now widely known as the Fiend—invaded Aragon and Navarre. Longdirk and Hamish fled south, but the rebel army followed, laying waste. When it laid siege to Toledo itself King Pedro of Castile agreed to humiliating terms. Nevil himself departed from Spain, leaving Oreste as his viceroy in Aragon. Seeking to escape to the north, Longdirk had doubled back and fell into Oreste's clutches at Montserrat, near Barcelona. *Demon Rider*. In the fall, Longdirk sailed to Genoa and there founded the Don Ramon Company.

1523:

The Company fought for (in turn) Verona and Ravenna in city squabbles.

1524:

The Company fought for Naples and Milan. Thinking Italy would be an easy conquest, Nevil sent an army under Varnius Schweitzer over the Alps. Longdirk was elected commander of the defenders' forces and won a resounding victory in the Battle of Trent, Nevil's first defeat.

1525:

Queen Blanche, a fugitive since 1510, fled from Savoy to Italy, landing in Pisa and proceeding to Siena to seek shelter with local royalists. While all Italy braced for the inevitable arrival of the Fiend himself, Longdirk negotiated a *condotta* putting the Don Ramon Company at the service of the Republic of Florence. *Demon Knight.*